RUBY

Marie Maxwell was born in London and, after living here, there and everywhere, now lives happily by the sea in Essex.

She has written seven other books under the name Bernardine Kennedy and information on Marie and Bernardine is available at: www.bernardinekennedy.com

RUBY

Marie Maxwell

A V O N

AVON
A division of HarperCollins*Publishers*
77–85 Fulham Palace Road,
London W6 8JB

www.harpercollins.co.uk

A Paperback Original 2012
1

First published in Great Britain by
HarperCollins*Publishers* 2012

Copyright © Marie Maxwell 2012

Marie Maxwell asserts the moral right to
be identified as the author of this work

A catalogue record for this book is
available from the British Library

ISBN-13: 978-1-84756-251-7

Set in Minion by Palimpsest Book Production Limited, Falkirk, Stirlingshire

Printed and bound in Great Britain by
Clays Ltd, St Ives plc

MIX
Paper from
responsible sources
FSC
www.fsc.org   FSC C007454

This is for Riley, my gorgeous grandson. His first dedication! xxx

I'd also like to pay a special tribute to the fabulous author and friend Penny Jordan/Annie Groves who died on New Year's Eve 2011. RIP Penny, you'll be sadly missed.

PROLOGUE

Southend Hospital, 1952

'Someone give me something . . . I'm in such pain . . . I can't breathe,' the woman on the trolley groaned. Her head rolled back and forth and she clutched fiercely at her chest. 'I can't breathe, help me . . .' As she spoke, all her strength seemed to float way from her body and she could feel herself being pulled towards unconsciousness. She tried to turn onto her side to curl up into a comforting ball but hands reached out to stop her and hold her flat on her back.

Her mind confused by the ever-increasing waves of pain, she was losing track of where she was. All she knew was that she was suffering the worst pain she had ever felt in her life. She felt as if her lungs were on fire. She could hear voices all around her but she was finding it hard to focus. An atmosphere of urgency pervaded, but the words she could hear made no sense.

1

She kept drifting between pain and oblivion: floating away peacefully to another place and then being pulled back with the fierceness of the pain.

Then the voices became louder and more urgent, and she felt herself being moved quickly. Bright lights flashed overhead, wheels rattled loudly underneath her and doors slammed behind her. Almost as soon as the journey had started, so it stopped, and people she didn't recognise grouped around her, touching her, pulling at her clothes. Then there was a pain in her hand, a mask over her face, and she was drifting away again. She just had time to wonder if she was dying, if that was it for her life – if that was all it had been about – before oblivion took her over and she succumbed to the anaesthetic.

'Time to wake up now,' a disembodied voice said. 'Your operation is over and we need to see you awake.'

She tried to shake herself awake but it was hard.

'Don't move. You've got dressings on your chest and your arm is in plaster. Just open your eyes so we know you're out of the anaesthetic and then you can go back to sleep.'

She forced her eyes open and focused on the nurse standing beside the bed.

'What happened?' The words came out slowly past her swollen tongue.

'You've had surgery. The doctor will talk to you about it later once you're transferred from post-op.'

Ruby

As she watched the ramrod-straight back of the nurse walking away, the memory of some of it started to come back to her. It was all disjointed in her head: the sudden crippling pain in her ribs that made breathing agony; the feeling that her chest had exploded; tumbling down the stairs and cracking her head; crawling along the hall to the open front door and then out onto the path looking for help. And then she remembered the fear . . .

'What happened to me?' she whispered, her chest hurting with every breath. 'Nurse? *Nurse* . . . ?'

By then the nurse was tending to a patient across the other side of the post-operative ward. She looked over her shoulder. 'Sshh, you're in recovery,' she said in a loud whisper. 'Don't disturb the other patients now. Go back to sleep and doctor will talk to you soon.'

'Why am I here?'

'You've had an operation. Stop shouting.'

'Operation for what?' Her voice was hoarse and her tongue felt as if it was filling her mouth so that she struggled to get the words out.

'I told you, *sshh*. I really can't tell you anything. Doctor has to talk to you and he will, later. He's talking to your fiancé at the moment.'

'To who?' She tried to clear her head. There was an image she was trying to catch hold of but it wouldn't stop long enough for her to focus on it.

'I'm sorry but there are seriously ill patients over here I have to look after, so stop the talking and rest,' the nurse snapped impatiently in a tone that proved tolerance obviously wasn't her forte in the middle of a busy night shift.

She closed her eyes in despair and let her head fall back onto the skinny pillow that had been placed under her head, but even that hurt. She reached up and touched her face, then had another flash of recall. She struggled to sit up.

'Someone tell me what's happened. I can't remember . . .'

'Stop this, you're disturbing everyone.'

Instead of the recall of events she was searching for, a wave of terror engulfed her and she started screaming, louder than she had ever screamed in her life, and the pain in her chest erupted.

'Tell me, tell me what's going on! I'm scared, I can't remember . . .'

This frantic call for help was answered with a dose of sedative that took her away from it all again.

Two men stood facing each other in the corridor. The older was dressed in a green hospital gown and short rubber boots with a surgical mask hanging down around his neck; the younger was wearing dark brown casual slacks and an open-necked shirt, a tweed sports jacket slung from one finger over his shoulder.

'Your fiancée has three broken ribs and one of these pierced her left lung. It was this that necessitated the emergency surgery. She's going to be in a lot of pain for a while but we can explain the implications of that to her later when we talk about her other injuries.'

'Will she be all right?'

'Well, we hope so. It's fair to say she could easily have died from the lung injury but we've done our best to put her back together,' the doctor said, a hint of contempt in his voice. 'At the moment she's as well as can be expected. First the fall with its accompanying injuries, possibly concussion, a head wound, a fractured arm, assorted cuts and bruises, a punctured lung and then the emergency surgery . . .' he stopped to take breath. 'She's been through a lot but she's stable and will be taken up to the ward later. We've had to sedate her again, she's so distressed by the, er, accident.' He made firm eye contact with the younger man. 'Tell me again how it happened?'

'I told you,' the man sighed as if this was really boring him, 'I don't know what happened. I wasn't there. No one was there. I arrived at the same time as the ambulance. I think a neighbour telephoned for it. He heard some sort of kerfuffle going on. Probably her falling down the stairs. She's so clumsy with those big feet of hers . . .' He smiled as he shrugged dismissively. 'I don't even know what she was doing there on her own, to be honest.'

'I see. But we are very puzzled by the bruises on her neck.'

'They'd be from when she fell down the stairs, wouldn't they?'

'It's possible, but unlikely. Anyway, that's not for me to decide. I just put her back together again.'

'You're absolutely right, doctor. That's not for you to decide.' The man held out his hand to indicate the end of the conversation.

'I suggest you go home now,' the doctor said. 'You won't be able to see your fiancée until tomorrow evening during visiting hours. Check at the reception desk for the hours. I don't know which ward she's going to be taken to. Will you be contacting her family?'

'She doesn't have any family.'

'I see . . .'

The doctor's tone was cold and he didn't take the proffered hand. He simply turned sharply and walked back through the doors he'd emerged from a couple of minutes before.

A look of anger flashed across the other man's face, and for a moment it looked as though he would follow the doctor, but instead he breathed deeply several times before turning round and heading down the corridor in the direction of the main exit. Once outside he sat on the wall, taking more deep breaths before lighting a cigarette and thinking about everything that had happened. He wanted to get it all straight in his head, just in case. After he'd ground the butt into the flowerbed he walked down the footpath and swung open the door to the phone box that stood at the main gate.

He fumbled in his pocket for coppers and then made

his call. 'Hello? It's me. I know it's late – or early, depending on how you look at it.' As he spoke he checked his hair in the mirror that was fixed on the wall above the phone and then pulled a comb out of his back pocket. 'I've had a strange old night but everything's OK now and I'm dying for a decent cup of coffee . . . among other things!'

He smiled at himself in the mirror as he put the phone back into its cradle, then he flicked the comb through his hair, slipped on his jacket and pushed the door open. He held the door back for the elderly woman waiting patiently outside.

'Thank you kindly young man,' she said. 'Have you just come out of the hospital?'

'I have. My fiancée's had an accident.'

'Ooh dear, I hope she's OK.'

'Oh, nothing serious. Just a bit of a tumble and a few bruises. I've told her to lay off the gin in future.' He grinned.

Shrugging his jacket straight, he pulled at his collar and walked away from the hospital where his fiancée lay battered and bruised.

PART ONE

ONE

Melton, Cambridgeshire, 1945

'Here comes the train. Mummy, Mummy, I can hear it, I can hear it!' As the small boy's shriek pierced through the general chatter on the crowded railway platform the conversations started to fade away and the train appeared around the bend in the track lumbering noisily towards the station. Children jumped up and down excitedly at the sight and sound of the huge steam engine, and adults automatically reached down to pick up their bags and baggage.

Ruby Blakeley wasn't feeling in the least bit excited as she pushed her own two small suitcases nearer the edge of the platform with her feet and then looked at the woman who was holding tightly onto her hand. She was feeling terrified.

'It's the train . . .' the girl sighed sadly. The woman pulled the teenager in towards her and hugged her tightly.

'Oh, Ruby, I've been dreading this moment. Uncle

11

George and I are both going to miss you so much. I still can't believe you're leaving us.'

'I'm going to miss you too, Aunty Babs. I don't want to go back, but I have to. There's no other way.'

'I wish there was something we could do to persuade your family to let you stay. We'd love you to work in the surgery with us. We need the help, and you could send money to your mother and support her that way.'

Ruby let herself be hugged for a few seconds before blinking hard and pulling back. More than anything she wanted to turn round and go back to the comfortable, loving home she had become accustomed to over the past few years.

'I know, but Mum said no. She said I have to go back. If I don't go she'll send Ray to collect me and you've seen what he's like. I suppose it is hard for Mum. Ray said I have to go and help her, what with Dad not coming back and Nan being there and everything . . .'

'Yes, dear, I know what Ray said, but having met him I think you and I both know he likes to exaggerate a little.' The older woman went on quickly, 'Listen to me, Ruby. I know you have to go but I want you to remember that we're always here for you. Any time you need anything, or you just want to come and see us, we'll send you the train fare,' she took hold of the girl's arm, 'or if things change and you want to come back and live here again. We'll keep your room, even if it's just for a holiday with us. This will always be your home.'

'Will you really? I'd like that,' Ruby said with a hopeful smile.

'Of course we will. Now don't you forget to keep in touch. We both think of you as our daughter. I never expected that to happen the day we took you into our home, but now . . .' Barbara Wheaton paused mid-sentence as her eyes welled up. She touched Ruby's cheek with her gloved hand. 'Now it's as if you were always with us, part of our family.'

'Thank you. I'll write, I promise. I'm going to miss you both so much.'

'And I'll write. Now you're sure you've got the paper on which Uncle George wrote everything down for you? We don't want you to get lost in London, and you mind who you talk to on the train.' She smiled and shook her head. 'I do wish you'd let us drive you back.'

'I'll be careful, I've got the paper in my bag and I'll be fine. Mum is going to meet me at the bus stop when I get to Walthamstow.'

At fifteen Ruby was slender and coltishly leggy with green eyes and dark red curls not quite tucked away under the brim of a grey beret, which matched her knee-length tailored coat. Her 'aunt' was taller in her high heels, her hair pinned into an elegant chignon, and her face subtly made up, but the women were of similar colouring and bearing, and, standing side by side, they looked just like the mother and daughter Ruby had often wished they were. It had been nice to be the cosseted only child in a loving home instead of the ignored youngest in a crowded unhappy house, but now she had to go back to her family.

Amid billows of smoky steam the train bound for London lumbered to a standstill and, after one more hug, Ruby clambered aboard with her cases and sat down in a window seat. Forcing herself to be detached she smiled and waved through the steamed-up glass as the train started to chug forward while Babs Wheaton stood perfectly still on the narrow platform dabbing gently at her eyes with one hand and waving with the other.

Just outside the station Ruby could see Derek Yardley, the Wheatons' driver, watching through the fence. As the train moved away she saw him raise a hand and wave. To all intents and purposes it was a friendly wave but she could see his stone-cold eyes staring directly at her. She hated him with a passion. He was the one person she certainly wouldn't miss, and she knew without doubt that he was pleased to see the back of her, too.

Ruby remained dry-eyed and outwardly unemotional but inside she felt sick and angry at the thought both of what she was leaving behind and of what she was going back to.

It just wasn't fair.

Five years previously, amid many tears and tantrums, the ten-year-old Ruby had fought desperately against being evacuated from her home and family in wartime East London to the safety of a sleepy village in the

Cambridgeshire countryside. Just the thought of going had been terrifying to the young girl, who had never been away from home for even a night. But once she had adjusted to the change, she had settled in and her time with Babs and George Wheaton had turned into the happiest of her life. She had stayed on long after the other evacuees had returned home.

But now the war was over and, despite pleading for Ruby to be allowed to stay indefinitely, her host family had been told that their evacuee had to return to her real family.

Ruby's eldest brother, Ray, had visited a few weeks previously and stated in no uncertain terms that it was way past time for the only daughter to do her bit for the cash-strapped family. Her mother wasn't prepared to agree to her staying away any longer.

Leaning back in her seat, Ruby closed her eyes. She was dreading it.

After five years living with the very middle-class country GP and his wife, who had picked her randomly from the crocodile of scared evacuees transported to the village school playground, Ruby had changed dramatically. She had morphed from a frightened shadow of a child into a self-confident and popular young woman with a good brain and a quick wit, although there was still a certain stubbornness about her that could surface quickly if she was crossed.

She had also grown accustomed to being loved and cared for, even spoiled, by her childless host parents.

It was all so different from her other home, a small terraced house in Walthamstow where she had lived for the first ten years of her life; the home where she had been brought up, the youngest child with three brothers who had constantly overshadowed her early years with their boisterous masculinity and smothering overprotectiveness; the home where her bedroom was the tiny boxroom and her role was to be seen and not heard, especially by her father. Ruby thought that her mother probably loved her in her own way, but she didn't have any time for her, and Ruby's enduring memory of those first ten years was of constant loneliness and anxiety. She hadn't actually been unhappy at the time because she didn't know any different, but now she knew how childhood could and should be.

Sitting in the carriage, carefully avoiding any eye contact with the other passengers, Ruby could feel that the old anxiousness returning, but she resisted the urge to nibble around the edges of her nails as she had when she was a child.

There was something niggling her, a thought that she couldn't quite get hold of. She could see how her mother would be run ragged and struggling to cope with a house full of adults, but she couldn't understand why anyone in her position would fight to add an extra person into the mix, an extra mouth to feed. It simply didn't make any sense.

When Ray had unexpectedly turned up on the doorstep

a few weeks previously to order her home, Ruby had been mortified. The gawky schoolboy she remembered had turned into a sneering young man. Ray Blakeley had gone from rowdy boy to ill-mannered lout, the kind of person Babs and George had always encouraged her to avoid at all costs.

'Ruby? There's someone here to see you. I've sent him round to the front door,' George had shouted through the hatch in the door that joined his village surgery to the house.

Ruby had run down the stairs from her bedroom expecting to see one of her friends in the lobby, but instead there was a young man. She looked at him curiously for a moment and then realised.

'Ray? What are you doing here?' She couldn't keep the shock out of her voice.

'Now that's not a nice way to talk to your big brother, is it, Rubes?' he grinned. 'No hello? No long time no see? No nothing at all?' With both hands in his pockets he looked her up and down critically and shook his head. 'I dunno, look at you done up like a dog's dinner. Looks like I got here just in time before you get any more stupid ideas above your station. Mum told me you're all la-di-dah now.'

'I've just got back from the town; I was just going to get changed,' she countered defensively.

'*Just got back from the town,*' he mimicked her voice

and enunciation with a wide grin. '*Just got back from the town.* Posh talk there girl.'

As a bright scarlet blush crept up her face, Ruby could feel herself shrivelling inside, reverting back to the trampled-over child she had been before her evacuation. But then she noticed Babs standing in the kitchen doorway, observing quietly, and her confidence returned.

'Aunty Babs, this is my oldest brother, Ray. He's come to see me,' Ruby said brightly, looking for a distraction.

Ray glanced dismissively at the woman before turning his attention back to Ruby.

'Oh, no, you've got it wrong, Rubes. I haven't come to see you, I've come to take you back home. Now.'

'But I don't want to go back.' As soon as the words were out she realised she'd made a mistake. 'I mean, I'm not ready. You can't just turn up without warning and expect me to go with you. I've got school and all sorts of things . . .'

'No choice there, Rubes darling. School's done for you, and Mum wants you back home, what with the old man more than likely dead . . . please God.' He paused and grinned before continuing, 'But you know that. Enough mucking around – she's writ often enough – so now she's asked me to come and get you; drag you, if I have to. Time to stop being all duchesslike and get back to where you belong.'

Babs stepped forward quickly, held her hand out and smiled.

'I'm pleased to meet you, Ray. I've heard so much about you. Dr Wheaton and I were so sorry to hear about your father. I have sent my condolences to your mother.' Her smile widened in welcome. 'But you've had a long journey and you must be famished. Come through to the kitchen and I'll make you some tea and find you something to eat. If I'd known you were coming I'd have had a meal waiting.'

As he ignored the proffered hand it was obvious Ray was confused by the welcome, and he stared suspiciously at this seemingly genial woman. But when Babs and Ray locked eyes for several moments Ruby could see that the gauntlet was down, although she wasn't sure who had thrown it.

'OK, must admit I'm bloody starving; but then we have to get back.' He looked back to his sister. 'You go and get your stuff packed as quick as you can while I have a feed. I can't muck around all day. And I hope you've got your train fare else you'll have to run behind.' He laughed as he held his hand out palm up towards Babs and rubbed thumb and forefinger together theatrically. 'Oh, and we expect a bit of payback for keeping our Rube here for so long . . .'

Ruby could feel crushing embarrassment taking over her whole body. Ray was behaving like a complete lout and she couldn't figure out why. He'd always been a bully but she didn't remember him being quite so bad-mannered.

'Oh dear, Ray, I'm really sorry but I don't think Ruby should travel today. She's been a bit under the weather the last few days.' Babs Wheaton's expression was suitably apologetic. 'There's a lot of mumps going about the village. We're not sure if Ruby's got it yet, but it can be really bad for young men. I wouldn't like to see you or your brothers go down with it. The side effects could be really nasty . . .'

As he thought about it Ray Blakeley screwed his eyes up and stared intently at his sister's neck. 'She looks all right to me, and she's just come back *from town*.' Again he put on the silly voice. 'She wouldn't be out and about if she were that bloody sick . . .'

Babs reached forward and placed her palm on Ruby's forehead.

'Your sister's such a good girl, she's putting on a brave face and pretending to be fine, but we're worried the mumps may be in the incubation period. We're not sure yet.' Again Babs smiled. 'But we'll soon see. Now let's go and see what I can conjure up to feed you, but don't sit too close to Ruby. Just in case.'

Her words hung in the air as Babs led the way through into the kitchen and motioned for the brother and sister to sit at opposite ends of the vast farmhouse table. As he looked around the homely room with a slight sneer on his face, Ruby studied Ray and tried to work out whether he was being deliberately uncouth for effect.

With his even features, dark brown hair and a jaunty

moustache, he looked older than nineteen. His clothes were clean, his shoes polished and he looked presentable enough – smart, even – but he had an arrogant swagger in his walk and more than a hint of aggression in the angry eyes that stared out from behind horn-rimmed spectacles. As she watched and listened, Ruby decided that, despite his being her brother, she really didn't like Ray Blakeley one bit.

As Ruby surreptitiously studied him from the other end of the table, Babs quickly made some thick cheese and pickle sandwiches and put a plate in front of him along with a chunk of cold apple pie, a big mug of tea and a white napkin tucked inside a ring.

Ruby watched in fascination as, ignoring the napkin, Ray stuffed the food in his mouth, washing each mouthful down with a swig of tea and dribbling as he talked with his mouth full. Within a few minutes the plates were clean and he looked at Babs, leaned back in his chair, wiped his mouth with the back of his hand and belched. 'Another cuppa'll really go down a treat, missus.'

It was at that moment that Ruby, overwhelmed with shame, knew he was being deliberately uncouth; that he was being provocative. She also knew that her mother would be equally horrified because none of them had been brought up to speak like that to anyone, let alone an adult, or to behave like that at the table.

As she stared at her brother in disgust a door next to the walk-in pantry opened and Dr Wheaton came through from his surgery at the other side of the rambling old house. His wheelchair clunked as he expertly wheeled himself across the stone-flagged kitchen floor and manoeuvred himself up to the table.

'Ray, this is Uncle George.'

'What happened to you, then? War wounds?'

'No. Polio. When I was a child.'

'Oh right. So as Ma says, this contraption is the reason you want our Rubes to stay here, so she can look after you? She says all the other kids are already home and you two want her as your skivvy.'

As Ruby froze, so George smiled. 'No. I don't need looking after. Ruby's still here because she wanted to finish her schooling here. She's very clever and doing well. We sent her school reports to your mother.'

'Yeah, well, it's not reports Ma needs, it's another pair of hands to help her out, and that's what Rubes has got, so off we go.'

Ruby looked from one to another before saying, to try to calm Ray, 'Uncle George is a doctor.'

But Ray just looked at her as if she were mad. 'I know that, you daft bint, but I've never seen a doctor in one of those. Who'd have thought it?'

'And I'm going to train to be a nurse when I'm old enough,' Ruby added.

'Course you are, Rubes, and I bet that's the doc's idea: a nurse in the house to save him a few bob. Shrewd, eh?'

Ruby

Ruby had to sit through another hour of embarrassment before Ray, having conceded that she could stay another couple of weeks until she was definitely confirmed fit, finally left, informing her he'd be back for her if she wasn't home within the month.

TWO

As Ruby was deep in thought, and going where she didn't want to go, the train journey into London was over in a flash and, following George Wheaton's instructions to the letter, Ruby caught the bus to the stop nearest to her road in Walthamstow. She looked around hopefully for her mother, but after a twenty-minute wait in the autumn evening chill she gave up and started walking.

The Wheatons had wanted to drive her back home but, after Ray's disrespectful behaviour, Ruby wanted to keep her two lives apart so she had determinedly refused. She had insisted that she was old enough to make the trip alone, but as she trudged along the streets and the two suitcases got heavier and heavier she regretted her decision. She kept picking them up and putting them down and changing hands, even though they were the same weight. When she was halfway there she dumped them on the pavement and sat down on one of them to catch her breath.

She looked around at the once-familiar surroundings that she had all but forgotten about when she was living safely in the open spaces of rural Cambridgeshire. Terraced houses with tiny front gardens edged both sides of the road, and the smell of coal smoke hung heavy in the air. Before her evacuation the area had simply been home, but now she viewed it objectively and it felt claustrophobic and grubby.

Amid the familiarity of the streets remnants of the war stood out. There were pockets of emptiness and rubble where houses and shops had once stood, and as she looked across the road at the bombed-out remains of two adjoining houses she thought about who might have been inside when the bomb fell.

Suddenly the recently ended war was real and the loss of life she'd heard about was on her own doorstep.

As she clenched and unclenched her aching hands and tried not to cry, a young man she had vaguely noticed walking along on the other side of the road crossed over and stopped beside her.

'They look far too heavy for a little thing like you to be carrying; here, let me help you. Where are you going?'

'To Elsmere Road, the far end, but it's OK, I can manage perfectly well on my own. I'm just giving my hands a rest,' she snapped defensively.

'That's just past where I'm going so it's daft for you to carry them on your own. When you've got your wind back we'll get going, but I'm not carrying your handbag.'

The young man's expression was friendly and his smile wide as he waited for her to stand up again. Once she was on her feet he quickly picked up the cases and loped easily along the street, leaving Ruby almost running to keep up. In no time they were by the familiar front gate to the Blakeley family home.

'Here, this is the house.'

The man put the cases down on the pavement.

'Thank you,' Ruby said, looking up through her eyelashes into a pair of navy-blue eyes. Under his intense gaze she felt strangely shy.

'You didn't tell me your name,' he said.

'I know I didn't,' she replied.

With his eyes still fixed on her, the young man held his hand out. As she took it he gripped firmly and, as he held on slightly longer than was necessary, Ruby felt a strange tightening in her throat that she couldn't identify.

'Well, I'm Johnnie, I'm from down the street. I live here; Walthamstow born and bred. Are you visiting?' he asked, still holding on to her hand.

'No, Johnnie-from-down-the-street,' she smiled as she withdrew her hand from his. 'I live here as well. I've been in evacuation for five years and I've just come back. It all seems strange, though. I know where I am but it doesn't feel like home any more. It's all different.'

'That was the war . . .' He paused for a moment and then raised his eyes upwards. 'Ah! I was a bit slow there! Of course you're Ruby; Ruby Blakeley, the missing sister who's been having such a time of it she didn't want to come home again. And none of your brothers came to meet you? They should be ashamed of themselves, leaving you to drag your own cases through the streets.' Johnnie Riordan shook his head slowly, his disapproval all too obvious.

'I wasn't dragging them, I was carrying them,' Ruby frowned. 'How did you know all that about me?'

'Your brother Ray has a very loose mouth; blabs all the time. Lucky he missed call-up; we'd have lost the war after he'd given chapter and verse to Hitler's spies.'

Ruby tried not to laugh. 'And you? Why didn't you go and fight?'

'Just missed out, but I've been doing my bit in other ways.' He winked.

'That's what they all say . . . So how do you know my brothers?' she asked curiously.

'Ah! That's for me to know and you to find out.' He winked again, and another very strange feeling fluttered gently through her chest. 'And I'm sure you will very soon, just as soon as you tell your brothers you met me. I'll be seeing you then, Ruby of the red hair!'

With a wide grin, a tip of his hat and a flamboyant backward wave the man strutted down the road in the direction from which they'd come. Ruby watched as he casually kicked a ball back to a group of children playing in the middle of the road and then disappeared into a gate halfway down the street.

She guessed he was older than she – he certainly looked it – maybe even older than her brothers, and he had an edge of danger about him that excited her momentarily; but she knew it wasn't the time to be thinking about handsome young men.

She was home, but all she wanted to do was turn and head back to the security of Melton and to the Wheatons, the substitute parents who had cared for her and loved her as their own.

She pulled back the wooden gate, took a couple of steps along the short concrete path and, after banging sharply on the door knocker, waited impatiently for what seemed an age before the door opened.

'Hello, Mum,' she smiled.

The woman looked at her for a moment before registering that this was her own daughter.

'Ruby! Hello, dear, you're early. I was just going to walk down to the bus stop to meet you, but you're back here already.'

'I was right on time. I waited for you for ages . . .'

'Not to worry. I had so much to do I must have got behind. But you're here now so in you come.'

The woman who had opened the door was small and round with wavy faded red hair pulled back from her face and tucked up in an old voile headscarf that was tied on top of her head. She was wearing an enveloping flowery apron and neatly darned woollen slippers.

Her appearance told Ruby that there was no way she

had been getting ready to go out, and she felt hurt that the mother who had stated how desperate she was to have her daughter back home couldn't even be bothered to walk down the road and meet her off the bus after such a long journey.

Sarah Blakeley held the door right back, then turned and shouted. 'Arthur? Your sister's here. Come and take her cases to her room.' She turned back to her daughter. 'Ruby, you go back out and shut the gate before those little urchins across the street start swinging on it again. I'm just sorting your brothers' tea and then we'll have ours after with Nan.'

Her eyes widened as she looked at her daughter properly for the first time. 'You've grown, Rube – I nearly didn't recognise you – and you look very glamorous, but a bit too old for your age. Did that Babs woman give those clothes to you?'

'Yes, she made me lots of clothes and altered some of hers for me.'

'Not really suitable for a fourteen-year-old . . .'

'I'm fifteen, soon be sixteen,' Ruby sighed.

'Still not quite right, though. I'll try them on later. I haven't had anything new for years.'

And that was the total of her welcome home from her mother after five years away.

Ruby stood for a moment on the threshold and stared straight ahead at the faded wallpaper in the narrow hallway and the staircase that disappeared off into claustrophobic darkness. She didn't even want to go in, let alone live there again. She wanted to run; but then she heard her grandmother.

'Is that you home, Ruby?' a voice called out. 'Come and say hello to your old nan.'

'Coming, Nan. Just going back to shut the gate.'

As her mother turned and walked back to the kitchen, Ruby's brother Arthur bounded down the hall past her and grinned. 'Hello, sis, decided to come home at last? Ray said you'd landed on your feet in that big posh house. He said you've gone la-di-dah and we've got to knock it out of you now you're back!'

At seventeen and not much more than a year older than his sister, Arthur had always been closest to Ruby in all ways and she had never taken offence at him the same way she had with her other brothers. He was a lump of a boy who had always had a certain slow innocence and openness in his nature, unlike Ray and Bobbie, who could both be mean and devious when the mood took them. She was pleased to see that, on the surface at least, Arthur seemed the same good-natured lad she remembered and she hoped that Bobbie, the middle brother in both age and temperament, had maybe grown up and away from Ray. Life back home would certainly be easier if her oldest brother was the only unpleasant one in the family.

'You could try, I suppose, or I could teach you how to be posh as well? It's not that bad, you know, there's nothing wrong with good manners.' She laughed as she put an arm around his waist and hugged him affectionately, much to his embarrassment.

'Get off,' he muttered as he pulled away, making her laugh.

'I've really missed you, Arf. You look so grown up now and you're so tall. It's a shame you didn't come to the country, you'd have loved being out in the open. I had a friend Keith who you would have loved playing with. He even had a gun to shoot rabbits and pigeons. It was great fun – even school – and Uncle George and Aunty Babs were so nice to me. I love them so much.' She paused as she realised exactly what she'd said. 'But I love you all as well, especially you, and even Ray.'

'We're boys. Dad said boys who were evacuated were cowards.' Arthur bristled and squared his shoulders. 'Dad said we had to look after ourselves and Mum, and that's what we did. We weren't girls . . .'

'Weren't you scared you might get killed with all the bombs?' Ruby asked curiously, still aware of the bombed-out houses she'd seen.

'No. We weren't scared. And now the war's over and we won! Ray said you weren't away because of the bombs, he said the posh people wanted you because the bloke's a cripple and she's barren. Ray said—'

'That is such rubbish,' Ruby interrupted angrily. 'Lots of different people took in evacuees and some of the hosts were really horrible to them. I was really lucky that I ended up where I was. Especially as no one from here bothered to check if I was OK.'

But Ruby knew that she was wasting her time. Arthur really didn't understand.

'Ruby, are you going to come and see me?' called Nan. Ruby turned away from Arthur and started towards the parlour.

'I'm just going to see Nan and then I'll tell you all about it,' she said.

Arthur picked up the cases and followed close behind her.

'You're supposed to be taking them to my room.'

'I am. Didn't Mum tell you? You're going to be sharing with Nan in the parlour. Ray's got your old room.'

'You're joking. I can't share with Nan. And what about the things I left?' Ruby turned and looked at her brother in horror.

'I think Ma got rid. Ray took your room as soon as you went away. Can't see him coming back in with me and Bobbie now he's the head of the house, can you?' Arthur laughed.

'Why can't Nan share with Mum?'

''Cos of the stairs, you idiot.'

'Why can't I share with Mum?'

Arthur laughed. 'I dunno . . .' Pretending to spar, he skipped around and punched his sister hard on the arm, the way he used to when they were children, but now he was physically a man and the punch hurt.

'Don't do that, Arthur,' she snapped at him. 'Don't hit me, don't ever hit me. We're not children any more. Adults don't hit each other.'

'Ooh, get you, Duchess. Ray was right. He said you think you're better than us now.'

Looking angry and still unaware of his own strength, he pushed at her and she stumbled backwards slightly.

'Well, I'm definitely better than Ray, I promise you that,' she snapped back angrily as she struggled to stay on her feet.

The door was open so Ruby turned straight into what used to be the front parlour, where they would all have dinner on high days and holidays, and formal tea when the parish priest visited, but everything that had been in there was gone, including the familiar battered piano that Ruby had loved to try to play.

Instead there were two narrow iron-framed beds with a bedside cabinet each, a wardrobe and a tallboy, which took up half the room, leaving just enough space for a chest of drawers with a jug and bowl atop and her grandmother's armchair in the small bay of the window. Arthur dumped the cases on the bed nearest the door and went out again without saying another word. Ruby knew she'd hurt his feelings but she was upset herself. She was, however, determined to make it up to him later because she knew he was the only one who she could rely on.

As she looked around all she could see in her mind's eye was her bedroom back in Cambridgeshire, the large and airy room with a wide comfy bed, a huge walnut wardrobe with drawers underneath, a matching dressing table and a ruby-red chaise longue that Aunty Babs had covered to match the curtains.

It was all hers but she'd had to leave it behind, and now she was standing in a room less than half the size, which she was going to have to share with her incapacitated grandmother. It just wasn't fair and, try as she may, she couldn't understand why they had wanted her back to cramp the house even further.

Keeping a determined check on the tears that were threatening at the back of her eyes, she went over to the bay where her grandmother was sitting.

'Hello, Nan. I'm back and it looks like I'm sharing with you. I'm sorry.'

'Oh, it's not your fault, Ruby dear. The war's meant we all have to make sacrifices, and Sarah was good enough to take me in so I can't grumble. Now come up close so I can see you; my eyes aren't what they used to be.' As Ruby moved closer the woman grabbed her hands and pulled her down. 'Ooh, you're a proper young lady, you are now, by the looks of it. Ray said you'd grown up. Now tell me all about it while you unpack. There's some coat hangers on the side. You're going have to use the picture rail for now to hang your clothes until I have a sort-out.'

'I'll unpack later, Nan, I'm so tired . . .'

'All night, dear. Then can you help me through to the back? We can have a cuppa before tea. I don't eat with the boys – they're too noisy and there's not enough room at the table. Me and your ma eat after they've all finished and gone out doing whatever it is that young men do nowadays. You'll be eating with us, I suppose.'

Ruby didn't answer; she just couldn't think what to say. She was both horrified and saddened as she looked at the elderly woman with stooped shoulders and cloudy eyes, who was peering up at her expectantly, waiting for an answer. One hand rested atop a wooden walking stick and the other gripped a vast dark grey crocheted shawl around her shoulders.

During the five years she had been away Sarah Blakeley had visited her daughter every other year on her birthday, but as Ruby hadn't been home at all she hadn't seen her grandmother in all that time, and she was shocked to see how much she'd aged.

It was on one of the birthday visits that her mother had told her that Nan, already a widow, had been bombed out of her own house in Stepney and come to stay with the family, and after her eyesight had deteriorated there was no way she could live alone. So there she had stayed, despite the overcrowded accommodation.

'Shall we go through to the back now, Nan? How do you want me to help you?'

'Just let me take your arm. It's the rheumatics, they kill me in this weather and make me feel ancient.' She laughed. 'Oh, it's good to have you home. You can help your mother around the house. Those boys are such hard work for her, what with her job and me being no use to her any more.'

'I've not come home to look after the boys, Nan. I'll help when I can but I'm going to be a nurse. I'm going to get a job and save up to start training when I'm eighteen.' Ruby smiled down at her grandmother hanging on her arm.

'Ooh no, Ruby, I don't think the boys'll let you do that. Oh no, dear, no.' The woman's voice rose sharply and she shook her head so violently Ruby took a couple of steps back. 'They said you were coming home to look after me and help your mother in the house. That's why they wanted you home . . . and they're a real handful for your poor mother, especially with no father to make them take heed.'

'I'm not doing that. If I can't go to school then I'm going to work.'

The old lady pursed her lips and blew out air noisily. 'I wish it was so, but I don't think so dear I really don't . . .'

Ruby stopped listening as she wondered how to stop Ray from taking over her life now, as Nan had reminded her, their father wasn't around to control the boys.

Ruby hadn't seen her father since the day she had been shipped off to Cambridgeshire, but she had rarely given him a thought. Frank Blakeley had always been so distant with her that she might as well not have existed in the family; it was as if she were invisible. He would, however, often rough and tumble fiercely with his sons to teach them to be men, and discipline them harshly for the smallest misdemeanour, his belt being the favoured tool of formal punishment, or his hand around the back of the head for an instant reprimand.

It was usually Ray who was the recipient of the fiercest beatings because he just would not give in. Ruby and Arthur would cower together, staying as quiet as possible when their father was beating Ray into submission, each of them praying for him to apologise and end it, but he rarely would. It meant that afterwards, despite the pain and the silent tears, Ray would be victorious.

Believing that girls were the responsibility of their mothers, Frank had never laid a finger on his daughter; but he had never interacted with her either. The news that he was dead had been a shock and she had felt sad – he was her father after all – but nowhere near as upset as some of the other evacuees had been when they had received similar news during the war. In the years she was in evacuation George Wheaton had been more of a responsible father figure to her than her own father had in the previous ten, and she adored him for it.

'Mum?' Ruby said as she helped her grandmother down the step into the back room. 'Are you there, Mum?'

She had expected her brothers to all be there to welcome her back; for her mother to be waiting for her; but no one seemed to be around.

The room was long and dim, with a single standard lamp alight in the corner; it was dominated by an impressive round table with large bulbous feet, which was covered in a shiny oilskin tablecloth and encircled by six hard-back chairs. The alcoves either side of the chimney breast had built-in dressers, which were filled with assorted crockery, serving dishes and the best sherry glasses. A wooden canteen of cutlery had pride of place on one side, and two large Chinese-style vases, which had previously stood either side of the fireplace in the parlour, on the other.

As her grandmother sat at the table and shuffled herself comfortable, Ruby went through the scullery to the back door, which was wedged open with an old iron pot. She stepped out into the back yard, trying to ignore the outside lavatory, which she knew she would have to get used to using again. Just the thought of it made her feel nauseous.

'Mum? Where are you?'

'Out here, Ruby, just getting the washing in. I should have done it hours ago. Can you come and help me?'

'Nan wants her tea. I said I'd make her a cup of tea while she waits. I thought the boys would be here to say hello.'

'Well, Nan will just have to wait until I've finished this, unless you want to heat it up for her. It's in the oven with yours. The boys have gone off somewhere like they always do and there's all this needs doing. Good job it's been a nice day, but it's already starting to get damp.' Her mother looked at her and smiled brightly. 'Now come over here and I'll show you whose clothes are whose. The boys don't like it if their clothes get all mixed up!'

'The boys, the boys. Don't you want to know what's been going on for me? I've been away for five years. *Five years*,' Ruby said flatly without moving. The washing line was stretched the length of the small back yard, which was part paved and part vegetable garden. A small corrugated roof extended out from the scullery and provided cover for the mangle. At the end, the gate that led out into the back alley was open.

'Don't be silly, Ruby, we've got plenty of time to catch up on everything now you're back for good. Back where you belong, not up there with those snobs. Here, hold this for me . . .'

Still smiling, Sarah pushed a battered laundry basket at her. Looking down, she remarked, 'Those shoes are a bit too grown up for you. You're only fifteen and they've got a heel . . .'

'And they're too big for you,' Ruby replied quickly with a smile, aware of the way the conversation was about to go. 'My feet are huge.'

'That's all right,' her mother replied seriously, still looking at her daughter's feet. 'I can stuff paper in the toes.'

Ruby didn't answer. She didn't want an argument, but she could see her mother was going to find it hard to accept that Ruby had gone away a child and come back an independent young woman with a mind of her own and ambitions to fulfil.

At that moment, standing in the back yard with a

washing basket of clothes in front of her, she knew that she couldn't stay in Walthamstow. It had been her home when she was a child but now that she had seen a different way of life it was alien to her. She'd tried to do the right thing but she could see that her return had actually been nothing to do with her personally. It was simply a power struggle, with her mother and Ray asserting their position over the Wheatons.

She watched as her mother quickly took the washing off the line and transferred it to the basket Ruby was holding out. She pretended she was listening to her mother's instruction about whose clothes were whose but she was already mentally composing her letter to George and Babs Wheaton, telling them she wanted to go back.

But even as she was doing it she knew that the letter would be the easy part. Persuading her mother and Ray would be the problem.

THREE

Ruby found life back at the Blakeley family home far more difficult to deal with than she had ever expected and, as the weeks passed, it got worse rather than better. She looked after her grandmother, helped around the house and ran errands for her continually overworked and dog-tired mother. She did her duty as she saw it, the duty she had gone home to do, but nothing seemed enough. Alongside that she generally irritated her bombastic brother, Ray, as much as she could, her view being that if she annoyed him enough there wouldn't be any objections to her leaving and going back to Cambridgeshire.

As the days passed she became increasingly obsessed with getting back to the Wheatons, and it always took several seconds when she woke up in the morning to remember where she was and then for the overwhelming sense of injustice to rise again. But her mother refused point blank to even discuss Ruby's return to Melton.

'Mum? I'm off to the High Street,' Ruby shouted, quickly pulling the front door closed behind her and hotfooting it away from the house. She wanted to escape before she was given an even longer list of things to do and items to try to buy. She resented always having to do the shopping, especially with rationing making it such a chore, but at least it got her out of the house and away from her mother's ongoing domestic grumblings, and Ray's tormenting, which was made worse by her middle brother, Bobbie, slavishly agreeing with his every word. Arthur remained her friend as best he could, but his fear of upsetting his oldest brother meant he would always run off and hide rather than get involved.

Ray and Bobbie worked at the same motor repair garage so more often than not they left together in the morning on Ray's beloved motorbike and arrived home together in the evening expecting their dinner to be waiting for them on the table, their clothes to be washed and ironed and their beds made.

And everything was always done. Their mother made sure of it.

Sarah Blakeley had easily accepted Ray's declaration of himself as 'Head of the Family', and Ruby saw he was turning into a clone of his father, the man he and his brothers had always been petrified of. He carefully shaped his moustache in the same manner, tipped his flat cap at the same angle, and when he shrugged on his late father's heavy overcoat the resemblance from a distance was perfect.

Ruby couldn't understand why he would want to be just like the father who had always treated him so harshly but she didn't comment; she simply observed and wondered why her mother didn't stand up for the women in the house.

She was deep in thought as she walked and was almost at the bottom of the road when she heard her name being called.

'Ruby! Ruby! Hang on a minute . . .'

She hesitated but didn't turn round; without looking she knew that it was Johnnie from down the street, the man who'd carried her bags and caught her eye; the man she'd only seen in passing since that day, but who she had thought about and also heard much about.

'Ruby!' he shouted again. 'Wait a minute and I'll walk with you, Ruby Red.'

This time she stopped and waited with a smile for him to catch her up.

As he drew alongside he looked at her appreciatively and she was pleased she'd come back from the Wheatons' with a decent selection of clothes and a secret lipstick. Clothes that had fortunately turned out to be mostly far too tight for her wide-hipped and ample-bosomed mother, despite the middle-aged woman trying her best to squeeze into them one by one.

'Hello. What's this Ruby Red silliness?' she asked.

'That's what I've decided to call you, Ruby Red. Red for short. You look like a Red. Anyway, you look nice. Where are you off to?'

With a grin Ruby held up the shopping baskets. 'Just running shopping errands for Mum and Nan, off to queue, queue, queue in the High Street. Again. My life is one long queue, hand over coupons, queue again.'

'See? I was right. Didn't take them long to get you back in harness. Big brother Ray said he was going to train you back into your place, as the family slave.'

Ruby laughed. 'Shut up! He never said it like that! Do you think I'm daft enough to let you annoy me? Ray told me all about you and what you're like, so don't bother.'

'Oh, so you were interested enough to ask him about me, then? I'm flattered.'

Ruby smiled up at him shyly as he fell in step beside her, his long legs taking just one step to two of hers.

'Not really! Anyway, I don't really mind getting the shopping for the moment. Ma has plenty to do with her job and everything. I do it for her, not the boys. And it's just until I can get a job and earn some money; just until I can start nursing training and live in at a hospital.'

'But they get the benefit of everything you do – don't you care?'

'I already told you I don't care.' Ruby lied easily, not wanting Johnnie Riordan to see her as downtrodden. 'In a way I feel sorry for Ray. He's just jealous he didn't get to live where I did during the war. His face nearly hit the floor when he saw it all when he came to order me home. It was so nice there – clean with lots of fresh air – it makes this bombed-out place look like a slum.'

'Oi! Hang on now, missy.' Johnnie stopped walking and faced her. 'I live round here, so does my sister and her kids, and it's all right, thank you very much. Apart from your bloody brothers, that is. If anything's wrong round here it's Ray and Bobbie. They lower the tone.'

Although he was half-smiling there was an anger in his words that made Ruby pull herself up. She suddenly realised what a snob she sounded.

'Sorry, I didn't mean it like that, I really didn't. I meant the size of the houses and the gardens and everything – it's all so much smaller here, and overcrowded. It's so different from where I was out in the country with open fields, fresh air and no bomb damage, I'm still getting used to it back here.'

'Apology accepted. I didn't really think you'd be such a duchess, despite what your brothers say.'

Johnnie resumed walking and Ruby strode alongside him.

'Good,' she smiled. 'I'm not like that at all! And yes, I did ask about you. I wanted to know who you were before I spoke to you again. But I have to say that I didn't ask Ray – as if I'd do that – I asked Mum, and she went and told Ray.'

'And am I all right to talk to?' he asked.

'No you're not. Ray went nuts and has forbidden me

to even look at you, never mind have a conversation. You are the villainous enemy, a spiv who he hates, who hates him, a really nasty piece of work and far too old. And you think you own the place.'

'Bloody hell, Ruby, far too old? I'm only nineteen! Though, thinking about it, I suppose the rest is true enough.'

Ruby kept her expression serious for a few moments before bursting into laughter.

Johnnie joined in as they quickly turned the corner, out of sight of the street, neither of them wanting to be seen with the other by their immediate neighbours, although for different reasons.

Despite the age difference they looked good together. Ruby was tall, at five foot seven, and certainly looked older that her years in the classy tailored clothes that she had brought back with her. Despite her slenderness she was shapely, with a tiny waist, neat breasts and wavy auburn hair, which was fixed back from her face with large grips and sugar water. Johnnie meanwhile was just under six foot, with broad shoulders. His fair hair was a little too long at the front, his features were even, and he had a natural loping grace that emphasised his long legs. They made an attractive couple as they walked along together, and Ruby felt comfortable with him alongside her, albeit with a large shopping basket looped over her arm between them just to be sure.

As they strolled slowly to the High Street Ruby told him a little about the Wheatons and her life with them.

Her time in evacuation had been spent in a small village so she had socialised with a far broader age range than when she had been living in Walthamstow. Her evacuation years, during which she'd had both dancing and tennis lessons, had served her very well, leaving her self-assured, graceful, and as comfortable around boys as she was with girls; but these assets now, in her original city surroundings, made her feel like a fish out of water.

Melton in Cambridgeshire, where Ruby had been sent to stay, was situated between Cambridge and Saffron Walden, and a long bumpy bus ride from either town. In typical village style, there was just one main street, but with narrow lanes and tracks running off, leading to outlying farms and cottages. The High Street was edged with an assortment of shops and houses, with Dr George Wheaton's surgery and family home at the top of the gently winding hill and the village school at the bottom. It was a slow and easy way of life, even in wartime, and because it was a few miles from the nearest towns, everyone knew everyone else and their business.

At the school, instead of clusters of children of the same age grouped around the playground, as there had been at Ruby's Walthamstow school, pupils of all ages, including the evacuee children, played together both in and out of school. There had been a natural wariness on both sides when the evacuees first arrived, but after the initial settling-in period, when there were natural divisions, an integration of sorts had happened. Keith and Marian Forger, the children of the local greengrocer, had very quickly become Ruby's closest friends.

Marian was two years older than Ruby and her brother, Keith, was Ruby's age. They lived with their parents over the shop in the village itself, and their cousins lived about a mile away in two adjoining cottages tied to an outlying farm where their respective fathers worked. Their family was close and all the cousins played and socialised together.

It was Keith who had held out the hand of friendship to the very scared ten-year-old Ruby on her first day at the village school, and she had had a huge soft spot for him ever since. He was short and wiry, with straw-coloured hair that never quite behaved, a splattering of freckles on his nose and hazel eyes. Ruby had adored him from the very first moment he'd smiled and befriended her, and, despite rapidly outgrowing him in size and maturity, she'd continued to adore him the whole time she was there.

Keith was a rough-and-tumble boy with no academic aspirations, who was happiest helping his father in the shop and with deliveries, while his sister, Marian, was the brains of the family. She was determined to go to university and become a doctor; she was also a brilliant comedienne and imparter of the facts of life as she knew them. The five farm cousins were all experts in animal husbandry so there was nothing Ruby didn't quickly learn about the birds and the bees and the ways of boys. The related group of children had drawn her in and become like brothers and sisters, and it had been nearly as hard to say goodbye to them as it had been to leave the Wheatons. But she'd promised she would keep in touch and had insisted she would be back as soon as possible.

As she gave Johnnie the description of her life in Melton, Ruby felt her eyes misting and a huge wave of homesickness swept over her.

'. . . And I'm going to go back just as I promised, as soon as I can persuade Mum and Ray that they don't really want me here after all. I mean, they don't want me, they just hate the idea of me being with the Wheatons and liking it.'

'Best of luck to you then,' Johnnie said sympathetically. 'I hope you manage to talk them round and then I can come and visit you. I've been to the seaside at Southend and up west to the city but I've never really been to the country apart from getting up to no good in Epping Forest a few times.'

'Oh, it's so different to here, all open spaces and everyone knows everyone. It's just nicer, I suppose. We all had so much freedom. It was just so different and—'

'OK, OK, that's enough, I'll take your word for it.'

Johnnie Riordan grinned as he interrupted her and held his hands up as if in defeat. He and Ruby had got to the queue outside the grocers. 'I've got to see someone, so you go and get started with your shopping and I'll meet you on the corner by the butcher's in about an hour and help you with the rest of it. I'd take you for a tea and a bun but we might be seen.'

Ruby smiled to herself as he walked away. There was something about him that cheered her up and made her feel like a grown up. An hour later she stood on the corner and tried not to look too pleased when he came strutting along the pavement towards her.

Doing the shopping with Johnnie alongside relieved some of the monotony of standing in the various queues to get everything on her mother's list. It was a relaxing and light-hearted few hours away from the house, but as she neared home she knew there was going to be trouble the moment she saw Ray waiting on the pavement outside. He was leaning against the gate jamb, his arms crossed and his face screwed up in anger. Ruby was relieved that she and Johnnie had parted company way before they reached their street.

Ray had one of those faces that would have been handsome if his nature had been different, but he exuded a thin-lipped violence that twisted his features and made him look unattractive and nasty.

As she looked at him she was suddenly scared, but there was no way she was going to let him see.

'Where the fuck have you been?' he snarled as he unfolded his arms. 'Mum said you've been gone hours.'

'Getting the shopping like Mum asked me, but what's it got to do with you? And anyway, shouldn't you be at work?' Ruby asked with a smile and a lot more bravado in her voice than she felt in her heart.

'It's got plenty to do with me. What have you been up to all this time?'

'Mind your own. You can't tell me what to do or when to do it.'

He moved closer to her. 'I'm the man of this house, head of the household, and you answer to me. Those retarded bumpkins out in the middle of nowhere might have let you roam the streets doing what you want but I won't. Your job is to help Ma and Nan. If you have to get shopping you go and then come straight back.'

Ruby gasped as she took in his words. 'Man of the house? Oh, do shut up. Do you know how daft you sound? This isn't the cinema, it's real life. You're my brother, that's all you are – just a brother. An equal, not a bloody overseer.'

Ruby laughed in astonishment as she went to push past him. She couldn't believe that her brother would speak to her like that.

'You're a kid, you're underage and you do as I say or else.' He moved in front of her, blocking her way with his body.

'Or else what? No, I do what I like and it's none of your business. I'm not your daughter or your wife. Now get out of my way if you want supper tonight, else I'll tip this lot out in the street and you'll have bugger all.'

For a moment Ray looked quite shocked. He hadn't expected her to challenge him.

'You dare talk to me like that, you little cow! Now get into your room and stay there until I say you can come out!'

Ruby stared hard at Ray and slowly shook her head. 'Not bloody likely. Get away from me . . .'

His hand flicked out and he grabbed her forcefully by the arm, dragged her down the path to the front door, then pulled her round until they were nose to nose.

'Get indoors and get into your room or I'll get Dad's belt to you.'

'You just try it, you lay one finger on me and I'll be out of that door for good. Don't forget, I've got somewhere to go.'

As soon as the words were out she regretted them. In the heat of the moment she had given Ray an insight into her thoughts.

'That's what you think,' he snarled. 'You ain't going nowhere, never in a million years. Nowhere!' His face was so close to hers she could feel the spittle on her cheek as he spat the words at her.

She tried to pull away from him but he just tightened his grip around the top of her arm and walked her over the doorstep into the hall before pulling his other hand back and slapping her across the face. As she reeled away he snatched the shopping basket from her before shoving her so forcefully into her bedroom she tumbled straight onto her bed. Then, before she could stand up, he took the key from the inside, slammed the door shut and locked it.

'Now you can stay there until I say you can come out.'

She rattled the handle with one hand and massaged her face with the other. She could feel her cheek swelling and her eye starting to close.

'Open this door,' she screamed as loud as she could. 'Open the door!'

But there was just silence from the other side.

FOUR

'Oh, Ruby, you silly girl, what have you done to upset Ray? He's got a fearsome temper, that lad. He's not one to be crossed.'

Ruby looked round and realised for the first time that her grandmother was also in the room and sitting quietly in her chair by the window.

'I haven't done anything. He's just being a pig because he *is* a pig. I hate him,' Ruby said, fighting hard not to cry. Not because she was upset or even because she was hurt, but because she was so angry and frustrated. How dare he do that to her? Hitting her was bad enough, but locking her in her bedroom like a child? She rattled the handle loudly and kicked out at the door, hoping that her mother would come and let her out.

'Let me out of here,' she screamed as loudly as she could. 'Mum? Arthur? Are you there? Someone unlock this bloody door. Ray locked me in and Nan's inside. Mum?'

'They won't open the door, Ruby, not if Ray's locked

it. They'll never cross Ray, none of them. They're all scared of him, even your mother; and anyway, he'll have the key in his pocket, like as not. No one'll dare ask for it.' Her grandmother's tone was wearily matter-of-fact.

'But why's Mum scared of him? He's her son, he should respect her, shouldn't he?' Ruby asked.

'Because that Ray's just like his father – your father – and she knows it. He doesn't respect anyone. He's nothing but a bullyboy and your grandfather would turn in his grave if he could see the way that boy carries on. My Ernie never liked your father right from the first day your mother brought him home, and he wouldn't like Ray, I know that for a fact. Truly like father like son. Peas in a pod, those two.' Pulling her shawl tighter round her shoulders she shook her head sadly. 'The others aren't really bad boys. Bobbie looks up to Ray, God help him, so he does as he's told, and poor Arthur doesn't really understand it all. But that Ray, he's bad through and through and no one can do anything about it.' She sighed, her whole chest heaving as if it was an effort. 'But it's your mother I feel for. My poor Sarah. A thug for a husband and now a thug for a son. Your mother is my only living child, even though we had three, so it hurts all the more to see her treated like that by one of her own children.'

Ruby sat on the edge of her bed and studied her grandmother, whom she knew could probably see only her outline across the room. For the first time since her return to London she was seeing her as a person; as Elsie Saunders, wife and mother, not just Nan who now lived with them all and with whom she grudgingly shared a bedroom.

Ruby had been so busy feeling sorry for herself that she hadn't realised how hard it must be for a woman of Nan's age to go from having her own home, where she had lived all her married life with her husband and where she had raised a family, to owning nothing and having to share a bedroom with a fifteen-year-old, eating her meals when she was told and being ordered around like a child by her own grandson.

It was too much for Ruby and she felt the tears of guilt break through and roll down her cheek. Standing up she went over the woman, leaned forward and hugged her tightly.

'Well, I never – what was that for?'

'Because I'm a selfish cow, Nan, and I'm sorry.'

Elsie Saunders' eyes also filled up. 'You're a good girl, Ruby, and it's a crying shame they made you come back here. Your mother shouldn't have done that and I told her so when Ray went to get you. She should have let you get away from this, even if she can't.'

'I want to go back there, Nana, I want to go back so badly, and they want me back. I could finish school and get qualifications. I want to train to be a nurse. It wouldn't mean I'd be gone for ever. Aunty Babs was teaching me how to sew my own clothes and grow fruit and vegetables, and I had real friends. But how can I go back now I know what's going on here? I can't leave you and Mum with Ray.'

Ruby started to cry. She didn't want to; she didn't want there to be any possibility of Ray finding out she was upset, but she couldn't help it.

'Don't you cry, Ruby love. Listen to me: you have to go back. You can't stop Ray being as he is, as your mother let him be, so don't sacrifice yourself. I saw what he did – my eyes are bad, but not that bad – and anyhow, I know that sound. He's his father's son all right.' She reached her hand up and gently touched her granddaughter's swelling face. 'Now, as we're locked in together, why don't you tell me all about your time away? We haven't had time for more than a few words since you've been back and it would be so nice to hear all about it.'

It was Sarah who opened the door a couple of hours later. 'Your dinner's ready and the boys have gone out. I told Ray he shouldn't have locked you in. He gave me the key.'

'Then why didn't you let us out? He locked Nan in here as well, and he hit me you know; hit me around the face. Look.' Ruby pointed to her swollen cheek.

Her mother glanced at her. 'That's going to really bruise up. I'll find the witch hazel. But you shouldn't have upset him. He told me what you said. You wouldn't have spoken to your father like that, would you?' The woman pursed her lips and shook her head slowly. 'Anyway, what's done is done. Just remember next time, Ray can get carried away but he doesn't mean it badly; he's just trying to look after everyone the best he can.'

'He is not my father. He locked the door with Nana in here. You should have let us out straight away.' Ruby was incensed and so was her tone but her mother simply shrugged.

'But there's no harm done, is there? And you'll know for next time. He is the man of the house now.'

'Oh, stop using that expression. There's nothing manly about him. He's just a thug and a bully. I hate him.'

Her mother didn't answer straight away; she simply frowned and looked from her daughter to her mother in bemusement, as if she really didn't understand what Ruby was so upset about.

'I don't think you understand, Ruby. Your brothers, especially Ray, work hard to keep this family going now your father's gone. Without them I'd probably end up in the workhouse. It's not asking much of you to help me look after them and your nan. Don't forget while you were living the life of Riley with the la-di-dah Wheatons, the boys were here working, I was working, and we were all trying to survive the Blitz.'

'But you sent me away. I didn't ask to go,' Ruby shouted.

'Yes we did. We sent you for your own safety, but you were meant to come back!'

Ruby stared at her mother. Sarah Blakeley was an attractive woman who had kept her looks despite everything she'd been through. There were lines across her forehead and around her eyes, and her lips were pinched, but she still retained her shapely figure and feminine legs that suited high heels. However, she rarely smiled spontaneously, her eyes were constantly unhappy and when she spoke her voice was a monotone. She wasn't enjoying her life, she was just going through the motions.

After her long chat with her grandmother when they were locked in the bedroom, Ruby had promised that she would try to be understanding of her mother, and at that moment she could see why the woman gave in to Ray on everything. It was the route to an easier life with fewer arguments. Arguments she knew she couldn't win. She had been bullied and ground down by her own husband all her married life so it had become part of her nature to accept it as her lot in life. Ray had simply stepped straight into his father's vacant shoes and she had let him. The treadmill for Sarah Blakeley just carried on with no end in sight and although Ruby felt for her she had no intention of getting on it herself.

In bed that night, with Elsie on the other side of the room snoring and snuffling and keeping her awake, Ruby pulled her eiderdown up to her chin and thought about her afternoon with Johnnie from down the street. Those had been the most carefree hours she'd had since her return. He'd made her laugh as she stood in the queues, bought her an icecream and then helped her carry the shopping. He was blatantly experienced in the ways of the world, maybe overly confident, and from what she'd heard was certainly involved in a great many dodgy dealings, but that added an element of danger that attracted her.

On the other side of the coin he spoke lovingly of his family and had a kindly streak that had been obvious the first time she'd met him. As she thought about Johnnie Riordan she couldn't help but focus on the resentment that existed between him and Ray and wonder if there was some way she could use her newfound friendship with Johnnie to get her own back on her brother.

It was easy for her mother to shrug off Ray's behaviour, but she couldn't. Ray had hit her and treated her as a child – her own brother had acted as if she was his child instead of a sibling – and she had no intention of letting that go without taking some sort of revenge that would punish him and, at the same time, distract him enough to allow her to make her escape back to Melton.

She knew that although Johnnie Riordan worked legitimately in a public house he was also a wheeler-dealer with a finger in many pies, some legal, some not. He bought and sold anything that might earn him a few bob, including the things that the ordinary man in the street had no access to in times of rationing and shortages. It had taken her a while to figure out why Ray hated Johnnie so much. Now she knew: it was because he was jealous; because he really wanted to be a part of those activities himself but he didn't have a quick enough brain to think things up for himself.

Ruby wondered if she could find a way to make that work in her favour, and as she finally dozed off a plan was coming together in her head.

'You know what, Roger, I'm gonna have to sort this out right now. I've got no choice. I can't let those pricks get away with it any longer, not now they're messing around close to home – to my home. If I roll over and let them carry on taking the mick like this then every upstart in Walthamstow and beyond will be trying to get his foot in the door – my door, on my turf.'

His irritation bubbling away, Johnnie Riordan slammed his fist down hard on the table, making the teacups rattle in their saucers and his brother-in-law jump nervously.

'But how's it your turf?' the other man frowned. 'You don't own Walthamstow, and anyway, what do you reckon you can do to stop them?'

'That's what I've got to decide. Any ideas?' Johnnie asked out of kindness more than anything. He didn't really expect a workable answer.

'I'm new at this lark so I don't know nothing; I'm not like you. It's hard for me after what's happened and I just don't bloody well understand any of it. I can't do it.'

The man sitting opposite Johnnie was so bewildered he looked as if he was about to burst into tears. Johnnie tried hard to keep himself in control. He was fuming at having found out that Ray Blakeley had apparently got his hands on some black-market alcohol to sell on. It wasn't that Johnnie didn't have enough of his own, it was that Ray even thought he could try to encroach on his territory.

'Don't whine, mate. I know it's hard for you to get your head round it, but when needs must and all that . . . It's not your fault you're a cripple now, and I feel bad for you, I really do, but your family still need providing for. I've given you a good way of doing that so you've just got to get on with it. You help me and I'll help you, but you've got to be committed.'

'But committed to what? What you do's dishonest. I was never clever, and I'm even dafter now, but that don't make me bent. I've never been bent.'

'It isn't dishonest, it isn't bent and you're not daft, just a war victim.' Johnnie struggled to keep his anger down. 'Well, yeah, OK, it is a bit dodgy but, like I said, when needs must; and right now needs must. I've got a living to earn and you've got a family to take care of.'

Johnnie was sitting in his sister's kitchen along with his brother-in-law, Roger Dalton. After they'd got home from the local pub Betty had made them a huge pot of tea, put it in front of them with a couple of home-made biscuits, while at the same time threatening them with their lives if they woke the two sleeping children upstairs.

Johnnie adored his elder sister and her children, and he even liked her husband, which was lucky, as he lived with them and contributed more than his fair share to the family budget.

Johnnie had been living with their widowed mother until the year before when, with very little notice, she had told him she was going off to be a live-in housekeeper in central London for a very wealthy elderly gentleman she'd met while working in the menswear department in Selfridges.

It had been a surprise but neither he nor Betty had been upset. Betty was pleased that her mother was enjoying her life again and had persuaded her beloved little brother to leave the temporary accommodation where he and their mother had been living since being bombed out of the old family home, and come to lodge with her instead. Johnnie was also pleased for his mother but, with an eye always on a chance, he had viewed his mother's change of circumstances more cynically and could see that her affluent employer was a connection that he might well be able to cultivate in time.

All in all it had worked well for the whole family.

'I reckon a good battering should do it, nothing too serious but enough to stop his fucking nonsense.' Johnnie leaned back in the chair and blew smoke rings in the air as he thought about it. 'That Ray likes to think he's a hard nut, but he's just another little punk without enough brains to be even a half-decent entrepreneur. As for Bobbie, he could be squashed underfoot in an instant. A few hard kicks up the arse should knock them down to size.'

'Entrepen what?' Roger looked quizzically at his brother-in-law.

'It's what I am and what I'm going to make you. Supply and demand. I've told you before, we find those who haven't got it but want it and then we supply it.'

'Supply what?'

'Oh, for fuck's sake, Roger, anything anyone wants that we can get our hands on. We're the middlemen. But you know all this; I've explained it over and over.' Johnnie sighed and banged the palm of his hand against his forehead in frustration.

'I know, but I've never heard it called that before. I thought it was just the black-market stuff.'

Johnnie sighed and leaned forward. 'Now listen to me, don't even mutter that expression under your breath, never mind out loud. We're businessmen – does that make it easier for you to understand? Anyone asks, we're businessmen. Don't say anything else. OK?'

Roger Dalton frowned and shrugged. He had never been the sharpest knife in the drawer but, before signing up to fight in the army, he had had a steady job in a local factory and had worked hard to provide for his family. Now, thanks to a random grenade, he was officially an invalid with a gammy arm that hung lifelessly by his side, a shattered knee that didn't bend, and an eye patch covering an empty eye socket while he waited to be fitted with a false one. But worse than the physical damage was the effect the explosion had had on him psychologically. Roger had returned from convalescence a nervous wreck who rarely slept and who jumped at the slightest sound.

He was getting better – mostly thanks to his wife – but Johnnie had also more than contributed to his painful recovery.

Johnnie was determined not to see his sister go without, so he was doing his best to help by getting Roger into a bit of wheeling and dealing alongside him, but it was hard work and he could only use him on the periphery of his blossoming business. There was no way Roger could cope with anything complex and Johnnie wasn't convinced he could be trusted not to talk inadvertently about his business to the wrong people.

'I saw you down the High Street talking to his sister earlier. Betty told me who she was. Is she like her brothers?'

'You never said hello – where were we?' Johnnie asked sharply.

'You were standing by the alley looking at her all daft, like. So is she like her brothers?'

'I wasn't looking at her like that, you idiot!' Johnnie said a little too quickly. 'But no, she's not a typical Blakeley. An old head on young shoulders, that one; all classy and bright as a button, thanks to spending five years away from the no-hopers in her family. I think she'll give the bloody Blakeley boys a run for their money eventually. She especially hates Ray so she's a good one to have on our side. We can make use of her if we play our cards right; get some info from her when we need it.'

'Do you want to go out with her then?' Roger asked

curiously. 'She's a bit of a looker, but don't tell Bet I said that.'

'Get off, she's far too young for me – not even sixteen yet,' Johnnie replied quickly, but with a lack of conviction. 'But there's something about her, the way she carries herself, her conversation . . . I dunno, she just seems way older than other girls her age. If I didn't know I'd have put her at twenty.'

'So you do want to go out with her?' Roger pushed with a wide grin.

'I said, she's too young for that, but I do want to be friends with her so I can keep tabs on the two toerags.'

'So are we going to have to batter 'em then? The Blakeleys?'

'No we're not, I'm going to get someone else to do it. We don't want to get in any bother ourselves, do we?'

Again Roger looked vague and Johnnie could feel his patience evaporating.

'Look, I've got to have a good think about it first. Maybe we could find Ray's stash and nick it. He has to store it somewhere, probably in that garage where they both work. He couldn't tell anyone we'd done it, could he? It'd drive him crazy and get him into some real bother.' Johnnie smiled at the thought, then stood up. 'Still, enough of that now, we'd better get ourselves off to bed before our Betty has a go. Me and her are off up west tomorrow to see Ma in her classy joint. Might even get to meet the rich toff she's working for.'

'It's not fair. I dunno why I can't go as well.' Roger's voice was childlike, his tone sulky. 'Why does Betty want to go with you and not me? I'm her husband.'

It irritated Johnnie when Roger behaved like this, but he tried to make allowances for everything he'd been through.

'Because you and Aunty Clara are keeping an eye on the kids for a change, and my motorbike don't take three.'

'But I want to go as well.'

'Too bad,' Johnnie interrupted. 'I want doesn't always get. Your missus needs a break sometimes, and I'm taking her out so stop bloody moaning on like a sissy.'

As soon as the words were out he felt guilty. 'Anyway, I've got a job you can do if you want an extra couple of bob; just an hour or so while the kids are at school.'

Roger's face lit up. 'What's that then?'

'I'll tell you about it in the morning,' Johnnie replied, giving himself a few hours to think of something that would help his brother-in-law's self-esteem.

FIVE

A large group of children all aged around ten stood in two raggedy lines. They faced forward obediently and, even though the boys feigned bravado, each and every one of the children was noticeably scared and nervous. Hands and feet fidgeted and eyes either darted around, taking in the unfamiliar scene, or stared down at their shoes.

Ruby Blakeley was in the middle of one line, her small suitcase and gas mask at her feet, tightly holding hands with the equally terrified small girl beside her. Her heart was thumping and tears were threatening to overflow once again from her already red eyes; all she wanted to do was run out of the gates and keep on running until she got back home. What had seemed a bit of an adventure when they had set off for the train station earlier that same morning had quickly turned into a nightmare once the reality of the situation sank in. They were leaving their families, homes and everything familiar to go and live far away with complete strangers.

Once the selection process got underway her thoughts became confused. On the one hand she desperately wanted to be picked, but on the other she didn't want to have to go home with any of the strangers who were milling around the playground, chatting with each other.

As they had neared the village, Mrs Sparrow, one of the accompanying teachers, had stood up at the front of the coach and briefly explained to the thirty children on board exactly what would happen once they had reached their destination.

'To make sure you all understand I'll repeat everything you were told earlier on the train, so listen very carefully. Those of you with red dots on your labels are getting off at the first village and the other half with blue dots will be taken to the next village with Miss Flynn. The other coaches, with the children who are accompanied by their mothers, have gone elsewhere. We'll be ticking your names off the list as you get off so don't any of you be trying to stay on board if you're in the first group.'

The usually stern teacher smiled down at the sea of small faces to ease the tension and paused while every child looked down at his or her name label.

'Once you're matched with your host family they'll take you to their home where you're going to live with them until London's safe again. These are kindly people who are doing their war duty so we expect you to repay them by *doing as you're told at all times, being helpful and behaving well. You'll be attending school while you're here, so you'll make some new friends; and don't forget, Miss Flynn and I will be staying with our groups for the time being. We know you're going to miss your families but you all have to be brave. It's for your own good, remember, to take you all away from the bombing.'*

A few minutes after she had finished speaking the coach pulled over to the side of the road and stopped. It was the moment of reality for the children, and some of the girls had started to cry openly while most of the boys chewed their lips, fiddled with their hankies and stared out of the windows, pretending not to care.

'All right, children. Red dots collect all your belongings and follow me. Quickly! Tell me your name and show me your label as you get off.'

The children scrambled off the coach and formed a crocodile before hesitantly following their teacher into the church hall next to the local school. After a brief respite, which included hot chocolate and biscuits, they were instructed to line up back in the school playground and the process began.

Only three children were picked before Ruby. Then she saw a woman point to her.

'Ruby Blakeley, step forward, please,' her teacher said, and she took the smallest step forward with her eyes firmly on the ground. 'Ruby! Manners!'

Swallowing hard, she looked up just as a tall, imposing woman stepped up to her and smiled.

'Hello, Ruby. I'm Mrs Wheaton. You're coming home to stay with me.'

Despite the lady's friendliness, Ruby was terrified, and she couldn't stop herself from shaking as she bent down to pick up her sparse belongings.

'You look frightened, Ruby, but don't be. Think of this as a nice holiday,' the woman said gently before taking Ruby's free hand and walking her up the main village street. She talked all the way, explaining about the village and pointing out the shops and landmarks, but the ten-year-old was so wrapped up in her own fear she found it hard to even concentrate, let alone respond.

'Here we are, Ruby, just in here. This is where we live. We don't have any children ourselves but your schoolfriends will be staying nearby. I was part of the committee that organised the billets so you just have to ask and I can tell you where they all are. And you'll make new friends at school.'

Ruby looked around as they approached the house. From the exterior it reminded her of 'the big house' up in Woodford, where her mother was employed as a cleaner. During the school holidays she had sometimes gone with her mother and waited impatiently on the wall outside, wondering about the inside, but not once had she been allowed over the threshold; and she had never met her mother's employer.

The Wheaton property was equally impressive, with thick wisteria growing up the walls, flowerbeds on each *side and a walled garden to the rear. The house itself was L-shaped and stood alone on a corner at the top of the main street behind a high but neatly trimmed hedge. A large black car was parked on the drive near a detached garage, a fat ginger and white cat curled up on the car roof. He opened his eyes, looked at the newcomer and closed them again.*

Talking all the while, Mrs Wheaton led Ruby along a curvy path to a hidden entrance on the side.

'We always use this entrance because the other one is the one the patients use to go into the surgery. I did tell you my husband is a doctor, didn't I? But there are also doors in the house that lead from one to the other.' She smiled. 'Oh, and the cat is called Fred. He's very gentle and lazy and loves children. Mr Yardley lives in the flat over the garage. He drives the car for the doctor and does all the odd jobs. You'll meet him later, and we usually have a nurse staying with us. There's a new one coming next week. She'll live in the room at the back of the surgery. That's why we only had room to take in one evacuee. It's a very busy house and surgery.'

With a hand placed in the middle of her back, the woman gently pushed a hesitant Ruby through an already open front door into a wide, square lobby with a tiled floor and half-panelled walls. Several dark wood doors led off it and there was an impressive staircase to the side that turned twice on its way to the first floor. Ruby's first impression was that it was enormous, so enormous she couldn't imagine sleeping even one night inside without being scared witless.

'I'll show you your bedroom in a minute, but first I want you to meet my husband. He'll be through in just a moment.'

Even as Mrs Wheaton spoke Ruby heard a clunking sound and turned around to see a man in a wheelchair heading across the tiled floor towards them. Ruby was petrified when she saw the man wheeling himself towards her. His head was down and she couldn't see his expression.

'George darling, this is Ruby Blakeley, the evacuee who's going to be staying with us. She's ten years old and from London. She's also very nervous, understandably. Ruby, this is my husband, Dr Wheaton.'

'Don't be nervous, Ruby,' the man said as he stopped his chair in front of her. 'I'm pleased to meet you. I hope you'll be happy during your time here; we look forward to having you for as long as you need to be here.'

The man held his hand out to her and smiled. His face was friendly and his tone soothing but, despite all the niceness, a huge wave of homesickness swept over her and before she could reach out and take the proffered hand she started to cry. Her shoulders moved up and down in time with the huge gasping sobs that she tried desperately to control but couldn't.

Mrs Wheaton immediately bent down and pulled the little girl to her; she hugged her tight and, whispering gently, she continued to hold her until the sobs subsided.

'There, I think the worst is over for you now so chin up. I'll show you your room and then we'll have dinner and get to know each other.'

Later that night Ruby lay curled up in her bed and thought about everything that had happened during that long first day. She was exhausted, but although Mrs Wheaton had made her a cup of warm cocoa she couldn't sleep. Her room was large and her bed was soft and welcoming, but she hated it and wished she was back home in the familiar boxroom, which she had to herself because she was the only girl. She also wished she had been able to bring some of her favourite personal things with her: the three china animal ornaments that had perched on her windowsill for as long as she could remember, the wooden box that contained all manner of secrets and mementoes, the mini-bolster that she liked to cuddle at night; but most of all she wished her mother was there with her.

When they'd started to gather in the school playground in Walthamstow, Ruby had assumed that all the children were travelling alone, but then she'd realised that some of the mothers had cases with them also.

'Why aren't you coming, Mum?' she'd asked tearfully.

'Don't fuss, Ruby. Only the babies have their mothers with them. You're a big girl now, you don't need me with you. Besides, I have to look after the boys.'

'Why aren't they being evacuated, then? There are big boys here.' Ruby waved her hand around to make her point.

'You know your dad wouldn't let them go. Just you,

because you're a girl. Now, no more tears. Look, everyone's walking; you need to find your place with your friends. I can see Mary Flaherty over there – go and walk with her.'

'Aren't you even coming to the coach with me?'

'No, I have to get back. I have to get to work or I won't get paid. You know what Mrs Harrison is like if I'm late. But you write to me as soon as you know your address and I'll write back. You won't be away long, I promise!'

The crocodile of children had started moving slowly, and Ruby took her place, but when she looked around to wave she couldn't see her mother anywhere in the sea of faces. There were so many children that no one would have noticed that Ruby's mother had gone, but still her face reddened and her disappointment was physically painful: her mother hadn't even kissed her goodbye.

Now she was in a beautiful bedroom that was probably six times the size of her boxroom back home. It was well furnished, with a proper wash-basin in the corner and a large yellow teddy bear with brown button eyes on the end of the bed. It was beautiful and luxurious beyond her imagination, but at that moment all she wanted was to be back at home with her mother in the crowded terraced house with an outside toilet and no bathroom.

Ruby Blakeley was unhappier than she had ever been in her life. She buried her head under the fluffy pillow and sobbed silently until she was exhausted. Daylight dawned just as she dropped off, and next thing she knew there was a knock on the door.

'Ruby? Are you awake? Breakfast is nearly ready. Ruby?'

'I'm awake.' Ruby replied cautiously.

The door opened slightly and Mrs Wheaton put her head around it.

'Then get washed and dressed and come down. I'll be in the kitchen. Dr Wheaton has an early surgery this morning and then Yardley, the driver, will take him on his rounds so it's just you and me. I'm looking forward to it.'

Ruby climbed out of bed and tiptoed across the landing into the bathroom. She'd never been in one quite like it until the night before and was overawed again with the inside lavatory with a shiny metallic chain, and the huge white bath with claw feet and gleaming taps. Even at the age of ten Ruby was worldly enough to take it all in and wonder exactly how rich the Wheatons were to have a house that size.

As she shyly took her seat at the table in the kitchen Babs Wheaton turned round from the range and put a plate in front of her with a fat rasher of bacon, a fried egg and a thick slice of fried bread. Just looking at it made Ruby feel sick but she knew she had to make an effort. The last thing she wanted to do was upset her host family on the first day.

'Did you get to sleep, Ruby? I heard your bed creaking during the night but I didn't want to come in and upset you.'

'I'm all right,' Ruby mumbled as she looked at the plate in front of her. 'I just feel a bit sick now.'

'Would you sooner have a plain slice of toast? You need something inside you, especially if you feel sick.'

Babs Wheaton removed the barely touched breakfast plate and replaced it with another that had just a slice of toasted bread with a scrape of butter on it and a glass of milk.

'Is that better? I know this is horrid for you but it will get better once you settle. In fact, today is a settling-in day for all the evacuees so we've both got a free day.' She paused and looked at the child sitting at her table. 'I think we should go for a walk round the village. I'll show you the shops and we can look at the church. We might even bump into the vicar and his wife. They also played a big part in arranging this evacuation and finding accommodation for you all.'

'I still feel a bit sick,' Ruby muttered cautiously, not wanting to go anywhere, least of all to meet the vicar and his wife.

'Then a breath of fresh air will do you good. Mind you, I think most of the children will be feeling sick today. It was a long journey for you all yesterday and you're all away from home.'

'Do I have to go to school tomorrow if I still feel sick?' Ruby asked hopefully.

'Oh, I think you'll be fine by tomorrow and, if not . . . well, Dr Wheaton will have a look at you. And you won't be going for the whole day. The school hours have changed because of having to fit in so many extra children; we can check when we get down there this morning.'

Babs Wheaton's tone was lightly firm and her smile was kindly, but Ruby knew instinctively there would be no point in arguing with the woman.

Walking back down the hill through the village, Ruby started to relax. They visited all the shops, and Ruby was impressed that Mrs Wheaton was introducing her as if she was a genuine visitor rather than a child who had simply been dumped on her.

That evening she was surprised when Mrs Wheaton explained about the evening meal; Ruby hadn't expected to be included for every meal and a part of her didn't want to be. The whole situation was far too overwhelming for a ten-year-old away from home for the first time.

'We don't stand on ceremony at mealtimes but we do expect promptness and good table manners. Now you sit here . . .'

Ruby took her seat nervously and sat perfectly still and quiet, with her hands in her lap and her eyes down.

'Now, young Ruby, tell us a little about yourself and your family.'

Ruby looked up through her eyelashes at the man sitting adjacent to her at the head of the table. Her mouth was dry and the nausea she had felt that morning started to rise again.

'We know your father is away at war and that you have two brothers at home—'

'Three brothers.'

'Ah,' Dr Wheaton smiled, 'the lone girl in a family of

78

boys. No wonder you're so quiet; I doubt you ever get a word in.'

Both Dr and Mrs Wheaton tried hard to bring her out of herself and into a conversation but she remained mostly silent and scared.

'Would you pass me the gravy, please, Ruby?' the doctor asked.

Silently Ruby leaned forward and picked up the glass saucer holding the jug, but her hands were shaking so much she couldn't hold on to it. As she went to pass it she felt it slip away and land in the middle of the table, splattering the thick hot gravy everywhere, including down Dr Wheaton's shirt. His wife jumped up from her chair and, with a quickly snatched tea towel, tried to minimise the mess as the doctor wheeled his chair backwards away from the table. But the brown liquid had already made its mark.

Paralysed with fear, Ruby could only watch the chaos she had caused. 'I'm sorry, I didn't mean it, I'm sorry . . .'

As the man moved his wheelchair towards her, so she cowered down in her seat fearfully. She was horrified she could have done such a thing, and terrified of the conse-quences. In her head she could hear her father's angry voice, and she could see the whiplash that was his hand as he banged one or other of her brothers around the head for the slightest perceived misdemeanour. A dropped gravy boat would have earned the boys a sound thrashing with his belt and Ruby a banishment by her mother to her room with nothing to eat or drink until the next day.

'Ruby, it's OK, it's just gravy. It doesn't matter,' Barbara said gently. 'It was an accident. We have them all the time in this house. I often drop things, and so does my husband. Now let's get this cleared up and then we'll start again.'

Eyes wide, Ruby looked from one to the other. 'I'm sorry.'

George Wheaton moved very slowly back beside her. He smiled and then gently ruffled her hair. 'Promise me you won't ever be frightened of either of us again, Ruby. Promise?'

'I promise.'

SIX

Walthamstow

'Any letters for me?' Ruby asked as she closed the front door behind her. It was always the first question she asked the moment she walked into the house. As she slipped off her coat and hung it on the hallstand she looked around hopefully.

'No, and I wish you wouldn't keep going on about it. I'm not as stupid as you think I am, Ruby. I know you mean letters from the bloody Wheatons and you know how much it gets me and your brother going when you keep asking. It's finished – all of it. You have to forget it.'

Head on one side, Ruby stared at her mother. She couldn't understand her constantly defensive stance towards the Wheatons, a couple who had done nothing wrong by her at all. Quite the opposite, in fact.

'I can't forget about it. And anyway, why should it bother Ray? Or you? I lived with them for five years, they

Marie Maxwell

looked after me as if I was their own daughter, and I really want to hear from them.'

'Well, they couldn't have thought that much of you as they haven't even written. Anyway, you should be pleased you had a real family to come back to. Lots of evacuees ended up in orphanages, you know. Homes were bombed, whole families killed, and that was it. Instant orphans. You've got all of us . . . well, apart from your father.'

Sarah Blakeley looked over her shoulder at her daughter and they locked eyes. She was kneeling halfway up the stairs, brushing the narrow carpet to within an inch of its life with a brush and dustpan, and Ruby knew the brass stair rods would be next for a vicious attack of Brasso, followed by the polishing of the banister. Every day of the week was marked by different chores and meals, and nothing was ever allowed to interfere with that domestic routine. Sarah's whole life was run to a meticulous timetable.

Ruby was convinced that her mother worked herself into the ground, both at home and at work so that she was permanently exhausted and therefore too tired to think about her grindingly monotonous life. Ruby felt for her, but at the same time couldn't understand why she didn't do anything about it. Being subservient to a husband was to be expected, but to answer in this way to a son was something else entirely and, as far as Ruby was concerned, not what her mother should accept.

82

'Yes I know, Mum, and I am grateful you're all alive and the house is still standing,' Ruby continued, trying but failing to keep her tone reasoned, 'but just because I have family here doesn't mean I can't have a second family there. They were good to me and you should be pleased.' Her voice got stronger along with her frustration. 'A lot of evacuees were treated like skivvies. I heard about one who only ever slept in a barn, even in winter, and he wasn't allowed to go to school, and he had to work all day on the farm to earn a meal.'

'Don't you shout at me. And *grateful*?' Sarah laughed drily. 'To *them*? I should be grateful that they tried to keep my only daughter? It was only because of Ray going up there that they let you come home at all. Just because they couldn't have their own they wanted to keep you to look after the crippled doctor in his dotage. They've ruined you, given you ideas above your station so you won't settle back here. They did it deliberately.'

Ruby knew her mother was repeating Ray's words and that it was pointless to argue, but she couldn't help it.

'That's not true, you know it isn't. It's just what Ray says . . .'

'It is true, Ruby, it is! Me and Ray both met them, don't forget. Both of them pretending to care but looking down on us all the while. Now stop keep going on about them and how wonderful they are. I mean, how come they've no kids of their own, him being a doctor an' all? Unless he's not a real man down there.'

Ruby was near to tears at the injustice of it all, but still she wouldn't back down.

'Why are you so horrible about them, Mum? They did their best for me and they still want to, I know they do. I could have a career, I could have—'

'Shut up, Ruby. Just shut up, shut up, shut up!' Sarah stood up. She stepped down the stairs and looked at her daughter, and Ruby could see the tears of anger in her eyes.

'I don't understand . . .'

'That's because you don't want to.'

Ruby paused when she saw what looked like genuine hurt on her mother's face. 'Oh, it doesn't matter. Just forget I said anything!'

Ruby stopped arguing. She could see that her mother would always follow Ray's lead and support his opinions. It puzzled her that her own mother didn't want the best possible for her, but she could also see there was no point in arguing about it.

But she was worried. She'd heard nothing from the Wheatons since their first letter and she couldn't understand how they could have forgotten about her so quickly. She'd written to them several times telling them how she felt, how she wanted to go back but wasn't allowed. She had opened up her heart and they hadn't responded, making her wonder if something was amiss.

Because her mother allowed Ray to have the upper hand in the household, Ruby's life was becoming increasingly unbearable. In fact, it was becoming the same as her mother's: a grind of mind-numbing domesticity. Her hopes of escape were pinned on her grandmother's support and the hope that the Wheatons still wanted her to live there.

She grabbed her coat again. 'I'm going to the phone box. I'm going to telephone them. They wouldn't have forgotten my birthday last week, I know they wouldn't. Something must be wrong . . .'

'Don't you dare go running off, Ruby. You come back here this minute! Don't you dare phone them. I'll send Ray after you . . .' her mother shouted after her as she slipped out of the front door without closing it, but Ruby took off down the road regardless.

She had no idea where she was going until she was halfway down the street and saw the open gate. On the spur of the moment she swerved in and cautiously knocked on the front door.

'Well, if it isn't Ruby Red!' Johnnie Riordan smiled as he opened the front door and saw her standing nervously on the step. 'Long time no see, missy. I thought you might have done a runner. What's up? You look upset.'

'Just out of breath,' she said. 'I'm sorry to ask, I want to make a telephone call but I left in a hurry and my purse is indoors and I don't have any money for the phone box. I can give it back to you but I don't want to have to go back for it right now . . .' she hesitated. 'Ray is due home soon and if I go back I might not get out again.'

'Course you can. Come in.' He stood back. 'You can come and meet my big sister, Betty Dalton, while you're here. She's great, is our Betty. Keeps us all in line.'

His voice raised at the end of the sentence and he looked over his shoulder.

'I'm not deaf, you know. I can hear you talking about me,' a voice echoed down the hallway.

'You were meant to,' Johnnie shouted back. 'I like to keep on your good side.' He looked back to Ruby and grinned. 'Come and meet Ruby Blakeley. She lives up the other end of the road.'

Betty Dalton came towards them and smiled cautiously. 'Hello, Ruby, nice to meet you. How are you settling back here? My brother told me all about your evacuation. You were really lucky, from what I've heard – so lucky, in fact, you nearly didn't come back!'

'Nice to meet you too, Mrs Dalton. Yes, I was very lucky,' Ruby answered nervously.

'Call me Betty. Have you got time for a cuppa?'

'Erm, I was just going to the phone box . . .'

'A quick one then. Come through to the back room. I've baked a cake and it's still warm. Does that persuade you?'

'That'd be nice, thank you very much,' Ruby said politely as she stepped into the house and followed Betty Dalton down the hall into the light and airy breakfast room. The houses in this part of the street were larger than those at the top end, with three storeys and inside facilities. The room was light and inviting with long sash windows decorated with pretty lace curtains and a dark red velour cover on the table in the side bay.

'Sit down and I'll make the tea.'

The woman went through to the kitchen, leaving Ruby sitting opposite Johnnie at the long rectangular table. She stared nervously at her hands, wondering what Ray would say if he ever found out she'd been inside the house of his sworn enemy.

Johnnie smiled. 'You look nervous but there's no need; Betty's not going to tell Ray you've been here.'

'How did you know I was thinking that?' Ruby asked.

'Because I know how you feel about Ray.'

'Here you are.' Betty brought a tray through and set it down. To Ruby's surprise she sat down with them.

As they made polite conversation Ruby looked from brother to sister. She was fascinated that there was no physical resemblance between them. Betty was not much over five foot, with pale skin, dark brown, tightly permed hair, and oval brown-flecked eyes. She wasn't unattractive, but there was nothing about her that stood out, in contrast to her tall, good-looking and charismatic young brother. Emotionally, however, Ruby could feel the link between the two. It was instantly obvious that the siblings adored each other, and she felt a little pang of envy. She'd seen the same connection between Marian and Keith Forger, her friends in Cambridgeshire, and it saddened her that she didn't have that closeness with any of her brothers.

Even Arthur was different now he was older and in the thrall of his two older brothers. If just the two of them were together it was almost like the old days when, despite being younger, Ruby had been the protector whom Arthur adored. But his fear of Ray and Bobbie was so great that if they were around he would either ignore her or bully her exactly as they did. It made her hate Ray even more.

'Tell me about your phone call – unless it's private, of course?' Johnnie asked once they were all seated at the table with tea and cake in front of them. Ruby looked cautiously at Betty, unsure of her.

'It's OK, our Betty's the soul of discretion, aren't you Bet?'

'Of course I am. I don't gossip me, but I'm not nosy either, so I'll go and find something to do if you want me out of the way.'

'No, it's OK', Ruby interrupted quickly. 'I wanted to ring the people where I was evacuated to but I left home without my purse. I've got the money at home but if I go back then I mightn't get out again. My brother . . .' she stopped. 'I mean, my mother . . .'

'It's all right,' Johnnie interrupted. 'Betty knows all about your brothers.'

'Arthur's OK,' she said defensively. 'He just follows the others. He's a bit slow – Mum always says he was born with the cord tied round his neck – and even Bobbie would be better if he wasn't around Ray all the time. Anyway, I had my birthday, and Mr and Mrs Wheaton didn't even send a card. I don't understand it. I haven't heard from them since I got back and I'm worried something's happened.'

Johnnie and Betty exchanged looks.

'What?' Ruby looked from one to the other. 'Do you know something?'

'No, don't know anything, but I can make a bloody good guess,' Johnnie said.

'Don't use bad language in front of ladies, thank you very much, John. You weren't brought up to do that.' Betty glared at him fiercely.

'Sorry, sis.' He looked from his sister to Ruby. 'Just wondering if your brother has possibly been nicking your letters.'

'He wouldn't do that.' But as soon as she spoke the words Ruby realised what she'd said, and laughed. 'Of course he would. I wonder why I never thought of that.'

'Because you're not a lying scheming piece of scum like Ray. Sorry, but I have to say it as it is.'

Ruby frowned. At times she hated her brothers but she still felt a certain sibling loyalty and Johnnie's rhetoric made her feel uncomfortable. She waited for Betty to intervene again but she didn't.

'I tell you what, Ruby Red, how about next week I take you to see them? We could go on my motorbike. It shouldn't take long if I put my foot down – an easy run, almost a straight line, I reckon.'

Ruby caught the glare of disapproval that Betty Dalton flashed at her brother.

'Ruby's family wouldn't approve of you taking her down to the High Street on that old boneshaker, let alone all that way, and quite rightly. You can't go upsetting them with something like that. It's none of our business and it's not right.'

'I could borrow a car. Bill Morgan would lend me his, if I asked nicely. I'm in his good books at the moment.'

'Bill Morgan? You know what I think of him,' Betty snapped. 'And what about petrol? Where will you get that, or daren't I ask? I'm telling you, John, you bring trouble to this door and you'll know about it. Just you remember that.'

'OK, OK, we'll go by train. How about that?'

Betty stared at her brother for a few moments. Then, without giving an answer, she stood up and walked out of the room, shaking her head.

'Sorry; all my fault, that. I shouldn't have said it in front of her; what the eye don't see the heart don't grieve over. She's very upright and righteous, is our Betty, but she's got a heart of gold underneath it all.' Johnnie pulled a face. 'But I mean it. I'll take you if you want, but the train is probably best. I've never been further than Wanstead Flats on the bike since I got it.'

Ruby laughed. 'The train would be best. It's a long way, and anyway, I have to ring them first and see if they still want to see me.'

'They'll want to see you. I bet any money you like your Ray's been playing at postman.'

Johnnie Riordan stood up, dipped into his trouser pocket and pulled out a handful of coins. After a quick glance at the money in his palm he took Ruby's hand and pressed the coins into it.

'That should be plenty. Do you want me to come with you?'

'Would you? But I don't want us to be seen. Ray's been worse lately and I don't want to ask for any more trouble than I've got already.'

'Go to the phone box at the top end of the High Street and I'll meet you there. I'll give you a head start and I'll use the back alleyway.' He laughed and touched her hand. 'I could pull my hat forward and turn up the old collar like they do in the films. I'm really good at not being seen!'

Ruby smiled in return. 'Yes, I expect you are,' she said.

SEVEN

Ruby pressed the A button in the telephone box and the coins clanked down. 'Hello, Aunty Babs? Is that you? It's me, Ruby . . .'

That was all she could say before she started crying. Just hearing Babs Wheaton's voice as she answered the phone was enough to set her off. Suddenly all the sadness and frustrations of her months back in Walthamstow came out, and she couldn't speak.

Johnnie was close beside her inside the red telephone box, and as she started crying he slipped his arm around her waist sympathetically before gently taking the receiver from her.

'Mrs Wheaton, I'm Johnnie Riordan, Ruby's friend. She's upset and missing you. She's worried she hasn't heard from you.'

He held the receiver between him and Ruby so they could both listen.

'What do you mean, she hasn't heard from me?' Babs

Wheaton said sharply. 'I've written every week since Ruby left and I sent her ten shillings for her birthday. I wondered why I hadn't heard from her. I even wrote to her mother because I was worried about her. I wish she'd phoned earlier.'

'Ruby's a bit upset but I've said I'll bring her to visit you, would that be OK?'

Ruby's tears dried quickly as anger took over. She was steaming mad – too mad to have a sensible conversation – so she left most of it to Johnnie. A queue grew outside the telephone box and eventually an elderly man banging on the glass made them bring the call to an end with a promise to phone again as soon as they knew when they'd be visiting.

Once the phone call was over Ruby was itching to get straight home and have it out with her mother and brother. She knew her missing letters had to have been Ray's idea, but it felt worse to think her mother was part of it.

'I'll kill him, I will, I'll kill him. How dare he do that? And Mum – how could she do that to me? No wonder she tried to stop me going to the phone box. I'm going home to give them what for. How dare they?'

As she ranted so Johnnie stood in front of her and blocked her from rushing off.

'Now calm down and listen to me. If you go storming in telling 'em all what's what and upsetting Ray, what good will it do? They'll know you know all about it and then you'll stand no chance of me taking you up to see the Wheatons. Take a tip from the expert: keep this information to yourself and then use it when the moment is right.'

'But I'm so angry. It's not fair!'

'You're going to bide your time. Never do anything in temper; it always backfires.'

'But I told Mum I was going to phone them,' Ruby said. 'She'll expect me to say something . . .'

Johnnie grabbed her by her shoulders. 'Listen to me, Red! Tell her you changed your mind. Say you couldn't get through, but whatever you do don't say you talked to them. She'll be so relieved she's not been caught out you'll be able to get away for the day. Be nice, act normal until we've been to see them, and then you can say whatever you like!'

As they walked along talking, Ruby automatically linked her arm through his the same way she used to with Keith when they were roaming down the lanes around the village. It was a few moments before she realised what she had done and she pulled her arm away, hoping that Johnnie hadn't noticed. One of the things she missed most about Melton was the casual way of life and the accompanying friendships that meant she was never lonely. Keith Forger was as much a friend to Ruby as his sister Marian was, and she missed their easy friendship so much.

Once Ruby and Johnnie were back in the danger zone

they separated and took different routes to Elsmere Road. As she neared the top of the road Ruby could see her mother standing at the gate in conversation with Mrs O'Connor, her next-door neighbour. As Ruby approached, Sarah Blakeley stopped talking and looked at her daughter carefully; Ruby could see the apprehension in her eyes as she studied her face.

'Well? What did she say?'

With a shrug Ruby walked past her mother and Mrs O'Connor and went indoors and, as she had expected, Sarah Blakeley followed her.

'Ruby, I'm talking to you. What did she say? More lies, I'll be bound. You can't trust them, you know.'

Ruby paused for a few moments. She really wanted to shout and cry but she didn't. She remembered Johnnie Riordan's words.

'I couldn't get through, and then when I went back to try again there was a queue outside the phone box so I gave up. It can wait. I'll try again another day.'

Ruby didn't turn round but the sigh of relief from her mother's lips was audible.

'Best leave it, Ruby. Maybe they just don't want to talk to you any more. All said and done you were only an evacuee – why would they want to have anything to do with you now they don't have to? Let sleeping dogs lie.'

Seething inside, Ruby forced a smile. 'Maybe . . . maybe none of my friends up there want to talk to me any more because I was only a poor old evacuee from London who only lived there for five years. Just little orphan Annie me, eh, Ma?'

'It's for the best, Ruby, really it is.' Sarah Blakeley completely missed the sarcasm in her daughter's comment. 'Shall we have a cuppa before I go to work? I'll make your nan one and take it through, then you and me can have a chat. We don't ever do that.'

It was hard for Ruby to carry on the charade, especially when she knew her mother was only being nice because she knew what she'd done – what Ray had done – but she tried to concentrate on Johnnie's advice.

'OK. I'll just go and check on Nana, see how she is.'

Ruby went into her bedroom and sat on the side of the bed, taking deep breaths. 'Don't get angry,' she muttered, 'don't get angry.'

'What's that, dearie? What did you say? I can't hear you.' The woman cupped her hand around her ear and turned her head.

Ruby raised her voice. 'Nothing, Nana. Just talking to myself!'

'First sign of madness, that is, girl, talking to yourself, along with hairs on the palm of your hand,' the old lady laughed.

'You'll not catch me out with that one!' Ruby said. 'Are you all right in here or do want me to help you through to the back? Mum's making a pot of tea.'

'I'll stay here. I like watching out the window, seeing

96

as best I can who's doing what. It's so long since I was out and about, sometimes I feel I'm in gaol.'

'I'll take you for a walk tomorrow, if you like, just to the corner and back.'

'I don't know about a walk. What I'd like is to sit in the chair out by the gate, but your mother says that's common.' She laughed again. 'What she means is, she doesn't want me gossiping to nosy Nora O'Connor next door about any goings-on in here.'

'Well when Mum goes to work tomorrow we'll both go and sit out front and be common, and you can chat to nosy Nora and give her something juicy to talk about down the market. How about that?'

'You're a good girl, Ruby.' She smiled affectionately at her granddaughter.

'I try to be, Nan, but sometimes it's so hard,' Ruby sighed. 'Why are they all so horrible? And I mean Mum as well . . . I've never done anything wrong but still they just want me to be unhappy.'

'It's not really like that, they're just envious. I know it's not right but that's how it is. When you were sent away they felt sorry for you, but then you landed on your feet. Your mother thought you preferred Mrs Wheaton to her, and all Ray could see was you living the life of Riley while he was being belted.'

'But that wasn't my fault. I didn't even want to go, and now I find out that they've been hiding my letters . . .' She stopped and glanced towards the door; the last thing she needed was for her mother to overhear her.

'Please don't say anything, will you, Nan? I've got to go. Me or Mum'll be back in a sec with your cuppa.'

Ruby took a deep breath, fixed a smile on her face and went off to do her own manipulating. Johnnie Riordan was teaching her well.

Taking a sip of tea she focused on the cup in her hand. Despite her anger she still didn't want to have to make eye contact with her mother when she knew that she herself was about to tell lies.

'Are you working every day this week?' Ruby asked. 'You're working more than ever before.'

'I can work more because you're here at home. It was hard doing everything before, but now it's easier . . .' She stopped and shrugged her shoulders, giving Ruby a chance.

'Mum, you remember Eileen, who I used to go to school with? Well, I met her when I was out just now and she's going for a job up west next week. She said some of the big department stores in Oxford Street are looking for shop-girls now they're rebuilding. Can I go with her?' She paused for a moment and looked at her mother, trying to gauge her reaction. 'She wasn't evacuated so I haven't seen her for ages. I thought maybe I could get a job myself. It's good money, she said; it'd help me settle back here if I had something proper to do . . .'

Ruby fiddled with her hair nervously as she turned on the emotional blackmail; she felt surprisingly little guilt at deceiving her mother, the woman who had so blatantly deceived her, and she knew she had to be convincing if she wanted to get away for the day.

The story she told her mother was half true. She had bumped into her old schoolmate Eileen, whom she hadn't seen for years and who really was going job-hunting, but Ruby had no intention of going with her. She was going to Melton with Johnnie.

'I really need you here, Ruby, you know that . . .' Ruby could hear a hesitation in her mother's voice and she was aware that it hadn't been an outright refusal. 'Three grown sons and a near-blind mother who's nigh-on a cripple is just too much for me to look after on my own. And I have my job . . .'

'If I got a job you could give yours up—'

'No I couldn't!' Sarah interrupted fiercely. 'That's the last thing I want to do, girl. It might be hard work at that bloody great place but it's the only life I have out of this house and that's when I need you here.'

'But you're always complaining how tired you are.'

'Yes, well, I am, but that doesn't mean I'm tired of the big house. I've got friends with the other help there and it's nice to have a bit of a natter about different things while we work. No, Ruby, your grandmother needs help all the time. She's getting worse by the day and I love my job so you have to be here.'

Ruby sensed that there was something she was missing, something her mother had given away by her tone, but she was too focused on getting her way to give it serious thought. She did, however, tuck the thought away in the back of her mind. She knew at that point that her mother was wavering and she hoped that with a little gentle persuasion she could be home and dry.

'I know it's hard for you but could I just go with Eileen to see what's happening and then talk to you about it? I'd love a day out, and I promise I won't do anything without talking to you. I'll just have a look around. I know Nan won't mind; she managed on her own before I came home.'

Sarah Blakeley took a deep breath and exhaled slowly. Ruby knew instantly that she'd won.

'All right, you can go – it won't hurt for you to have a bit of a day out – but don't go telling your brothers. They don't mean it badly, they just worry about how much I have to do and they worry about you being out on your own. They're all good boys really . . .'

Ruby knew that was nonsense but it wasn't the time to nitpick. She was going to go to Melton with Johnnie one way or another. She wanted to visit the Wheatons, of course, but she also liked the idea of spending the whole day with Johnnie Riordan without them having to look over their shoulders for fear of being spotted together.

'Oh, thanks, Mum!' Ruby jumped up and flung her arms around her mother and hugged her.

'Get off, you silly girl. There's no need for all that nonsense.'

'Can I just go round to Eileen's and tell her it's OK? I'll be really quick.'

'Go on then. If the boys come in I'll tell them you're running an errand for me.' With a sharp intake of breath she jumped from her seat in panic. 'Oh dear God, just look at the time! Ray and Bobbie are due in any minute. I'd better get the dinner sorted, but you get off and tell that Eileen you can go with her.'

Despite her brusque words Sarah smiled and looked decidedly pleased at the interaction, making Ruby turn away with a tiny tinge of guilt. But she quickly brushed it off. She had been let down by her family once too often, and there was no way she could ever forget that, whatever the reason. There was no going back.

As her mother rushed around preparing dinner, Ruby got out of the house as quickly as she could and ran down the road to Betty Dalton's house.

'Can we arrange the day?' she asked Johnnie excitedly. 'I've told them I'm going up west and Mum agreed.'

'See? You should always listen to me. I know these things. I'm off to work right now. I'll see what I can fix for getting us there. Betty says not to use the bike.'

'I think Aunty Babs'd have a fit as well. Best go by train.'

'However you like, Red, this is going to be fun and we both need a bit of that.'

EIGHT

'You still up for it?' Johnnie Riordan asked the man who was leaning on one elbow on the other side of the bar skilfully rolling a cigarette.

'Just waiting for you to give me the go-ahead.'

'You haven't been around. Friday afternoon do you? The boss does his business in the morning, those in question are there alone and late to leave; they have other business.' Johnnie smiled but it wasn't with humour. 'I don't want anyone else involved and no one else to know anything. Got that? Not anything about anything. Just you and them.' Johnnie didn't look at the man as he spoke quietly.

'Yeah, Friday it is, then. Everything else as we said previous?' the man asked before concentrating on striking a match then lighting the skinny roll-up that was more paper than tobacco. He inhaled deeply as he waited for a reply.

'Yes, as I said. Nothing too serious, just a good warning,

but you may have to persuade them to hand over what I want. They need a lesson.'

The man smirked. 'Thy will be done.'

'Don't take the piss, Eddie. Makes you look like an idiot.'

With a glare and a quick shake of his head Johnnie pushed a bottle of beer across the bar towards him, scooped up a few coins and turned away. He took a few steps sideways towards the elderly man he had spotted out of the corner of his eye waiting impatiently further along the bar for service.

'And a very good evening to you, Mr Morgan, sir. Sorry I kept you waiting. What's your poison? Same as usual? But no taking it home for the missus, eh?' he asked jovially, referring to the man's ongoing joke about his wife.

'Not a chance, Johnnie boy. She's poisonous enough as it is; don't need no more dripping off that tongue of hers.' The man laughed and Johnnie joined in. 'And where's young Sadie tonight? You're all right in your way but I like to see a pretty face when I'm supping.'

'She's out with some flash bloke who wants her to work in his club up west. She's got her eye on improving herself, has Sadie, and she sees one of the swanky clubs as the way to do it.'

'I'd better have a word with her then about swanky clubs and the scum that hang around in them, give her a bit of advice before she gets herself in trouble. She's a good girl but a bit daft. Be a shame if she was taken advantage of.'

Johnnie shrugged, unsure if he'd dropped Sadie in it but not really caring; keeping in with the boss was far more important. Sadie had a bit of a thing about him but although he quite liked her it was never going to go any further than a bit of fun.

Bill Morgan was always impeccably dressed to the point of sometimes being mistaken for a dandy, but those that dismissed him did so at their peril. He looked like everyone's favourite dotty uncle, but he was a ruthless career villain who was always treated with wary respect by those who knew him. He owned the Black Dog pub where they were, but had very little to do with the everyday running of it. Instead he treated it as his private office.

Into his seventies he was still fit in his body and sharp in his mind, albeit with some arthritis in his knees and hands. Apart from always wearing a cravat, his biggest affectation was using an ornate walking cane with a solid silver handle moulded in the shape of a running lurcher, a nod to his lowly origins in a gypsy caravan in Yorkshire. Bill Morgan used the cane when walking but it was also the perfect weapon to make a painful point if anyone disrespected him, and many had received a nasty slice across their cheek from the razor-sharp point on the innocuous-looking handle.

Although mostly retired from the physical involvement of his trade, he still kept a finger in most of the dubious pies across a wide area of East London, and as a result lived in considerable luxury with his wife of fifty years in a vast detached house in Wanstead, overlooking the open spaces of Wanstead Flats and just a short car drive from the Black Dog.

'You setting up something I should know about?' He nodded his head in the direction of Eddie Stone as Johnnie set his usual Whisky Mac down in front of him.

'Nothing relevant, Mr Morgan. Eddie's helping me out imparting some advice to a couple of upstarts from down my way who think they can just take what I've worked hard for.'

'Some of the young pups need a bit of a kicking now and then to keep them in line . . .' Morgan paused and looked at Johnnie carefully. 'Mind, you're a bit of a pup yourself, so you'd best be careful whose toes you tread on.'

'Just protecting my interests. I'm not treading on anything. These are just fly-boys trying to be cut corners. *My* hard-earned corners, as it happens, on *my* patch,' he said defensively, not enjoying the implied criticism from his mentor.

'A word of advice, Johnnie boy,' the man said quietly. 'I like you; you're ambitious and you're bright with a bit of education behind, but you're still young and a bit too keen to flex muscles you haven't grown yet. It won't do you any good to get ahead of yourself and get in bother.' He paused for effect before continuing, 'Don't run before you can walk and, more importantly, remember him over there,' he nodded his head to where Eddie Stone was still standing, 'he can't always control himself. Not his fault, mind, but this game is all about being in control.'

Johnnie shrugged and smiled, but his smile wasn't as wide or as self-assured as before. He tried to decide if Bill Morgan was advising him or warning him. The man was a big name in London, equally admired and feared, and the last thing Johnnie wanted to do was upset him.

'I've got to take care of my business. I can't let them think they can do whatever they like.'

The older man shook his head. 'Ways and means, lad, ways and means. So take heed. I can help you in the long run same as I can help young Sadie, but I need to know you're sensible. I like you both, as it happens. You'd make a good couple'. He stared at Johnnie eyeball to eyeball for a couple of seconds before turning away. 'Anyways, I'm expecting company, so think on. If anyone asks I'll be in the snug.'

Bill Morgan picked up his drink in one hand, his cane in the other and walked across to the door in the corner of the public bar. Before he even got there someone had jumped up and pulled the door open for him, and as he disappeared into the small bar Johnnie knew he'd spend the evening there, along with a select few, equally important companions.

Johnnie Riordan loved his family and would do absolutely anything for any of them, but outside of that circle he had little loyalty, few emotions and a ruthless streak that belied his youth and the moderate, churchgoing upbringing his mother had given him.

Success and money were important to him and he was focused on achieving both. During the day he hovered eagerly on the periphery of crime, looking for a gap in the market; a local Jack-the-lad, able to get almost anything for anyone if the price was right. Post-war shortages and rationing affected everyone and many were prepared to pay over and above for the things they wanted. Johnnie didn't see that anything he was doing was criminal as such, and he hated being called a spiv, he just saw it as being paid to provide a service.

Even at school he had been wheeling and dealing in the playground, and then, as now, he'd seen himself as a bit of a Robin Hood. It was his way of easing his Catholic conscience.

At other times Johnnie kept his working life relatively clean by working in the Black Dog, a dubious establishment with a bit of a reputation, on the borders of Walthamstow and Wanstead in Essex. But it was legitimate employment and a good cover for Johnnie's other activities. Although his wage as general dogsbody and bottle-washer was a pittance, just being there and mixing with the dodgy clientele made him some excellent contacts.

One of these was Bill Morgan himself and the other was Eddie Stone, a failed boxer who was down on his luck after coming home from the war broke and depressed, and who'd happily sell his own mother if the price was right. Eddie was unpredictable and had a vicious streak, but no-one was really sure if he'd always been like that or if his boxing injuries had been more damaging than anyone had realised.

Not wanting to dirty his own hands, Johnnie had spoken to him about the job he wanted doing, a lesson taught to Ray and Bobbie Blakeley, and carefully arranged for it to be done when he himself was well away and with an alibi. Their sister, Ruby.

He wanted the Blakeley boys brought down a peg or two but he also didn't want to blot his copybook with Ruby. Despite his Jack-the-lad reputation, Johnnie Riordan wasn't a ladies' man; he was far more into his business, his future and earning money. It wasn't that he didn't have the opportunity and he had the odd fling here and there – especially with Sadie Scully, when they'd shared a shift and the backroom was empty after hours – but anything more than that wasn't what he was looking for.

However, Ruby had a manner about her that he'd never come across before and she was intruding into his thoughts far more often than he wanted. There was something about the girl that kept pulling him towards her. Offering to take her to Melton had not been entirely a gesture of goodwill. He wanted to spend some time with her away from the local prying eyes, who may well tell Ray Blakeley, the man to whom Johnnie preferred not to give any ammunition. The man who Eddie Stone was going to deal with on the very day Johnnie and Ruby were miles away.

'Any chance of service here?' Eddie asked in the tone that always irritated Johnnie.

Johnnie smiled none the less. 'What do you want?'

'What do you mean, what do I want? I want a fucking drink, that's what I want.'

'Of course. Coming right up, sir. Anything you want, sir . . .' Johnnie's tone was pure sarcasm but it went straight over Eddie's head.

'About time too!'

Johnnie got the man his beer, took his money and made two mental notes. He would never use Eddie Stone again and he would also at some point teach him all about manners.

NINE

As the train turned the final bend Ruby pulled down the carriage window and leaned out; she could see Babs Wheaton standing on the edge of the short platform, waiting for the London train to arrive. She was wearing the familiar beige coat that Ruby had long coveted and a matching hat perched at a jaunty angle with a large feather pinned to the front. The coat was shaped tightly into her waist with a row of black velvet buttons all the way from neck to hem and a neat velvet collar, and knowing that she had worn it specially made Ruby well up. She waved frantically as the train pulled in and, after jumping out as the train was still moving, she ran over and hugged her tight. Babs hugged her back for a few seconds before holding her away with both hands and looking her up and down.

'My, how you've grown, even in this short time. Just look at you – you're nearly as tall as I am with my high heels on!'

'And you're wearing my favourite coat!'

'Maybe this time I'll let you take it with you, now you're just a little older.'

'But not the hat.'

As they laughed Johnnie stepped up beside them both and held his hand out.

'Aunty Babs, this is Johnnie Riordan. He's the friend you spoke to on the phone when I was so upset. He helped me arrange the visit.'

Johnnie smiled confidently and tipped his hat. 'Very nice to meet you, Mrs Wheaton. I've heard a lot about you from Red here.'

'Red?' Babs raised an eyebrow and looked at Ruby before taking Johnnie's proffered hand. 'Nice to meet you, Mr Riordan. It was kind of you to go to the trouble of helping Ruby. Dr Wheaton and I appreciate it.'

Babs smiled and briefly shook the young man's hand, but it wasn't quite the friendly smile Ruby was used to. Her mouth smiled politely but her eyes were narrowed with querying disapproval. As she took her hand away and looked back at Ruby her natural smile returned.

'Let's go, Ruby dear. Yardley's waiting for us outside. He's looking forward to seeing you again, and so is Uncle George, of course. He's in surgery but he'll be with us for lunch, emergencies permitting, and Marian and Keith are going to drop by after lunch . . .'

Johnnie stepped back as they walked to the car and stood politely to one side when Ruby briefly greeted Derek

Yardley with a curt nod before she and Babs climbed into the rear of the car. Only when they were settled did he then get into the front passenger seat. His manners were impeccable and Ruby was both impressed and relieved, especially after the way Ray had embarrassed her when he'd visited, but she felt that Babs Wheaton, the woman she viewed as a second mother, wasn't equally impressed.

During the drive back to the village Babs gave Ruby a brief outline of everything that had gone on in the months she'd been away, while Johnnie asked Derek Yardley all about the car. Both conversations were stilted and super-ficial, and there was a distinct atmosphere that Ruby didn't understand but which made her feel uncomfort-able. She sighed with relief when the car finally turned off the road.

'Beautiful house, Mrs Wheaton. I've heard so much about it,' Johnnie said as they pulled up outside the house Ruby knew she would always think of as home.

'Thank you. It's my husband's family home. He was brought up here; his father was the village doctor before him.'

'The war didn't affect you out here in the sticks then? No offence, of course. I say that 'cos Red was evacuated here so it must have been safer than London.'

Ruby stiffened at his words; she knew what Johnnie meant by 'out here in the sticks', but the way he said it made it sound like a criticism of this place she loved.

'We weren't directly affected by the Blitz, no, and we

fared better than London and many other cities and towns, but like everywhere else we lost family and friends. It's a blessing it's all over, though, and we can start to get back to some normality.' Babs' tone was polite as she turned back to Ruby. 'Come along, dear; let's go in.'

As Ruby walked along the path beside Babs she glanced back and noticed Johnnie had stayed back by the car and he and Derek Yardley were standing almost head to head in deep conversation. A wave of panic swept over her. The last thing she wanted was for Yardley to have an opportunity to talk to Johnnie Riordan.

'Johnnie, come on, catch up . . .'

The two men shook hands and Johnnie walked quickly, catching them up as they turned the corner leading to the back door.

'What were you talking about?' Ruby asked.

'Sorry about that. I'm interested in cars and motorbikes, and we were comparing notes. He knows his stuff, that man; we've got a lot in common.'

'No, you haven't, you've got nothing in common with him,' she snapped, but then countered her comment with a smile.

She tried not to be irritated at the way Johnnie was seeing the visit. She wanted him to stay in the background and let her have a brief sample of her old life; instead he was involving himself in it and she felt unreasonably territorial. She turned away sharply.

'Can I go and say hello to Uncle George?'

'He'll be coming through for lunch providing there are no emergencies, so best wait until then,' Babs replied.

Although she knew that what Babs was saying made sense, Ruby still found it hard to hide her disappointment.

'I'll wait until lunch then. Do you need any help?'

'You could lay the table. You know where everything is.'

The general awkwardness continued as they made superficial conversation and Ruby quickly regretted bringing Johnnie Riordan with her. They all carried on through the motions until after lunch, when Babs stood up.

'Johnnie, do you mind if I take Ruby off for a few minutes? I really want her to meet the new nurse and I'm sure you'd sooner sit here and chat with Dr Wheaton.' She looked at her husband. 'Is that OK with you, George?'

'Sounds like a good idea to me, darling,' George Wheaton said, 'Don't forget I've got a call this afternoon, but there'll be plenty of time for Yardley to drive Ruby and Johnnie to the station for the London train.'

George Wheaton was a kindly man and his face reflected that. His brown eyes twinkled when he smiled, which was often, and Ruby had rarely seen him angry. Because of using a wheelchair his upper torso was extraordinarily broad and strong, but it was a gentle strength that he never used in the wrong way. Ruby loved watching him spread his long graceful fingers across the piano keys as he taught her how to play. She loved him as a father but she also admired him for achieving everything he had, despite his disability.

Smiling first at George and then at Johnnie, Ruby stood up. She was surprised when Babs headed to the front door instead of one of the interconnecting ones, but she didn't comment as she followed her out into the garden. Together they walked slowly around to the surgery door, but instead of going inside Babs beckoned for them to sit on the bench under the covered porch just outside.

'I wanted to spend a few minutes with you alone. It's hard to talk properly in front of a stranger . . .'

'But Johnnie isn't a stranger – well, not to me. He's been a good friend from the day I went back to Walthamstow and he carried my cases along the road. He lives just further down with his family. We're neighbours.'

'I know, dear, you said that, but George and I don't know anything about him so to us he is a stranger.'

'You make that sound bad, but he's the only friend I have there. I really miss having Keith and Marian, and Johnnie is nice to me . . .' She could feel her throat starting to tighten so she swallowed hard. The last thing she wanted to do was cry.

'Tell me about him then.' Babs said. 'What does your mother think of him?'

'She doesn't know him and she doesn't know we're friends. Ray and Bobbie hate him so she'd just side with them. It's easier to say nothing.'

'Do you know why they don't like him?'

'Because they're jealous of him.'

'Why are they jealous? What does he do for a job?' Babs asked gently but curiously.

'He's a businessman,' Ruby said quickly and defensively.

'Ah, right . . . But what sort of businessman?'

Ruby frowned, unsure how to answer. 'I don't know, but he works in a public house in Wanstead to earn extra. He helps support his sister and her family – her husband was crippled when he was in the army. That's good, isn't it?'

'Of course it is. I just wondered what his business is—'

With her naturally quick temper rising in defence Ruby interrupted her, 'Why are you asking me all these questions? Why don't you ask him?'

'It's not really my place to question him, Ruby, but it is my place to worry about you because we care about you.' Babs touched her arm but Ruby pulled away. 'I'm just not sure if you should be hanging around with someone older than you, and I also don't feel comfortable helping you deceive your mother.'

'But she deceived me,' Ruby snapped. 'She said you hadn't written when all the time Ray had been stealing my letters and she knew. How can that be right? Is that what mothers do?'

'It's not right, but then again two wrongs don't make a right, and she is your mother. I love you dearly, Ruby, and I so wanted you to stay with us; but now you are back with your mother, she is responsible for you and

I feel very guilty that you're here and she doesn't know.'

Ruby was startled. It was the last thing she had expected when she and Johnnie had set out that morning to make the journey to Melton. She'd chattered excitedly all the way, telling him what to expect, but now it was all going wrong.

'I thought you were going to be pleased to see me, like I was to see you.' She knew she sounded sulky but she didn't care. Her disappointment was overwhelming.

'Oh, we are! But I'd be happier if your mother knew you were here, especially as you're with a young man. It makes me feel quite uncomfortable.' Then Babs smiled. 'But now I've said my piece and we can get back to where we were. Shall we go back in? We need to enjoy the little time we have before you go home, and don't leave it so long next time. Maybe I'll write to your mother and formally invite you to come for a holiday, all above board.'

'She won't let me.'

Ruby looked down and tried not to show her disappointment. It was all going wrong and she couldn't think of anything to say. It shouldn't have been like this. Babs and George Wheaton should have been thrilled to see her, whatever the circumstances.

'Ruby darling, I don't want you to take any of this the wrong way. Uncle George and I want to see you and to be part of your life – we love you – but I'd like it to be done properly, and properly isn't you sneaking away with a young man no one knows anything about. I know you're upset, and I'm sorry, but I had to tell you. You're only just sixteen, after all.'

Ruby looked down at her watch. 'Can we go for a walk through the village? I want to show Johnnie around.'

'Of course, we'll go together. Hopefully we'll bump into Keith and Marian. They both miss you as much as you miss them.' She took both Ruby's hands in hers. 'Friends?'

Ruby didn't answer but as they stood up Babs Wheaton put an arm around her waist and, ignoring the resistance, pulled her in towards her for a few seconds.

'I shall try hard to get to know your friend.'

Once they were on the train heading back to London, Ruby was close to tears.

'They're not usually like that,' she said. 'I don't understand it. I thought they cared for me, but maybe Mum and Ray were right, I was just the stupid little evacuee . . .'

'Ray is never right. Even I could see how much the doc and his wife love you. They were just being protective,' Johnnie laughed. 'Ray is an idiot who thinks he's brighter than he is, but he'll get his comeuppance, and when he does you'll enjoy it.'

Ruby looked at Johnnie Riordan curiously.

'It's just not right, is it? How can he dictate my life to me? And it's not right that Mum lets him.'

'Ray thinks he's a big man but he isn't. He upsets people, the wrong people, but he'll learn otherwise.'

'No he won't. He's always been a bully; he's not going to change now, unless . . .' she paused and looked at him, 'unless he did something wrong, unless the police were to know he's doing things he shouldn't be doing.'

'Hang on there, Red. If you mean what I think you mean that's a serious road to take, involving the Old Bill. That's not the way we do things where we come from.'

'I just want him to leave me alone.'

'Oh, he will. As soon as he's got something else to think about.' Johnnie smiled. 'Someone'll sort him out good and proper one day.'

'I hope so, I hate him. He makes my life misery and enjoys it. He deserves a taste of his own medicine.'

'And Bobbie as well?'

'I hate him for doing everything Ray says. Monkey see, monkey do. But I know he wouldn't be like that without Ray.' Ruby looked at him, waiting for a reply, but he simply shrugged; he put his arm around her shoulder and pulled her towards him very slightly. Instinctively she stiffened and pulled away just enough for him to loosen his hand and move it onto the back of the seat.

'They're good at upsetting the wrong people so they'll both be in real trouble soon enough.'

'I hope Mum hasn't found out I wasn't where I said I was today,' she said, changing the subject. 'They'll all go bananas and I'll never get out of the house again!'

'She won't find out.' Johnnie looked at her and smiled.

'Hope not . . .' Ruby smiled back shyly.

'I tell you what, it's been a nice day even if we spent hours getting there and back, and you're right about the doc and his wife – they're OK – and that Yardley, the chauffeur, me and him are cut from the same cloth, I reckon. He's a bit of a card, isn't he?'

'Hardly a bit of a card and you're not cut from the same cloth. Yardley is bad.'

'I bet he's a bit of a duck-and-dive merchant in his spare time. Perfect set-up there, car to get him around, a garage to store stuff and the respectability of working for the doc. He's got it made.'

Ruby shook her head and pulled a face. 'Well, I wouldn't know that, would I? Uncle George helped him out by giving him a job because of his bad lungs, and they think of him as family and they trust him.' She paused for a second. 'More fool them. He's bad.'

'Why do you say that? Seemed OK to me.'

'I don't want to talk about Yardley.'

'Not too keen on him, then?'

'I just said, I don't want to talk about bloody Derek bloody Yardley, OK?'

'OK.' Johnnie looked at her sideways but she just focused on the steamed-up window. There were some things she didn't want to talk about and she wasn't going to let Johnnie push her into it.

'Interesting view, that. Well, I think it might be, if we could see it.'

She turned towards him and, despite herself, she laughed. 'You're a nitwit, you know that, don't you?'

'Maybe, but my sis says I'm a nice nitwit.'

This time when he gripped her shoulder Ruby let him pull her close. Leaning her head on his shoulder she suddenly felt really grown up. Especially when he softly kissed the top of her head and touched her neck with his fingertips; she felt goose bumps rising on her skin and she reddened, aware that he could probably feel them as well.

Her heart was thumping all the way down the road, and by the time she opened the front door her fear was so great she felt as if she were about to have a heart attack. Once she was back in the High Street the reality of everything she'd done and the possible implications hit her. She was suddenly petrified that her mother might have found out that not only had she been to visit the Wheatons, but she'd gone with Johnnie Riordan, Ray's sworn enemy, and, in the heat of the moment, she'd done far worse.

It had seemed such a good idea at the time, but as she walked in through the door at nearly midnight she could feel her heart palpitating in her throat as she imagined Ray waiting behind the door for her, waiting to backhand her.

'Mum? Are you there? Mum, I'm sorry I'm so late but the buses from the West End were up the Swannee. We had to walk for miles and we got lost. It was ever so frightening.' She paused fearfully and listened. 'Mum? Are you awake?'

As she stood at the bottom of the stairs, looking around and praying nervously that there was nothing in her expression to give away her guilt, so her mother leaned over the banister at the top.

'Ruby? Oh, thank God you're here. Come upstairs quickly. I don't know what to do . . . Your brothers need help, you have to help. This is beyond me. Oh my Lord, this is awful . . .'

TEN

It was already dark in the narrow, unmade lane that led from the main road to the line of ramshackle engineering-style workshops behind a disused section of bombed railway track. The only lights were the dim beam escaping from under the doors of one of the units, and the dying embers of a rusty brazier outside the large central unit that was home to a carpentry shop. Blacksmiths Lane itself was a dead end with the units forming a banjo at the far end, but there was another hidden route for anyone prepared to clamber over the remains of a wooden fence and slip through a gap in the overgrown bushes at the back, which shielded the eyesore of assorted workshops from the allotments behind.

It was amid the rubble behind these bushes that Eddie Stone was waiting impatiently for the right moment. He'd done a walk-by the day before, feigning interest in having an armchair repaired, so he knew exactly where he had to be, when he had to be there and how to get in and out without being seen. He also knew what he was going to do.

There was no disputing he desperately needed the money but he couldn't help looking forward to a bit of a dust-up at the same time. It had been a while since he'd had either.

When the last of the other units was locked up, and the occupants were out of sight and sound down the lane, Eddie ground his cigarette into the dirt under the heel of his soft-soled shoe, flexed his shoulders and arms, and prepared to slip through the brambles to surprise Ray and Bobbie Blakeley and earn his desperately needed payday from Johnnie Riordan.

On the way past he stopped and rubbed his hands together over the still-warm brazier before taking the last few steps to the grandly named Collins and Son, Garage and Workshop. His research told him that despite the name neither David Collins, senior nor David Collins, junior actually worked there. They did, however, own every single unit in the lane. They also owned the land and all the businesses in all the units.

David Collins, junior visited all the units most days just to check on that small part of the family property and business empire. Although his visits were dreaded by his employees, at least his routine was always the same: smartly turned out, he'd drive up at the same time, swagger in and out of every unit, looking down his nose at the workers as he did so. On Fridays he would visit and hand out the pay packets with benevolence, as if he were handing out charitable donations. Nobody liked him – he was arrogant and dictatorial – but nobody ever said a word because at least they all had jobs and the lazy Collins son was preferable to his cantankerous and unpredictable father, who hired and fired as the mood took him.

The unit with the lights still on was the one Eddie was going to pay a visit to. It had a corrugated-iron roof and double wooden doors with rusting metal bolts and hinges on the outside that had seen better days, and three motorbikes parked up outside. One belonged to the brothers and the other two were there to be patched up as best they could be.

That was the job that Ray and Bobbie Blakeley were paid to do and they were good at it. They patched up motorcars and motorbikes that were really fit only for the scrapheap. It was a job that needed brawn more than brains, and no qualifications. They just worked long hours, learning how to do it as they went along.

The pay, typical of the Collins', was as minimal as they could get away with, but Ray and Bobbie topped up their income by using the long-forgotten lockers at the back for their own sideline business. The small working space was so crammed full of tools and equipment that the battered and greasy lockers that lined the back wall weren't visible to anyone who didn't already know they were there.

'Hello, boys,' Eddie said as he slipped in through the unbolted doors into the workshop and quickly pulled them to behind him.

Ray was sitting at a small wooden desk near the doors and Bobbie was perched on the corner as Eddie appeared. Initially they both looked bemused; they'd stayed late because they were expecting a customer they didn't want anyone to know about, so it took a moment for either of them to react.

'Yeah?' Ray asked as he took in the man. Dressed all in black, the six-foot-four ex-boxer with no neck and shoulders like a silver-back gorilla was a scary sight, but Ray wasn't instantly concerned. He had an arrogance about him that made him none too observant and he stayed in his seat staring confrontationally at Eddie. Bobbie, however, instinctively stood up and started to back away.

'I've been asked to pay you a visit to clear up a little misunderstanding that Mr Riordan is concerned about.'

'Reckon you're in the wrong place, mister, so unless you've got some genuine business here, get out.' Ray nodded his head towards the doors, a gesture of dismissal.

Eddie Stone laughed; he loved a challenge. He flexed his shoulders in a circular movement, then with one long reach of his arm he grabbed Ray round the neck, pulled him from the chair and punched him full force straight in the midriff before letting go and watching him drop

126

to his knees. As Ray groaned so Bobbie jumped forward.

'What are you doing? Leave him alone. You're in the wrong place.'

Eddie Stone's eyes moved to the younger lad. 'You said what?'

As Bobbie sidled towards his brother so Eddie hit him with a professional upper cut to the side of his jaw. He stumbled back with blood dribbling from his mouth and fell onto the floor opposite his brother.

'What do you want?' Ray groaned from his kneeling position. 'There's nothing here worth nicking. The boss has already gone with the cash box. It's just us – we only work here – there's nothing . . . nothing.'

Eddie grinned as he lifted a boot-clad foot and kicked Ray in the chest. It wasn't an overly vicious kick but it was hard enough to crack a rib and send Ray flying across the workshop. Then he turned to Bobbie and gave him a hefty kick in the kidney area.

'But that's not all you do here, is it? I know you're up to no good, and naughty boys that get up to no good get punished.'

Staring at each of them in turn, Eddie reached out and picked up a large spanner. He grinned as he gripped it tightly and batted it against the palm of his other hand.

'Now, you and I are going to have a little chat. Well, more than a chat really . . .'

Eddie started to swing the spanner, knocking things off the various surfaces. His long arms and massive hands gave him both control and strength of the weapon, and tools and engine parts went flying, including a hammer that bounced fiercely off Bobbie's shoulder.

'Don't! Please don't. Leave us alone, we haven't done anything . . .' Bobbie was one step from tears and he put his hands over his head in terror as Ray clambered to his feet and tried to shoulder-tackle Eddie.

'Don't, Ray, you stupid git!' Bobbie shouted. 'He'll kill us . . .'

'Clever boy! At least one of you's got some brains,' Eddie laughed as he whacked Ray right across his knuckles with the spanner. 'Now give me what you know you shouldn't have and I'll be gone. But if not, then the bikes outside look like they need seeing to . . .'

He didn't need to finish the threat. This time there was no arguing. Bobbie ignored his brother and told Eddie exactly where to look. Eddie scooped up the boxes, which contained twenty-four bottles of black-market whisky and gin, and headed towards the door.

'The lesson of the day for you boys is that Mr Riordan's unhappy. He wants you to stay off his turf. You want to wheel and deal, you don't do it round here. Got it?' He looked from one to the other. 'I said, have you got it?'

Ray and Bobbie lifted their heads in unison and nodded.

Eddie winked at the prostrate brothers and left as quickly as he had arrived. The whole episode had lasted only a few minutes but in that short time Ray and Bobbie had both been badly hurt. However, that was the least of their problems.

The cases of whisky that Eddie had taken hadn't been paid for, and for that they knew they'd be in even worse trouble.

Ruby took the stairs three at a time and nearly ran into her mother, who was standing on the landing wringing her hands.

'Something's happened to my boys. They're hurt and I don't know what to do. They don't want to go to hospital but they must, they have to, they're hurt . . .'

'All of them? What happened? ' Ruby asked.

'No, it's Ray and Bobbie. Just go and see if you can do something to help them, please!'

'Why me?' Ruby was puzzled at her mother's insistence.

'You said you wanted to be a bloody nurse – you lived with a doctor – you know what to do . . .'

Ruby went into Ray's bedroom, the tiny boxroom that used to be hers, and saw him lying fully clothed on top of the bed. He was lying on his back with his knees up and bloody hands clasping his midriff. She could see his hands were injured and his face was deathly pale. As she moved forward to take a closer look her mother stood stock-still in the doorway with her hand clamped over her mouth.

'Get out, Ruby,' Ray shouted as he opened his eyes and

saw her leaning over him. 'Get out of my fucking room and mind your own business, you stuck-up little bitch. Get out . . .'

Ruby shrugged. 'OK. I was only going to help.'

With her mother almost glued to her back, she went into the other bedroom to see Bobbie, who was sitting on the edge of his bed close to tears, while Arthur was tucked down tight in his bed curled up in the foetal position facing the wall with his hands over his ears, trying to pretend nothing was happening.

'Bloody hell, what have you two been up to?' Ruby asked. 'You need a doctor—'

'No,' Bobbie interrupted sharply. 'Don't tell anyone. It's nothing, you mustn't tell anyone. Please, Ruby, don't tell.'

'Is Arthur OK?' Ruby asked over her shoulder.

'He's just scared,' Sarah said. 'He doesn't know anything. He was here with me and your nan but he saw them come in all covered in blood.'

Ruby turned to her mother, who was standing behind her gulping in air and making noises as if she were hyperventilating.

'So what happened? Did they crash the motorbike?'

'I don't think so. Ray said someone jumped them on the way home, but I don't see why they don't want anyone to know. Will you try and talk to Ray again? Bobbie'll just do whatever he says. They've been beaten so bad – why would anyone want to hurt my boys?'

In a split second Ruby had a lightbulb moment and

everything fell into place. She was horrified at the implications of her thoughts, but still wanted to laugh.

Johnnie Riordan. He had to be behind this.

'I'll patch them up. You're right, I used to help Uncle George in the surgery so I know what I'm doing, but you'll have to tell them to let me.' Ruby looked at her mother, who was leaning on the wall struggling to light a cigarette. 'Ray'll hate having me look after him but if he doesn't he might get blood poisoning, and there's nothing I can do if he's hurt inside. If either of them gets worse then you have to get proper help, whatever they say.'

It was all she could do to keep the satisfaction out of her voice. Maybe now they'd got other things to think about they would leave her alone and let her live her life.

After much persuasion from their mother, and with hatred in his eyes, Ray allowed Ruby to perform some basic first aid on his hands. Her mother fetched some iodine and a bottle of aspirin from the medicine cabinet and then went down to the scullery for a bowl of warm water. While Ruby bathed Ray's hands Sarah tore an old pillowcase into strips for bandages and watched as Ruby wrapped them around.

Once the basics were done she moved onto Bobbie, who had lost a tooth and bitten his tongue quite badly. He also had a large bruise forming on his left side. But despite the pain they were both in, Ray was adamant there would be no doctor and that they both had to be able to go into work the next morning, although neither of them would say why.

Later that night Ruby and her grandmother were sitting in their bedroom.

'So the boys are in trouble, eh? About bloody time that pair came unstuck and were taken down a peg or two. I wouldn't wish them real harm but I hope this is a lesson learned.' Elsie Saunders was sitting up in her bed wearing a pink crocheted bed jacket and her ever-present hairnet. With her teeth in the denture pot beside her bed she looked older than her years and she spoke with a lisp. She peered across at Ruby, who was sitting cross-legged on her bed. 'And I'm not going to ask how your day was because there's something that doesn't seem right about any of this and I don't want you to have to lie to me.'

'I wouldn't lie to you, Nan.'

'Yes you would, my girl, same as you've lied to your mother, but that's between you and your conscience. I hope you haven't overstepped the mark, that's all.'

'You don't think I had anything to do with Ray and Bobbie, do you? How could I do that? I'm pleased they were battered but it was nothing to do with me! I was shocked when I first saw them.'

'Seems fishy to me that you beg and plead for a day away and it's the very day something happens. I may be old and decrepit in body but I'm not stupid. I see a lot – far more than your mother, in fact – and when I do venture to the front door I hear things.'

'Honest, I promise you, Nan, I don't know anything

about what happened to the boys. Cross my heart and hope to die.' Ruby was starting to feel scared all over again.

'Ruby, my little precious, never push your luck by saying things like that. I don't want to know what you're up to so long as you're not in trouble.' Elsie's expression was serious as she stared at her only granddaughter. 'And violence never solved anything.'

'I'm not in trouble, but Ray and Bobbie are, and of course I'm pleased,' she laughed. 'I patched them up so now they're both in my debt and I can do whatever I want!'

Ruby leaned her head back, closed her eyes and thought about what had happened just a couple of hours earlier on the way home. When she had let herself get carried away with Johnnie Riordan in the park, with the moonlight glimmering through the shelter of foliage that hid them from the sight of any passing people. She relived how she had let him kiss her, touch her . . .

She crossed her arms and hugged her secrets close to herself. Suddenly she felt grown up and in love, and she knew Johnnie felt the same because he had told her.

She smiled happily. Suddenly her future looked a lot brighter and it didn't matter so much that the Wheatons had let her down; she had Johnnie to look out for her now.

When they'd got back to Walthamstow they decided to take the circuitous route back to Elsmere Road via the alleyways and the park so that they wouldn't be spotted by anyone. As they strolled through the almost deserted park hand in hand, Ruby just didn't want to go home; she wanted the moment to last for ever. There was no conversation, but the silence between them was comfortable.

'Shall we sit for a while?'

'I need to get back.'

'I know, but a few more minutes won't hurt. This is so nice, just you and me and the moon.'

As Johnnie looked at her expectantly so Ruby looked up at the full moon shining overhead and smiled. She sat down on the bench and Johnnie sat beside her. He was so close to her she could feel the warmth of his body through his clothes.

'I was about to have a cigarette but I'm going to have to do this instead . . .' Johnnie leaned round, took her face gently in both hands and kissed her, gently at first and then harder, much harder. Ruby was lost; she knew she should resist and go straight home, but she couldn't . . .

Afterwards she was filled with remorse and she hated herself because she'd done exactly what the Wheatons had always warned her not to do. She'd let herself down.

'I have to go home,' she said, not looking at him. 'We shouldn't have done that. It was wrong.'

'Oh, Red, don't say that. I know how I feel about you and I know you feel the same.'

'Do you love me?' she asked with tears in her eyes.

'Of course I do.'

The next morning Ruby stayed in her room until she heard the slamming door that told her the boys had gone to work. She went through to the back, hoping that her mother would still be too distracted to ask any questions about her day in London with Eileen.

'How're Ray and Bobbie? I heard them go off to work.'

'Bobbie's gone but Ray's still in bed. The poor boy can barely walk. Bobbie's going to cover for him if Collins shows up. I don't know what this country's coming to when two hard-working boys get battered like that for nothing.'

'Hmm.' Ruby was determined to be noncommittal. 'What do they think happened?'

'Ray said they were ambushed by a gang of men in Blacksmiths Lane as they closed up. He thinks they were wanting to burgle somewhere and came across the boys working late. He's so worried they'll get the blame if anything was nicked so he wants it all hushed up. They don't want to lose their jobs.'

'So do they know what was taken?'

Instead of answering, Sarah Blakeley started crying again. 'Will you go and see how Ray is? You'll know better than me.'

Ruby was getting really irritated with her mother but she did as she was asked.

She knocked on the bedroom door and went in to find Ray trying to get dressed.

'You shouldn't be up. You need to stay in bed.' she said

gently, but he ignored her. 'Ray, please, get back in bed. If you rest you'll get better but—'

'Get out of here, Ruby. You've done your duty, like Mum made you. Now leave it.'

Ruby was horrified at how ill he looked, doubled up in pain. Suddenly his suffering wasn't quite so funny any more.

'Get back in bed, you idiot. Bobbie's at work, he'll sort it all out there. Think how Mum'll feel if you keel over.'

He looked at her and his face was ashen.

'What happened, Ray? I mean, what really happened?'

'We were jumped, that's it. Random.'

'I don't believe you.'

'I don't give a monkey's what you believe, you stupid kid. Get out.'

'You need to see a doctor, you look really white—'

'GET OUT.' As he shouted, so Ray leaned forward and was violently sick all over his feet and the bedside rug.

Ruby said nothing – there was nothing to say – but the idea that Johnnie Riordan could have been behind the attack was no longer amusing.

Regardless, she was in love with him.

ELEVEN

Melton

'Ruby! What are you doing here?' Babs Wheaton exclaimed as she walked up to the back door and saw the bedraggled girl sitting on the doorstep in the pouring rain. 'Why didn't you go indoors, you silly girl? You're drenched.' But her responsive smile quickly dropped away when she registered Ruby's distressed expression and the small sodden bag on the step beside her. Babs dumped her shopping baskets on the ground and leaned across the girl to push the unlocked door open.

'Whatever's wrong? Oh dear, let's get you inside and warm you up. You're soaking wet and you'll catch your death. I can't believe you didn't just let yourself in to get warm . . .'

With her hair hanging all around her face in rat-tails and her dripping wet cotton frock and cardigan clinging to her body, Ruby looked like a little street urchin. Babs smiled in reassurance and reached out a welcoming hand as Ruby continued to sit stock-still on the step, her shoulders hunched and her arms wrapped tightly around her shaking body. Then after a few moments she put a hand out in response and let Babs pull her up and lead her gently over the familiar threshold straight into the warmth of the kitchen. Despite feeling scared and in the depths of despair, she also felt relief that she was back where she felt safe. She knew she still had to explain the situation, but for the moment she just felt relieved to be back in the place she would always think of as home. She just hoped that Babs and George would continue to let that be.

'How did you get here?' Babs asked as she led her over to a fireside chair beside the range and gently made her sit. 'You should have telephoned. I hate the idea of you travelling alone.'

'I got the train and bus. It's taken so long, but I haven't told Mum and I thought you might tell me not to come if I didn't ask her first. Johnnie lent me the fare.' She said it almost as a challenge, but Babs didn't rise.

'Of course I would have said you should tell your mother, but I wouldn't have rejected you, not ever. You know that. Whatever made you think I would?'

'Last time I came I wasn't welcome here, and when Ray said you wouldn't want me any more I thought perhaps he was right: that I was just your good turn for the war . . .'

'That's a lot of piffle and you know it. Now I'm going to make a pot of tea and you can tell me what's happened. I can see it's serious.' Her expression was troubled as she looked closely at Ruby, who wasn't making any eye contact. 'Is it Ray? Has he done something to you again? What's been going on?'

Ruby didn't answer. She was so scared and embarrassed she just couldn't think of the words she needed. Instead she sat motionless with her knees together, her hands clenched in her lap, and looked at her feet.

'All right, you don't have to tell me anything if you don't want to – I can see you're distressed. I'll do you something to eat and make up the bed in your room and we can talk in the morning.'

Ruby took a deep breath. 'No, I'll do it now. It's nothing Ray's done – this isn't his fault – but I'm scared of what he'll do if he finds out. I'm in such big trouble, Aunty Babs – really, really big trouble – and I don't know what to do. You're the only person who can help me.' She hugged herself even tighter as if for protection, then started to sob quietly.

'It surely can't be that bad, dear, and even if it is there's nothing we can't deal with, is there? Tell me what's wrong.'

'I'm sorry. You're going to hate me . . .' She chewed her lip and looked everywhere except at Babs Wheaton.

'Go on.'

'I'm sorry . . . I think I'm having a baby. I think I'm pregnant and I don't know what I'm going to do.'

Walking over to the kitchen table, Babs Wheaton leaned on it with both hands and then lowered herself onto a chair. Her eyes opened wide with shock as the words slowly sunk in.

'I'm so sorry. I didn't know where else to go. Ray will kill me if he finds out. I've left for good, I can't go back there, and if they find out they won't want me anyway.'

'Are you sure about this? Have you been to the doctor yet?'

'I think I'm sure, but I haven't been to the doctor. I went to the library and looked it up, and I've got the symptoms, and I did . . . you know, I did do . . . *IT*. I know how it happens, I just never thought it'd happen the first time, the only time. I promise, it was only once, and when I was at school they said . . .'

Her words were mumbled and trailed off, and her face was scarlet with embarrassment at having to talk about things like that to the person she loved most, the person whose approval was so vital to her.

'But you're only just sixteen. Who is it? Is it that one who brought you up here? Johnnie? Did he take advantage of you?'

Ruby paused. She wondered about lying, about shifting the blame so that she wouldn't be such a disappointment, but she couldn't do it. She didn't want to lie to the woman she truly wished was her mother.

'It was Johnnie, but he didn't take advantage of me. He didn't make me. I really liked him and it just sort of went too far. It was after we left here last time, I was upset and—' she stopped and searched frantically for the right words. 'And things happened.'

'Well, things shouldn't have happened, and if you're having a baby then he's going to have to marry you whether he likes it or not. There's absolutely no alternative,' Babs stated angrily. 'Honestly, he should have known better. You're just a child. I dread to think what Uncle George will have to say about this.'

'He's only nineteen, he just looks older.'

'That's still too old even to be courting you, let alone . . . let alone . . .' She couldn't get the words out. 'I knew my instincts were right about him. Well, if you're pregnant he has to marry you!'

Babs Wheaton flitted nervously back and forth across the kitchen as she spoke, her distress evident in her movements.

'But I don't want to marry him, I don't want to marry anyone,' Ruby said. 'And I don't want him to know because then he'll think he has to.'

'He *does* have to. An illegitimate baby? It can't happen. It will ruin your life.'

'Can I just stay here and then have it adopted after it's born?'

Babs' eyes widened. 'Heavens above, Ruby, that's a question from out of the blue. This isn't something I can deal with just like that. But apart from that, I don't have the authority. You're under twenty-one and I'm not your mother or even your guardian.' She smiled sadly. 'I'll have to tell George. He needs to know and he'll know what to do. He's used to dealing with this sort of thing. He's going to be so disappointed with you.'

'I knew you'd help me,' Ruby said, looking up at Babs.

'I'm promising nothing, Ruby. This is serious and not something to be dealt with over a mug of cocoa. And anyway, we don't even know if you are pregnant. So, first things first. Where does your mother think you are?'

Ruby dropped her eyes and didn't answer so Babs continued, only thinly disguising her concern. 'You know this is the first place they'll look. We'll soon have your brother on the doorstep creating merry hell just for the fun of it. What if they call the police? You'll have to go home then.'

'They won't. I left a note. I said I was going to Manchester with a friend, that I wanted to get away from being a drudge. It was a good letter.' For the first time Ruby smiled.

'Ruby, this isn't funny. I can't deny I'm disappointed. You're a clever girl, with everything going for you.'

'I know, I'm sorry.' Ruby said.

'It's not me you have to apologise to, it's yourself.' Babs paused and shook her head. 'But what's done is done. I'll talk to Uncle George later tonight and we'll go from there. He's out on a call at the moment so it's you and me and a big bowl of soup. Just by chance I made your favourite this morning.'

She touched Ruby's face gently and then ruffled her hair. 'We'll sort this out. I don't know how yet, but we will. I just wish you'd never had to leave here in the first place.'

It was all that was needed for Ruby to jump up and throw herself crying into Babs' arms. The woman hugged her close, in exactly the same way she had when Ruby had been a ten-year-old scared and lonely evacuee.

Later that night, as she snuggled down in the familiar bedroom, which was exactly the same as the day she had left it all those months before, she thought about what had happened.

Aunty Babs was right; she had let herself down and she should have known better. After five years living in the country and spending time on farms, she knew only too well how babies were conceived, and yet still she'd let it happen. Not only that, she'd given away her virginity on the spur of the moment to someone she didn't even know very well, and it didn't matter one iota that she loved him.

For the first time since she was a child she put her hands together and prayed. She prayed the Wheatons would help her, she prayed that she wouldn't have to tell her mother and she also prayed that they wouldn't insist on telling Johnnie Riordan.

Ruby had been so absorbed with Johnnie Riordan and her feelings for him that it had taken a long time for her to realise that she might be pregnant. She knew what she had done, and in the back of her mind she knew what the consequences of that could be, but she was sure it couldn't happen the first time. Her biggest concern was that Johnnie would think she was cheap, that he would despise her for giving in so easily, so she had labelled it a mistake and was determined that it wouldn't happen again.

There was also the distraction of the atmosphere at home, and Ruby had put her feeling of nausea down to the underlying sense of misery throughout the household after the incident with Ray and Bobbie. She guessed they were both in some sort of trouble and that it was probably to do with Johnnie, but she didn't know and didn't want to know. She didn't want anything to spoil her feelings for him.

She was head over heels in love.

It was only when the waistband of her fitted skirt was distinctly tight and she realised her lack of monthlies that she put two and two together and it hit her like a hammer-blow to the head.

'What's wrong, Ruby? You know you can tell your old nan,' Elsie Saunders said to her granddaughter when she realised the girl was crying into her pillow. Her eyesight wasn't what it should be but there was nothing wrong with her hearing. 'Come on, I don't like to hear you all upset. Tell your nana what's wrong.'

Ruby had felt panic soaring in her throat; she desperately wanted someone to confide in but she knew it couldn't be anyone who lived in the house in Elsmere Road. Even if her grandmother was sympathetic, she knew that she'd feel obliged to tell her mother.

'It's Ray and Bobbie . . .' Ruby lied. 'They're both so vile to me, I can't stay here any longer. I really tried to help them when they were beaten but they don't care. I want to go away from here, to do my nursing. I don't want to be here.'

'Well, dear, if that's what you really want then you have to tell your mother and see if she'll change her mind.'

Ruby pulled her eiderdown further up under her chin and shivered. 'She'll never let me. I'll have to run away.'

'Then you have to make the decision, don't you?' Elsie said before turning over in her bed and facing away from Ruby. 'I don't want you to go anywhere, lovey, but I can see what those boys are doing to you. Your mother should have left you where you were and I've told her that.'

Ruby didn't answer and within a few minutes the woman was snoring and she was wide awake, thinking about what she'd said. If she was pregnant, as she suspected, then there was no alternative but to run away.

'Ruby? We need to talk to you. Ruby?' The gentle knock was followed by the door opening an inch.

Curled up in the chair in the corner of her room, the room she'd missed so much and longed to go back to, Ruby rubbed her eyes with the back of her hand and sniffed.

'Do you want me to come downstairs?'

Babs pushed the door right back and stood in the doorway.

'Yes, come on downstairs. We need to have a talk.'

'Are you going to tell Mum?'

'Come on downstairs, Ruby, and we'll talk about it all.'

It had been two days since Ruby had turned up on their doorstep and uttered those immortal words, 'I think I'm pregnant'. Two days of uncertainty and disappointment for everyone, although after the initial embarrassment of having to first tell Babs and then talk about it clinically with George, Ruby was just relieved that she wasn't having to deal with it alone. She knew George and Babs were talking about it when she was in her room and, because Babs had disapproved of her visiting behind her mother's back earlier, Ruby had constantly worried that they would try to send her home. But she had already made up her mind that she wasn't going back, whatever they said. If she had to run away from everyone then she would. Nothing would make her go back.

At least the Wheatons had agreed on the first night that Ruby could stay while they decided what to do for the best, but there were strict ground rules. No one was to know she was back in the village, not even her friends, and she was going to have to stay indoors just in case her family, specifically Ray, came looking for her. If no one knew she was there then no one could let anything slip.

The next day Dr Wheaton had checked her over in his

surgery in private after hours and confirmed that she was indeed expecting a baby, but that she was also fit and healthy.

'Sit down, Ruby. Uncle George and I have come to a decision. You can't stay here and keep your pregnancy a secret – it's just not possible – so we've spoken to Uncle George's sister, Leonora, who lives near Southend down in Essex. Remember, she came to visit us? We think you should go and live there with her until the baby is born and then we can arrange for it to be adopted.'

'But I don't know anyone there.'

'That's why it's for the best. We have to consider your future and this is best, unless you'd sooner go into a mother-and-baby home?'

Ruby didn't answer. She knew she was backed into a corner of her own making.

'Leonora owns a small hotel so you can also work there to pay your way. Then you can come back either to here or to Walthamstow, and get on with your life. No one need ever know if you don't want them to. It'll be best for everyone, especially you. It will give you choices you won't have if anyone finds out about a baby.'

'Why would she help me?' Ruby asked, feeling increasingly nervous at the thought of going to live somewhere strange. Again.

'Because she's a very nice lady. She's family and so are you.'

'I'm sorry, I'm really sorry . . .'

'Well, what's done is done, and we're pleased you felt you could come to us.'

'I was so scared. I'm still scared. What if Ray comes looking for me? He'll kill me stone dead, that's for sure.'

'No, he won't. Not even Ray—'

'He will. He and Bobbie were beaten and robbed at the place where they work and they've both been even worse since then. Ray is just angry all the time.'

'That's awful. What happened?'

'I don't know but they were hurt badly and now Ray is quite fearsome. He's always shouting and swearing, and everyone's scared of him. He even lashed out at Mum and blacked her eye. It was Arthur who pulled him off. Bobbie is just quiet, not really there at all.'

'Well, he won't get near you, take my word for it!' Babs stated emphatically. 'Now when Uncle George comes in for his lunch we'll talk this through, but you have to stay out of sight while we put everything in place. It will be only for a couple of weeks, anyway, while we make all the arrangements. You need clothes and things for the time being. We're thinking that you could be a war widow. Then you won't have to explain your pregnancy to anyone. You look a lot older than your age, so that should work.'

'I should just have run right away. I'm causing you all so much trouble—'

'No, you shouldn't have run away and you know it. This will work out. You'll see.'

Ruby shrugged and closed her eyes in silent resignation.

When she had realised that she could be pregnant with Johnnie's baby her first instinct had been to tell him, but once she gave it some thought she knew it would be pointless. Johnnie Riordan was young and ambitious, and there was no place in his life for her.

As time had gone on and she had got to know him better, Ruby had discovered that while he undoubtedly liked her, he had also been using her as a way of keeping tabs on her brothers. It had never been spoken about but she knew without doubt that Johnnie had been behind the attack on them and, much as she had wanted Ray to suffer, it bothered her that Johnnie was capable of authorising such violence.

That knowledge hadn't stopped her being in love with him, but it had given her an insight into his character, his ruthlessness and his huge ambitions. Ambitions that certainly wouldn't include a shotgun marriage to a sixteen-year-old.

She had thought about confiding in her grandmother but she knew Nan would have trouble keeping it secret, however much she might have wanted to.

In the end she had run to Babs and George Wheaton, the only people she knew she could really trust.

It had never even briefly occurred to her to confide in her mother.

*

'Johnnie, I've got an interview at a hospital in Manchester to see about nursing. Can you lend me the train fare? I'll pay you back, I promise, but I'm skint and you know I can't ask Mum 'cos she'll tell Ray and it'll all start up again. He's been strange since he and Bobbie were battered: much quieter, which is nice, but so much nastier.'

Ruby and Johnnie had been sitting side by side on the park bench close to where they had made love that very first time, but it was daytime and there were people about. They sat a distance apart, not touching, but Ruby was still aware of his closeness.

His eyes had narrowed slightly at her words. 'I didn't think he could be any nastier – well, not to you, anyway.'

'More quietly angry instead of his old raging temper . . .' She paused, aware that she'd sown a seed in Johnnie's mind. 'But what about the fare to Manchester? Can you help me?'

'Why Manchester? That's a long way away.'

'Oh, that's only for the interview,' she lied easily. 'I'll be training in London if they accept me, and living there. It's how these big hospitals work.'

'I'll come with you. We could have another day out together—'

'No, no,' she interrupted quickly, 'I know you're busy. I just want to sneak away without anyone knowing. I want to get all the facts before I say anything.'

'Good idea, Red.' He took her hand and gently rubbed his thumb up and down hers. 'You really need to get out of that house and get a job you get paid for. They just use you, and I hate seeing it.'

Ruby could feel her resolve weakening. She so wanted to tell him, for him to declare it was fine and they'd get married right away. But she held firm.

'I know. One way or the other I'll pay you back but I don't want anyone to know where I am. I don't think they'd ever ask you but just in case they do you have to say you don't know anything.'

'Of course I'll lend you the money and I really hope you get the job or whatever you call it, and my lips are sealed.' He studied her face for a moment. 'You are coming back, aren't you? This isn't you running away? You really can trust me, Red.'

But she already knew she couldn't. Not only did she know about what he'd done to her brothers, she also knew all about Sadie Scully, the barmaid at the Black Dog. Johnnie's sister, Betty, had made a point of telling her.

He'd leaned forward to kiss her on the lips but she'd moved her head just enough for him to kiss her cheek instead. Ruby Blakeley had learned the hard way that, however much she wanted it to be otherwise, she was not going to see Johnnie Riordan ever again.

She was going to leave Walthamstow. She wasn't going to Manchester and she also wasn't going to come back. Ever.

TWELVE

1946, six months later

'Oh, she is so pretty. Look, George, just look at her little rosebud lips and button nose . . . She looks just like Ruby but her hair is so fair, it's almost invisible. I expected another redhead. She is beautiful and so healthy. You've done well, Ruby, you clever girl . . .'

'Yes, she's perfect, a bonny bouncing baby, definitely.' As he spoke George Wheaton gave a warning look to his wife before glancing quickly at Ruby, who was standing alongside them at the glass partition that fronted the nursery where all the swaddled newborns were lined up in their cribs like fresh produce in the shop window. Only the names on the cribs identified which one was which.

Babs and George stood side by side gazing adoringly at the baby tagged as 'Baby Blakeley, Girl', but instead of looking at her daughter Ruby was determinedly looking the other way. She had no intention of connecting any more than was absolutely necessary with the infant from whom she would soon be separated for ever.

'They all look the same to me, and anyway why would I want to look at her? It's not as if I'm keeping her. She's not mine.' Despite her barely disguised frustration at her situation Ruby shrugged as if she didn't care.

'Have you definitely made your mind up then?' Babs asked. 'Have you spoken to anyone about adoption?'

'I haven't said anything and I'm not going to while I'm still in hospital. They all think I'm a poor little war widow so they're being really nice to me. Not like Gracie, the girl at the other end of the ward who's just had an illegitimate baby. They're so horrible to her and now she's got to go back to the mother-and-baby home that's just like a prison.'

'Well, it's going to be hard for you too, Ruby, whatever you do. You do know that, don't you? Giving a baby up is hard for anybody.'

'Yes, I know that. I'm not stupid you know.'

Ruby could feel a surge of anger rising up in her. It was as if they didn't think she was capable of realising the enormity of her situation at that moment. She had given birth to a baby she was going to give away and never see again: a beautiful and perfect baby girl who, under different circumstances, would have been her pride and joy.

Despite her youth and circumstances Ruby had felt a maternal surge the moment she had held her daughter for the first time. She had tried to fight it, and had been fighting it every minute since, but it was still there.

'I know you're not. I was just making sure you do what you want to do. If it's any consolation, Uncle George and I both think that giving her up is the best thing you can do for both of you. Other than marrying the father, of course.'

Ruby's head swivelled sharply. 'No. Oh, you haven't told him, have you? I don't want Johnnie Riordan having any part of my life. Or hers.' She paused. 'Not that he'd want to.'

'Of course we haven't said anything – not to anyone. Not a soul – but we do want you to be sure you know what you're doing. Adoption is for ever. You can't change your mind sometime in the future.'

'I know. It's the best thing to do and it's what I'm going to do, but I don't want to do anything until we've left here. I couldn't bear to be treated like Gracie has been. They've been so nasty to her and she's had no visitors. Not one.'

Babs shook her head. 'That must be horrible for the poor girl. I'll go and have a word with her on the way out. If the nurses think George and I know her they might be nicer. It's wrong, I know, but . . .'

'That's a kind thought, Babs,' George said before turning to Ruby. 'Have you chosen a name for this little one yet?'

'Why would I do that? There's no point in me giving her a name and then someone changing it as soon as they take her.'

Babs and George Wheaton exchanged glances.

'We have to talk to you in private, Ruby. There's something we have to tell you. The nurses have said you can come outside with us for a walk, so we'll go somewhere private.'

Being a doctor himself, George had been able to pull strings that allowed both him and his wife to visit 'his niece' freely in the nearby maternity home where she'd gone to have the baby. It was another thing that annoyed Ruby on Gracie's behalf.

Babs pushed George's wheelchair as they made their way along the main corridor to the double doors that led out into grounds. As they walked they all made stilted small talk. Ruby spoke quickly and fired questions about Marian and Keith, and Babs and George told her a couple of amusing but completely irrelevant anecdotes about the surgery. It was all very superficial as the three of them all skirted around the most important subject of all. The baby.

It had been a perfect pregnancy and an easy birth, with Ruby feeling fit and well physically, and more than ready to leave the hospital when the time came. All she had to do was actually set the wheels in motion to arrange the adoption of her daughter.

When the plan had been formed all those months ago for her to go to stay with George's sister, Leonora, in Essex, Ruby had accepted she had little choice but to go if she were to have the support of the Wheatons so she had persuaded herself it was another evacuation.

Being sent to Melton had turned out OK so she was determined that a stay in Southend would be equally satisfactory if she just focused her mind on the end result. A few months in exile, then she would have the baby adopted and could start her life again, hopefully back in Melton with her friends. But whatever happened she knew she could never go back to the overcrowded terraced house in Walthamstow, where she wasn't wanted and which was just a stone's throw away from Johnnie Riordan, the love of her life and the father of a beautiful baby daughter who looked just like him.

She tried hard to block him out of her mind but she often wondered what he was doing and whether he missed her. However, she knew he had to be part of her past, just as her family were now. Pregnant and in exile, all she had had was Aunt Leonora, who, despite her honorary title of aunt, was really just another total stranger.

Leonora Wheaton was the spinster of her family, the oldest child of four who had never married because she had become the carer who stayed at home and looked after her ailing mother. After she died Leonora had inherited the family home where she had lived all her life, but instead of staying there she had sold everything and fulfilled her long-held dream of running a seaside hotel. She had bought a run-down seafront property near Southend and turned it into a quiet upmarket establishment for genteel single and widowed ladies, who may otherwise have found having a holiday impossible. It meant Ruby fitted in there perfectly and no one asked any embarrassing questions about her condition.

She was a kind-hearted woman and a natural-born carer, so she was good to Ruby and went along with the deception because she loved her brother, but she hadn't been completely able to hide her dismay at the young girl's situation.

As they reached a deserted area of the hospital grounds Babs stopped and faced Ruby.

'This is really important, dear. Uncle George and I have been talking and we think we have a solution.'

Ruby turned away. 'I'm not changing my mind. I can't look after a baby, I don't want a baby and I'm not going to marry Johnnie. I'm sorry.'

'We understand that. But the solution we're offering may well suit everyone,' George said. 'Babs and I think, well, we wondered—'

But before he could finish his wife interrupted, 'You're beating around the bush, George. Let me tell her. Ruby, we want to adopt your baby. We want her, we want her so much . . .'

Stunned, Ruby looked from one to the other. It was the last thing she had expected them to say, and something that had never even crossed her mind.

'I don't understand. You're saying *you* want her? You never said before. Why would you want to take my baby?' Ruby could feel her warning antennae on alert.

'It's not that we want to take your baby, Ruby dear – that sounds so cruel – we want to adopt her, to have her as part of our family and give her a good life. We feel attached to her already because she's yours, and we hate the idea of her going to strangers.' Babs said quickly and intensely.

'Why didn't you say that earlier? Why wait until now?'

'Because neither George nor I dared to consider it as a possibility. We didn't want to pressure you into anything, you had to make your mind up yourself; but if you're determined to give her up then surely it's better that we take her home with us, to bring her up as ours. Better than her going to strangers. We were never lucky enough to have a child of our own; you were the nearest we came to parenthood . . .' as Babs' voice broke George took Ruby's hand in his.

'Ruby, no one need know anything apart from us; no one will know she's yours. I have contacts who can arrange the adoption. Then you can get on with your life, knowing your baby is truly loved and well looked after.' George held her hand tighter. 'And you know we'd do that, don't you?'

Ruby looked from one to the other as she tried to take in just what they were saying to her. Was the couple who meant so much to her ready to push her aside to have the one thing they had apparently always wanted? A child of their own?

She tried to get this new notion together in her head.

When she had gone to visit them with Johnnie, Babs had been insistent that it was wrong for Ruby to deceive her mother, yet when she became pregnant they had whisked her off and hidden her away. Had they done that because they knew from the start that they wanted the baby? Would the baby replace her in the Wheatons' affections?

She walked over to the low wall that separated the lawn from a wide paved footpath and sat on it very gingerly, at the same time wrapping her dressing gown tightly around her still swollen body. She chewed her lip and looked into the distance as she determined not to cry. George and Babs followed her.

'So you don't want me to come back to Melton then? You just want my baby.' Ruby could hear the whine in her voice, the childish challenge, but at that moment she felt like a child again. She could taste the betrayal.

Babs and George Wheaton moved simultaneously to either side of her, and Babs, too, sat on the wall. George took her hand again and gripped tightly.

'No, it's not like that. Of course we want you – we want both of you – but you said you were giving her up anyway so it makes sense to let someone who loves both of you take care of her. Ruby, we love her because we love you. You can be her big sister, her guiding godmother. We're both getting on a bit now and you can be the younger influence for her.'

'Just think about it, Ruby,' Babs said. 'We're not going to make you do anything you don't want to do, but you could stay here for a couple of months and then come back to live with us eventually, and no one would be any the wiser. Think about it, at least.'

Frowning, Ruby looked from one to the other, feeling their expectation.

'No, it's OK, you take her. I suppose she'll have a good home.'

'No, no, Ruby, you have to think about it. You can't make such a big decision just like that,' George said with a distinct note of caution in his voice, but Ruby wasn't interested.

'Yes I can, I'm leaving hospital tomorrow morning and I'm not taking her with me. I'll just leave her here. You can take her in the morning when we leave here and I'll go back to the hotel. If Aunt Leonora'll still have me, that is.' Ruby bit her lip, determined not to cry.

'Of course she will; and don't worry about anything, we'll arrange it all . . . if you're sure. We'll come back and collect you as soon as the interest in the village has died down, as soon as there's no way they can make any connection between both of you.'

'OK.' Ruby shrugged but she knew it would never happen. If they adopted the little girl then things could never be the same, however much they all wanted them to be. 'Have you heard from Ray? Or Mum?'

'No, nothing since Ray telephoned all those months ago being obnoxious, but there's something else we need to tell you. Johnnie Riordan visited a few weeks ago, looking for you. He just turned up on the doorstep out of the blue.'

'You didn't tell him, did you?' Ruby's head turned from one to the other. 'I don't want him to know anything. *Anything!*'

Ruby felt sick as she once again brushed away the picture of her and Johnnie with their baby, which kept invading her thoughts. It wasn't going to happen, so she had to live with it.

'No, of course we didn't, even though he seemed very determined to find out about you. He was very polite, of course, but that's his way.'

'Did he say anything about Mum or Nana?'

'He said he'd spoken to your grandmother and that she was well.' Babs answered. 'She told him everything was much the same apart from Ray, who was still behaving very badly. I have to confess we felt really uncomfortable lying to him, knowing that you were having his baby. I wish you could have married him, Ruby, kept the baby . . .'

Ruby shrugged. 'I have to get back now. I'll see you tomorrow.'

She stood up cautiously and, without looking at them again, turned to walk back to the ward and her last day with her baby.

The next morning Babs and George Wheaton collected Ruby and her baby daughter from the hospital and they all went back to the hotel where Ruby had been staying during her pregnancy.

It was a four-storey terraced building right on the seafront on the borders of Thorpe Bay, and had been tastefully and expensively renovated. The ground floors housed the communal lounges, dining room, kitchen and reception area, two more floors were single guest rooms, and the top floor was Leonora's spacious private flat where Ruby had been staying. There were just two live-in staff and their quarters were down in the basement. The hotel was Leonora Wheaton's life and she spent most of her time in the office behind the small reception desk on the ground floor.

Because of George's wheelchair they couldn't go up to the flat so they were all cramped into the office on the ground floor in an embarrassed silence as Babs gave the baby her first bottle away from the hospital and carefully got her ready for the drive back to Melton with Babs at the wheel.

'Do you mind if we called her Margaret? Then she can be Maggie or Meg. What do you think? We think it really suits her.'

'I don't care what you call her,' Ruby answered abruptly. 'Just take her and go. Please? I can't stand any more of this. Just go.'

Babs handed the baby to George while she collected everything up.

'We'll talk on the telephone . . .'

'I'm sorry, but I just want this over with.'

'Ruby, you know you'll always be a daughter to us, don't you? You'll both be our daughters. Nothing's changed.'

'If you say so,' Ruby answered. But she knew it wasn't true. Everything had changed.

That night Ruby allowed herself to cry for the first time over what might have been. She cried for the loss of her baby, she cried for what might have been with Johnnie, she cried for the change in her relationship with Babs and George Wheaton; but she didn't shed a single tear for her mother and brothers. As she saw it, none of it would have happened if they hadn't dragged her away from her carefree life in Melton back to Walthamstow.

At that moment she desperately wanted to make them pay for how they had ruined her life.

THIRTEEN

Walthamstow, the month before

As Johnnie Riordan was driving his motorcycle down Elsmere Road he saw Elsie Saunders, Ruby's grandmother, sitting on an upright chair in the tiny front garden of the Blakeley house. It was the first time he'd seen her sitting outside so he went home, parked his bike, and, after a few minutes' hesitation, walked back up the street and stopped at the gate. Her concentration was on the knitting needles that were clicking furiously in her lap so she didn't notice him standing there.

'Good afternoon, Mrs Saunders. My name's Johnnie Riordan. I'm a friend of Ruby's. I live down the street at my sister's house. Don't know if you know her – Betty Dalton? Married to Tony?' He smiled disarmingly, turning the charm up high.

The woman peered up at him but didn't answer. Johnnie

164

wondered if she was having trouble seeing him so he stepped closer and gently touched her arm.

'I wondered if you'd heard anything from her.'

'And what's that got to do with you? She never said anything about you to me. Not a clue who you are.' She glared up at him through the new spectacles she was adjusting to.

'I'm a friend. We got to know each other when she came back from her evacuation. Just a bit worried 'cos she sort of disappeared.'

'Not your job to worry, young man.'

'Well, no, but we were friends and she's been gone for months. I didn't expect it to be that long. I thought she was going away for a couple of days, but so long as she's OK . . .'

'Well, Sonny Jim, seeing as what happened before she went I doubt she'll ever come back, poor kid, but if she does I'll tell her you were asking.'

Her tone was dismissive as she shrugged and pulled a face; immediately Johnnie started laughing. 'I can see where Ruby got her fighting spirit from.'

'In this house it's stand and fight or lie down and let the buggers walk all over you. Ruby fought back; me and her mother just lie here and let them do whatever they want.'

She placed her knitting on the wall and wriggled forward on her chair. As she started to stand up Johnnie leaned forward to help her but she swatted him away impatiently, grabbed the front wall with both hands and heaved herself up.

'Ruby told me things, you know, but she didn't want Ray to know we were friends. I know a lot about what she went through and why she didn't want to be here. She told me you were the only one who understood. If there's anything I can do to help?'

'You can pass me that walking stick.' The elderly woman looked around, checking that no one else was nearby to hear her words. 'I'll say if I hear anything, so if you see Ruby you'll tell me, will you? I just want her to be all right, that's all. She's a good girl and they did wrong by her.'

'I know. I'll tell you if I hear anything.'

After she'd fully turned to go indoors Johnnie had walked slowly back down the street, thinking hard about Ruby Red, the classy and clever young girl whom he'd met by chance and instantly been fascinated with. The attraction he had felt for her wasn't the same feeling he'd had with other girls, and he had enjoyed the slow burn of the embryonic relationship, but then he'd made the mistake of losing control and having sex with her despite her being only sixteen.

He had realised the next time he'd seen her that she was ashamed and embarrassed, and he hated himself for making her feel that way, but there was no going back.

Initially he'd felt so guilty he'd been almost pleased

when she'd gone away, but then she hadn't come back and now she was at the forefront of his thoughts again. He wondered if the urge to find her was because he was backed into a corner with Sadie, who, encouraged by Bill Morgan, was eagerly making plans for a party at the Black Dog to announce their engagement.

An engagement that Sadie wanted, that Bill Morgan wanted, but not one that Johnnie himself wanted. But he saw it as a chance to ingratiate himself further with Bill, who treated Sadie as the daughter he'd never had.

He leaned on the lamppost outside his house and watched a young courting couple walking along, completely absorbed in each other. He realised he had never felt like that with Sadie Scully. He liked her a lot and they had fun together, but he wasn't in love with her.

Then it hit him like a bullet between the eyes. He was in love with Ruby Blakeley.

He decided then and there to go to Melton as soon as he had a free day. He knew he would be better able to judge the Wheatons' reactions to his questions if they were face to face. But first he would have to arrange for a day off from the Black Dog and also find an explanation that would keep the very possessive and volatile Sadie happy.

A week later he walked up the path to the Wheatons' front door and knocked. As he waited he saw Derek Yardley looking out of the window of his flat over the garage. He smiled and waved, but the man just frowned and dropped the curtain.

'Good day, Mrs Wheaton,' Johnnie smiled confidently as she opened the door. 'I'm wondering if you know anything about Ruby. She's missing.'

One look at the shocked expression on her face and he knew that the Wheatons were somehow involved with Ruby's disappearance.

'I'm worried about her and I know you know where and how she is.'

'I'm sorry, Mr Riordan, but Ruby doesn't live here. We haven't seen her for a while.'

'But is she OK? Why didn't she come back?'

Johnnie stayed where he was, hoping that Babs Wheaton's natural good manners would get him into the house. The woman wasn't being unfriendly and her expression was neutral, but there was a determined line to her mouth.

'I'm sorry you've had a wasted journey, Mr Riordan. You're welcome to come in and have a cup of tea before your journey home but I really don't want to talk about Ruby. It's not my place. Have you asked her family?' She stood back and motioned for him to go in.

'I've spoken to her grandmother. She's worried about her welfare, but I think she's also pleased Ruby has made a run for it and got away!'

'Do you take sugar in your tea?' Babs Wheaton asked with a smile, effectively ending the conversation.

When he left an hour later he was none the wiser; Babs Wheaton had given away nothing, although she hadn't denied that she knew where Ruby was. Johnnie hovered around for a few minutes after Mrs Wheaton had shut the door and then went across and knocked on the door of Derek Yardley's lodgings over the garage. Then he knocked again. And again.

'Hello, mate. Long time no see.'

Derek Yardley tried to smile but it just didn't happen. Johnnie knew that guilty look and it surprised him, but at the same time he was intrigued. The man was hiding something.

'I'm looking for Ruby Blakeley – have you seen her?'

'No.'

'No suggestions where she might be then?'

'No.'

'Can't say I believe you, but no matter. I'll be back, so you have a think in the meantime, eh?'

The two young women were sitting side by side on the seawall swinging their legs and looking out to sea. They were both wearing similar but different coloured outfits of patterned cotton frocks, light cardigans and summer sandals, but whereas Ruby's clothes were good quality, almost new and well-fitting, Gracie's were faded and over-worn bordering on threadbare.

'What happened to your baby, Ruby? Why isn't it living with you?' Gracie McCabe asked curiously.

'I don't want to talk about it. It's over and done with, and now I want to forget all about it and get on with my life. Like you do,' Ruby said firmly.

'It didn't die, did it?' Gracie's jaw dropped as the thought occurred to her.

'Of course not. I'd have said, wouldn't I?' Ruby sighed loudly and raised her eyes skywards. 'And stop saying "it". *She's* a girl and I gave her up to be adopted, if you must know. Same as you with your baby boy, who's a *he*.' She emphasised the words but smiled at the same time.

'But why would you have your baby adopted, you being a war widow and all that . . . unless you're not a widow at all!' Gracie studied her closely for a few moments, then continued, 'I thought about saying I was a widow but when I had to go into the home they wouldn't let me. The bloody nuns thought I had to feel shame and be punished for my sins. And, God, was I punished. That's why I just left the baby there and did a runner. I wasn't going to spend another six weeks in purgatory being punished before they took him away. Ten days in hospital with him were bad enough.'

'Don't you want to know what they've done with him? Haven't you got to sign papers and things?'

'They wouldn't have told me that, anyway. They just arrange it all and you do as you're told. I knew he was going to be adopted so that was it. Do you know what's happened to yours, then?'

Ruby shook her head. 'I don't want to talk about it.

Neither of us has our baby any more. That's it, there's no going back now, is there?'

'I suppose not.' Gracie replied with a deep sadness in her voice that Ruby could understand. Despite her protestations of indifference, every time Ruby closed her eyes she could see the little bundle of shawl, bonnet and rosebud lips that was her firstborn as she said her final goodbye. She knew that image would stay with her for ever and she was sure that Gracie would be feeling the same, despite them both proclaiming their joy at their current freedom.

The day Ruby had left the hospital she'd given Gracie her address at the Thamesview Hotel, and asked her to keep in touch, but it had been several weeks before the young woman had eventually turned up on the doorstep. She'd made light of her situation but Ruby could read between the lines and guessed that she'd had it rough. Having seen how Gracie had been treated in the hospital, she could only imagine how it must have been for her in the mother-and-baby home.

'I've not offended you, have I?' Ruby asked. 'I just want to forget any of it ever happened.'

Gracie swung her legs back over the wall and stood up on the pavement. 'Of course not. I just don't understand why you won't confide in me. I'm not likely to tell anyone, am I? Me being in the same situation and all.'

'I just can't. One day I will. Promise!' She looked at Gracie and smiled. 'It's not you, it's me.'

Gracie smiled back and then nudged her. 'I know, how

about we go for a walk to town and have a look in the Kursaal. There's this bloke working there – I saw him last week when I was taking a walk – he's so good-looking. I bet he's a gypsy, he's all swarthy and mysterious, like, and I swear he looked at me, you know, proper looked, like he fancies me.'

'Aren't you off men after what happened?' Ruby frowned.

'If you fall off your bike you get straight back on, that's what my ma used to say, so that's what I'm going to do,' Gracie said with an exaggerated shrug, making Ruby laugh properly for the first time in months.

'OK, OK, you win. I need some fun as well but it's not going to be the man sort of fun for me. I'm done with all that for ever. I'm going to be an old spinster with a Pekingese. And an aspidistra in a gazunder.'

Ruby got ready to cross the road back to the hotel. 'You wait here and I'll just go and grab my bag quick and hope I can get in and out without being seen or heard by any of Leonora's Ladies. They all tell tales on me, and I'm supposed to be helping with afternoon tea.'

Ruby put her forefinger up to her lips and gave an exaggerated wink. She was fed up with the questions. She was fed up with still having to act out being a nineteen-year-old grieving war widow who'd suffered a stillbirth. She was also fed up with Aunt Leonora alternately smothering her and then expecting her to act as an unpaid lady's maid.

She'd co-operated with everyone but now she had the urge to rebel. She wanted to be out and about having fun like other girls her age, like Gracie, not hanging around in the kitchen at the beck and call of the lady guests, then being sent off to bed at nine thirty like a schoolgirl.

Before the Wheatons had left, taking her baby daughter with them, there had been a discussion about the future and George had promised to open a Post Office account for Ruby with enough money to keep her going until it was the right time for her to go back to them. Leonora had disapproved strongly of a young girl having access to a large sum of money and had wanted to control it, but Ruby had dug her heels in. She saw it not as a gift, but as a small payment for handing over her baby, and she fully intended to use it to go out and enjoy herself and pretend that the past months had never happened. She also thought that having money to spend would help to wipe Johnnie Riordan from her memory.

But until Gracie turned up she hadn't had the opportunity.

After Gracie had walked out of the mother-and-baby home she'd quickly found a live-in job in the vast Palace Hotel at the top of the hill overlooking Southend Pier and the seafront. It was one of the most lowly and poorly paid jobs in the hotel, with long hours of back-breaking cleaning and polishing of the communal areas, but she had a bed to sleep in and food to eat, and the occasional afternoon off.

The two young women had initially bonded in the hospital and after meeting up again their friendship had continued to grow, not only because of their similar situations but because they really liked each other. The circumstances of their pregnancies and adoptions were different but their feelings were the same and that meant they understood each other in a way no one else could.

'Right, let's go before I get spotted!' Ruby said as, laughing, she ran down the hotel steps and off along the seafront with Gracie hot on her heels.

Ruby had fallen in love with the Thames Estuary town of Southend. After the drabness of post-war Walthamstow and the sleepiness of the Cambridgeshire countryside, the seaside town was a hive of excitement just waiting to be explored, and now she had someone to explore it with.

Gracie had been born and brought up there and, at twenty, she knew exactly where to go to have fun. Ruby hadn't admitted her real age so Gracie still thought they were nearly the same age. She knew she would have to confess at some point but she was scared Gracie wouldn't want to be friends with someone four years younger than she was.

'What shall we do? I've got some money, we can go wherever we want.'

'Let's walk to town and see what's happening. I've got to get back to work at five, but we could have some chips on the beach and then have a go on the roller coaster? That's where the young man works. He is so

174

handsome, all moody-looking with green eyes and a tattoo on his arm.'

'Sounds dangerous to me.'

'Yes, I know, but I need some danger and excitement in my life after the home and the hospital and all that.'

'Do you think I could get a job at the Palace as well?' Ruby asked. 'I have to get away from Aunt Leonora. She means well and has been really good to me but she's just there all the time. It'd be nice to do whatever I want. I've never been able to do that.'

'I dunno. I was lucky 'cos I know one of the chefs and he persuaded them. Lots of people are looking for jobs with board now, what with the bombing and everything. We lived in Westcliff up by Chalkwell Park and were bombed out. Mum's rented a new place down near the seafront, but I've been banished. None of the family want to know me 'cos of the baby and other stuff. They think I'm a right tart but I'm not, I was just stupid. I shouldn't have got caught out, specially with a bloody soldier passing through.'

Gracie was a very plain girl. Her mousy hair was dead straight and more often than not it was greasy and lank. She suffered badly with acne though it never seemed to bother her; she was a livewire with a huge personality and Ruby enjoyed being with her. She wanted to ask a bit more about Gracie's baby's father but she knew she wasn't ready to talk about Johnnie, so she said nothing.

'Me, too.'

'But if you were a widow then you were married, so then it was all right for you to have a baby.' She paused and squinted sideways. 'Something's not right about your story. Why are you living with this aunt and why did you have your baby adopted? You're no more a war widow than I am, Ruby Blakeley.'

'I told you, I don't want to talk about it. Keep on and I'm going back!' Ruby looked down at the pavement and Gracie didn't push it.

The tide was out as they walked along the seafront with the weak autumn sun just about warming their faces. They stopped as they neared the Kursaal amusement park to watch some children playing in the mud. The little girls had their skirts tucked in their knickers and were giggling and ducking as the boys threw mud pies at them.

'They'll be in trouble when they get home. I remember when me and me sisters used to do that. Ma'd go bananas when we got home with mud caked up our legs and in our hair.'

'It looks fun. I used to get all muddy but not from the beach. I lived in the country . . . Do you get on with your family? Apart from having the baby, that is.'

'Yeah, on the whole I suppose. And me mum'll come round sooner or later. She always does when one of us does wrong! We all fight like cat and dog but then we make up.' Gracie laughed. 'Want a fag?'

'I don't smoke.'

'Oh, come on, give it go. It's hard at first but once you get used to it it's great. Let's sit on the beach and I'll show you how to do it.'

They walked for a little way and then ducked down between two empty beach huts, away from the breeze that was blowing in from the Thames Estuary. In unison they tucked their skirts under their knees and perched on the cold pebbles. Then Gracie pulled two cigarettes out a packet of five, lit them both behind cupped hands from a single match and passed one to Ruby.

'Now suck the smoke all the way into your lungs. It'll make you cough but you'll soon feel so relaxed and it looks so sophisticated when you do it right. As soon as you've learned we'll go to the Kursaal and show 'em. Have you been on the roller coaster yet? It is so noisy and scary.'

'No, I haven't been anywhere except to the shops in the High Street. Not since I was in hospital. Not even before I was in hospital and I was sent into exile—' Ruby stopped mid-sentence.

'So you're not a bloody war widow. I knew it.' Gracie clapped her hands. 'So go on, tell all. What happened to you? You tell me your story and I'll tell you mine.'

But before she could answer Ruby suddenly started coughing and spluttering as the smoke from her first cigarette hit her lungs.

'It gets better . . .' Gracie dissolved into laughter, with Ruby coughing and laughing at the same time. 'Now tell.'

'No, I've got a better idea. Let's carry on walking. My lungs are on fire . . .'

'I'm not moving until you tell me.'

Ruby hesitated. The promise between Ruby and the Wheatons had been not to say a word to anyone, ever, but Gracie was different: she'd been through the same.

'OK, I've not been widowed, or even married. I'm sixteen, not twenty, and Aunt Leonora isn't my aunt. I got caught out and she helped me. Now, let's go . . .'

Ruby jumped up and ran off, Gracie in hot pursuit, but they hadn't run far before a voice rang out.

'Gracie, Gracie, stop!'

The girls looked round in unison and saw two young men heading towards them.

'Oh God, it's Sean. He's a porter at the Palace and keeps asking me out. What can we do? I don't want to be lumbered with him now, I want to talk to you, you secretive cow!' Gracie said out of the corner of her mouth as she waved half-heartedly.

'Nothing you can do. He's closing in on you,' Ruby murmured. 'Who's that with him?'

'Dunno, but not bad, eh? Think that one's mine,' Gracie murmured.

'You can have both of them. I'm not interested in any men. Never again . . .'

With no other option they stopped and waited for the two young men to catch them up.

'Hello there, Gracie. Fancy seeing you here! And who's

your friend? This is my cousin Patrick, who's visiting from London for the day. I'm showing him the delights of the Golden Mile.'

'Hello, Sean. Hello, Patrick. This is Ruby, she's a friend of mine who lives up in Thorpe Bay.'

'Oh, very nice is Thorpe Bay. That's where the money is,' Sean said, and his tone made Ruby instantly cautious.

'No money, me. I'm also staying with a relative,' she said with a polite smile.

'So where are you living when you're not on your holidays by the sea?' the other young man, Patrick, asked her, but Ruby chose not to respond. The last thing she wanted was personal questions from a stranger.

'Don't tell me then!' he grinned.

After everyone had shaken hands with everyone else, they all stood facing each other in an awkward silence, unsure of what to do next. Eventually Sean took the lead.

'Would you girls like to go for a drink or something? We could go to the pub? Or the cafe?'

Gracie looked at Ruby and then back at Sean and Patrick. 'Not the pub, but the café at the end of the pier would be fun. We want chips and then I have to be back at work.'

The group of four walked along to the pier and caught the train that trundled back and forth. At the pier head they bought cups of tea and bags of chips, and went to sit on one of the benches that faced the sea.

'Look, I can see the Thamesview from here. I wish we

had binoculars,' Ruby said as she looked across the estuary.

'What's the Thamesview?' Patrick asked.

'It's a landmark,' Gracie said quickly. 'The border between Southend and Thorpe Bay.'

Ruby smiled at her gratefully. The streetwise Gracie was always much quicker than she when it came to covering up. 'Shall we walk back? Did you know this is the longest pier in the world? It's over a mile.'

'And you want to walk it?'

'Yes. It'll do us all good. Lots of sea air in our lungs to clear out the fag smoke!'

The four of them strolled all the way back to the seafront and then went their separate ways, Gracie to the Palace and Sean and Patrick to the High Street.

When Ruby was on the bus on her way back to the hotel, she realised she had enjoyed herself. Really enjoyed herself for the first time in so long. Sean had made no secret that he was interested only in Gracie, so Ruby and Patrick had been thrown together and had chatted about everything that wasn't in the least bit personal. Gracie had kept glancing at Patrick all the while but Ruby didn't mind. She wasn't interested in having a serious boyfriend, but she enjoyed being part of a group again, being silly and acting like the carefree young girl she used to be in the good days in Melton. The days before she'd had to leave her school and all her expectations and go back to Walthamstow.

Ruby

Patrick had made noises about the four of them going out dancing one night, and the more Ruby thought about it the better that sounded.

FOURTEEN

'I've made up my mind, Aunt Leonora. I'm not going back to Melton.'

'Why ever not?' Leonora Wheaton asked sharply. 'Babs and George are looking forward to you going back, and you getting to know Maggie. Have you decided to go home to London instead?'

'No. I'm going to stay here, in Southend. I've got used to the place and I've got friends again. Anyway, I don't think it's fair on any of us for me to be around Maggie all the time. But don't worry,' she laughed, 'I don't mean I'm going to stay here.'

Leonora looked hard at Ruby. 'But how can you stay in Southend if you haven't got anywhere to live?'

'I've been offered a job at the Palace with Gracie, and I can live in there. It's a shared room but I don't mind.'

'That doesn't sound a good idea, Ruby. You're still far too young to be living like that when you don't have to.

Gracie has no choice, poor thing, but you do. And your baby? You don't really mean that, do you?'

'Yes, I do. She's not my baby any more so why would I want to see her every single day? It's not fair to expect me to pretend that I'm her sister. What if I make a mistake and say something wrong? I can't do it.'

As Ruby welled up she was surprised to see the woman's normally stern expression change slightly. Leonora Wheaton was usually brusque and unemotional in her dealings with everyone, be it the chambermaid, the milkman or the visiting vicar of the parish. No matter what the situation, her demeanour remained the same.

She was a large, upright woman with salt-and-pepper coloured hair, which she always wore pulled back from her face, pinned tightly behind her ears and rolled around the bottom. Her outfit of choice without fail was a tailored costume over a long-sleeved, high-necked blouse and a very fearsomely structured corset. Her concession to summer was to remove the jacket. Her complexion was naturally pale and she always wore lipstick, a touch of powder along with a spray of floral perfume, and a large diamanté brooch in the shape of a lizard.

But despite always being so rigid and formal, she noticeably softened when Ruby mentioned the baby.

'It's just so sad, dear, but at least you know where she is and how she's getting on. You'll always know that, and George and Babs will be perfect parents to her, the same as they are to you. You just have to think of that poor Gracie, who wasn't lucky enough to have the support you had. She knows nothing about her baby and she never will.'

'I do know that,' Ruby said sharply. 'But now they've got the baby they always wanted I'll just be in the way.'

'No you won't. That is just being childish and silly, Ruby, and I know you're not silly. It's true they always wanted a child but were never blessed, but that doesn't mean they don't have enough love for you both. Some parents have five, six, seven children – can they only love one of them?' She looked at Ruby and raised her eyebrows. 'But it's not my place to say any more about it. You must talk to George and Babs and discuss this with them.'

With that Leonora stood up and carefully straightened her skirt before looking in the large mirror that hung over the open fireplace, patting her permed hair without actually moving it, and reapplying the bright red lipstick, which seemed out of character with her otherwise staid appearance. Ruby knew that was meant to be the end of the conversation but she wasn't going to let it go as easily as that.

'Well, I know I want to stay in Southend and I'm going to. It feels like home now.' She smiled. 'But I'm really grateful for everything you've done for me. You've been so good. I don't know what would have happened if you hadn't helped me. You didn't have to, but you did.'

To Ruby's surprise a deep flush made its way from Leonora's neck all the way up to her forehead.

'That is such a nice thing for you to say, Ruby Blakeley. And believe it or not, it's been a pleasure to have you here. You've grown on me, young lady!'

Ruby was pleased. She felt settled and was glad Leonora liked having her there. Since meeting Gracie, Ruby was enjoying her new life in the lively seaside town. The two girls had become close friends and were going out together at every opportunity. They went to dances and the cinema, they even went to the theatre, but there was nothing they enjoyed more than spending an afternoon at the Kursaal on the seafront, sometimes just the two of them and sometimes with young men. But although Gracie sometimes took it further Ruby never did. She wouldn't even let a young man kiss her, let alone go any further. She had promised herself she would never get into that awful situation again. Yes, she thought to herself. Southend was home.

Pressing her lips together to set her lipstick, Leonora turned around to face her. 'Has your money from George run out yet? Is that why you need a job?' she asked.

'No. I haven't spent much of it. I'm saving up, and if I take the job I can carry on saving. I've helped out here, I've seen what Gracie does in the Palace, and I can easily do what she does.' She looked at Leonora earnestly, seeking approval. 'I want to learn all about the hotel trade. I want my own hotel.'

'Not so long ago all you wanted was to be a nurse.'

'Yes, but only because that was all I knew. I had the idea that I'd become a nurse and then go back and work with Uncle George, but that was just a stupid kid's dream. Now I know different. I want a hotel just like this one day.'

'High expectations, young lady. I was lucky to have an inheritance. I could never have afforded this without it and after all those years looking after my mother I had the domestic experience as well, which was lucky in its own way. And I was already getting on in years.' Leonora laughed drily. 'No, dear, I approve your ambition but you should go off and do your nursing training. That would be a good basis for many things, especially for marriage and children. You may meet a nice doctor – lots of nurses do. That's why they're nurses.'

'I'm not going to get married. I don't need a man to look after me. I want to be able to look after myself. I want a job, a career. Like you.'

'But that's not how it is nowadays, not now the war's over and the men are able to work again. There aren't so many jobs for the women.' Once again she glanced in the mirror. 'Now we have to go down and see to the guests. We'll talk again tonight.'

Ruby looked at her and realised that the conversation really was over.

Leonora walked ahead down the narrow staircase from the flat to the main hotel accommodation and then down again to the ground floor; as Ruby went into the kitchen so Leonora went into her small office by the reception and sat down at her desk. At the age of fifty-five, unmarried and, until the death of her mother, never having had a life outside the family home, she had an understandably narrow view of modern life. She tried to keep up with the world she had never previously had much access to, but it was hard. She'd had little opportunity to make a social life, and she had no experience of the younger generations. She was more comfortable dealing with the genteel ladies who stayed in her hotel rather than opening it up to holidaying couples and families.

She had only agreed to having the pregnant Ruby to stay with her because she adored her brother George, and would do anything for him. Despite her reservations, she had, however, grown fond of the young girl and had got used to having her around to help out. She enjoyed her youthful company and conversation and it was as if she were reliving her own lost youth.

She had fretted over Ruby's pregnancy, the birth and then the adoption and she had been delighted that baby Maggie was with George and Babs and not with strangers. She had been sucked in to their lives, and now the time was drawing near she found herself dreading the girl's departure.

The hotel's small office window looked out across the sea, and on a clear day it was possible to see right across the estuary to Kent. She would often sit and stare and imagine what her life could have been like if she had had some freedom in her youth, especially when she saw the passenger ships heading out to open sea en route to countries she had only read about in the many books she'd collected over the years. In her daydreams she was on a ship travelling off on an adventure to the great unknown, sailing to such exotic destinations as India and China, Africa and America. As she watched she could see herself sipping tea on deck with the ladies and dining with eligible male companions who were off to transform the colonies.

It was these now unachievable dreams that made her want something more for her young charge. Leonora Wheaton disapproved strongly of the fact that Ruby was unmarried and a mother, especially at such a young age, but she also admired the way she had dealt with it.

She opened a drawer, pulled out a ledger and spent an hour going through it, adding up, working out and thinking hard. She pushed her chair back resolutely and went out to the reception desk where Ruby was standing talking to one of the guests. Leonora watched for a moment as Ruby interacted perfectly with the elegant woman, and as soon as the conversation was over Leonora called Ruby into the office.

As she closed the door Ruby went straight into her naturally defensive mode.

'I wasn't doing anything wrong. Miss Delaney was asking me about the buses.'

'It's nothing like that. I want to put something to you.' Leonora paused for a moment and took a deep breath.

'If you're sure you want to stay in this area, then you can stay here and work for me properly. As my assistant. I can't pay you much but you'll have board and lodging and training. You will have to take your turn at everything; this is such a small hotel I can't have specific employees for specific jobs.'

Ruby stood and stared. She was completely taken aback and she wasn't sure what to say. Her decision to move out had been made because she thought she had no choice, and suddenly she had an alternative but she wasn't sure it was the alternative she wanted. Part of the appeal of staying in the town was the thought of the freedom it would bring her. She and Gracie had plotted and planned where they would go and what they would do once she was away from Thamesview and free to go out and start having fun.

'Oh, I don't know what to say. This isn't what I was expecting . . .' Ruby stuttered when she realised that Leonora was waiting for some sort of response. 'I wasn't hinting or anything . . .'

'I know you weren't and I can see you're shocked, so off you go and think about it. Then if you decide we can talk about your role, which will have to combine work and training.'

'I've arranged to meet Gracie at the pier – I have to go, she'll be waiting for me – but I'll come straight back.'

Leonora smiled but Ruby could see the woman was disappointed that she hadn't jumped at the offer.

As she turned to leave the room Leonora called her back. 'Ruby dear, I'm not doing you a favour. I'd like you to stay.'

Ruby hadn't arranged to meet Gracie but she wanted to get away to think. Even if her situation at Leonora's hotel changed she couldn't imagine the woman who had been her guardian, as such, easily letting go of the reins.

She walked along to the nearby parade of shops and went into the small café where she and Gracie sometimes sat for hours with a pot of tea and a plate of biscuits topped up occasionally by the owners, Mr and Mrs Alfredo, if there wasn't a queue. If it was a sunny day the lace curtains were clipped back from the windows and everyone who went in always wanted the window seats. Ruby and Gracie always sat in the alcove at the back without a view of anything except the kitchen so they were rarely moved on.

'Ah, it is the beautiful Ruby.' Mr Alfredo held his arms out in welcome across the counter. 'But where is the also lovely Gracie?'

'She's not here today. Do you mind if I sit in here on my own? I don't want anyone to get the wrong idea . . .'

'If they get the wrong idea then Mrs Alfredo will immediately teach them the right idea. You go and sit and I'll bring you tea. Go, go . . .'

Ruby smiled. It would be very easy to be flattered by the charm of the moustachioed Mr Alfredo but she'd spent long enough in there to know that he greeted everyone as if they were all long-lost cousins and their offspring. While he gesticulated and complimented, so Mrs Alfredo tutted and rolled her eyes. It was a routine, almost a music-hall act which the two of them had perfected over the years.

She crossed to the other side of the café which was empty apart a young couple sitting at a table in the window, oblivious to everything going on around them. Once she was seated and had a cup of tea in front of her, Ruby watched them surreptitiously as they leaned into each other across the gingham-covered table and held hands. She noticed the shiny gold wedding ring first and then saw the woman gently touch her stomach.

Recently wed and pregnant.

As she watched she couldn't help but think of Johnnie Riordan. The familiar wave of pain that always swept through her body whenever she thought of him and Maggie started in the pit of her stomach and spread up though her chest. She blinked fiercely, aware that the next stop for the wave was always her eyes. It just never really went away. She often lay in bed at night and fantasised about the three of them being a family, and that thought hurt just as much as it had the day she had handed Maggie over to Babs and George Wheaton.

It was that pain that helped her make up her mind.

Having fun with Gracie was such a short-term thing and she really didn't want a serious boyfriend. Although she was only just seventeen she felt a lot older; older than

Gracie, even. Her friend seemed to have overcome everything that had happened to her and locked it away in the far reaches of her mind; she bore little resentment to the father of her baby, who had quickly abandoned her when she told him she was pregnant, to her mother who threw her out of her home, or even to the nuns who treated her so badly. 'Back on the bike and riding . . .' she'd laugh if Ruby asked how she was feeling.

Ruby always went along with the gaiety and pretended to feel the same but inside she felt stripped of all emotion. She couldn't imagine ever getting over it as Gracie seemed to be doing.

'Thanks, Mr Alfredo,' she said as she rushed past the counter. 'I've left the money on the table.'

'Wait, Ruby, wait! I want you to meet my son. He's at university, you know! He's very clever; he's going to be a big important lawyer when he qualifies.' His pride was obvious as he turned and shouted out in the direction of the internal stairs that led up to the accommodation above the café. 'Tony? Tony, come down and meet my most beautiful customer, my favourite customer.'

The young man who sauntered down into the café, hands in pockets, was classically handsome in features and obviously Mediterranean in colouring. Confident in his stature, his clothes were casual but smart, and he was perfectly groomed; he had a mass of thick black hair controlled by Brylcreem, light olive skin and deep brown eyes that looked directly into Ruby's as he moved to stand behind the counter. Ruby's first impression was that he looked just like a movie star, but she instantly dismissed the thought.

'Tony, this is Ruby . . . Ruby, this Tony, my son. He's home from university for the holidays and helping his *mamma* and *papà* with the business,' Mr Alfredo said.

'Pleased to meet you, Ruby,' Tony Alfredo said with a smile that showed his very white teeth but didn't reach his eyes. Ruby guessed he was fed up with being regularly wheeled out to be shown off.

'Pleased to meet you too, Tony,' she smiled, and then turned back to his father. 'I'm sorry but I have to run. I've got something I have to do but I'll see you soon.'

She blew Mr Alfredo, senior a light-hearted kiss and winked at his wife, who smiled and predictably rolled her eyes.

She could feel Tony Alfredo's eyes on her but she resisted the urge to turn round and look at him again. The flicker of interest she felt wasn't what she wanted.

As she reached the Thamesview she ran up the steps, into the lobby and and then straight through into the office.

'Aunt Leonora, I've thought about it. I'd love to work here and I'm so grateful to you for giving me the chance. I want to learn absolutely everything and I promise I won't let you down.'

'Good,' Leonora said. 'Now which one of us is going to tell Babs and George that you're not going back to Melton?'

PART TWO

FIFTEEN

1951

'But Ruby, you must come back for Maggie's birthday tea party. I really want you here; we all do.'

'I don't know if I can. The hotel is busy and Aunt Leonora is still unwell.'

'I'm sure you can manage this one day. Maggie really wants you to come. She's written your name on her list.' Babs Wheaton was at her persuasive best. 'We've missed you, darling. It's been so long. We'll send Yardley to collect you and Leonora. It will be nice for her to see Maggie as well.'

'I'll do my best. Gracie might be able to take over if she can get the day off from the Palace. Sometimes I wonder how we'd manage without her being prepared to work twenty-four hours a day. My saving Grace, she is,' Ruby laughed.

'Marian was asking about you the other day. She's

engaged now. Keith is still single and he's grown into such a fine young man. He's doing National Service but I don't know where he is. Oh, Ruby, he looks so handsome in his uniform . . . And, of course, there's Maggie; such a little madam, that one. She rules this house. You must come home.'

'OK, you win,' Ruby laughed. 'I'll be there but we don't need Yardley. I can drive the hotel car now. I'll bring Aunt Leonora if she's well enough but I am worried about her. Do you think Uncle George will examine her?'

'If she lets him. Leonora can be very difficult.'

'Difficult isn't the word at the moment, but she is poorly and I'm worried. You'll notice when you see her – if she comes.'

Ruby replaced the phone onto its cradle and leaned back against the wall. She didn't want to go and play happy families at Maggie Wheaton's fifth birthday, but she knew it was something she had to do: a duty.

The little girl had been brought up knowing Ruby as her distant big sister and godmother, so the occasional visit was something she had to endure to keep everyone happy, but it was hard and every year it got harder rather than easier. As Maggie had changed from a baby into a beautiful small person with a voice and a personality, Ruby was even more aware of what she was missing, but she knew it was the best thing for daughter, who was having a happy childhood with two comfortably-off parents who adored her.

But still it hurt.

As time had passed she had done her best to detach herself from her previous lives in Melton and Walthamstow simply because she didn't want to think about what had gone before, but every so often something happened and she was back on the hospital ward holding the bundle in her arms.

A remark, a look, a small child of a similar age playing on the beach could instantly spark an unexpected memory. There was always a current photograph of Maggie on the sideboard at the hotel, but it was Leonora who would take the old one out of the frame and replace it with the new. Anyone who asked was told that Maggie was Leonora's niece and Ruby's goddaughter.

The only person outside of the Wheatons who knew the details of Maggie's parentage was Gracie, but it had never been discussed since the day Ruby had told Gracie she wasn't going to move to the Palace Hotel and work with her, that she was going to stay at Thamesview, and then told her all the reasons why. Gracie had hugged her friend and promised to keep her secret. And she had. The one good thing to come out of it all was Ruby's deep and enduring friendship with Gracie.

She went through to the kitchen where Gracie was again helping out.

'Gracie, I have to go upstairs. Mrs Burton may be leaving early but I know you can take over on reception.'

'Oh, yes, me on reception. Aunt Leonora'll have a real

touch of the vapours when she finds out about that!'
Gracie laughed. Then she saw the expression on Ruby's
face. 'What's up? You look as white as a sheet, like you're
going to faint.'

'Don't exaggerate. A bit shocked, maybe, but not about
to collapse! Aunty Babs just telephoned. She wants me
to go up to Melton for Maggie's birthday. I really don't
want to but I suppose I have to. It'd look strange if I didn't
as I'm her godmother. And some fresh country air might
be good for Leonora.'

'Instead of the fresh sea air blowing up a storm right
outside this front door?' Gracie laughed.

'All right, that was a silly thing to say, but this chest
thing is taking so long to shift and she won't go to the
doctor. I'm hoping she'll let Uncle George have a look at
her. I'm going to go up to see how she is and how she
reacts to going to Melton.'

'Good luck with that. Have you got a tin-hat ready?'
Gracie laughed loudly. 'Sorry, you know I don't mean it.
Shall I go to the chemist and get her a tonic?'

'Maybe later.' Ruby looked at her friend and smiled
affectionately. 'Thanks, Gracie. I don't know what I'd have
done without you helping out.'

'Go on with you,' Gracie said. 'Go and see the Lady
Leonora.'

'Tut tut, you make her sound like a pleasure steamer!'

Ruby was still smiling as she walked up the stairs,
thinking how much she loved Gracie McCabe.

200

Leonora was sitting in her favourite winged leather armchair with her feet up on a large tapestry footstool and a heavy blanket over her legs pulled right up to her hunched shoulders. She looked so pale and fragile that Ruby was worried anew.

'How are you feeling?' she asked as casually as she could.

'Just a little tired. Do stop fussing, I'll be fine by tomorrow.'

'Oh, good, because Aunty Babs has just rung, they want us both to go to Melton for Maggie's birthday party on Sunday. It's the first party she's ever had. I can drive, if you trust me!'

'Well, *you* have to go, of course, and you can take the car, but I'm not going. There's far too much work here for both of us to be away.'

'It's not until next weekend, and it's only for the day, so you might feel better by then,' Ruby said without looking at her. 'I'll make you a pot of tea now and then bring your supper up later on a tray.'

'I'm not an invalid, you know. I just have a chill, and I can do my own supper, thank you. And I'm perfectly capable of sitting at the table. I've never resorted to a tray on my lap in my life.' To show her disapproval she inhaled and exhaled as loudly as she could before reaching a hand out and turning the volume on the wireless up high.

Ruby bit her tongue. Over the years, Leonora had

mellowed and become almost amenable but since she had been unwell she was back to the intransigent, difficult person she had been when Ruby had first gone to stay with her. She sometimes reminded Ruby of her grand-mother back in Walthamstow: she was tough as old boots because of everything she'd been through in her life but with a good heart tucked away inside. Ruby had grown increasingly fond of her and understood her absolutely, but still she occasionally lost patience with her.

'I'll stay and have a cup of tea with you. Gracie is in charge downstairs.'

'Gracie?' Despite her lethargy Leonora visibly bristled. 'She'll drive all my guests away. They'll all go and leap off the pier in protest.'

'That's just what she thought you'd say, but she's more than capable, as you know. She's helped out more than enough times, and your ladies always love her.'

'She's common.'

'So am I.' Ruby snapped back.

Leonora shrugged back down under the blanket and glared ferociously but Ruby knew it was because she was feeling frustrated at having to hand over the reins of her beloved hotel to someone else, even if it was Ruby, who had worked hard alongside her for five years, and Gracie, who was more than proving her worth in being a general dogsbody in her spare time.

Ruby made the tea, set it out on a tray and put it on the side table beside her aunt's chair.

'Shall I pour for both of us? Gracie can manage, you know, and I said I'd be an hour so she's not expecting me.'

Without waiting for an answer Ruby sat on the chair next to the other side of the table and stirred the teapot.

'I'd really like you to come to Melton with me. It's going to be so hard and it would help if you were there. You understand the situation so well.'

'I'll see how I am. I know it's just a chill but it's wearing me out. I feel so useless.'

Leonora's tone had Ruby wondering if she was actually trying to convince herself that she just under the weather rather than really sick.

Suddenly Ruby wanted to go to Melton and she wanted to drag the recalcitrant Leonora along with her so that George could give her a check-up.

'How is she?' Gracie asked when Ruby went back down.

'I'm not sure. I want to talk to you about Maggie's birthday. If I can persuade Aunt Leonora to come with me, would you take over here for the whole day? A long day?'

'I can ask for the day off, but would you really trust me here for a day? And more importantly, would Lady Leonora?'

'She'll fret, but she frets when it's me.'

They both laughed. Gracie was nearly as fond of Leonora as Ruby was.

'And as for fretting, when are you seeing Tony again?' Gracie asked. 'He's been fretting a bit himself since

Fanny-Ann upstairs has been out of action and you've been too busy for him.'

'He's not happy that I'm so busy but that's just too bad.'

'Well, you know what I think about him, but the feeling's mutual so I don't care.' Gracie's tone was matter-of-fact.

'You do seem to rub each other up the wrong way all the time.'

'Hmm. So how do you really feel about him? How far is it going to go? All the way down the aisle?' Gracie turned the corners of her mouth down and pretended to shudder.

'Don't be mean,' Ruby laughed. 'I like going out with him, but that's it at the moment. I don't want to be married. I've said before, just me and a Pekingese in my old age.'

'You'll change your mind, I know you will, but I hope it's not that arrogant twit you decide on. A smelly snuffly Pekingese would be much nicer.'

'Meanie. Anyway, I'm off to do things that need doing.'

They smiled at each other before going off in different directions to work, Gracie to the kitchen and Ruby to the office and reception.

Tony Alfredo was the only bone of contention between Ruby and Gracie. He was the man Ruby was going out with him, but Gracie didn't like or trust him, and she made no bones about it.

Ruby had become friends with Tony Alfredo very

slowly, starting five years before with just the occasional outing during his university holidays when he was visiting his family. As an occasional companion the charming young law student had been perfect, but then he'd returned to the family home to live with his parents and started working in London, commuting by train every day, and he expected to see her far more often. He had become more demanding, and although Ruby still liked his company she was uncomfortable with his intensity.

He hated her going out and about, especially with Gracie and her friends from the Palace Hotel, yet he would never go out with them, despite Ruby asking him. They had fun when they were together and he took her to places she wouldn't normally go, but he was too demanding when Ruby couldn't spend time with him. Despite her constantly trying to find the middle road, Tony just wanted more, and he would push and push until she gave in. She knew she had to sit down and have a talk with him, but she knew it would be hard, and at that moment she wasn't in the right frame of mind.

As Ruby helped Leonora out of the car a whirlwind that was a child ran out of the house and then stopped dead beside the car door, looking expectant.

'Hello Maggie! Many happy returns of the day to you. Are you having a lovely birthday so far?' Ruby managed a wide smile, despite feeling her stomach lurch right up into her throat. It was such a physical feeling Ruby was grateful that she could busy herself helping Leonora out of the car and not have to make any prolonged eye contact with the child immediately. She needed some time to acclimatise herself both to seeing Maggie, who had grown so much, and to being back in Melton, the village she loved.

It was the same every time she went back: she felt physically sick with expectation, unsure of how it was going to be.

Leonora had started to feel better in the days before Maggie's birthday so it had been easier to persuade her to go to the party and leave a very scared Gracie in charge of the hotel. But as they got closer to Melton so Ruby's nerves had started to take over and when she turned onto the village High Street all she wanted was to do a U-turn and head straight back to Essex.

But of course she didn't. She carried on following the familiar route to the house.

'I'm having a birthday party. Four of my friends are coming and Mummy's made jelly and cake for everyone. You can have some as well.'

'I can't wait! And you look so pretty in your party frock. Shall we all go inside and see Mummy and Daddy?' She looked at the little girl. Her daughter. 'Say hello to Aunty Leonora. She wanted to see you on your birthday as well.'

'Hello, Aunty Leonora.' As the child held out her hand

and smiled, all Ruby could see was Johnnie Riordan. There was little in her features or colouring to connect her to Ruby, but there was no denying her paternity. The child's hair was blonde and straight, and tied back from her face with a bright red ribbon that perfectly matched the colour of both her T-bar shoes and the edging of her white cotton frock, which Ruby just knew was home-made by Babs. She wanted to cry as she looked at the perfect little girl standing in front of her, but before she could shed a tear Babs came out. Ruby knew she'd stood back for a few minutes to let her say hello to Maggie, and she was grateful for her thoughtfulness and perfect timing under the circumstances.

She walked forward and greeted her sister-in-law politely first, before hugging Ruby affectionately. 'Oh, I'm so pleased to see you, both of you. I thought we'd have a slow light lunch to get our strength up before the other little girls arrive and the party starts. The children will be excluded from the sitting room so Leonora and George can spend some time together.' Babs lightly squeezed Ruby's hand to acknowledge that she'd listened to Ruby's request for George to check his sister over.

'Ruby, do you want to come and see my new pram? I've put my dolly in it already.'

'I'd love to, and I've got a birthday present for you as well, and,' she paused and looked down at Maggie, 'so has Aunty Leonora. But you have to go indoors first. Go on, no peeking. Off you go.'

The little girl laughed and ran off into the house, followed by Leonora, leaving Ruby alone with Babs to get the presents out of the car boot.

'How are you getting on?' Babs asked. 'I've missed you so much, and I still worry about you.'

'I know.' was all Ruby could think of to say. Melton was no longer her world and Maggie was no longer her daughter; the whole situation felt wrong. As they walked together to the house Ruby saw Derek Yardley leaning against the Wheatons' car, watching her; as she caught his eye so he smiled, or rather his mouth made the shape of a smile, but he didn't say anything, he simply stared until she looked away.

'I don't think Yardley knows what to say to you. You've turned from a gawky little schoolgirl into a beautiful young woman. He was always very fond of you . . .'

'Hmm.' Ruby's murmur was noncommittal as she looked away from him and walked faster towards the open back door of the house. 'You did tell Yardley I was just giving Aunt Leonora a lift, didn't you? I don't want him to know where I live or what I do.'

Babs looked puzzled. 'We've never said anything. It's nothing to do with him, but it's been so long anyway, he'd never put two and two together now. No one would.'

Derek Yardley had been the Wheatons' driver for so many years they thought of him as part of the family. Ruby had no intention of saying anything against him, especially as she didn't live there any more and didn't have to have anything to do with him, but she disliked him intensely and was ever uncomfortable around him. But because George and Babs depended on him so much she kept quiet.

'OK Maggie, let's go and look at your new doll's pram,' Ruby said. 'And you've got more presents to open . . .'

Ruby watched Maggie and was fascinated at the self-assurance of the little girl. She was gorgeous and confident, and Ruby found herself thinking to the future, seeing her daughter growing up to go to university, qualifying as a doctor to take over from George and keep the family surgery going in the village. Because of circumstances and finances, Ruby's parents had never had any aspirations for her and it thrilled her that Maggie would have everything going for her. There would be no limits for Maggie Wheaton.

Everyone watched indulgently as Maggie opened her gift from Ruby and whooped with excitement at the beautifully dressed baby doll. She placed it straight into the pram and wheeled it around the room.

'She loves it,' Babs smiled. 'Look at her, such a wonderful choice.'

Then she opened her gift from Leonora, which was a compendium of games. Ruby had known what the birthday present was – she'd even bought it from the toyshop on Leonora's behalf – but with everything that was going on she hadn't given it too much thought.

'Oh, look, Maggie, all those games,' Babs said. 'It's got your favourite game in the box. Draughts . . .'

Draughts. The word hit Ruby like a bullet between the eyes. Nausea rose and she breathed deeply. In and out, in and out.

'Who do you play draughts with?' Ruby asked Maggie, trying to keep her tone moderate.

'I always play with Mummy and Daddy.'

'Do you play with anyone apart from Mummy and Daddy?'

'No, but I might play with my friends now I've got a big box. Look, Mummy, Snakes and Ladders. Will you teach me?'

As her face became hotter so Ruby could actually feel her heart palpitating erratically in her chest. Suddenly the old wound, which had seemed long since healed, was ripped open again.

SIXTEEN

1942

'*What are you up to, young Ruby?*' *Derek Yardley asked the twelve-year-old, who was kicking a tennis ball at the edge of the path in boredom. Babs Wheaton was helping her husband in the surgery, Marian and Keith had gone home for their tea, and Ruby was on her own with nothing to do.*

'*I'm waiting for Aunty Babs.*'

'*I don't want that ball hitting the car I've just cleaned. Do you want to come up to my flat and wait for her? It's just about to rain. We could listen to the wireless or play a game of draughts.*' *He walked over to where she was playing and smiled as he patted her gently on her back.*

'*I'm all right here. It's nearly teatime.*'

'*I'll leave the windows open and then you'll hear Mrs Wheaton call you.*'

'*OK,*' *Ruby said without any more hesitation. Yardley,*

211

as he was called by everyone, was almost family and she had known him as long as she'd known Aunty Babs and Uncle George.

Derek Yardley was a compact and wiry man in his early thirties, with a neat moustache and short hair. He was softly spoken to the point of mumbling, and he rarely made eye contact with anyone. Country born and bred, he had a very narrow outlook, was not very sociable and didn't stand out on any level. He'd not had to serve in the Forces because of health problems, and he had no family so he was the perfect live-in driver for George, with his own disability. He did everything for the doctor that he couldn't do himself: he helped him in and out of the car, lifted his wheelchair and helped him on his rounds. He looked after the car impeccably and did some odd jobs. He was indispensable to both George and Babs, and they acknowledged it by treating him well.

Ruby followed him up the outside stairs at the rear of the garage and in through the door at the top. It had previously been the hayloft, but the Wheatons had converted it into a compact flat that was just big enough for one person. A heavy curtain attached to the ceiling separated the living area from the bedroom. There was a washbasin in the corner and an outside toilet behind the garage, but no cooking facilities, so Yardley ate the same meals as the family although he never ate with them. He simply collected his plate and returned it after he'd eaten. If it was a day when the elderly housekeeper was there *then he'd have a cup of tea and a slice of cake with her in the kitchen, but other than that he led a separate, isolated life.*

'Here, Ruby, you sit on the sofa and I'll get the draughts out.'

Ruby had never been in his flat before. She had automatically sat down at the drop-leaf table by the window, but she did as she was told and moved to the sofa, watching as Yardley set the game up on a rickety side table that he'd pulled forward. He then sat beside her on the small lumpy sofa, which was against the wall on the far side away from the window.

'There you are. What do you want to be, black or white?' he asked.

'I always choose white when I play with Aunty Babs.'

'White it is for you, then. You go first.'

The man and the child had been playing the board game and laughing for a few minutes when Derek Yardley made his move. First he slid one hand along the back of the sofa and then moved it onto her shoulder. It was surreptitious and although Ruby sensed something not quite right it wasn't enough for her to say anything, but she was distracted enough to move her white draught without concentrating, leaving Derek Yardley to jump over two and take them.

'I won!' he whooped. 'Now you have to pay a forfeit. You have to give me a kiss.' He laughed before leaning forward and kissing her hard on the lips with his mouth

open, forcing his tongue between her teeth. She tried to pull away and turn her head sideways, but he grabbed hold of her hair and forced his tongue right into her mouth; then in one quick movement his hand was up her skirt and touching her inside her knickers, his fingers probing around before frantically tugging at the elastic to force them down.

'Don't,' she said nervously, unsure of what to do. 'You're hurting me.'

'It's OK, Ruby, just relax. It's what grown-ups do all the time.'

'I'm not a grown-up,' she said fearfully. 'I want to go now. My tea will be ready.'

'But you look like a grown-up. I bet you've done this before – all the city kids do it all the time – I can tell you know what to do, Ruby. Come on, do it for me . . .'

He leaned right over, moving his arm from behind her and putting it across her neck. As his breathing quickened so his face flushed and he started wheezing so hard she could hear his lungs rattling. He pulled his hand away from her knickers, arched his back and grabbed inside the already undone fly buttons on his trousers.

But at that moment a voice echoed from below.

'Ruby? Ruby, where are you? Tea's ready . . .'

Derek Yardley turned and hesitated just long enough for her to slip out of his grasp and reach the door, which she was horrified to find was locked, although the key was still there. As she fumbled to open it she looked back over

Ruby

her shoulder to see Derek lying back on the sofa with his upright penis poking out of his trousers and a strange look on his face. Ruby stared a split second in horror before throwing the door back.

'One word, and I'll tell them you came up here, that you asked for it,' he spat as she stepped out onto the top of the outside staircase. 'One word, you filthy little London brat, and I'll fucking kill you. One word . . .'

Ruby stifled a scream and ran down the steps and around to the front of the garage from where she could see Aunty Babs, who was still calling her.

Ruby took a deep breath. 'I'm here.'

'Thank heavens for that,' Babs laughed. 'I thought for a minute we'd lost you. Have you been good?'

'I was in the field out the back with Keith and Marian, they've just gone.'

'Come on then. Teatime.'

As she went back to the house, Ruby looked up at Yardley's window, expecting to see him peering out, but there was no sign of him.

He didn't ever try to do anything again, and it was only as the years passed and she got older that she became aware of what had actually happened, but still she never said a word to anyone because she could see how lost the Wheatons would be without Yardley to do everything for them.

She was also worried that they might not believe her after so long.

It was easier to pretend it had never happened and just

keep away from him as much as possible. Sometimes there was no way of avoiding him and it was then that she remembered, and was aware that actually his resentment was far stronger than hers. It was also as she grew older that she realised he actually hated her for knowing what she knew about him.

The rest of Maggie's birthday passed in a blur for Ruby. She enjoyed it on one level because the little girl had such a wonderful birthday and she could see how much Babs and George loved every moment of it, but on another level she was fighting the distractions in her mind caused by the resurfacing of her long-buried memories.

She made an effort and pasted on a smile, but all she could see was a beautiful, friendly little girl living in a house that was just a few steps away from the resentful Derek Yardley, who had tried to abuse her when she was a child. She just hoped he never discovered the secret about Maggie's parentage.

Despite everything going on around her she tried to trawl her memories of that time, to analyse what had happened. Was it only she who had attracted him? Had she done something to encourage him as he'd implied, or did he like children? Any children? Had he done it to anyone else? Just the thought of it made her feel sick.

'Has Yardley ever had a girlfriend, do you know?' Ruby asked Babs as they stood side by side in the kitchen, cutting tiny crust-free jam sandwiches.

'Not that I know of, but what an odd question. Any reason for it?'

'No, just wondered. I suppose I'm surprised he's still here and living over the garage at his age. Wouldn't you think he'd have been married by now?'

'Oh, I think he's too much of a loner for that. He has a bit of social life in the village. He goes to the working men's club and to church, and on his day off he does some gardening for the vicar. I don't know what else he does but he's been with us for so long now and he's helped George so much.'

'Uncle George helped him: he gave him a job and somewhere to live.'

'That's why it works. They're good for each other.' Babs smiled at her. 'This is nice, just standing here talking. I really miss having you around to talk to. I know it's hard for you but I really wish you'd visit more often, maybe even stay for a few days?' She paused and when Ruby didn't answer she pretended not to notice. 'Anyway, shall we take the sandwiches and lemonade out to the children in the garden?'

As Babs picked up one tray, so Ruby picked up the other. 'Let's go.'

As they got ready to leave Ruby wanted to snatch Maggie up and take her away from the vicinity of Derek Yardley. She knew that the right thing to do would be to tell George and Babs, but it was so long ago and she still had her old childhood fear of not being believed, of being thought of as the outsider causing trouble. And Yardley had been part of the Wheatons' lives for far longer than she had, and George especially depended on him. She couldn't do it.

They all walked out together to the car, and as she opened the passenger door for Leonora to get in she caught sight of Yardley standing beside the Wheatons' gleaming black Vauxhall, pretending he was tending to it. But she knew he was watching her, the same way he had always watched her.

'I'm just going to have a word with Yardley,' she said. 'I won't be long.'

'Can I come with you?' Maggie asked.

'You stay and talk to Aunty Leonora. I'll be one minute.'

As she walked over to him she smiled as if she were going to greet a friend.

'Once you warned me, now I'm warning you. If you lay one finger on Maggie then you'll live to regret it. I'll make your life a real misery.'

Yardley's smile was equally insincere as he faced her. 'Now that's a bit uppity of you, isn't it? I mean, what's it to you? You're not part of that family,' he nodded his head in the direction of the Wheatons, who were all standing in the driveway, 'not like I am, and what I do is none of your business, Miss Dirty Evacuee. None of your business.'

He rubbed his hands together as if he was rubbing dirt off but Ruby was determined not to be riled. She didn't want anyone to see the confrontation, so she shrugged. 'But you made it my business when you did what you did. Remember my brother Ray who came to visit? Well, there are another two just like him at home. Three nasty violent thugs. So remember that if you ever touch Maggie like you touched me I'll know and I'll send them all down to deal with you.'

She turned and left him standing where he was, but she could feel his eyes boring into her back.

With the smile still glued to her face she hugged everyone, climbed into the car beside Leonora and drove off down the drive.

'Did you enjoy the visit?' she asked Leonora as they drove through the village towards the main road.

'It was nice to see Maggie but I wasn't happy that you tried to take advantage of George being a doctor. If I wanted to see a doctor I would, and I don't.'

'But he's your brother, he's bound to be worried about you. You should have taken advantage of him being a doctor on hand!'

'Don't be ridiculous.'

With that Leonora put her head back and closed her eyes. Within a few minutes she was asleep leaving Ruby with plenty of time to think about the day that had ended so badly for her.

When they eventually got back to the hotel she helped Leonora upstairs to her flat and then went back down to find Gracie.

'How's Maggie?' Gracie asked.

'She's lovely. She's so pretty, and clever beyond her years. There were four others there and she was way ahead of them. It must be because Aunty Babs spends so much time with her. She's five, can you believe it? Five years old.'

'Yeah, I can,' Gracie said sadly.

Ruby's jaw dropped. 'Oh God, I'm so stupid; your own baby. I'm so sorry, Gracie. I was so wrapped up in myself . . .'

'Oh, it's OK. I don't often think about him. I think he's probably fine. But I have to think that, don't I? Sometimes I think you're really lucky knowing all about Maggie, but then at others times I think I'm the lucky one 'cos I can forget most of the time.' She smiled and touched Ruby's arm. 'Did she like her presents? I bet she did. And how's Lady Leonora? Did she buck up a bit once she was with her family?'

'You know, one day you're going to slip up and say that in front of her, and then you'll be in such trouble!'

'But I don't mean it, do I? Anyway, how is she?'

'Tired, but I think she enjoyed it. Have you got to get back or do you want to stay here tonight? There's an empty room on the first floor, but don't tell anyone.'

'Oh, yes, please. I was dreading dragging me poor aching body all the way back home tonight. These ladies are far more demanding than what I'm used to. Gracie this, Gracie that, it never stops.' But she grinned as she said it, and Ruby knew she had actually enjoyed being in charge of the hotel.

'Go and take the key. It's time for all of us to get some kip. And thank you for today. I couldn't have gone without you!'

'Get away . . .' Gracie laughed. She reached over the desk, snatched up a room key from the board and ran up the stairs.

Ruby made sure everything was as it should be before handing over to Henry, the night porter. It had been a long and emotional day.

As Ruby had put the car in gear and driven out of the drive, Derek Yardley had carried on pretending he was engrossed in buffing the paintwork on the already gleaming car, but he was actually watching everything through his eyelashes. He had noticed how Ruby was included in the family gathering while he was left firmly on the outside. He'd seen how she'd been part and parcel of the birthday celebrations, both inside the house and out in the garden, while he had been handed some sandwiches and cake on a plate to take away and eat on his own.

He resented the fact that he'd been a loyal employee to the doctor and his wife for over fifteen years and yet he remained no more than that. He wanted so much to be a part of their lives, to be included the way Ruby Blakeley was, to be their surrogate son, but instead he was just an invisible employee.

As he watched the car disappear out of sight all he could think was how he could get back at Ruby and make her life as miserable as she had made his. He had been delighted when Ruby was ordered back to London, but it hadn't been the end he had expected. She was still back and forth, and even though she wasn't in Melton any more she was still treated as family. Even when the Wheatons had adopted the baby the talk was still of their precious Ruby. The final straw for Derek Yardley was when they gave her the role of godmother, while he remained just the employee who drove the car.

It had all been brewing in him for so long when, to add insult to injury, he'd had to stand still and smile as she insulted and threatened him. He couldn't believe that Ruby Blakeley, the little nobody evacuee from the back-streets of London, the kid who was absolutely no better than he, had actually had the nerve to speak to him so disrespectfully about something that had happened so many years ago.

Something that he knew could still ruin him in the eyes of the Wheatons.

Yardley's biggest talent had always been his ability to hide his feelings completely, so on the face of it he remained the pleasant and accommodating driver who was always there. Every day he carried on smiling and behaving as he had always done, but every day his resentment and his paranoia increased.

He was angry that Ruby continued to be treated as one

of the family, while he was living in a poky flat over a garage with an outside toilet and a tin bath. He was angry that after Ruby had left the Wheatons' home they had then taken in another child, this time an orphan baby, and adopted her.

Because of the time he'd worked for them – dedicated his life to them almost – Derek Yardley had anticipated an inheritance of sorts when the childless couple eventually passed on, but now he could see that slipping away. For that he placed the blame on Ruby, and for that he was determined to do her down.

His thoughts immediately went to Johnnie Riordan.

SEVENTEEN

Up in the flat at the top of the Thamesview Hotel Ruby went out onto the balcony and picked up the binoculars that Leonora always kept to hand. Despite it being dark outside she held them up to her eyes but she couldn't focus properly because the lenses were blurred and damp from her tears. She rubbed her eyes quickly with the back of her hand and sniffed. She really couldn't take it all in.

It had been one of the worst days of her life.

That morning, just three days after the visit to Melton for Maggie's birthday, Ruby had gone back up to the flat for an early tea break and been surprised to see that Leonora wasn't up and around. Even though she'd been feeling unwell and unable to manage the stairs, the pernickety woman had always made sure she was washed and properly dressed before settling in the chair in the sitting room or out on the balcony. Ruby had quickly checked the kitchen and bathroom and the balcony before going to her bedroom and knocking on the door.

'Aunt Leonora? Are you OK? Shall I bring you a cup of tea in bed?'

She had waited for several seconds before knocking again and rattling the door handle. 'Aunt Leonora?'

When there was still no response she opened the door and peered in.

As soon as she had seen Leonora Wheaton lying flat on her back in her bed with her eiderdown on the floor, one arm hanging over the edge of the bed and her eyes open and lifeless, she knew the woman was dead, but still she had frantically tried to wake her. She gently shook her body and then cautiously touched her icy-cold face.

'Wake up. Please wake up, please. You can't leave me, you can't . . .'

As the panic had built up inside Ruby felt herself losing control, so she ran out of the flat and called over the banister, 'Help! Someone, help! Aunt Leonora's unconscious. She won't wake up!'

Although she had known without any question that she was dead, Ruby simply couldn't bring herself to say the words out loud.

It was only later that day, after death had been confirmed and certified, Leonora's body removed and the formalities dealt with, that reality had forcefully hit Ruby.

Aunt Leonora, her mentor, companion and unlikely friend, whom she had lived with for over five years, was gone.

Deep in thought, and with the binoculars grasped

firmly in her hand, she walked around the flat, picking things up and putting them down, looking at the things that she'd always seen but never really taken notice of before. Leonora had always kept the flat uncluttered for convenience, but there was still the family photograph in which George was a young boy on his feet before the polio struck; the model of a sailing ship with cotton sails and tiny brass portholes; the shelf of travel books, a selection of postcards and a framed photo of Maggie.

As she looked at everything with different eyes Ruby realised exactly how much she had grown to love the outwardly cantankerous old woman and how much she was going to miss her.

Ruby had listened and watched, and she alone knew that behind the carefully constructed façade of church-going severity was a woman with unfulfilled dreams of a glamorous life far away on another continent, with a dashing gentleman on her arm. She'd seen the faraway expression on Leonora's face when she watched the liners through the heavy binoculars, which were always to hand. Ruby knew that when she was out on the small balcony of the ordinary seaside hotel she was no longer a prim and proper spinster but a beautiful young woman gazing out from the salt-stained balcony of a liner, headed off into the great unknown.

Ruby walked back out there again, sat on Leonora's chair and looked out to sea. Leonora's sea. She was still sitting there deep in grief when the door flew open.

'Ruby! Jesus Christ, I only just got your message and I came straight here. I can't believe it. I knew she was poorly, but dead? That's so awful,' Gracie cried as she ran full speed across the flat towards her friend. Ruby stood up and they hugged each other and cried.

'I know, I can't believe it either. I don't know what to do, I feel so useless, but the hotel still has to be run. We've got only three guests but still there are things to do. Gracie, I don't want to go downstairs . . .'

'Don't worry about that. I'll go down and check in a minute, and then I'll stay with you tonight. Have you spoken to George yet?'

'Yes, they're coming down here tomorrow. There's the funeral to arrange and also her business affairs. Uncle George has to deal with the solicitor and everything. I think she was very organised in all that, you know how she was . . .'

'I suppose she was worth a few quid – quite a lot of quid, probably. Will the hotel and everything go to them?'

'Yes, they're the only family she has apart from a couple of obscure cousins up north somewhere.' Ruby paused and looked down. 'Gracie, I know it's selfish even to say it right now, but what am I going to do if they want to sell the hotel? Where will I go? I can't go back to Walthamstow, and I can't go back to Melton with Maggie there. It'd be too much for me to have see her every single day.'

'Blimey, Rube, I hadn't even thought of that!' She

looked at Ruby in horror. 'No, George wouldn't do that to you. He knows this is your home and your job. Maybe he'll let you stay here and run the hotel for him.'

'You keep forgetting I'm not family. They owe me nothing. I owe them for everything they've done for me.' Ruby said as she stared at her friend.

'I don't think they see it like that,' Gracie said quickly. 'Well, I hope they don't. I mean, look what you've done for them. They've got Maggie – that's got to be worth much more than a bleeding hotel in Southend.'

'What's this about the hotel and Maggie?'

Ruby and Gracie jumped up in unison and turned round. Neither of them had heard Tony Alfredo enter the flat and walk across to the balcony where they had been sitting with their backs to him. Both of them immediately worried he might have heard the words and put two and two together.

'This is a private conversation, haven't you never heard of knocking? That's just so bloody rude.'

Ruby looked from one to the other, terrified that Tony might have some idea what Gracie meant. But instead of responding to Gracie he looked her up and down dismissively before going over to Ruby and kissing her on the cheek. He was still wearing his pinstripe suit, and with his highly polished shoes, gleaming white shirt and perfectly groomed hair he looked every inch the solicitor. Even amid the sadness Ruby couldn't help but think how handsome he was.

'I'm sorry to hear about your aunt. Dad told me. It was so sudden and I know you were fond of her. What happened?'

'It was a massive heart attack, they said. It was instant – she wouldn't have known anything about it – but I still feel guilty that I wasn't there,' Ruby answered quickly, to stop Gracie giving a smart answer.

'I must admit I was surprised you didn't bother to tell me yourself,' Tony said, with a hint of undertone. 'I'd have come straight back from work. It seemed odd I had to hear it from my father. I felt quite sidelined.'

Ruby shrugged slightly. 'Well, it only happened this morning and it's been hectic ever since. I'm sorry you're upset, though. I didn't think.'

'Is her legal situation all in order?' he asked, putting his arm around Ruby's waist.

'I've no idea. Uncle George is coming tomorrow to deal with everything.'

'I hope he's got your best interests at heart. This has got to be a profitable business and it's an expensive property.' He paused. 'So what's Maggie got to do with it?'

He smiled as he looked from Ruby to Gracie and then back again, watching both their faces as he did so. Ruby knew then that he'd registered Gracie's comment and was analysing it.

'What's Maggie got to do with what?' Ruby asked.

As always, Gracie was quick off the mark. 'We were

just talking about how much she's going to miss her Aunty Leonora who lived by the sea in a hotel. Every little girl's dream, that – free holidays!'

Tony didn't respond to Gracie; he didn't even look at her. It was as if she wasn't even in the room.

'Well, if you need help with the legal side I can help you, Ruby. You need to have your own representation.'

'Why would I need that?' Ruby frowned, genuinely bewildered.

'You may have a claim on the estate. You're entitled to something for all the hours you put in here. You've done all the work for so long.'

'Oh, give the old legal flimflam a rest,' Gracie snapped. 'Can't you see she's upset at losing Leonora? All that other stuff doesn't matter a bloody fig.'

'Shut up.' Tony retorted dismissively. 'It's nothing to do with you.'

'Well, it's got bugger all to do with you, that's for sure, you ignorant pig.'

'Stop it, the both of you,' Ruby said with a break in her voice. 'The lawyer is dealing with everything, along with Uncle George. It's nothing to do with me. If I have to move on then so be it. You both seem to think I'm entitled to something but I'm not.'

Ruby turned away and stepped back onto the balcony.

'I'm sorry.' Tony followed her out and kissed her on the cheek. 'I was just trying to help. I only came to see how you are but I realise I'm not appreciated so I'll come back tomorrow when you're not so emotional. My parents both send their condolences, by the way.'

'Tell them thank you.' She forced a smile.

He kissed her again and, ignoring Gracie completely, left the room as quietly as he'd come in.

'I wish you'd get on with him,' Ruby said. 'Especially now. It's going to be difficult enough as it is.'

'Sorry. He is such a snob and he looks down on me all the time. And he was sneaking around. I don't like him but I'll try to be nice in future.' But Ruby knew Gracie didn't really mean it.

Over the years Gracie had gradually changed both in appearance and attitude. She had filled out into a very shapely young woman with slim legs, curvy hips and a quick and endearing smile. Her mousy hair was brighter and blonder, and it wasn't greasy any more. She wore it shoulder length and gently waved, which softened her features and, along with carefully applied make-up, helped detract from the acne scarring on her face. She was vivacious and bright-eyed, and everyone who met her liked her.

Everyone except Tony Alfredo.

Although she still worked at the Palace Hotel on the busy seafront, she also spent a lot of time helping out and learning about the business at the quieter and smaller Thamesview Hotel in Thorpe Bay. Because they worked together and played together she and Ruby had become as close as sisters and had never once fallen out with each other, but it was this closeness that irritated Tony and he made no secret of it. He simply didn't understand why Ruby still enjoyed a lively night out at the Kursaal with Gracie when she could be alone with him.

Tony Alfredo still lived with his parents, although they no longer lived over the café. They had bought a small house close by in a road behind the seafront, where Tony was waited on hand, foot and finger by his doting parents, in whose eyes he could do nothing wrong.

Attractive and ambitious, he had an obvious charm and no hesitation in using it to get what he wanted. Old for his years in many ways, and often staid in his rigid Italian Catholic outlook, he wanted far more commitment from Ruby than she was prepared to give at that time, and made no secret of it. But although his charm and eligibility were undeniable, it was all wasted on Gracie, who simply declared him oily and devious.

'I've seen creeps like him before,' she'd say. 'Just because he speaks nice, wears a suit and works in London don't mean he's not just as much a fly-boy as the boys at the funfair.'

'But you like the boys at the funfair.'

'Not any more. I learned the error of my ways and dumped them; so should you.'

Ruby always laughed it off and emphasised that she actually enjoyed Tony's company, but whatever Ruby said, Gracie McCabe didn't trust him and made no secret of it.

Ruby

In return, Tony Alfredo made no secret of the fact that he despised her and her lifestyle.

It was a standoff.

Melton

Babs Wheaton held her hands out, palms up, and shook her head. 'I am at a loss here. How exactly are we going to handle this, George?'

'We'll deal with it as Leonora would have expected us to: fairly and properly,' her husband answered with a gentle smile. 'She trusted us to carry out her wishes and that's what we'll do. We understood her and knew her well enough to know what she wanted; what she meant.'

'Of course we will. I think I'm just surprised. I wish she had confided in us so that we could have been prepared, for Ruby's sake. It's going to be a very sudden transition. Ruby has only ever thought of herself as Leonora's assistant, and she's still so young.'

'I don't think it ever occurred to her that she would die any time soon – well, it didn't occur to any of us, did it? She thought she was under the weather. But even if we had known in advance we'd still be in the same situation now.'

George Wheaton was sitting at an impressive antique roll-top desk, which dominated the second reception room at the back of their house. It was an informal, comfortable room with large, well-worn furniture, and the one they used far more often than the formal sitting room at the front. As George shuffled papers across the desk from one pile to the other, his wife paced the floor.

Leonora's solicitor had briefly outlined everything to George on the phone, and he and Babs were trying to get all the facts straight for themselves before telling Ruby.

'You're right, of course, darling. If she'd known how ill she was she'd have gone to the doctor, I'm sure, or even let you examine her when she was here. What exactly did she say when you spoke to her at Maggie's party?'

'I told you, nothing much at all. She refused to confide in me about her health, just said she had a cough and cold. I did tell her to go and see her doctor but she always was contrary. When she was a child, Mother used to call her Contrary Mary.' George Wheaton looked down at his desk and ran his fingers across his forehead; the shock had hit him hard.

'I was always the sickly one and I always thought I would go first. Everyone did, even when I was a child.'

'I know you're going to miss her, darling – so will I – and poor Ruby will be bereft,' Babs smiled sadly. 'That was such an unlikely relationship. I never thought when we sent her there that they'd actually become so close.' She laughed lightly. 'I imagined Leonora packing Ruby back to us as soon as she possibly could, but in the event she wanted her to stay and treated her as much like a daughter as we do. Strange.'

She pulled a chair from beside the fireplace and sat

beside her husband, placing her hand gently on his leg.

'But all this will business – I don't know if this is good or bad for Ruby. I'm worried her family will crawl out of the woodwork again. Can you imagine what would happen if her family got wind of this? And then there's that Johnnie fellow. I didn't trust any of them to start with, but now this has happened. Considering everything, Ruby's done so well at the hotel and in her life. I don't want this to be a burden to her.'

'Well, we don't have a choice. We have to go back to Southend again and talk to her face to face. It has to come from us and it has to come before the funeral or the formal reading of the will.'

'I'm worried, George. Ruby has been so happy lately, and then there's Maggie. I'm scared this may change the way it's all working . . .' Babs' voice trailed away.

'Maggie is our daughter, legally signed and sealed. Let's not look for things to fret over.' George wheeled himself backwards away from the desk and then turned the wheel-chair so he was facing his wife. 'Leonora meant well and we have to abide by her wishes and accept that it will be for the best for Ruby.'

Babs stood up. 'Maybe we should take this as a reminder to us to get our own affairs in order in case anything unexpectedly happens to either of us.'

George smiled at his wife, his affection for her written all over his face. 'We're already all in order, my darling. Now if you could telephone Ruby and tell her we're going down to Southend again tomorrow, I'll go through to the surgery and throw myself at the mercy of the locum again!'

As they had talked and tried to decide the best way to go about making sure Leonoras Wheaton's will was executed according to her wishes, neither of them had realised that their driver, Derek Yardley, was standing near the open window, tucked away out of sight beside the blooms of the gnarled wisteria growing up the outside of the house.

He'd originally stepped out for a cigarette but the sound of voices had pulled him across the garden and he was doing what he did best. Snooping.

He couldn't hear every word but he heard enough to draw a conclusion that made his head spin. Ruby Blakeley, the random evacuee who had inveigled her way into the family, was in for a windfall from the lately dead aunt and they were worried about her family and Johnnie Riordan finding out. That told him the inheritance had to be big.

When he eventually slipped away from the window he was seething, but at the same time a plan was forming in his head to pay back the Blakeley bitch.

Later that day, when he knew that George was safely ensconced in his surgery and Babs was down at the church hall with Maggie, he'd slipped in the unlocked back door and headed straight for the desk in the hall near to the telephone where Babs Wheaton kept her assorted note-pads and address books.

He flicked through until he found what he was looking for, scribbled the information on a scrap piece of paper and sneaked out again with his prize clutched in his hand. He couldn't believe he hadn't done it before.

EIGHTEEN

The next day, after a long sleepless night, Ruby stood at the window in the office, watching the road outside and waiting for the Wheatons' car to pull up. Gracie had taken over the day-to-day business of the hotel and was busy dealing with it all while Ruby nervously waited for them. She felt like a child again, desperately needing them to support her and reassure her that everything would be all right, to promise that they would look after her, whatever happened.

For the third time in her life Ruby felt lost, with nowhere to go. She wouldn't ever go back to Walthamstow, and Melton was out of the question, with Maggie there. The only option she could see for herself was to find a live-in job at another hotel; to be a small fish in a big pond after several years as Leonora Wheaton's assistant.

She went from the window to the desk, which was dominated by an imposing typewriter, shuffled a few papers and then went back to the window. The wait was nerve-racking and, to add to her distress, when the car did pull up, she saw Yardley was driving. She didn't want him to see her upset and she certainly didn't want him inside the hotel, but she knew George and Babs would expect him to be invited into the kitchen for a drink and a snack after the long drive. It had been a secret that she was living here, but suddenly it didn't really matter any more, especially if she was going to have to move out.

She quickly wiped her eyes once again, powdered her nose and went outside to greet them. She managed a watery smile as she welcomed them and, without actually looking at him, she made the offer to Yardley, which, to her relief, he declined, pleading the need to stretch his legs.

George told him to be back in an hour to take him to meet the solicitor and deal with the formalities of the impending funeral. He turned and walked off in the direction of Southend itself as the Wheatons and Ruby went inside. Ruby found it strange to be sitting with them in Leonora's hotel without her being there; she had to force herself not to think about her lying all alone in the chapel of rest less than a mile away.

'I wasn't expecting you back until the funeral. I'm worried now!' she laughed nervously. 'Is it bad news?'

'Not at all, dear,' Babs said. 'George has a meeting with the solicitor that you have to go to as well, but first there is something you should know . . . something we have to talk to you about.'

Ruby's heart started to thump. 'I knew it. The hotel's got to be sold and I have to move out. It's OK, I was expecting it,' she said quickly.

Her hands shook as she pulled a cigarette out of the packet she'd been holding and flicked away at the silver table lighter several times before there was a flame. She inhaled deeply and leaned back before blowing the smoke slowly up into the air.

'This is all so horrible. I'm still so upset about Aunt Leonora, I can't think straight. Thank God there are hardly any guests to look after at the moment. Do you think we should close for a couple of weeks? It's too sad.'

'I know,' Babs said, 'we're all upset, especially as it was so unexpected. She was one of those ageless people who always seemed as if she would go on for ever. But one consolation is that she knew nothing about it, although I do wish it hadn't been you who found her.'

Tears welled up in Ruby's eyes. 'It was horrible. She was just lying there. I knew as soon as I saw her even though I've never seen anyone dead before.'

'I know,' George said sympathetically. 'But, Ruby, we have to talk before I go to the solicitor—'

'Can I stay in the flat until I find somewhere else?' she interrupted sharply. 'Maybe the new owners will give me a job. I know what I'm doing now.'

'If you'd just listen for a moment we might get somewhere. I've spoken with the solicitor, her solicitor, and Leonora has mentioned you in her will . . .'

But Ruby wasn't listening at all. She just didn't want to hear what they had to say so she chattered on, putting off the evil moment of truth that she was sure was coming.

'I've already asked Gracie to put her ear to the ground; she knows so many people in so many hotels and boarding houses all over town. I might even get a decent job at the Palace now I've got the experience.'

'Stop it, Ruby! Just stop interrupting and listen to what we have to say.' Babs looked at her husband. 'George? Can you please tell Ruby about Leonora's will? You understand it all better than I do.'

'Ruby, listen to me and don't say a word. Leonora made a new will recently. I don't think she thought she was going to die so soon. I think she was thinking about you in the future. And Maggie . . .' He looked at her. 'Ruby, Leonora's will states that—'

'The hotel's going to be sold,' she interrupted again, trying her best to pretend she didn't mind. But she did. She minded so much it hurt.

'Calm down and listen, Ruby. You're acting like a child.' George was getting impatient with her. 'Babs just said Leonora has left you something – well, she's left the hotel to you. *To you.* It's all very complicated but the general gist is that the hotel is yours so you'll be staying here and running it. If that's what you want to do, of course.'

'But that can't be right. I'm just a kid. I'm not even a relation . . .' Ruby's eyes were everywhere, her hands were shaking and she was palpitating. It was all too much for her to take in. She pulled another cigarette out but this time George picked up the lighter. He flicked it once and the flame glowed. As Ruby leaned forward with the cigarette in her mouth for him to light he took the opportunity to continue what he was saying.

'No buts. You have the hotel, Maggie has a trust fund for when she's twenty-one, and Babs and I have been left some investments and insurances. I hadn't realised how shrewd my sister was in business. Cleverer than me, that's certain!' George laughed. 'There are stipulations, of course. You can't sell it for five years, and Babs and I as executors have been asked to oversee everything for those five years to give you a little support.'

'Are you sure you've read it right? It should be yours. You're family, and it was the family house that bought this place, she told me.'

'Yes, but it was hers to do with as she wanted,' George said quietly. 'And you *are* family and you've worked hard here. We're proud of you. You deserve this opportunity, and what would we do with a hotel in Essex? Our lives and the surgery are in Melton, we're very comfortable, and we're all used to village life, including Maggie.'

'You could sell it. That's what I was sure was going to happen. I can't believe it. The hotel is mine? Really?' Ruby was excited at the thought of owning the hotel, but her excitement was tempered by the sorrow of how it had come about.

'Yes, really. There is a reserve to go with it for

242

emergencies, but other than that you're going to have to work like a Trojan to run it, and you're going to need someone alongside you, as you were for Leonora. We also need to talk about the implications.'

'What implications?' Ruby asked curiously. Her head was in overdrive but she tried to concentrate.

'First, there's the commitment of you having to manage Thamesview completely, no easy task for anyone, let alone someone as young as you. Then there's fortune-hunters. You're an attractive, single young woman who is now of independent means; a businesswoman, an owner of property. You're going to have to be very aware because there will doubtless be men who will want to court you for the wrong reasons.'

'Never! It's a hotel, not the crown jewels,' she laughed in embarrassment.

'Oh, it's very likely!' Babs said firmly. 'So it may be best if you're discreet about your inheritance. And talking about young men, are you still seeing the chap that you told us about? Tony?'

'Sort of. But he's not a fortune-hunter, he's a solicitor, and I've known him for years, ever since I came here.'

'Where does he live?'

'At the family home, just a road back from here. His parents own the café in the parade of shops up the road. They used to live over the shop but they've moved to somewhere bigger; they are such nice honest people, though they have spoiled their son.'

'He doesn't know anything about Maggie, does he?'

'No, of course not. I'm not stupid. No one knows except us and Gracie, and I'd trust her with my life,' she replied sharply, annoyed that they would even think she'd betray them and Maggie.

'I'm sorry – we're all being oversensitive at the minute – but you're going to have to be more aware than ever before. Even with people you know.' Babs said.

'Tony's all right. Once he's more experienced he'll earn a fortune. He's ambitious.' She stopped for a moment. Then: 'Can I tell Gracie?'

'Not straight away, nor Tony.' George said. 'Best not to tell anyone until it's all formalised. Now we have to leave for the solicitor.' He looked at his wife. 'Can you see if Yardley is with the car?'

As she stood up Babs Wheaton smiled at Ruby. 'This is going to be a challenge for you, but I know you're capable and we'll be there to help.'

While George, Babs and Ruby had been up in the flat talking through the details of Leonora's will, Derek Yardley had walked along the seafront, taking in the air and looking for a postbox. When he got back to the hotel he crossed the road, sat on a nearby bench and, almost in a trance, watched the world go by.

He watched the mix of people walking along the promenade, some with dogs on leads, others with babies in prams, elderly couples arm in arm just taking the sea air.

Despite a chill in the air there were children and adults alike paddling in the sea, absolutely caught up in the moment and savouring the freedom from everyday life. It was so peaceful, and he leaned back on the bench and imagined himself living there in the comfort of a seafront property with perfect views and the bustling social life of the town just up the road.

A picture-postcard place to live.

And now Miss Ruby Blakeley, the snivelling little evacuee kid, was not only going to live there on Wheaton money, his permanently listening ears told him that she was going to own the whole hotel.

He wondered how long she had been living there and he also wondered why. Something just wasn't right about the whole situation, but he couldn't figure out exactly what it was. He sat there and seethed with resentment and anger. The anger was, however, tempered a little by the knowledge that Ruby Blakeley had a couple of shocks in store.

Deep in thought and warmed by the sun, he was annoyed when he saw Babs Wheaton appear on the steps and look across at him. As she waved so he stood up, carefully straightened his uniform, fixed a neutral expression on his face and walked back over the road to the hotel where the car was parked.

Once again he manipulated George Wheaton's wheel-chair into the boot of the car and then followed the directions that took them to the line of shops and offices on Thorpe Bay Broadway. During the short drive he made a point of catching Ruby's eye in the rear-view mirror as often as he could. His expression was neutral but he made sure she knew he was watching her and he enjoyed the power he could see he had over her.

On the way back he again looked at Ruby and could almost feel her discomfort, her desire to get away from him. That annoyed him, so as she climbed out of the car back at the hotel he caught her eye once again, gave a sly smile and winked. She pretended not to notice but the tiny action was somehow so sinister it took her breath away.

'Well, we have to go shortly, darling. It's a long drive, as you know,' Babs Wheaton smiled as they all went back inside. 'But I'm pleased Gracie is staying with you. She's a lovely girl and you're lucky to have her as a friend. And vice versa, of course.'

'I know. I love her dearly. I don't know how I'd get on without her, especially without Aunt Leonora.' Again the tears filled Ruby's eyes. 'I never really thanked her for all she did for me . . .'

'She knew how you felt, and she felt the same about you. The best way to thank her is to take care of her hotel from now on in, to look after her gift to you. Now a quick cuppa and then we'll be off and we'll see you on funeral day. George will make all the arrangements but if you have any suggestions then ring us.'

Ruby

As they left, Ruby avoided any more contact with Yardley. She was aware of him trying to catch her eye but she was determined not to let it happen again. She wasn't going to let him overshadow her mourning of Leonora Wheaton.

NINETEEN

When Ruby opened the curtains on the morning of Leonora's funeral she was relieved to see a perfect sunny day dawning. There wasn't a cloud in the bright blue sky, the waters of the Thames Estuary were mill-pond calm, and Leonora's favourite view was as clear as it could be.

Purely by chance the high tide peaked as the funeral cortège pulled away from the hotel. Ruby looked out of the car window as the hearse moved slowly along the seafront and smiled sadly, pleased that it was so perfect as Leonora Wheaton left her beloved hotel for the very last time.

It had been a strange few days as Ruby tried to come to terms with both Leonora's death and her will. Such extremes of good and bad.

George and Babs had had to go back to Melton because of both the surgery and Maggie, but Gracie had been staying at the flat with Ruby. They had both been rushed off their feet, which stopped Ruby thinking too much, and it had also made it easier for her to sidetrack all conversation about the future of the hotel. She had nearly given in a few times, but in the end she told no-one, as George and Babs had asked. But she was waiting impatiently for the moment after the funeral and the formal reading of the will when she could. She hated having secrets from Gracie.

The moving service in the local church and the burial in the pretty churchyard outside passed in a blur, but the saddest moment for Ruby was travelling back to the hotel without Leonora. It didn't seem right.

Gracie McCabe had stayed behind and laid out the funeral tea in the dining room at the back of the hotel and, dressed from head to toe in respectful black, was standing waiting at the door as the mourners arrived back, pointing everyone in the right direction. There had been a good turnout at the church and everyone who attended had been invited back to the reception.

As Ruby went in, Gracie took her hand. 'How are you?' she whispered.

'I don't know really. I need to talk to you after all this. The solicitor will be here soon and then I can tell you everything . . .'

'So you know what's going to happen then?'

'Yes, but I can't say anything until after the formal stuff. I'll tell you later, I promise!'

Gracie was doing a good job of co-ordinating the food and also managing the reception desk, while Ruby and the Wheatons circulated amid the sea of black clothes and sad faces. Many were members of the church where Leonora had been a regular on Sundays, along with any of the hotel guests who had wanted to attend the service.

It was over an hour later, and most of the mourners were still there when Gracie came into the room and whispered to Ruby, 'There's a bloke in the lobby asking for you, Ruby. He says he's—'

'That'll be the solicitor,' Ruby interrupted. 'He's here for the formal reading of the will.'

'No it isn't. I think it's your brother Ray out there. Well, he said he is! What do you want me to do with him?'

Ruby nearly passed out on the spot.

'Oh dear God! Ray? How do you know it's Ray? What did he say?'

'Just that his name's Ray and that he's your brother. He's insisting on seeing you. I told him there was a funeral reception going on but he just laughed.'

Tony had been watching the interchange and, sensing something was up, came straight across the room to stand beside Ruby. Although he hadn't been at the funeral he had walked along to the reception to pay his respects.

'Problem?' he asked as he placed a hand in the centre of Ruby's back protectively.

'Nothing we can't handle,' Gracie smiled.

'My brother has turned up out of the blue. He's in the lobby waiting for me,' Ruby said.

'I didn't know you were in contact with your family. Do you want me to turf him out?' Tony asked.

'I don't know what to do. How did he find me?'

'You tell me . . .' he asked, looking at her suspiciously.

But as he spoke, so the familiar figure of Ray appeared in the doorway with his hands in his pockets and a huge grin on his face. He was slightly more rounded and his face was puffy and pasty, but there was no denying it was him.

'Hello, Rube. What's holding you up? Ain't you pleased to see your big brother?'

As Ruby looked at him her heart started to beat faster. Ray Blakeley, her brother. So much flashed through her mind in a few seconds that she couldn't keep track. She guessed that was what it must be like to have your life flash past your eyes.

His voice was loud enough to stop all conversation in the dining room, but as everyone turned in the direction of the loud voice George wheeled himself over with Babs by his side and a confident smile on his face.

'Well, I never.' Ray laughed out loud. 'Uncle George and Aunty Babs, the child stealers! I knew you were behind our Rube disappearing, you lying bastards.' He shook his head and laughed. 'Still, I love a family party. Is there a drink for me? I mean, I'm family, aren't I?'

'This is a private reception. We've just come from my sister's funeral so, I'm sorry, but I have to tell you you're not welcome.'

'OK, I'll wait out there in that fancy great armchair and cause a bit of a rumpus. I can always talk to some of the posh bints I've seen hanging around looking a bit lost.'

'You have no right to be here, Ray. Now please show some respect. I've told you, this is my sister's funeral.' George said quietly.

'And I just want to speak to *my* sister,' Ray said.

'It's OK,' Ruby said quickly, aware of the potential for trouble, 'I'll talk to him. I don't want a scene in front of everyone.'

'I'll come with you,' Tony said with a wide fake smile and a very slight flexing of his shoulders that he knew Ray Blakeley would understand. 'Just to support you.'

'No, Tony, I don't need any help. I can deal with Ray – he's my brother.'

Ruby was in shock but she had no intention of letting anyone know how she was feeling, especially Ray. She couldn't believe that he had found her, let alone turned up on the day of the funeral, and just before the formal reading of the will. She had to get rid of him before Leonora's solicitor arrived with all the documents. She could only imagine what would happen if her family found out about her inheritance.

'Come on then, come through to the office,' she said to Ray. Then she leaned over George's wheelchair as if to push him. Hardly moving her mouth she whispered, 'When the solicitor comes take him straight through to the lounge and shut the door. I won't be long.'

High heels clacking sharply on the tiled floor, she marched straight across the small lobby to the office, with Ray right behind her, but despite his inimitable swagger he looked unsettled out of his own environment and in his sister's. The last time they'd been together she had been young, scared, secretly pregnant and about to run away. As she looked at him she realised that for the first time ever she had the upper hand over her brother. She was on home ground whereas he was on unfamiliar territory and among total strangers.

'Take a seat.' She pointed to a bucket chair near the door and, needing the security of a barrier between them, walked round and sat behind the desk.

'Very important, Rube. I'm impressed,' Ray smiled.

'What do you want, Ray? I'm not really sure why you're here.'

'Because you're my sister. Because you ran off without a word and left Ma and Nan worried sick, not to mention Robbie and Art. Ma thought you'd probably been done in up north; me and the boys thought you were probably on the game somewhere.' He laughed but she didn't react. Ruby knew he was only baiting her.

'Not a thought for any of us, had you? And as for Mr and Mrs High and Mighty declaring with a straight face they didn't have a clue . . .'

Ruby smiled. 'They were helping me, being kind to me. They really cared about me, which is more than can be said for my real family. What a sorry tale you're telling, but none of you had any thought for me when you were treating me worse than a stray alley cat. Still, that's in the past. Done. Forgotten. So why are you really here? I don't understand. How did you know where I was?'

Ray Blakeley crossed his legs, folded his arms and smiled.

'A little bird told me!' he said. 'Now I'm asking how you came to be here. I thought you ran off to be Florence Nightingale and tend to the sick. Now, as far as I can see, you're a waitress to Lord and Lady Muck out there.'

Ruby ignored his dig, happy to realise that he no longer had any power or control over her. 'Are any of the family with you? Is everyone OK?' Ruby asked.

'Bit late to be asking that, Rube, after all this time not bothering.' He frowned. 'But you're not telling me what all the bloody Wheatons are doing here. What are you doing here? They told Ma they didn't know where you were and now it's all happy families beside the seaside.'

'It's their hotel and I work here.' Ruby lied easily. 'But now I have to get back to the funeral, so if you're done . . .'

'Any messages for anyone?' he grinned.

'No. I'm sure you'll tell them everything.' She stopped. 'Just remember me to them. I missed Ma and Nan. Is Nan still OK?'

'Same as she was, but older and deafer.'

As she stood up so did Ray, but the angry attitude she knew so well just wasn't there in the same way now; he was all bluster. She walked beside him to the doors and then out onto the steps.

'I'll be back, you know. You don't escape us that easily.'

His words were thrown angrily at her, but as he turned away she noticed something in his expression, something she'd never seen before. Ray Blakeley looked vulnerable. She looked at him closely and noticed that his clothes were very well worn, and there was a sad, dishevelled air about him. He looked like a chubby neglected version of the Ray she remembered so well.

Something had happened to change him.

She suddenly remembered him sitting on the side of his bed, beaten to a pulp and scared witless by Johnnie Riordan.

Something was wrong with her brother. He'd given in far too easily. As she watched him make his way down the steps she noticed for the first time that he had a limp.

'Ray, wait!' she called. He turned on the pavement outside. 'How did you get here?'

'On the train.'

'Just to come and see me? I'm flattered,' she smiled.

'Don't kid yourself. I came with someone else. I'm meeting 'em back in the pub up the road.'

'I have to finish with the funeral, but come back later if you want.' She looked at her watch. 'At five o'clock, for some tea before you go home.'

His eyes narrowed with suspicion. 'Why?'

'I don't know. Maybe because a funeral focuses the mind, maybe because you're family – I don't know – maybe because I'd like you to. But it's up to you.'

Overwhelmed with guilt she walked back into the hotel, feeling so very unhappy. It was all too much for one day.

'You have to go through,' George said as she went back in. 'Babs has taken Mr Wallington to the lounge but time's getting on and we have to get back. I'm sorry Ray turned up today of all days. How did he find you?'

'He said someone told him, but I can't imagine who.' She walked back to the door and looked out. There was no sign of him.

'I know it's distressing having Ray appear out of the blue like that, but we'll talk about it properly later: first we must do the legalities.'

'What legalities are those?' Tony asked. Ruby had forgotten he was there.

'I'll tell you later.'

'Do you need me there for you?'

'No, I bloody don't!' she snapped. 'I'm perfectly capable. Now just let me do what I have to do . . . please.'

Tony stared at her for a few seconds, his frown so fierce his eyebrows were nearly touching, and for a split second Ruby felt nervous, but then he just turned on his heel and walked out of the hotel.

'Now you've done it,' Gracie said.

'Oh, I don't care right now. But don't you go, will you? I have to talk to you as soon as I come down from this meeting. Can you keep an eye out for Ray? I don't want him to know what's going on.' She pulled a face. 'I told him to come back in two hours for his tea . . .'

'Well, he is family, I suppose,' Gracie said. 'I can understand it, but I don't think Tony-me-laddo will if he gets wind of it!'

Leaning against the wall outside, Derek Yardley was trying hard not to react. With his arms folded across his chest and with one foot crossed over the other he watched as best he could as the events unfolded. He'd never expected to be lucky enough to be a spectator when it all hit the fan, and it amused him especially that Ray Blakeley had unwittingly timed his entrance to perfection.

He couldn't hear everything that was being said so he moved a little closer and tried to read the various faces as everyone stood in the lobby.

When he'd driven George and Babs down to Southend earlier in the week Derek Yardley had been his usual invisible self in the driver's seat as they talked discreetly about the situation, but it didn't matter. For once he had felt strong and powerful and that was because he knew what he had in his jacket.

He'd kept his old feelings of inadequacy and rejection under control for so long, but the confrontation with Ruby and then the news of her inheritance had brought it all back. Once again he was the sickly worthless child no one cared for or noticed.

He'd parked the car and gone for a walk around the block until he'd found a pillar box. He pulled two already written plain postcards out of his pocket and kissed them happily before posting them in the box with a flourish. That would teach her.

'You'll find RUBY BLAKELEY at: The Thamesview Hotel, Eastern Esplanade, Thorpe Bay, Essex.'

One postcard was addressed to Ray Blakeley and the other to Johnnie Riordan.

Ray walked out of the hotel and Yardley had just moved to follow him when Babs Wheaton called to him, 'Don't go anywhere, Yardley. We've got to leave very shortly. Come through to the kitchen, there's a plate for you.'

Yardley cursed under his breath but turned back obediently. Firstly, he really wanted to talk to Ray Blakeley, and secondly, he hated being sent to the kitchen while Madam Ruby flounced round importantly having meetings with solicitors.

A plate for you. How he hated those words. They summed up everything that he hated about his treatment.

He loved both George and Babs Wheaton, who had done so much for him during his many years with them. He loved them so much he would gladly kill for them, but he hated everyone else in their lives.

Especially Ruby and the child Maggie. The usurpers.

TWENTY

Wanstead

Johnnie Riordan frowned as he reread the words on the postcard and then turned it over several times, scrutinising it carefully. He was looking for a clue but he didn't recognise the handwriting and the Southend postmark meant nothing to him. But there was no denying it was meant for him.

He was bemused, but also grateful to his sister for handing it to him when they were alone. However, he also didn't want to react to it in front of her.

'What do you make of it, Johnnie?' Betty asked as he stood, deep in thought, with the postcard in his hand. 'Do you think Ruby sent it to you?'

'No, that's not what she'd do. If she wanted to contact me after all this time she would have gone to the house.'

'But you don't live there any more.'

Johnnie laughed. 'You know that and I know that, but

Ruby doesn't. No, I know trouble, and this just reeks of someone trying to stir something up. Ray Blakeley maybe? He'd love to drop me in it now I'm his boss,' he laughed. 'God, how he hates that.'

'But in that case he'd be dropping himself in it as well. Is he that dim?'

'Well, maybe it's someone trying to drop Ruby in it, then. Oh, I don't know and I don't care. Ruby was someone I felt sorry for. She was different, and I liked that, but she must have wanted to disappear off the face of the earth and she did.' He looked at it again and smiled. 'At least we know she's alive. I had wondered if Ray had done her in.'

'Have you ever asked Ray about her? I mean, you don't know why she disappeared. Maybe he does.'

Johnnie laughed. He was just about to tell her about talking to Ruby's grandmother but decided against it. 'No, I wouldn't ask him and raise his suspicions. No, Ruby's of no interest to me any more and I don't know why anyone would think she would be. I'm certainly not going to do anything about it.'

'Pleased to hear it!' Betty said. 'But I had to give it to you because it's addressed to you. Best to just tear it into tiny pieces and forget it ever came. You know what Sadie can be like.'

'Yeah, I know all right. She'd have my guts for garters and a belt before I even finished explaining the whys and wherefores. She'd never believe it was nothing to do with me.'

'It's because she loves you. She just goes about it all wrong.'

'I know, but she doesn't trust me and that's damned frustrating.'

'Well, that's Sadie! Where is she now? Did you tell her I was coming over?'

'Taken the kids to the park. You know how she is about you. And Ma. She thinks I love you both more than I love her.'

He shrugged and smiled, as did his sister. Neither said anything but they both knew that actually Sadie was right. He didn't love his wife as much as he should. In fact, he didn't love Sadie at all. It was a marriage of convenience on his side. But he didn't feel guilty about it. He treated her properly and provided well for her and their two small sons so she had no legitimate cause to complain.

Betty had caught the bus from Walthamstow to Wanstead to visit her beloved brother at his house just one street away from where Bill Morgan, his employer, who was now also his landlord, lived. Betty had tried to warn him against putting all his eggs in one basket but Johnnie Riordan's ambitions and the promise of a promotion at work and a nice house for him and Sadie to start married life in had cancelled out any concerns.

After his last attempt to find Ruby had ended in failure he'd simply put her to the back of his mind. He'd had feelings for her that he'd never had for anyone before or since, but he was sensible enough to bury them and put all his energy into his ambitions to better himself. And he had done that very successfully, though he had had to sacrifice most of his independence and cosy up with Bill Morgan, the owner of the Black Dog and the man who had bought all the businesses in Blacksmiths Lane from his rival David Collins.

Bill Morgan had put Johnnie in charge of overseeing them all, along with collecting the rents on some of his other investments, effectively making him Ray and Bobbie Blakeley's boss.

Johnnie had enjoyed the irony but at the same time had tried to be fair to them, and as soon as he'd dropped the bombshell that he was going to be in charge he'd increased their wages a little. But he'd also closed off their black-market skulduggery, which he'd had the advantage of knowing all about, and the Blakeley Brothers were caught between the devil and the deep blue sea. If they wanted to keep their jobs they had to be legal.

Pleased not to have to work behind the bar at the Black Dog any longer, Johnnie Riordan threw himself into his new job with gusto. He loved it but the downside was that, as a condition of employment and a higher-than-average wage, he had to accept Bill's rule of iron. Not only did he have to work extra-long hours, he also had to bow to Bill Morgan's matchmaking skills and, against his better judgement and his sister's advice, marry Sadie Scully, whom Bill adored in a paternal way.

Nine months later she'd given birth to his first son,

Martin, and less than a year after to his second, Paul. Johnnie adored his little sons, but he knew they'd come along so quickly because Sadie wanted to ensure he was totally tied to her.

'So, do I get a cuppa from my little brother then? Or do you want me gone before Sadie gets back and throws another pink fit?' Betty ruffled her brother's hair affectionately.

'Get off,' he laughed. 'I'll put the kettle on. And I want you to stay and see the boys, whatever Sadie says. Silly cow that she is . . .'

'I don't want to cause a fight but I would like to see my nephews. We all want to see them so you must bring them over. How about tea on Sunday? Ma's coming to stay for a few days so she'll be there to see them as well.'

'That sounds nice. Tea on Sunday. I'll tell Sadie. We both know she'll say no but she can like it or lump it.'

Betty laughed lightly and looked at her brother for a few seconds before speaking.

'Johnnie, I know things are different now, and I really hate to ask, but is there any chance of some work for Roger? He's driving me mad, under my feet all day doing nothing. Money is really tight.'

'I'll see what I can do. How do you think he'd feel about helping in the pub as a potman? I know he gets touchy but it'd bring in a bit.' He took his sister's hand. 'You know I'll always help out, always. You just have to ask . . .'

'No, Johnnie. If you can find something for Roger that's wonderful, but I don't want handouts, really.'

At that moment they heard the front door open. Johnnie went out to the hall to help Sadie with the double Silver Cross pram, a present from Bill Morgan when the second baby was born. It was Sadie's pride and joy.

'Shouldn't you be working?' she said angrily as she pushed the pram down the hallway without looking at him.

'Not yet. Betty's here. I told you she was coming over this morning.'

He gave her a warning look but it made no difference. It worried him that Sadie was always so angry but he just didn't have time to pander to her jealousies. Every day it was something different. He'd been accused of having affairs with every woman he came into contact with, even the old woman who helped out cleaning the pub.

'Well, my boys are sound asleep and I'm not going to let her wake them, the interfering old cow.'

With that she pushed the pram into the room and sharply pulled the door shut.

'*Our* boys, thank you very much, but that's OK, we're all going over there for tea on Sunday so she can see them then. And their cousins want to see them as well. Ma's going to be there,' Johnnie smiled, keeping his voice calm. He didn't want Sadie having a go at his sister, but at the same time he wasn't going to let Sadie undermine him.

'No we're not.'

'We are. Now get in there and be civil to Betty.'

His tone meant Sadie did exactly as she was told, albeit with bad grace.

Two years older than Johnnie Riordan, Sadie was big in size and personality with masses of platinum-blonde hair. She was only five foot three, but she always wore high heels, pinned her thick hair up high with combs, and wore full make-up every single day. It was all of this, combined with her favourite fitted outfits, that had made her the perfect barmaid and Bill Morgan's favourite. In his eyes she could do no wrong, a situation of which she took full advantage and of which Johnnie was wary. But Bill Morgan had never really seen the demanding, selfish side of Sadie, the same side that was jealous and volatile. Johnnie had never seen that side either until after they'd tied the knot and he had no way of backing out.

She always controlled herself in public; she was the epitome of the jolly bubbly blonde barmaid and was like an affectionate puppy in front of Bill, but one wrong word at the wrong moment from Johnnie in private and she could fly like a banshee, attacking him verbally and physically.

'I'm going to give Betty a lift home and then I've got to go straight to see Bill at the pub. I'll be late tonight so put my dinner in the oven and kiss the boys good night from me.'

Sadie ignored Betty completely and glared at her husband, her face enveloped in a sulk.

'Late again? Surprise, surprise. Anything rather than come home to your family. Who is it going to be tonight?'

'Don't be stupid. You know what Bill's like: business has to be done in the Dog. He thinks that's his office and it's open until closing time.' He kissed her on the cheek. 'See you later, I'll try not to wake you.'

He ushered Betty out of the door before Sadie could respond, but they both heard the bang as something she'd thrown down the hallway hit the front door.

'I don't envy you going home tonight!' Betty grinned as they got into the car that was also owned by Bill Morgan.

After he dropped his sister off at her home Johnnie started to head back to Blacksmiths Lane to check on the units, but on the spur of the moment he decided to take a detour. He turned and drove into Walthamstow High Street, parked the car and walked straight to the park where he and Ruby had gone after they had got back from Melton.

The park where he'd made love to Ruby Blakeley the one and only time.

He walked over to an empty bench and sat down plumb in the middle to try to avoid anyone coming to sit next to him. Leaning back he closed his eyes.

He counted back and guessed it would have been about six years before . . . six years, and such a lot had happened since then, but sitting there it seemed as if it was only the day before.

He knew the minute they'd both stood up and straightened their clothes that he'd done the wrong thing. He hadn't planned or expected it, but at the time he'd been carried away by both Ruby and the circumstances. He could see he'd taken advantage of her but it hadn't seemed like that at the time.

The visit to Melton had opened Johnnie's eyes to life away from the London he'd lived in all his life and it had also shown him Ruby in different surroundings. It had all been so exciting that, for the first time in his ruthless young life, he'd let his heart rule his head. She was a sixteen-year-old virgin and he was three years older, and already well experienced, courtesy of Sadie Scully. It was wrong and he knew his sister would have been horrified if she'd ever found out.

The train journey home that had seemed so romantic, the smell of her shiny clean hair when she leaned on his shoulder, walking in through the park gates holding hands, the first kiss, the anticipation . . . he could remember it all so clearly. But then not long afterwards, just as he'd started to think they could have a future together, just as she'd started to intrude into his thoughts all the time, she'd disappeared. But at the same time so had his guilt, because he had no constant reminder of his foolhardy behaviour.

Ruby Blakeley had become a pleasant memory.

He pulled the postcard out of his pocket and studied it. He had no intention of following up on this information

– he had a wife and two children and a good job with Bill Morgan – but he still couldn't help wondering again about her. What she looked like, what she was doing, and what had gone wrong. He wondered why she was apparently living in a hotel when she'd gone off to be a nurse, whether she was married, if she had any children. He smiled nostalgically as he remembered the young girl who had fascinated him from the first moment he'd seen her sitting on her suitcase at the bottom of the street, and then disappeared just as he was falling in love with her.

Suddenly fearful of the feelings that one simple card had reawakened in him, he tore it into several pieces and almost ceremoniously dropped it in a nearby rubbish bin. Then he went back to his car and drove away.

Johnnie Riordan was living a good life, and as long as he stayed on the right side of Bill Morgan and did his bidding without question it could only get better.

Now all he had to do was forget what he'd read and stay away from Ruby Blakeley.

TWENTY-ONE

'You own the bleeding hotel? She's left it all to you? Oh, dear God in Heaven, what a shock! Not that you don't deserve it, but blimey, that's some inheritance. I thought you were going to say she'd given you the car or her fur coat or something, but the whole fucking hotel?'

Gracie was happily incredulous as Ruby finally shared the news with her. The solicitor had headed off back to his office and the Wheatons had left for Melton, so Ruby and Gracie were alone for the first time. It had been prearranged that there would be no dinner provision that evening and the few guests that were there had either gone out or to their rooms after the funeral tea, giving the two women time to sit down and discuss the turn of events.

'I couldn't tell you until after the formal reading of the will. I wanted to but . . . anyway, I've also got a reserve fund in case it all goes wrong. I suppose she knew I wouldn't be able to cope . . .'

269

The tears started to well up again as she thought about Leonora, the woman who didn't like the dark, spending her first night all alone in the churchyard. Ruby had thought about putting her precious binoculars in the coffin, but she couldn't bring herself to part with them so instead she'd placed inside the ragdoll that Leonora had kept on her bed and a postcard of a cruise liner that one of her lady guests had sent her from India several years before.

'I know I should be pleased about the hotel,' Ruby sniffed, 'but I feel so bad that this is all because she died. And I'm so scared. It's all beyond me, really. I don't know if I can manage it. I wish George and Babs were nearer.'

'Of course you can manage. You've been doing it for years already,' Gracie tried to reassure her.

'Yes but with Aunt Leonora watching over me like a hawk and jumping when I did something wrong. Doing it on my own is going to be a different kettle of fish, that's certain.'

She looked at Gracie sitting beside her in the cramped office that had always been such an oasis of calm, but had seen so much action in the past couple of weeks. It wasn't a small room but it was full to capacity. The desk was old and creaky, and at an angle, with a chair either side, placed so that Leonora could see the view from the window and also into the lobby when the door was open. A floor-to-ceiling bookcase was crammed into an alcove and weighed down with folders and files and everything to do with the hotel. Aside from a couple of extra chairs tucked in the corner there was nothing else. It was Leonora's little kingdom and Ruby felt uncomfortable being in there without her, even though she had been many times before.

'I know I've been helping here, but there's so much to learn. I mean, look at all those files and things. I don't know what's in most of them.'

'Easy-peasy! You already know it all, even if you don't think you do. One step at time . . .' Gracie smiled. 'You've got a solicitor and an accountant to help you, as well as Babs and George.'

'Can I ask you something? Uncle George agrees that I need someone to help me so I was wondering, would you come and work here properly? If you did my old job then I might muddle through doing the rest. But I can understand if you don't want to,' Ruby added quickly, not wanting to put Gracie on the spot. 'I know the Palace is big and lively, and you've got lots of friends there. It can be as dead as a dodo here out of season. In season too, sometimes.' She laughed nervously, desperately wanting Gracie to say yes.

Gracie didn't answer straight away. Instead she started chewing around the edge of her fingers, the way she always did when she was nervous. 'I'll have to think about that one. I love helping out here but I don't know if I'd go nuts being here all the time. It's a bit sort of grim sometimes when Leonora's ladies are demanding stuff and nonsense.'

'Listen, Gracie, don't worry about it. I don't want my question to make you feel put on the spot,' Ruby said quickly, panicking that she might push Gracie away completely, 'but some ideas might help me. There are some things I want to change. I suggested some changes to Aunt Leonora ages ago but she was having none of it. But I can't do anything just yet. It would be disrespectful.'

'I know what you mean, but do you know what I think?' Gracie jumped up and marched on the spot. 'I think we should go for a walk and talk about it; we both need some fresh air. You look dead on your feet.'

'I can't in case Ray comes back.'

'I thought you didn't want anything to do with any of them.'

'I didn't, I don't . . . Oh, I don't know. I suppose it's because Aunt Leonora died so suddenly it made me think about my mother and grandmother. It would be nice just to know how everyone is, even if I never go back there.'

'Are you going to tell him about the hotel?'

'Not a bloody chance. The boys'll be on the doorstep in a flash, looking for free holidays!'

As they both laughed so Henry, the occasional night porter, who'd come in early to help out, knocked on the door.

'Someone here for you.'

'OK, I'm on my way.'

Ruby and Gracie walked out together. They were still dressed from top to toe in black, and both had their hair still tied back from when they had had their hats on for church. Ruby fleetingly wished they'd had time to change and not look so drab but it was too late to do anything about it.

'You came back,' Ruby said to Ray, who was standing by the desk. She smiled slightly but didn't offer a hand and neither did he. 'I didn't think you would.'

'Thought I might as well come and see what's what.' He shrugged and curled his lip slightly, feigning indifference, but Ruby wasn't fooled. She knew him too well. Ray's curiosity had got the better of him.

'Let's go to the dining room. I put some food aside for you in case you came back. It's only from the funeral tea but it's really nice.' She looked at him, trying to judge his expression. 'Oh, and this is Gracie, a friend of mine. We work together sometimes.'

Gracie smiled and held her hand out. 'Pleased to meet you, Ray.'

'I bet,' he said as he took her hand and shook it before quickly dropping his back down to his side as if he'd been shocked. With both women being nice Ray was completely wrong-footed.

Ruby led the way to one of the tables in the dining room, then went and fetched some cake and sandwiches for him along with a pot of tea. She placed the tray in front of him and sat down next to Gracie.

'Why'd you do it, Rube? Run off like that.' He didn't look up as he poured himself a cup of tea.

'You know why. You and Ma forced me to come back from Melton where I was happy and then you treated me like dirt. I didn't want to be your skivvy. I wanted to finish my education and have a life.'

'Well, get you. Still Miss High and Mighty.' As he said it he glanced down at her hand and Ruby knew he was checking for a wedding ring. 'Well, you didn't get yourself much of a life, did you? From what I can see you're just a waitress in a run-down boarding house!' He sighed deeply and shook his head.

'I'm happy,' Ruby smiled. 'Well, not today because of the funeral, but I like living here.'

'You shouldn't have gone like that.'

'Whyever would I have stayed?'

'Because we're family and that's where you belonged. You know that, and if the doc and his wife hadn't got you you'd have known your place. You had a duty to the family but you ran off and left us to manage. Family should have been the most important thing for you, same as for the rest of us.'

Ray leaned back in his chair and looked at her. It was a challenge.

'No, I didn't belong, and you didn't need me, as well you know. You just all resented that I'd had another life; but it wasn't my fault Dad didn't let you boys be evacuated, and it wasn't my fault that he battered you all and not me.' She stared at him for a moment and then shook her head. 'But that's all in the past. I've moved on and I bet everyone else has.' She waited for a few moments for him to speak but he said nothing. 'So what's been going on back home, Ray? Has something happened to bring you here?'

'Curiosity, once I knew where you were,' he said.

'Who told you?' she asked.

'You already asked that; it's for me to know and you to find out!' he replied childishly.

'Oh, well, never mind, it doesn't matter.' Ruby shrugged, determined not to give any leverage for anything. 'How is everyone? Are you going to tell me?'

'Ma's married again.' His tone was flat and suddenly everything became clear. Ray's demeanour was because he had been usurped as head of the family.

'Who'd she marry?'

'Some bloke she worked with. That's why she loved that job at the big house so much. He's the fucking gardener.' He looked at Gracie. ''Scuse language, no offence.'

Ruby nearly fell off her chair. Ray being respectful?

'None taken.' Gracie smiled and stood up. 'But now I'd better go and help in the kitchen. Edith's struggling out there on her own and you two must have lots to talk about.'

Ruby knew that wasn't strictly true. Last time she'd looked Edith was sitting out in the garden with her feet up on a stool having a cigarette and a cuppa, but she appreciated Gracie's show of tact.

'So what's his name?'

'Who?'

'The bloke Ma's married, of course.' Ruby laughed, determined to keep the mood light.

'Frankenstein. No, sorry, it's Donald. He's Scottish and a right ugly bastard, but Ma thinks the sun shines out of his you-know-what.'

'Is he good to her?'

'I suppose. Don't see her that much. She doesn't care about any of us any more. It's all to do with him.'

And Nan?' Ruby asked.

'Older and going a bit gaga. Spends all her time looking out the window, especially since she got some decent glasses.' He grinned and there was a hint of the old nasty Ray. 'Looking for you most likely! She don't like Donald all that much either.'

'What about everyone else?'

'I'm married, living in Leytonstone. Bobbie was engaged but she did a runner and he's in lodgings. Only one at home is Artie. Lives in his own world, does that one. Him and Nan are well suited. He looks after her since he lost his job. But you're asking all the questions . . . What about you?'

'I live and work in this hotel and I'm not married.'

'So that's it then. All caught up,' he said.

'Hardly, but it'll do for the moment. I noticed your limp – what happened?'

'Why do you ask?'

'Oh, stop being so snippy. I'm just asking. It's called talking.' Ruby shook her head. 'Maybe we should have tried it before.'

Suddenly she was finding the whole conversation really wearing. It had been a long day and she wondered if she'd ever find out why Ray was really there. She also wondered if she cared. She just didn't want to play the silly games any more.

'Motorbike went one way and I went the other. Wrecked my knee and the bike. Bike's mended but I'm not, so no National Service for me, but I married the nurse so some good came out of it.' Ray's response was so normal Ruby wondered if there had been a breakthrough.

'Are you working?' she asked.

'Same place, me and Bobbie, but that Johnnie Riordan who used to live down the street is boss now. He works for some old villain who's got a finger in every pie. The bloke bought the whole of Blacksmiths and put him in charge. Bastard wears a suit and swans round in a decent car while me and Robbie scratch by but, as the missus says, it's a job and beggars can't be choosers.'

Ruby could barely breathe as she took in what Ray was saying. *Johnnie Riordan*. The name reverberated in her head.

She wanted to ask Ray about him, she wanted to know everything, but didn't dare even speak his name. Her secret was just too big to compromise by showing an interest. Forcibly she pushed the information away and watched her brother as they sat across the table from each other.

It seemed strange to her how things had changed. Although she'd tried to hide it Ruby had been terrified when he'd come in through the doors earlier in the afternoon, all bluff and insults like the old Ray she'd run away from, and yet now they were having an almost normal sibling conversation.

'Well, this has been strange, hasn't it, Rube? But I've got a train to catch . . .' Ray stood up and pushed his chair back.

'Do you want me to give you a lift to the station?' Ruby asked, surprising herself as the words came out.

'Blimey, girl, you really have gone up in the world,' he said.

'I'm just offering you a lift to the station in the hotel car, that's all.'

'No, thanks, I'll walk. I've just got a bit of a limp, I'm not a fucking cripple.'

'That wasn't what I meant and you know it, but suit yourself,' she said easily, but she was disappointed not to have the chance of a little more time to find out more about everything that had happened in the years since she left.

Especially what had happened to Johnnie Riordan.

Later that night Ruby was upstairs in the flat with Gracie, who was staying overnight again.

'Your brother didn't seem that bad,' Gracie said tentatively. 'Mellowed with age, do you reckon?'

'Being demoted from his self-appointed role in charge of the family probably did for him. That must have hurt. I'm shocked Ma was brave enough to marry again but then I did always wonder about the pull of the Big House, as we always called it. Now we know. But good luck to her. She had nothing in her life.' Ruby suddenly laughed. 'Well, I didn't think she had. And Ray's married. I never even asked her name. Maybe they were right, I am a selfish bitch . . .'

'Today isn't the day for any more emotional stuff. Forget about Ray and all that for the moment. Deal with Leonora and the hotel today.'

'It's been so strange from start to finish.' Ruby lit a cigarette and then waved it at Gracie. 'See what you've done to me? I'm a bloody chain-smoker now!'

'Give over, you love it! But maybe it's time for you to make peace with your family now you've slain the giant. I did that with my family. Not that I have much to do with them, but I could if I wanted. Common as muck, they are; not good enough for me any more now I'm mixing with the posh folk in Thorpe Bay.'

As Ruby spun her head round and looked at her in horror, so Gracie screamed with laughter.

'Gotcha. No, the peace has been made but it's not the same. Can't be after the baby and the home they sent me to. More bothered about the neighbours' gossip than me.

279

But we send cards for birthdays and Christmas. It'll be like that with you and yours. It's hard to go back once you've grown up and moved on but there's that bit in the middle that's nice and neutral.'

'I'd like to see Nan. She won't be around for ever and she was the one who encouraged me to get away else I might still be there, but I'd never be close to the others.'

She thought about telling Gracie what Ray had said about Johnnie Riordan but then decided it was best left. The less she discussed it, the easier it was to forget again.

'Have you thought about my offer?' she asked Gracie to change the subject.

'Sort of, but I'm not sure, Rube. I'll think about it and let you know. Hey, your mate Tony'll have a breakdown when he finds out about you having the hotel and him not being involved. He was desperate to give you advice! Are you going to tell him?'

'Not straight away. You're right, he'll want to give me advice and I'd like to keep this separate from my love life. No, let's keep it between you and me. I'll just let him think the same as Ray – that I'm managing it for Uncle George.'

TWENTY-TWO

Ruby strolled slowly along the seafront until she got to the steps and then walked down onto the beach. The tide was on its way out so just before she reached the soft damp mud she quickly slipped off her sandals and walked barefoot, feeling the mud seep between her toes. She loved the early mornings on the beach, especially when she needed to think in peace. She was wearing her favourite shirt dress with a full skirt, which she gathered up in her hands like a child to avoid getting mud on the hem. It was early morning and hardly anyone was around to notice the tall attractive redhead holding her skirt up around her thighs while she waded up to her ankles in the mud.

She had decided that much as she had loved Leonora she had no intention of following her overly formal dress code to work, so she just wore her normal clothes, albeit the ones that were unobtrusive and looked professional. That morning, knowing the accountant was scheduled for a long, complicated visit, she'd chosen her favourite pale green dress with three-quarter-length sleeves and an open shirt collar that stood up high against the back of her neck and flattered her pinned-up auburn hair. Her stockings and beige court shoes were laid out in the bedroom for when she got back to the hotel.

She loved the beach and the proximity of the sea. Like Leonora before her, she couldn't imagine living anywhere else now; she would even sit out on the balcony as Leonora had with her beloved binoculars up to her eyes and watch ships and boats sailing by, especially when the tide was up and the fishing boats were making their way either in or out. To her mind it was the perfect place to live. The only difference was that Ruby knew that one day she would sail on one of the cruise liners that headed out to sea via the Thames Estuary, whereas Aunt Leonora had never got the chance.

It had been four months since Leonora Wheaton had died and Ruby had settled into her new working routine far more easily that she had expected. Gracie had dithered for only a few days before agreeing to work for her, and they shared the flat on the top floor. But while the two young women were still close friends and worked well together, each had her own social life. Ruby had very little spare time but most of what she did have she spent with Tony Alfredo, while Gracie still spent time with her old friends from the Palace, especially Sean, to whom she'd started to grow close, against all the odds. He was now the head porter and although he'd had other girl-friends over the years, and Gracie had not been especially nice to him, he still held out for her and it made her think far more kindly towards him.

As she turned to start walking back Ruby saw Tony standing on the steps from the Promenade, watching her. He was dressed casually in slacks and a white V-necked cricket sweater over an open-necked shirt. There wasn't a hair out of place on his head. Tony Alfredo always looked immaculate.

'Take your shoes off and come and join me!' Ruby shouted.

'Not likely,' Tony shouted back. 'It's too filthy for me.'

'It's good for you. Mud is all the rage nowadays. Very healing.'

He smiled as she padded back to the steps where she'd left a small towel and a child's bright orange beach bucket full of water. She tucked her skirt up so she was sitting on her knickers and carefully rinsed the mud off her feet before drying them and putting her sandals back on.

'You look like a naughty child sitting there like that, not very ladylike at all,' Tony said with a smile on his face and just a hint of criticism in his voice.

'Better than going back covered in mud. Leonora's ladies would not be amused, I can tell you.' She smiled. 'Anyway, what are you doing down the beach this early on a weekday? Haven't you got a job to go to?'

'I've got a day off and I came looking for you. I

promised to do the café books for my father but I thought I'd see if you'd like to come for coffee and cake there before I start. Gracie told me you were over here,' he said calmly, expertly covering his real feelings about Ruby's friend. 'Papa's been complaining he doesn't see enough of you now that uncle of yours is working you into the ground.'

'He's not working me into the ground, I'm doing it myself. I really want this to be a success and I've got lots of ideas.'

'Well, come over to the café and you can tell me all about them. I'm interested.'

Ruby still hadn't told Tony about her true role at the hotel. She hadn't lied, she just hadn't elaborated on her previous generalisation that she was going to carry on working there. She wanted to be honest and open with him but was aware that his personality would make it impossible for him not to interfere so she continued to let him think that George Wheaton owned the hotel and she was managing it for him. It was just easier that way.

Ruby stuffed the towel into the bucket and they walked along the promenade together to the café.

'Oh, Ruby, Ruby, where have you been, my beautiful one? It's been so long . . .' Mr Alfredo ran over to her with his arms outstretched. 'Tony tells me you are working too hard, too hard for a beautiful young woman. You should have a man to take care of you.'

'I'm very well, thank you. I am working hard but I enjoy it. Just like you and Mrs Aldredo enjoy your café.'

'But Mrs Alfredo has me to work beside her. You are all alone in that hotel with so many women. There's no one to appreciate you. You must let my boy help you.'

'That's enough flattery, Papà,' Tony said firmly. 'We're here to have morning coffee, not to have a lecture on the joys of working together.' He looked at Ruby. 'Shall we have the table in the window?' he asked, but the decision was already taken.

'I shall bring your order over. You two go and sit, talk, enjoy . . .'

Ruby was never sure exactly how much of Mr Alfredo's Italian lilt was exaggerated but he always made her smile with his extravagant compliments and hand waving. She envied Tony his besotted parents, but sometimes, when he was being mean, she wondered at how they had overindulged him. In their eyes he could do no wrong, and he had grown up thinking exactly the same. He was supremely confident in himself and his abilities, to the extent that it never occurred to him he could be wrong or that someone could disagree with him. But it was also that confidence that made him so good at his job.

Tony Alfredo was always the perfect companion when they went out together and Ruby enjoyed his company. He would take her to nice restaurants and dances, and sometimes to the theatre in London. He was charming and intelligent, and always immaculately turned out; the perfect gentleman who could always make her laugh and feel special. However, just occasionally, when she disagreed with him, he could turn in a flash from being a suave and sophisticated young man into a sulky and spoiled child with a bad temper.

'You were going to tell me about your plans,' Tony said.

'I have to talk it through with Uncle George but I want to change the hotel. I don't want it to be ladies only any more. That's so old-fashioned now. I think we should open it up for couples. It'd earn more if there were two people in every room, and if we didn't do dinners—'

'I suppose Gracie's behind this,' he interrupted.

'It's nothing to do with Gracie. Surely you don't think I'm so silly that I'd do something I didn't agree with on the say-so of someone else?' She smiled as she spoke because she could see Mr Alfredo looking over at them, trying to eavesdrop on their conversation.

'I don't think that's such a good idea, Ruby. Thamesview is well known. It has a good reputation and many of the guests come back year after year. I bet Leonora Wheaton had to struggle to build it up again after the war. You'd lose all that. You'll end up like every other seaside boarding house along this stretch of the esplanade.'

Ruby took a sip from her drink, unsure where the conversation was going. She'd expected Tony to be all for modernising the hotel.

'But it's just so sedate,' she said, feeling irked that he didn't agree with her.

'Is that wrong, then? I think it makes it different. And Thorpe Bay isn't in the centre of town, not the best place if you want a family seaside holiday.'

'Well, what would you suggest then, to bring it into the twentieth century?' Ruby asked curtly.

'That you get your uncle George to invest some cash into the property. It needs decorating inside and out, and the furnishings all need replacing. The armchairs in the lounge look as if they might collapse, the carpets are falling apart and the curtains are out of the ark—'

'I can't believe you're saying that.' Ruby interrupted. 'I love the hotel—'

'I know you do, but George has to be realistic about his investment. He has to either invest in it or sell it. The clientele will move on if it's not renovated to reflect the prices.'

'Suppose that's not an option? Suppose Uncle George doesn't agree?'

'Then it's his problem isn't it? He shouldn't be in the business if he can't think ahead constructively,' Tony said with a dismissive shrug.

As they talked further Ruby was distracted; she knew she was doing the wrong thing by talking about it but not telling him the whole story. She decided to change the subject to avoid saying the wrong thing.

'I'm thinking about going to visit my mother. Ray will have told her about his visit so it might be a good time to break the ice. I feel happier with the thought than I did at the time, when Aunty Leonora had just died.'

'Is that a good idea? You said you never wanted to see any of them. Why the change of heart?'

'Because seeing Ray and talking to him, I've realised that I have nothing to be scared of any more. And I'd like to see my grandmother again before it's too late.'

'So you're not just being nosy about your mother's new husband? Your stepfather?'

'Oh Lord.' Ruby sat up in her chair and gasped. 'I hadn't even thought of that. A stepfather . . .'

'Someone else to come and scrounge off you now they know where you are. You're doing well for yourself, you don't need those people in your life.'

Ruby suddenly felt irrationally defensive. First he'd told her the hotel was a dump and now he was criticising her family. But she said nothing; she knew it was her own fault. He only knew what she had told him about her family, and none of it had been good. She wanted to say that things had changed, that she'd been sixteen when she'd run off and now she was older and knew better. She wasn't scared of anyone any more.

'Anyway, time marches on and I've got to get back now. I'll think about what you said and talk to Uncle George.' Ruby stood up and kissed Tony on the cheek. 'Good luck with the book-keeping. I'll see you tomorrow evening still?'

'Of course. Cinema and dinner. I'll call for you at seven.'

'That'll be nice.'

Ruby slid out quickly while Mr Alfredo's back was

turned. She couldn't face another round of compliments and hugs from him or his wife.

She turned right and meandered back past the line of shops, looking closely as she walked. She realised that they looked as decrepit as the hotel did from the outside, and she was ashamed she hadn't noticed it before.

She'd arrived down in Southend after the war when the town was slowly returning to normality and trying to encourage the visitors back. Leonora had told her a little about the trials and tribulations of the town in the wartime lockdown but Ruby hadn't been interested; she had been too wrapped up in her own misery to care. But now she was looking around and noticing how the townspeople must have suffered. Especially those with small hotels like the Thamesview.

She crossed the road so she was opposite the hotel and stood looking up, really studying it for the first time. Suddenly she was shocked at how neglected it looked. Tony was right. The paint was peeling off the woodwork, the railings needed attention and there was a general air of grubbiness about it. She could see that Leonora had made the right decision in continuing to focus on widows and single woman, and many of them returned year after year, but there weren't many new guests. She would have to talk to George and see what he thought.

'Tony the Great was here looking for you,' Gracie said as Ruby went back into the hotel.

'I know. He found me on the beach paddling in the

mud like a five-year-old. We went to the café. It wasn't open but the parents let us in anyhow. Tony's spending the day doing their books for them. He's good at things like that. He has a very organised mind.'

'You seem bright and happy. Do I sense wedding bells in the air?' Gracie laughed. 'Oh dear God, I don't think I could have him as a boss. Makes me feel like Little Orphan Annie when he looks me up and down.'

'Oh, he's all right in his way,' Ruby replied. 'He's just been spoiled. Anyway, I could ask the same of you. Are you going to marry Sean? You're getting on a bit, you know. You're older than me, you'll be up there swinging your legs on the old maids' shelf soon.'

When Gracie didn't answer immediately Ruby opened her eyes wide and stared. 'No . . . Has he asked you? Why didn't you tell me, you secretive cow?'

'He's not asked outright but I know what he's thinking.'

'And? If he does ask?'

'I don't know. He's hard-working, not bad-looking and he loves me. What more do I want? I was head over heels once and look where that got me. As soon as I told him I was expecting he was off and I ended up in that bloody awful place. Sean wouldn't do that to me . . .'

'You're not pregnant now, are you?' Gracie asked.

'Of course not. I'm not that stupid, you know.'

Ruby went over to her friend and hugged her tight.

'Blimey, what's that all about?'

'Because I sometimes forget that you had an even worse

time than I did. If it's any help, I think Sean is a really nice bloke and I think it's better to have someone who really wants you than to go looking for the moonlight-and-roses stuff and then get dumped.'

Gracie stared at her. 'Some speech that, missy. I'll try and remember it!'

'You do,' Ruby said with a smile, before turning on her heel and going to the office to think about getting the hotel done up and also how to pay for it.

TWENTY-THREE

'I've been thinking about taking you to the seaside for the day, you and the boys, what do you think?' Johnnie Riordan asked casually as he and Sadie were sitting side by side in front of the fire. She was hand-sewing blue satin ribbon onto the edge of a romper suit for the baby and he was flicking half-heartedly through the pages of the newspaper. 'We could take a picnic for the beach.'

'Oh, that'd be so fantastic, Johnnie. The boys haven't been to the seaside yet and I haven't been for ages!' Sadie shrieked, and leaned across to kiss him hard on the cheek. 'When? Where?'

'Southend. On Sunday. I've told Bill that I have to have at least one whole day a week with you and the boys and he's agreed. He knows it's hard for you so he didn't mind too much when I laid down the law to him.'

'Aw, I love Bill, but it is boring being stuck here all the time with just babies to talk to. I miss the Black Dog.'

'Well, Sunday it is then; a day out. Let's hope it doesn't rain.'

'I don't mind. It's been so long since we went out on a day trip.'

Johnnie couldn't help but smile. It cheered him no end that Sadie was so happy at the thought of a family day out, but at the same time there was an underlying niggle of guilt because he wasn't doing it for her. He was doing it for himself.

Johnnie had tried hard to put the postcard out of his mind and concentrate on his life as it was, but it had nagged away at him constantly from the moment he'd seen it four months before.

Ruby Blakeley. Thamesview Hotel. He told himself over and over that the girl he once knew was now history and that he had no interest in her; that he just wanted to know she was OK. He'd thrown the card away for fear of Sadie finding it but the address was imprinted in his mind and there was no way he could erase it without checking it out. He needed to resolve his feelings and put Ruby Blakeley back into the past.

'Time for bed, Mrs Riordan,' Johnnie said with a wink as he stood up, aware that Sadie was in a good mood. 'Up those stairs with you . . .'

'Come on then, Mr Riordan, show us what you're made of,' Sadie laughed.

He quickly checked the locks, clicked off the lights and then followed his wife up to the bedroom, smacking her gently on her backside as they went. When she was like this it was like the old days. They'd had a highly charged relationship that thrived on excitement and instant sex, but back then her moods had always stayed within the boundaries of normal highs and lows.

But she'd changed the moment they were married. She was no longer Sadie Scully, the barmaid, the life and soul, whom everyone fancied, but Mrs Riordan, the wife with two small children and wider hips than she'd ever had. He didn't mind her hips at all, but she did, and it depressed her.

When they were in their own little bubble Sadie was as happy as could be; it was when the outside world, especially Johnnie's family, intruded that she dropped right down into the depths of paranoia and depression.

Next morning Sadie was already downstairs cooking breakfast and dancing around to a tune on the wireless when Johnnie came downstairs. It bothered him that she had such extremes of mood, but at least if she was happy then he wouldn't get too much of a grilling when he went to work.

'Still looking forward to Sunday, I see,' Johnnie laughed, and hugged her from behind as she stood at the stove frying eggs. 'Well, so am I! We could go down the pier, get the train, go on the boating lake, drive from one end of the seafront to the other . . . Do you remember when we went there before we were wed?'

'I remember. That was when it was just us. Now we've got children and you don't fancy me any more.'

'Not true. We did all right last night, didn't we?' He hugged her again. 'Do you know anyone with a fold-up type pram that can fit in the car? I'm sure I've seen them. Or even a carrycot on wheels for the little 'un. I can carry Martin when he's tired, and we could even top and tail them.'

'I dunno. I don't know who to ask.' Sadie frowned.

'I'll ask Betty. She'll have one in the loft; she never throws anything away.' As soon as the words were out of his mouth he knew he'd put his foot in it.

'I don't want my boys in someone else's pram, especially hers.'

'OK.' he soothed. 'It'll just be easier or we'll have to carry them both. That Silver Cross thing would need a lorry to take it anywhere.'

He laughed to try to distract her from her irritation before it built up into something else. Again.

She put his breakfast on the table and grinned. 'Go on then, ask Betty, but don't dare ask them to come with us. This is going to be just us and the boys. A real family.'

Sadie was still in a good mood when Sunday came round and Johnnie watched as she happily gathered up everything for the day and piled it all into the Ford Consul. She was dressed up to the nines, with full make-up, high heels and her hair piled high. He thought it was a bit too much for a day at the seaside but he didn't say anything, he was just relieved she was happy. She packed his precious car full to overflowing, and Johnnie was pleased that Bill Morgan wasn't around to see it looking like a removal van, but within a few minutes they were on their way to the seaside.

When they drove down Chalkwell Avenue to the start of the seafront Sadie was like another child in the car, clapping her hands and laughing. Nine-month-old Paul was asleep in the carrycot in the back and two-year-old Martin was on his mother's lap in the front.

'Look Marty, it's the sea . . . look at the sea . . . look at the boats!' She turned to Johnnie. 'They're fishing boats, aren't they?'

'I'm not sure. They might be cockle boats. I don't know the difference, but whatever they are they'll go out on the tide later on.'

'I'd love to go on a boat.'

'We could see if the pleasure steamers are running. If not it'll have to be the boating lake.' Johnnie looked sideways and laughed. 'What do you want to do? Go for a drive along the front or park up and go somewhere first?'

'Let's park and go for a ride on the pier. Marty will love the train, then we can have our picnic on the beach at Westcliff.'

Johnnie hid his disappointment well. He wanted to drive along to find the address on the postcard. Just to have a look.

'OK. We'll just drive along and get our bearings and look for the best place to go for our picnic on the beach later on.'

He drove slowly from end to end with his arm on the open window, trying to look casual, but he was actually looking hard for the sign 'Thamesview Hotel'. He drove all the way along the front up to Shoeburyness, then turned round to drive back. His disappointment was hard to hide but he did his best.

Then on the way back he saw it: a large white three-storey property set back from the pavement. The first-floor balconies jutted out over the front garden and were protected by permanent canopies. It was a large property that at first glance looked too small to be a hotel, but an ornate sign on the front that said 'The Thamesview Hotel for Ladies' in big black letters told him he'd probably found the right address.

The only thing he didn't know was if Ruby Blakeley really lived there or if the postcard was some sort of joke. The building just didn't tally with where he had imagined Ruby would be.

'This looks a really nice place for a picnic. It's not crowded. Shall we come back here after the pier?'

'Looks a bit quiet to me,' Sadie said.

'But after all the excitement of doing all the things we want to do, the boys will need a nap and we might need a bit of peace and quiet.'

'I suppose . . .' Sadie said without much enthusiasm.

'We'll decide later then.' Johnnie appeased her as he always did.

He continued driving back towards the pier and then parked as near to it as he could.

They crammed both children, one each end, into the borrowed carrycot and caught the train to the end of the pier before walking all the way back and spending time in the amusements on the other side of the road. Johnnie did his best to make sure everyone had a good time but he was really just itching to get back to the part of the beach that was opposite the hotel. It certainly wasn't the best part of the beach for a picnic, with a concrete slope and just a small strip of sand before the mud, but he convinced Sadie it was perfect. He collected two deck chairs and carefully positioned them near one of the seaweed-covered breakwaters, then put the carrycot with a sleeping Paul in the shade of it.

Then he sat in the deck chair that gave a perfect view of the hotel doorway and left the other, which faced towards the sea, for Sadie.

She'd packed quite a spread into the picnic basket, and as she laid it all out carefully on the rug Johnnie started to feel guilty all over again. His conscience was shouting at him to gather everything up and go right back to the

other end of the promenade, as far away from the
Thamesview Hotel as he could get, but once it was all
spread out he told himself it was too late. He had no
choice but to stay there.

The longer they sat there the more Johnnie started to
relax and enjoy himself. Martin was happily trying to
make mud pies with his baby bucket and spade, and he
was making Sadie laugh. It was a perfect family day out
and Johnnie promised her they'd do it more often.

And then he saw her.

It was the hair that he saw first and then the person.
He wasn't sure he would have recognised her if it hadn't
been for the hair. The dark red hair was the first thing
he had noticed when he'd seen her sitting on her suitcase in Elsmere Road and it was the first thing he
noticed now.

Red, he had called her then. Ruby Red. The coltish
young girl who was far too young and innocent for him.
Now she looked so tall and ladylike that it jolted him.
He stretched out in the deck chair and watched carefully
so Sadie didn't see him looking. She didn't know Ruby
or anything about her, but she hated Johnnie even
glancing at another woman so he knew she'd sit up and
take notice if she got even a hint of Johnnie's wandering
attention.

He didn't move a muscle as Ruby walked down the
two front steps of the hotel with another woman about
her age and the two of them crossed the road almost

where the Riordan family were sitting with the remains of the picnic between them. His heart thumped with the fear of being caught, of Ruby seeing him and saying hello. It was so fierce he was sure Sadie would hear. He wanted to run but there was no way of escaping without being spotted.

'Are we mud-paddling today, my Lady Ruby of Thamesview, or is wandering round with your skirt in your knickers on a Sunday a bit beneath you now?' The other woman's voice carried, as did her laugh.

Ruby laughed. 'Stop taking the mick, you. I'm up for a paddle if you are!'

'I've got me best slacks on,' the other woman said in mock horror.

'Roll them up. If I can tuck my skirt up then you can roll your trouser legs.'

''Spose I've got no choice.'

Without even glancing at them the two women walked within a few feet of the Riordan family to the edge of the mud, took their shoes off and left them on the sand. Ruby gathered her skirt up and the other woman carefully rolled the legs of her slacks up to her knees and held on to them.

'Come on then,' Ruby said with a wide grin. 'It's not that cold!'

Johnnie didn't move a muscle as he watched them walk out onto the mud together and then stand there squelching their toes and giggling, the unknown woman with her trouser legs up by her knees and Ruby with her skirt clutched up in a bundle around her thighs.

'I tried to get Tony in to do this the other morning but he refused point-blank.'

'Beneath his dignity, of course. Tony never lets his hair down that I can see.'

'Not often, but he's a nice man deep down . . .' Ruby giggled and kicked at the water that was pooling in the natural gulleys as the tide came in. 'Aaah, we're going to get cut off by the tide. We'll drown in a sodding great whirlpool of mud and sludge and our bodies will never be found.'

'Don't be daft, we're only a few feet from shore. We could go out to the Ray and have a swim,' Gracie said, referring to the natural sandbank in the distance.

'Never in a million years. It's all right for you, you can swim!'

They laughed together, oblivious to the beachgoers out on the strip of sand. There weren't many but those that were there were watching and laughing as well.

All apart from Sadie Riordan.

'Look at those stupid cows,' Sadie suddenly said. 'Have they got no shame? Acting like schoolkids at their age. All dressed up and nowhere to go, my mother used to say.'

Her voice was so loud that Johnnie knew they must have heard her, but if they had it made no difference; they carried on doing what they were doing.

'If they splash one of the kids I'll tell 'em their fortune.'

Johnnie wanted to say something, to tell Sadie how miserable she was, but he was scared to open his mouth. Instead he sank further down in the deck chair with his arms crossed and his chin on his chest, hoping Sadie would think he was dozing off. Turning his head to one side he watched Ruby dancing about and having fun, and he felt really choked. He knew he shouldn't have gone looking for the past. He should have left it buried.

It took a few moments for Johnnie to realise that Ruby and her friend were playing up to Sadie's continuing comments. They didn't look at her but Ruby hoisted her skirt higher and started marching while the other woman laughed long and hard.

'Bloody ridiculous, I think. Just look at them, stupid women . . .' Sadie snarled without looking at him. He didn't know how to stop her because to comment would make her worse. Suddenly the other woman started to head towards them. 'Don't Gracie,' Ruby said. 'It doesn't matter. And anyway we can't have any of the ladies spotting us out here getting into a brawl.'

But Gracie carried on regardless. 'Look, you, just 'cos you don't know how to enjoy yourself don't mean we can't. Now shut it.'

Sadie was up out of the deck chair in a flash.

'Don't, Sadie. Don't spoil the day. Please don't, not in front of the children . . .'

Sadie hesitated for a moment and then sat down again, albeit with a face like thunder. Gracie looked from one to the other and then, with a shake of her head, turned away. Johnnie sighed with relief; when Sadie wanted to fight she usually went for it without any thought, but this time she held back. Bill Morgan called her spirited, and Johnnie himself had always believed that up until they were married, but the more he got to know her the more he realised that she was that deadly combination of volatility with no self-control.

Mortified, he buried his chin back into his chest. He just wanted them to go away.

He knew the sender of the postcard had been right, and that this was the place; he knew this woman was Ruby Red, and he knew that she was safe and well and seemingly very happy. Much happier than he.

He told himself that was all he'd wanted to find out, all he'd gone there for. He just shouldn't have taken Sadie and the kids on his jaunt into the past.

'We'll have to back over the road like this, you know. Let's hope we don't get spotted. It's not in keeping with our positions, is it, Lady Ruby?'

'Probably not!' Ruby picked up a handful of mud and started to mould it into a ball.

'Don't you dare . . .' Gracie laughed, and ran the other way.

As Ruby looked towards Gracie her eyes skimmed past Sadie. Johnnie knew she was glancing at the woman who had nearly started a confrontation but then her glance went past him.

Then she did a double take and he knew instantly that she'd recognised him.

Scared, he met her eyes and pleaded silently. She paused for a split second and then quickly dropped the mud, snatched up her shoes and, after doing a detour to avoid getting too close to him, she started marching back up towards the promenade.

'Hurry up, Gracie,' she shouted over her shoulder. 'We're late. You're going to have to catch me up.'

Once both women were out of sight Johnnie sat forward in the deck chair. He didn't dare look round, especially as Sadie was glaring in their direction to see where they were going, but he didn't have to look because he knew exactly where they were heading.

He also knew that now he'd seen her he'd be back. Ruby Blakeley still had the power to draw him in.

TWENTY-FOUR

'What's the matter?' Gracie asked breathlessly as she caught up with Ruby. 'Something's happened, I know it. Was it the crazy woman back there? She was just jealous because she's got a boring husband and two kids and isn't allowed to have fun any more. We'd never give her a room here, miserable cow!'

'It wasn't that,' Ruby said as she carried on walking.

'Well what then? You just turned and ran off like the devil was hot on your heels.'

'I don't want to talk about it. I'm going to get washed and then we have to make a start on dinner. It's just you and me tonight, but with only four guests it shouldn't be too hard!'

'Don't tell me you turned and ran back to get the dinner on,' Gracie said. 'Don't forget I know you, Lady Ruby.'

'I said I don't want to talk about it, not now. I'll tell you later, promise.' She paused. 'Do you mind getting started with the vegetables? I've just remembered something I haven't done. I won't be long . . .'

Gracie looked at her. 'I don't believe you, but off you go. I'll get it out of you later.'

Ruby smiled. She knew Gracie was right: she'd pick and pick away until Ruby gave in for a quiet life.

Trying not to run, she went straight into the office and closed the door. Because of the balcony above she knew that no one could see in the window unless they were up close to it, but still she stood to one side and peered around the curtain in the direction of the beach. Because of the steep slope she couldn't see anything below the level of the pavement but she carried on looking and waiting and cursing the people walking and driving by on both sides of the road.

As she watched and waited so she reran the whole event in her mind. It had been such a shock to see Johnnie Riordan again she had felt physically sick. She'd seen the family there, heard the woman making silly comments and wanted to look at her. But then she'd seen the man with her.

It was the shape of the man's head, his fair hair, his long angular body folded up in the deck chair. Her recognition had been instant and after the shock her immediate instinct had been to smile and acknowledge him as she would any old friend, but his fearful eyes had told her not to.

Because of that she could only assume that the tarty,

aggressive woman he was with was his wife and that the two tiny children were his. She hadn't had time to study the woman but it made her feel sad to think of the lively ambitious man she'd known being too scared of his wife even to acknowledge someone from his past.

And they had two children. If they were his then there were two children related to Maggie.

Half-siblings to his daughter whom he knew nothing about.

She shook her head away from that thought and pondered on why he had chosen that that particular strip of beach to have his family picnic. But as she thought about that so she wondered at the coincidence of her brother Ray *and* Johnnie Riordan both finding out where she was. The last two people she had ever wanted to find her. There they both were, in or near an obscure little hotel on Southend seafront, but nowhere near the regular day-tripper areas.

The more she thought about it, the more concerned she became, and the emotional impact of seeing him was overshadowed by the realisation that it was nigh on impossible for it to have been coincidence that, after all those years, both Ray and Johnnie found where she was and had turned up within a few months of each other.

Ray had said that 'a little bird' had told him; maybe the same little bird had told Johnnie. Maybe it was someone trying to cause problems for her. But she had no idea who or why.

Suddenly Johnnie appeared at the top of the steps

carrying a carrycot towards a car that was parked nearby. He pushed it onto the back seat and then went back for all the other stuff while the woman, who was done up like a dog's dinner, appeared with the little boy on her hip and climbed straight into the car.

Once she was in the car and everything was packed in the boot, Ruby saw Johnnie look across at the hotel; he stood behind the open boot where the woman couldn't see him and just looked in her direction, deep in thought. Then fiercely he slammed the boot down, climbed into the driver's seat and Ruby heard the engine start. As he pulled away she saw him take one last look across at where she was standing.

She knew then that there was no coincidence.

'Gracie, can I ask you something?' she said when she had calmed down.

'Of course you can. Is this to do with earlier when you had a funny turn on the beach?'

'Sort of, but not really. Who can you think of who'd want to cause me some upset?'

'No one that I know of. You don't go round upsetting people like I do,' Gracie said, looking sideways at her friend. 'What makes you think that?'

'I was wondering who could have told Ray where I was. He wouldn't say how he knew.'

'I can't think of anyone. You're not an enemy-gathering person.'

Ruby frowned and went over to the kitchen sink. 'Have you done all the vegetables? You shouldn't have, I said I wouldn't be long.'

'Oh, bugger the vegetables, there's something you're not telling me. Come on, Ruby, we're friends – thick and thin – who know each other's darkest secrets.'

Ruby took a deep breath. 'You know that family on the beach, the brassy woman who was chuntering on like an old granny about us?'

'I knew it was something to do with her, but we did carry on just to annoy her even more, show-offs that we are,' Gracie laughed. 'Daft bint.'

'It's not to do with her, it's to do with the man who was with her. Did you look at him?'

'Yeah, hen-pecked and scared. He didn't move a muscle while she carried on, just pretended not to notice. Yellow belly—'

'It was Johnnie Riordan,' Ruby said. 'There, I've told you. It was Johnnie Riordan.'

'Johnnie who?' Gracie said, and then it dawned. '*Noooo*. Are you sure? How can you be sure? He didn't look like the spivvy jack-of-all-trades you'd described. That bloke looked more like a well-trained dog.'

'Of course I'm sure. I had his baby, didn't I?' Ruby said calmly.

'Sorry. Just wondering when it happened . . .'

'You know when it happened. You and me both,' Ruby glared.

'No, not that. I mean his castration! Bet he can sing bloody good soprano now.' Gracie starting singing high.

'He did look a bit scared of her, I must admit,' Ruby said with a slight smile. 'But that's all by the by. I've got a puzzle for you. After all these years what do you think are the chances of him just happening to turn up on the beach out front? I mean, first Ray shows up and now Johnnie.'

'Maybe they're the fortune-hunters George and Babs warned you about.'

'Don't be daft. For a start, they don't even know I've inherited. No one does.'

'As far as we know no-one knows. Word can get out, although I promise you I've not said a single word to anyone.'

'I know,' Ruby said. 'But I think I'm going to go back to Walthamstow for a visit. To see Ma and Nan, make some peace. It's time. And if I can find out from Ray how he knew where to find me that'll be a bonus.'

'And Johnnie?'

'That door is shut. Looks like he's made himself a nasty little bed to lie in.'

'Are you going to tell Tony about Johnnie and Maggie?'

Ruby looked at her friend and shook her head. 'Never in a million years. He's not the sort of man to be that understanding, is he?'

'No, I guess not.' Gracie smiled but her tone was sad. 'Mind you, I haven't told Sean either.'

'Some secrets are best left where they are, buried in the past.'

'How would you feel about not living at the hotel any more?' Tony Alfredo asked Ruby.

'What a strange question. I have to live at the hotel: it's my home and my job.'

Ruby looked across the table at him. They'd been for a walk to the nearby Southchurch Park and then gone back to the café. It was packed out with mostly holiday-makers so they were tucked away at a tiny table right next to the kitchen. Ruby was relieved it was so hectic because it meant Mamma and Papà Alfredo hadn't got time to take any notice of them.

'Papà has said I can live in the flat upstairs here. He wants to let it out, so who better than his son? And it's fully furnished, a perfect first home.'

'Why would you want to do that when you've got a mother who does everything for you and desperately wants to keep you tucked safely under her wing?' Ruby laughed. 'Everything you could ever want is in that house. I bet you've never so much as picked up a saucepan!'

'But I don't want to live at home any more. The time has come to move on and settle down away from home.' He paused and fumbled in his pocket. 'With you. I want to live with you.'

'But I live with Gracie.' Ruby frowned, not quite sure of what he meant.

'I want you to come and live with me in the flat upstairs.' He pulled out a box, opened it and stood it in front of her. 'I want you to marry me!' He put his hand to his mouth. 'Sorry, I mean . . . please, please, Ruby Blakeley, will you be my wife?'

Shocked into silence, Ruby picked up the box and looked at the diamond ring tucked into the velvet. There were five diamonds in a row, the biggest in the middle and two smaller ones on each side. It was neat and pretty but not ostentatious, and Ruby was mesmerised, not by the ring but by everything it meant. She was dumbstruck by the proposal, which the last thing she'd expected.

Tony Alfredo was not a man who showed his emotions. Although Ruby knew he liked her and liked being with her, he had never even said that he loved her, never talked about the future other than in the loosest terms. There was no doubt that they got on well together, but marriage . . . ? Ruby's brain was in overdrive.

As she looked at the ring she thought of Johnnie Riordan with a wife and two children, a Ford Consul and a day out at the seaside. She could see him in her mind, slumped down in the deck chair, terrified of what his mad wife would do if she said so much as hello. This was the man whom she was sure had ordered the attack on her two brothers that left them both battered and bloodied and in need of medical attention. He may have been the father of her baby, but Maggie now belonged to the Wheatons and Johnnie belonged to his wife.

The door was closed and she wanted it to stay that way. She didn't want temptation, and being married to Tony would make sure she didn't succumb.

'Well?' Tony asked. 'What do you say?'

'Yes, Tony. Yes, I will marry you,' she whispered. She smiled as he took her hand across the table and slid the ring onto her third finger, enjoying the delight on his face. The fact that she could still see Johnnie Riordan in her mind's eye was irrelevant. Marrying Tony Alfredo would be a good way of ensuring he was out of her head.

'Can I tell the parents?'

'Ssh, not now. They're rushed off their feet. We can tell them later.'

'I love you. You'll enjoy being a solicitor's wife; you'll love having lots of babies.'

The dark eyes that she always found hard to read gazed into hers possessively and she panicked, instantly regretting her answer to his proposal.

'And I love you too,' she said uneasily. 'And I love the ring, but I'll have to put my hand in my pocket as we leave. Your dad has a very eagle eye.'

'We have to make decisions now. First thing will be that George has to find someone else to manage his hotel. You can't do that and be a solicitor's wife. Maybe dim Gracie could take the reins in the short term.'

Ruby didn't answer. Not because of how he'd referred to Gracie, but because she had temporarily forgotten that Tony didn't know she actually owned the hotel. She owned the hotel, the business, absolutely everything connected to the hotel, yet the man she'd just agreed to marry didn't have a clue.

'I can't give up Thamesview, I really can't, because –' she started to say, but he leaned forward and placed a finger on her lips.

'Ssh. Your loyalty is fantastic but it'll be my job to look after you. Not the Wheatons'. You're not their little pet evacuee any more, you know. And then we have to arrange the wedding and sort out the flat as we want it.'

Ruby smiled at him and listened as he carried on planning their lives together. She let it all waft over her; she would tell him all about it the very next day.

'You what?' Gracie shouted when Ruby told her later that night. 'You're out of your mind. You don't love Tony. It's all that business with Johnnie-the-ex that's brought this on.'

'No it isn't. He'll be a good husband. I don't want to be like Leonora, with just the hotel in my life. I want a husband and children, same as you do. Sean isn't the love of your life but you're thinking about settling down with him. You're just waiting for him to ask and then you'll be off down the aisle.'

'That's different. I actually really like him as a person, and he likes me,' Gracie laughed.

'Oh, come on, be happy for me. You can be chief bridesmaid.'

'Are you sure he's not just after your money?' Gracie asked, suddenly sombre.

'Hardly. He doesn't even know I own this place. He thinks I'm just the manager.'

'Whaaat? Oh, Ruby, what is wrong with you? He will go mad when you tell him.'

'Why?' Ruby asked, as if she didn't know the answer.

Gracie threw her hands up in the air. 'Because it's going to look as if you don't bleeding trust him,' she shouted. 'You know what he'll do, don't you? He'll throw a sulk first and then he'll want to take it over. You'll lose everything if you marry him.'

'I'll tell him, I promise, and I'll discuss it with Uncle George.' She pulled a face. 'The biggest problem is he wants me to move into Mamma and Papà Alfredo's flat with him, the one over the café. It's only up the road but—'

'Oh, you are priceless, Ruby Blakeley,' Gracie interrupted with a huge exaggerated sigh. 'Priceless. I'm going to go to my room, get down on my knees and say a prayer for your sanity and your safety, you daft ha'porth. You're going to need all the help you can get from the Good Lord above to get out of this mess!'

TWENTY-FIVE

Melton

Derek Yardley was up in his flat looking out of the window at the scene of domesticity in the Wheatons' garden below. It was a cold autumn day but still George and Babs Wheaton were out in the garden with Maggie. George was in the summerhouse with a blanket over his legs, his wife was gardening and Maggie was running around excitedly with her new lurcher puppy, a stray that Babs Wheaton had brought home after finding it freezing cold and shivering in the field out the back.

Yet another stray.

They'd given it a home because they felt sorry for it; much in the way they had taken in Yardley himself all those years before, except that even the puppy really was part of the family. Looking down at them, all he could see was a perfect family unit and Yardley resented that he wasn't part of it, that he was even lower in the pecking order than an abandoned flea-ridden gypsy puppy.

He wanted to be a part of it somehow, so he pulled on his well-worn donkey jacket and went down the wooden stairs and through the open gate to the garden. He walked around the edge of the lawn towards where they were at the far corner.

'Good afternoon, Mrs Wheaton, Mr Wheaton,' he said respectfully as he approached.

Babs looked up from her weeding and smiled. 'Good afternoon, Yardley. What can we do for you?'

'I saw you from my window and thought you might like me to help you with the wheelbarrow.'

'That's thoughtful of you but it's your day off.'

'I haven't got anything else to do. I like to be busy.'

'In that case, yes, some help would be nice. I'm trying to sort the vegetable garden out but it's so time-consuming and it's getting a bit chilly. See that pile of leaves there? If you could rake them that would be such a help.' Again she smiled. 'And if you gather up the windfalls, I'll bake you an apple pie in appreciation.'

As they worked side by side he started to relax. He felt that he was part of the family again, the way he had been in the days before Ruby and Maggie, when it had just been the three of them. He always blamed Ruby because she was the one who made the Wheatons feel dissatisfied with the way things were. It was because of Ruby that they adopted orphan Maggie, as he liked to call her. It

317

was because of Ruby he was no longer the only one. He hated her.

It wasn't that he was all that much younger than either of the Wheatons in years, but he was in intellect. His reading and writing skills were poor after minimal schooling, and his social skills were even worse. Babs Wheaton had spent time with him, teaching him the basics he'd missed and, despite his own disability, George had taught him to drive, but Derek Yardley had remained socially inept.

Derek Yardley had been a sickly child born prematurely to farming parents who lived on the breadline and who had no time to compensate for his lack of schooling. Lung congestion, they had called it, when he had wheezed and coughed and had been too ill to get out of his bed. His mother would boil some water, pour it into a bowl and then place him and the steaming bowl under a towel. Much of his childhood had been spent either in the kitchen under the towel or alone in the bedroom he shared with two healthy brothers, who were always either at school or working on the Cambridgeshire farm. No one had ever had any time for Derek Yardley.

As a result he was not only small for his age, and socially inept, but also inherently resentful of life.

At thirteen he'd run away with as many of his clothes he could wear at once and never gone back. He quickly taught himself how to live rough and he'd survived by doing odd jobs when he was well, and sleeping in the woods in his makeshift shelter when he was poorly. He loved his den, which was made of collected wood and any old rags he could find all moulded together with mud to make a reasonably waterproof shelter. He'd learned to hunt for food by trial and error and had become skilled at roasting rabbits over an open fire and sewing the pelts together for warmth in the winter. No one knew where his hideaway was so he was left alone in his solitude unless he went out into the villages looking for work.

He'd lived that way for several years until the day he'd collapsed both physically and mentally while working in the village next to Melton. Dr George Wheaton had not only treated him, he'd taken him under his wing and helped to mend him.

Derek Yardley adored the couple who had made him feel like an ordinary human being, and he had never been as happy as he was in those early years being sheltered by the Wheatons. They fed him, tended his illness and taught him all about cars; then they gave him a job and his own home. They had not only saved his life, they'd replaced it, and he saw himself more as a son than an employee.

But that had all changed when they'd brought in Ruby Blakeley and really embraced her into the family; in his mind he was convinced the London evacuee had replaced him.

Now he felt as if he were fighting for survival all over again. He'd been happy in the woods at the time but now he knew different, and he couldn't imagine not having his job and home. He didn't ever want to go back to having nothing.

Babs and Yardley carried on doing the gardening while George dozed and Maggie bounced around with her puppy.

'I've been thinking, Yardley, it seems a long time since you had a holiday. Why don't you take some days off and go somewhere? It would do you good, I'm sure. We all need to get away sometimes.'

'I'm fine, Mrs Wheaton. I don't like holidays, I like to work.'

'I know you do, and we all appreciate it,' she said. 'I tell you what, I'll have a word with Ruby. She's at that lovely little place in Southend that used to be Dr Wheaton's sister's hotel, where we went for Mrs Wheaton's funeral. Well, you couldn't stay there because it's ladies only, but I'm sure she could recommend somewhere. The sea air would be good for your chest as well . . .'

Halfway through what she was saying his mind switched off so he didn't really hear the words, he didn't recognise her thoughtfulness, he just heard Babs Wheaton trying to get rid of him.

Instantly his back was up and he was angry all over again.

'I don't like the sea, I like the country, I like it here . . .' he muttered without looking up, but he didn't think she'd heard him because she was across the garden, laughing with Maggie as they tried to catch the puppy.

'Well, I think we've finished here now, Yardley,' she shouted across to him. 'Thank you for your help. An apple pie it is for you!'

He turned away and walked back up to his flat, feeling as if he'd been dismissed.

Apple pie. He sneered as he walked up his staircase. He didn't want apple pie, he wanted things to be as they used to be before Ruby Blakeley came along.

His head was throbbing with the familiar pain as he went inside. Revenge was all he could think of, but his head was hurting too much for him to formulate anything. He looked in the drawer for his bottle of aspirin. He took three with a glass of water to be sure, then lay down on the lumpy sofa with his head on a small cushion and his legs hanging over the end. He would think about Ruby Blakeley in the morning.

Babs had opened up the door of the boiler in her kitchen, and George and Maggie were sitting warming their hands in front of the glowing coals while Babs prepared supper for them all. The curtains were drawn and the puppy was curled up in his bed fast asleep, tired out from all the exercise.

'Maggie darling, I think it's time you went and had a good wash after all that playing in the garden with Scruffy.'

The little girl turned down the corners of her mouth. 'But, Mummy, I don't want to. I want to stay here with Scruffy.'

'No supper for you then. We'll have to give it to this

little doggie here instead.' George shook his head and pulled a sad face, making her laugh and run for the stairs.

Babs looked round the door to make sure she'd gone. 'George, I have to confess I'm a little worried about Yardley. I'm concerned he's going back a bit to how he was when you first treated him. I can't quite put my finger on it but something's not quite right. Even Ruby was asking questions about him when she was here.'

'Can't say I've noticed.' George looked at her. 'He's just being Yardley, surely. He's always been different, that's how he ended up here in the first place.'

'I know, but I am going to keep a close eye on him. It's been a long time since he had any of his mental problems but I think we need to watch him . . . for his sake as much as anyone else's. Maybe give him a check up? He can't say no to you if you suggest it.'

'Fair enough, but here's no reason for it to happen again. His problems were caused by his circumstances. Living alone in the woods for years would affect anyone. The one single factor would be if he was stressed, and he certainly doesn't have any stress here.'

'I'm still going to keep an eye. Especially with him driving you on your rounds.' Babs looked thoughtful. 'Next time I speak to Ruby I'm going to find out what made her ask about him. Unfortunately we were too busy with Maggie's birthday tea to really talk, and then Leonora died and everything was forgotten.'

Babs Wheaton loved her husband just as much as she

had when they were courting. The couple had a strong marriage and adopting Maggie had added to it. They both adored her. Babs also admired George tremendously. He had overcome being crippled by polio as a child and, against all the odds, had gone to medical school and qualified as a doctor so that he could carry on when his father, the village GP, retired.

A popular figure in the village community and a much-admired GP, George was always doing over and above his duties. Babs loved the fact that he was kind and caring and that he always tried to see the best in everyone, but it was this very trait that was now making Babs feel she had to be extra observant.

Something wasn't right about Derek Yardley. Her instincts told her that he had changed recently and, with hindsight, her conversation with Ruby was now worrying her. She wondered what it was that had made Ruby ask the questions she had.

'I'm going to telephone Ruby to double-check. You don't mind, do you?'

'Of course not, if it puts your mind at rest,' George smiled.

After she put the phone down she went back through to George.

'Well? What did she say?' he asked.

'I didn't get round to asking about Yardley.' Babs' expression was thoughtful. 'She said that she and Tony wanted to come and see us. George, they're engaged. She wanted to tell us face to face but as I'd phoned she told me.'

'Oh, that's interesting. Can't say I'm surprised he's asked her – I'm sure lots of young men would like to marry our Ruby – but I am surprised she said yes. What do your instincts tell you about Tony Alfredo?'

'I don't like him one little bit, as you know, but Ruby's a big girl now. All we can do is cross our fingers . . .'

'And make sure the ownership of the hotel is watertight. Solicitor or not, I don't trust him as far as I can run, and that's certainly not very far at all, is it?'

Babs laughed. 'Yes. At the funeral he trying to inveigle his way into every conversation. He asked too many questions for a stranger. The hotel definitely needs to be wrapped up legally.'

TWENTY-SIX

Ruby stood on the doorstep for several minutes while she plucked up the courage to knock on the door. It had been so long since the day she had just upped and left that she wondered if perhaps it was best to leave it be, to turn and walk away a second time. None of them had contacted her after Ray had found her, although he had telephoned her once. But then again she hadn't contacted them.

She knocked twice and waited. Then she knocked again.

'There's nobody in.'

She looked around and realised the voice was coming from next door. Nosy Norah.

'Well, knock me down and call me Charlie, it's young Ruby, I'd recognise that hair anywhere. How are you, lovey? Long time no see, eh?'

Ruby smiled. 'I'm fine, thank you, and it's nice to see you too. Do you know where everyone is?'

'Probably at Whipps Cross. Elsie was carted off in the ambulance a couple of weeks ago.'

'What happened to her?' Ruby asked. 'Is she all right?'

'She had a fall and broke something – her leg or her hip. It's afternoon visiting today so that's where they'll be.'

Ruby started to walk back down the short path but Norah had no intention of letting her get away that easily.

'You look smashing, a right proper lady. Best thing you did was to get away from those brothers of yours, your nan used to say. Mind you, your mother's done all right for herself. Really nice man she's married, always passes the time of day and even tends my bit of back yard at the same time as your mother's. And she doesn't have Ray and Bobbie there no more, which is probably a blessing.'

Ruby smiled. 'Thanks, Norah. I'll try again later.'

'Why don't you go down to Whipps? Elsie really missed you; always talking about you. She'd be chuffed to see you.'

'I might just do that.'

With that she turned and started walking to her car, which she'd left away from the house for fear of them thinking she was showing off. As she got to it she tried to talk herself out of doing what she was thinking, but it didn't work so she walked down the road to Betty and Roger Dalton's house.

'Ruby Blakeley,' Betty said as she opened the door. It was a statement rather than a welcome.

'Hello, Betty. I came to visit my family but no one's in so I thought I'd knock and see how you are . . .'

'Johnnie doesn't live here any more.'

'I know that, I know he's married . . .'

Betty smiled. 'I thought you might! It's probably not the wisest thing, but would you like to come in?'

'I would, I really would,' Ruby said, puzzled by the less-than-enthusiastic reception. As far as she was concerned, Betty knew nothing about her and Johnnie except that they were friends.

Betty stood back and gestured her in.

It seemed strange walking down the familiar hallway to the back room. Everything looked exactly the same: the wallpaper, the carpet runner, the hallstand by the door.

'So what have you been doing, Ruby? You left a bit sharpish, leaving everyone wondering . . .'

'I'd had enough so I just went. I live down in Southend now.'

'I know.'

'How do you know? Did Ray say something? I know he works for Johnnie now.'

'Do you now . . .' she said, more as a loaded statement than a question before continuing, 'No, it wasn't your brother. A postcard came here for Johnnie telling him where to find you. But he's married now, lives in Wanstead with his wife and two children. He married Sadie who used to work with him at the Black Dog. He's got a good job, a nice car, he's settled and doing well.'

'I'm so pleased for him. He was destined to do well, with all his ambitions,' Ruby said as lightly as she could.

Suddenly it all fell into place.

Sadie. Ruby had never met her but she'd heard all about her from Johnnie. She was the barmaid he worked alongside at the Black Dog, the one he said wouldn't leave him alone, the one he said had pursued him so relentlessly but he had dismissed categorically. And now he was married to her . . .

'I'm pleased he's happy. He was nice to me when I was having such a bad time, and I remember him fondly . . . I'm engaged now.' Ruby held her hand out across the table to show Betty the ring. 'My life is finally together so I thought it time to see Ma and Nan and make the peace.'

'Congratulations, Ruby. I hope you'll both be very happy,' Betty said, her manner thawing slightly. 'I'll put the kettle on. Do you still like cake?'

Ruby laughed. 'You remembered.'

Once the conversation started to flow Ruby told Betty about her life after she'd left. Selectively, of course. She didn't tell her that she'd had a baby that she'd had to give up – Johnnie's baby – or that she had inherited the hotel where she worked. It was all very general and light.

'Betty, can you tell me anything about the postcard you said Johnnie got? Only Ray got one as well, and he came and found me. No bad thing, as it happens – it broke the ice – but I don't think it was meant to be a good thing.

I think someone is stirring something but I don't know who or why.'

'Hmm. Plain postcard which just said your name and the address of a hotel. Posted in Southend . . .' As she said the words so Ruby could see Betty's brain furiously clicking away. 'Johnnie went to Southend recently, took Sadie and the boys for a day out. Did he go and see you?'

'No. I haven't spoken to Johnnie since before I left,' Ruby answered confidently. 'We weren't friends of long standing, there was no need to keep in touch.'

'No, of course there wasn't,' Betty said with a hint of a smile.

The two women made some light conversation about her husband and the children for a while longer before Ruby decided it was the polite time to leave. She could see she was making Betty feel uncomfortable.

'It's been nice to see you again, Betty. Maybe we can catch up again next time I visit.'

Betty smiled as she held the front door open but she didn't answer.

As Ruby left the house she noticed a green Ford Consul parked just up the road. As she got closer she looked at the registration plate and was sure it was the same car she'd seen Johnnie and his family driving away in. She was so busy looking at the car itself she didn't notice the man in the driving seat until she was right beside it.

'Hello, Ruby Red.'

'Hello, Johnnie from down the street,' she replied, feeling the familiar thump start up in her chest

'I don't want Betty to see us. Cut through the alley and I'll pick you up by the High Street.'

Before she could answer he quickly drove away without a backward glance.

She stood stock-still watching the car disappear down the road. There was no question in her mind that she should just go back to her own car, get in it and drive away. That was the right thing to do. Johnnie Riordan was a married man with two children, and she was newly engaged to Tony Alfredo. Her head told her to carry on going but her heart said otherwise, and her legs took her straight to the familiar alley.

Johnnie Riordan leaned over and opened the passenger door from the inside and Ruby got in. He quickly pulled away and, without saying anything, drove to the edge of Epping Forest, pulled off the road and tucked the car out of sight of passing traffic under the cover of the trees.

He turned to face her. 'Well, Red . . . what can I say? Long time no see.'

'How about saying that we shouldn't be here? That you're a married man with two children and I'm engaged to be married?'

Mentioning the children was hard for Ruby. She wanted to tell him all about Maggie, the beautiful little girl they had made together, but of course she didn't.

'You could say that, but . . .' he trailed off.

She twisted in her seat to look at him and was surprised to see him looking so very sad.

'How did you know I was here?'

'I didn't. I pulled up as you turned into Betty's gate. Nearly had a heart attack. But anyway, tell me all about yourself,' he continued. 'It's been so long, I've often wondered about you.'

'It's not been that long . . . A few days back you were sat on the beach outside my hotel.'

'That was a stupid thing to do. Crazy. I shocked myself afterwards but it had seemed like a good idea at the time,' he laughed. 'I thought I might get a glimpse of you, see how you were doing. I never expected you to all but climb over my legs to get to the bloody water. Dancing in the mud . . . what were you girls playing at? That was so crazy, I couldn't believe it was happening.'

Ruby smiled. He still had the ability to make a good joke out of anything. 'The joy of living at the seaside. I love it there so much. Your wife didn't take too kindly to it, though.'

'How did you end up in Southend?' he asked, but Ruby ignored the question.

'I came back today for the first time, I was looking for the family but no-one was in. Nosy Norah said Nan's in Whipps Cross. I was all fired up to walk into the lion's den and it was empty.' She laughed.

'I didn't know that. Your brothers never said anything.'

'Why should they?'

'Come on, stop snapping like a crocodile. I'm not the one in the wrong here. You came to see me however long ago it was to borrow your train fare and that was it. Gone. You were never seen again, not even a postcard. You just disappeared.'

'You're right. I'm sorry. I never paid you back.' She laughed, feeling the old easiness of his company again. 'And speaking of postcards, Betty told me you got one. Whoever sent it to you, sent one to Ray as well. It can't be someone who actually knows you because neither of you lives at the old address any longer; it must be someone who knows me and is stirring it.'

'Did Ray cause a problem?'

'Long story! He turned up by coincidence at the funeral reception of a very close friend. But it was all smoothed over. A bit of a shadow of himself really.' She stared at him. 'Just like you, in fact. Where's the "I'm going to rule the world" Johnnie gone? Surely marriage can't be that bad?'

Johnnie Riordan didn't answer. He simply looked miserable and shook his head.

'You said you're engaged?'

'You didn't answer my question. Where's Johnnie Riordan?'

'I think he died a little when Ruby Red left without a word and never came back and he had to settle for something else that he didn't want.' He sighed. 'I can't complain though because it was all my own fault. I made an idiot of myself, Ruby Red. I did what Bill Morgan wanted instead of what I wanted. Now he owns me and my life. He chose Sadie and I married her, I work for him, live in one of his houses and drive one of his cars. I don't have anything that's mine.'

He leaned across and pulled her towards him gently. She relaxed and let herself fall into his arms as he kissed her fiercely with a passion that ignited everything in her again. She responded eagerly – she just couldn't help herself – but when he tried to take it further she pushed him away.

'No . . . we can't. You're married, I'm engaged.'

Reluctantly he pulled away. 'I know. You can't imagine how much I wish we weren't.'

'There's no going back, Johnnie, and we shouldn't be trying. It's wrong – you know it is – and neither of us is like that.'

He loosened his tie and rolled the window down, and for a few minutes neither of them said anything.

'We'd better go back,' Ruby whispered gently. 'If you could drop me somewhere nearby. My car's back in Elsmere.'

'What car have you got?'

'Morris Minor.'

'Hmm, not bad for a woman.'

Ruby picked up her handbag and playfully swung at him with it. The heat of the moment had passed.

'Can I see you again? Just so that we can catch up.'

'I've already said, you're bloody well married; I'm engaged to be married. It's playing with fire . . .'

'I know. Next Friday, I've got to go see someone up in Essex to collect some rents for Bill Morgan. I'll be with you at lunchtime. Shall I come to the hotel?'

'OK.' The word was out of her mouth without her even realising it.

Ruby looked at her watch and decided she still had enough time to go and see if her mother was back, so when Johnnie dropped her off she walked through the alleyway. But just as she went to turn onto the street she saw her mother and a man walking down towards the house. He had his arm around her and she was leaning her head on his shoulder. She was just about to say something when she noticed that her mother was crying. Big fat tears rolled down her cheeks as she sobbed loudly. As they got to the house Nosy Norah came out of her gate.

'What's happened, Sarah? Is it Elsie?'

'Yes. She passed away this morning,' the man said. 'We didn't know until we got there.'

'Oh, I'm so sorry, my love. Come on in and I'll make you a nice sweet cuppa for the shock. Your Ruby was here just now looking for you,' she heard Norah say.

'Ruby? Do you mean my Ruby?'

'Yes, dear. Very elegant, she looked, all grown up and driving a car. I saw her getting out of it. Mind, I didn't know it was her until she came knocking.'

'What did she want?' the man beside Sarah asked, his strong Scottish accent telling Ruby he was indeed Donald the new husband. Her stepfather.

'She said she was looking for you,' Norah said. 'I told her you were visiting at Whipps with Elsie. I thought she might go there.'

'Well, she left it too sodding late if she did,' Sarah cried.

Ruby took a step back, unsure what to do. It was an all-or-nothing moment; she knew if she turned away she would never go back there again.

She stepped out and walked towards them.

'Mum.'

Sarah, Donald and Norah all turned towards her.

'If you want me to go I will. I'm so sorry about Nan . . .' She felt her eyes prickling and then suddenly two big fat tears rolled slowly down her cheeks. 'I'm sorry, I didn't know, I'm sorry . . .' she sobbed.

'And so you should be,' her mother said without moving.

It was Norah who made the first move. She stepped forward and put her arm around Ruby's waist.

'Come on now, dearie, no need for that. Elsie wouldn't want you crying over her any more than she'd want you all fighting.' She looked directly at Sarah.

'Shall we all go inside?' the man beside Sarah said calmly.

The deep timbre of his voice suited him perfectly. He was tall and broad, with tanned leathery skin that told of a life working outdoors. His hair was mottled black and grey, as was the full beard and moustache that framed his jaw. At first glance the man looked intimidating but Ruby had already noticed the kindly dark green eyes that looked at her sympathetically. She took to him immediately.

As Sarah turned on her heel and walked up to the front door, so Donald McIver stood back and motioned for Ruby to follow, leaving Norah standing alone on the pavement. Ruby turned and smiled and mouthed 'Thank you' before walking cautiously into the once-familiar house that used to be her home.

It wasn't very different from when she'd left. The runner in the hall was new, as was the stair carpet, and the paintwork looked brighter, but the biggest difference was that Ruby didn't feel intimidated as she walked down the hall towards the back of the house. The constant niggle of fear that had always been there when she entered the house was gone.

'I'm sorry about Nan . . . I just don't know what else to say.'

'Well, you should be sorry. She missed you and now she's gone, not knowing if you were dead or alive.' She looked Ruby up and down. 'You look like you've done all right for yourself so you could start by telling us where you've been.'

'I'll put the kettle on . . . By the way, I'm Donald.' The man held his hand out to Ruby and she took it gratefully.

She could see he was going to be a good mediator between her and her mother.

'I'm Ruby, though you know that already,' she smiled, then looked back to her mother, who was pulling out the chairs from the familiar dining table.

'Didn't Ray tell you?'

'Tell me what?'

'About me?'

Ruby stared into her mother's eyes and then laughed humourlessly. 'He didn't tell you. Same old Ray. He found out where I was living and came to see me a few months ago. I thought he'd changed, I really did!'

'I don't believe you. Ray would have told me. You're just trying to put the blame on him because you got here too late for your nan.'

'OK, try this for size. Donald is your husband now. He's a gardener, works with you at the big house, Ray had an accident and married his nurse, Bobbie's in lodgings and Artie's been looking after Nan since he got the sack from the butcher's shop . . . Oh, and Ray and Bobbie have to behave themselves at work now. No more dodgy dealings.'

'How do you know all that?' Sarah asked suspiciously.

'I told you, Ray found out where I was and came to visit. I just thought he'd tell you. Shall we all sit down and have a talk? I'd like to clear the air, I really would.'

'Then that's what we'll do, won't we, Sarah? Life's too short for grudges,' Donald said purposefully.

'Yes, Donald.' Her mother looked at him and smiled, and Ruby could feel the tears prickling away again. She couldn't remember the last time she'd seen her mother look content.

TWENTY-SEVEN

Ruby was distracted to the point of losing track of what she should be doing. Her brain was spinning constantly, she couldn't sleep and she was losing weight, but what she did know was that Gracie was worried about her and that Tony was angry with her.

However much she tried to explain her feelings about her grandmother's untimely death to him, he simply couldn't understand how she could be so upset over someone whom she hadn't seen for so many years, and then he'd compounded her misery when he'd told her it would be for the best if she didn't rekindle family relationships. She'd been especially surprised at that, considering how close he was to his own parents.

But she tried to be understanding and make allowances for his behaviour because she could see why he was frustrated. At a time when they should have been happily planning their wedding together she was having trouble even thinking about it, let alone doing anything.

They were newly engaged yet she had already lost interest, and for this he blamed her reconnection with her family.

An element of that was true. Ruby was upset that she had missed seeing her grandmother for the last time by just a few hours and she hated herself for it. She hated herself for not going straight to the hospital when Nosy Norah had told her that her grandmother was there, but most of all she hated herself for having absolutely no will-power when it came to Johnnie Riordan. She had betrayed Tony and he had betrayed his wife, and it was wrong.

'But, Ruby, how were you to know about your nan?' Gracie asked impatiently as they talked about it while going through the booking forms for the new season. 'Did Norah tell you she was dying? No. Did Ray let you know she was in hospital? No, and he should have done – and, yes, he should have told her he'd seen you – but none of it happened and none of it can be changed so stop feeling so bleeding guilty about everything.'

Ruby leaned back and closed her eyes to try to ease the tiredness caused by lack of sleep that was over-whelming her.

'I should have gone to see them all after Ray came here. I'd built it into such a big thing, but I was sixteen when I left, a kid who didn't know better. Now I do. I was such an idiot. I should have gone back . . .'

Gracie looked at her and shook her head in frustration. 'You're telling me all this, but I know there's more to all this guilt than your nan dying. So what is it you aren't you telling me this time?'

'There's nothing,' Ruby said vehemently. 'Just leave it alone. You keep going on and on all the time and I just want to work in peace. Our bookings are down and I have to think about getting the decorating done.'

'I thought the decorating was going to be done early next spring?'

'Yes, it was, but Tony said that's too late. It needs to be started right away, then we can get the carpets down.'

'Oh, bugger Tony and what Tony said. This is your hotel . . . and I bet he doesn't know that yet, either!'

'That's not the point. Anyway, he's coming over later so I want all this paperwork done first. We're going to discuss the wedding. And he wants to schedule the engagement party. He wants a big fancy do at Garons in the High Street.'

Gracie huffed loudly. 'Oh, come off it, Rube. You're not still going to go through with this fiasco, are you?'

'Of course I am. I agreed to marry him – how can I possibly call it off almost as soon as it's happened?' As she said the words so her face crumpled and she started to laugh and cry at the same time. 'Oh God, I'm sorry. You're right, this is one big mess and I don't know what to do. Why do I get myself into these situations, eh?'

She was standing at the reception, leaning on her elbows with her head in her hands, pretending to study the columns of figures in front of her.

Gracie put her arm over her shoulders. 'Stop feeling sorry for yourself and let's go upstairs. I'll just tell Edith she can be in charge for a while. That'll please her no end. She doesn't often get the chance to be out front and scare the guests.'

Ruby laughed. 'She is a bit of a battleaxe, isn't she? But she works hard.'

Making sure the door to the flat was properly locked this time, Gracie made a pot of tea, then sat quietly beside Ruby and waited. It wasn't long before she told Gracie everything about bumping into Johnnie and what followed.

'He said he's coming to see me on Friday, just so that we can catch up, and then put it all behind us. A sort of Last Chance Saloon visit.'

'Catch up, my eye. He wants more than a catch-up else he wouldn't have been sat on the beach outside here looking like an abandoned puppy dog.'

'He did look a bit sad, didn't he?' Ruby cracked a smile. 'But that wasn't because of me, it was because of that silly Sadie.'

'Ruby, Ruby, listen to me. I can guess how you feel about Johnnie just by listening to you. You can't marry Tony, you can't. It's not fair. Not that I care about him, of course – you'll be well rid – but if he ever finds out . . . Honestly? You are playing with fire. You'll not only get burned, you'll be bloody torched,' Gracie said.

'But there's no future for me and Johnnie. He's married

with kids, and you've seen the wife. And married is married in my book. Adultery isn't for me. I just feel this pull to him . . . OK, dammit, I want to see him just once more, then that's it: he can have Sadie and I'll have Tony.'

'First love and all that shit, it never really goes away,' Gracie said.

'Hmm. Not quite how I'd put it . . . But I'd almost forgotten about him. I'd inherited a bloody hotel, I was starting to feel content with Tony, and I know Maggie's happy even if she isn't mine, as such. Johnnie was just a memory . . .' She clenched her fists. 'I could kill the bastard who sent those postcards and disrupted my life. Everything was fine until then.' She stood up and walked out onto the balcony. 'Until Leonora died.'

Gracie walked out and joined her but this time she kept an eye on the door, even though she knew it was locked. She didn't trust Tony Alfredo one bit.

Ruby reached for the binoculars and looked out over the sea. A storm was threatening and she watched the small boats bobbing about like toys in a bath. She loved living up here, at the very top of a building that was right on the seafront; she didn't want to move, even if it was only a few doors down. She couldn't do it. Thamesview was hers.

'Well, I think whoever it was who sent the cards did you a great big favour, even if that wasn't what they meant to do,' Gracie interrupted her thoughts. 'It's brought it all out into the open. You don't love Tony and you shouldn't even be considering marrying him. He's got a dark side Rube, I can smell it when he's around. I know you think I'm mean but it's not just that I don't like him, I don't trust him. There's something bad there.'

'That's not fair! Tony's a nice man. It's not his fault I'm so complicated. But the question is still, why did whoever it was send those postcards? Who knew about both Ray and Johnnie? I mean, Ray's my brother but no one knew about me and Johnnie.'

The two of them ticked names off on their fingers, trying to narrow down the list.

'It had to be someone who knew where they both lived and that you were here.' Gracie frowned as she tried to think it out. 'There can't be that many. The family in London didn't know you were in Southend. People in Southend thought you were from Melton. People in Melton thought you were in London. How funny that is!' she laughed. 'The only ones who knew it all, especially about Johnnie, are the Wheatons and me.'

'It definitely wouldn't be Uncle George or Aunty Babs, and it's not you . . .' Ruby screwed her eyes up and suddenly her hand flew up to her mouth. 'I know who it was. Oh God, I bet I bloody well know who it was . . .'

'Well, tell me then.'

'Yardley the driver. It has to be him. He'd met Ray and Johnnie when they went to Melton, he drove the car and heard all the conversations that went on in there; and he hates me.'

'But how would he know the addresses of Ray and Johnnie?' Gracie frowned. 'Mind you, they were both out of date. It was just chance that Ray had gone to visit your mum that day and she never got to see it.'

'I bet Aunty Babs has everything written down some-where. She is so efficient at things like that. He could easily find that sort of information if he wanted it. They trust him and he can do whatever he likes.'

'But why do you think he hates you? I don't understand.'

'He just does. I can't explain right now. He's strange and I think he thought I was taking his place somehow. Oh, I don't know,' Ruby said, unsure if she was trying to convince Gracie or herself. 'If it was him then I think it's probably because he was having a stir. I don't think it was sinister.' She sat with her face buried in her hands. She wanted to confide in Gracie but she couldn't. She had to talk to Babs first.

'I wish I'd seen one of the cards. He's semi-illiterate – I'd have recognised his weird writing anywhere. Bugger it.'

'Do you think he's dangerous? Do you think he knows who Maggie is?'

'Don't say things like that, please. I'll talk to Aunty Babs about it. I just have to get the order of things straight before I fire everything up. Another couple of days won't hurt.'

'And what about Johnnie? Are you going to put him off as well? Mr Married Man.'

'Gracie! You're not my mother! I'll do what I decide to do, about Johnnie, about Tony, about Yardley, about Nan's funeral . . . There. That's how much I've got going on, so put that in your pipe and smoke it.'

Gracie smiled. 'Good to see you've still got some gumption about you, girl!'

Derek Yardley was once again maniacally polishing and buffing the Vauxhall to within an inch of its life. He saw Babs Wheaton look out of the window that overlooked the garage and was certain that he was being watched. He didn't like it one bit. In fact, he was feeling very scared. He'd often fretted about being invisible, but now it seemed that she was watching his every move, checking up on him, asking him questions. He was getting increasingly paranoid, wondering if Ruby had said anything to them.

Were they watching him because of Maggie? Did they think he would actually touch a child, their child? Did they believe Ruby Blakeley's story? The questions kept whirring repetitively in his head. He'd never done anything else wrong, never, but now his life was going to end because of that one stupid incident so long ago.

He was scared, but he was also offended because it wasn't true. Or not true in the way she saw it. Yes, he had tried to kiss her and touch her, but he hadn't expected her to mind. He had thought she liked him as much as he liked her.

At the age of twelve Ruby had been clever and pretty, and knew far more than he. He would watch how she behaved with her friends, especially with Keith, the lad from the greengrocer's, and he would want to be out there with her, chasing through the fields and racing bicycles.

He'd watched as the mousy ten-year-old evacuee had turned into a lively, amusing girl with a wit and wisdom way beyond her years, and it was about then that he'd stopped seeing her as a child and thought of her as something more. He had sat up in his flat fantasising about her and imagining what it would be like to have a relationship with her, to have sex with her.

He had liked her so much and had wanted her so badly, but then when she rejected him the feelings had quickly turned to a hatred that was coupled with the fear of losing everything he had with the Wheatons.

As Yardley was buffing the car and thinking, he saw Babs Wheaton look out of a different window. He couldn't think what to do. He was scared witless and convinced it was only a matter of time before he lost his job, his home and his standing in the village as the doc's driver. His life.

He carried on polishing and did his best to look unconcerned. After a few minutes he put the dusters away and he did what he had done so many times before when he was stressed and knew he wouldn't be needed for a few hours. He got his beloved pushbike out of the garage, wheeled it to the end of the drive and then cycled hard and fast to the woods between Melton and the next village and then made his way to the location of his old shelter, hidden deep in the woods where no one ever ventured. He had lived there for so many years it was his security blanket and the only place where he could always clear his head of the crushing headaches that he suffered under stress and think clearly.

Although basic, his makeshift den was reasonably weatherproof, with protection from the canopy of the trees above and the well-weathered roof and walls of mud mixed with moss and layered onto crossed branches. Well hidden, miles away from any public access in the densest part of the woods, and meticulously blending into the surroundings, it was visited by no one. Whenever he went there he'd tidy up and make sure it was ready for his next visit. He'd sweep dry leaves into his makeshift mattress to refill it, gather some fallen branches for his fire, add some more mud to the walls and ceiling, and renew the covering foliage. He'd even got a couple of raggedy old blankets, an eiderdown and a pillow, which he covered in an old tarpaulin every time he left. Each time he visited he took something new with him to leave behind. This time it was a battered old saucepan that he'd bought at the church jumble sale. He never slept there any more but he had to keep it up to scratch. Just in case.

The den was his security blanket and he couldn't

Ruby

imagine a life without knowing it was there waiting for him.

Once his chores were done and he was satisfied he lay back on his mattress and waited for his headache to clear. Then he started to formulate a plan.

TWENTY-EIGHT

Tony Alfredo's face was screwed up with anger. Ruby had never seen him like that before, and as he marched back and forth across the room with his fists clenched she could see exactly what Gracie meant. There was a darkness about him that was suddenly frightening. He barely resembled the handsome and rangy Anthony Alfredo, with his sexy Roman colouring and charming smile.

He reminded her of Ray.

'Are you telling me that you *own* the Thamesview? And you never said anything?'

'Well, yes, but I don't see what difference that makes . . . You knew I worked here and I still do. Why would you mind?' Ruby asked.

'Why would I mind?' he asked nastily. 'Are you mad? You keep something like that from me and ask why I mind? We shouldn't have secrets. I don't have secrets from you, you know everything about me. Why didn't you tell me?'

'Maybe because I knew you'd be like this. Oh, I don't know, it just wasn't important so I never got round to it,' Ruby said with a shrug that seemed to incense Tony even more.

'Do you really not understand? I am your fiancé. We were planning our future together as a couple and you didn't think something like this would be important? I don't believe you. This has to have been a deliberate attempt to undermine me.'

'It wasn't, Tony, I promise.'

He stared at her in disbelief. 'You knew I wanted you to give up working there as soon as you became my wife, and now I find out you actually own the place.'

'I'm sorry you feel like that, Tony, but I don't understand why it makes any difference. I've not got control of it, anyway. Uncle George and Aunty Babs have that for five years. What I do is just a job, like I said.'

'That's not legal. He can't have control of something that's yours. He's not your guardian.'

'It was Aunt Leonora's wish. Her will was very specific about what she wanted.'

'That doesn't matter if it's not enforceable in law. I need to see the will.'

From being apologetic for the situation Ruby was suddenly angry. 'This isn't to do with you, this is family business.'

He laughed nastily. 'They're not your family. Your family live in the dirty backstreets of East London, not in a bloody great house in the country like the Wheatons. You're getting a bit too big for your boots for my liking.'

Ruby looked down at her hands. She couldn't believe he'd thrown such a low blow.

'I don't care what you say, it's still Wheaton family business.'

'No, from now on it is my business. When we're married I'll be responsible for the hotel. It'll be ours in law.' He stopped marching about and looked out of the window. He didn't look at her. 'You said there's a reserve fund – how much money is in it?'

'I don't know. Tony, stop it. I don't want to talk about it. You're making mountains out of molehills. Can we just talk about the flat and the wedding?'

'The flat's irrelevant now that we know you own a great big hotel. How inadequate do you think that makes me feel, my wife having more money than me?' He held his arm out and pointed around the room. 'I'm showing you a poky little flat owned by my parents, and you're laughing behind your hand because you own a whole damned hotel.'

He had started to pace again, his shoes clicking rhythmically on the stiff, brown-patterned linoleum, which was laid throughout all the main areas of the flat. Ruby hated it; in fact, she hated the flat, which was dingy and old-fashioned. The only thing going for it was the view, but there was no balcony.

As he paced he puffed angrily on a cigarette, despite usually being only a social smoker.

'Tony, I'm leaving now. I'll talk to you when you've calmed down. I don't like you being like this. You're reminding me of Ray when he used to rant and rave.'

She picked up her handbag and scarf and started walking towards the door, but in an instant Tony was blocking the way with his body.

'You can't go and leave all this hanging in the air.'

'Get out of my way, Tony. We'll talk tomorrow.'

She tried to get past him but he was across the room in a flash with his arms out blocking the doorway. 'You're not going anywhere. We have to talk this through.'

'Yes I am, I'm going home. I don't want a scene. We can talk tomorrow.'

His hand shot out reactively and gripped her around the neck, but just as quickly he let go.

'I'm sorry, I didn't mean to do that. I love you, Ruby. You can't do this to me . . .'

'I don't think you do love me, not really. I'm sorry, Tony, I can't marry you now, not after this.' She looked him straight in the eye. 'The engagement is off.'

She pulled the diamond ring from her finger, but rather than give it to him she laid it gently on the utility sideboard his parents had left in the flat. Her heart was thumping with fear but she tried to keep her voice calm. Anything to get out of there and away. The fear was rising in her, just as it had when Ray was attacking and trying to control her. Suddenly she saw the handsome and eligible Tony Alfredo as a threat and she was horrified.

'I'm really sorry but if you don't let me go I'll call the police,' she said as calmly as she could as she ducked under his outstretched arm and out of the room, trying to pull the door shut behind her, but she pulled it onto his fingers, which were gripping the edge of the door-frame, making him yelp with pain.

Ruby had known Tony Alfredo and his parents for over five years, most of the time she'd lived at the Thamesview, and although she knew he could often be overly self-assured and occasionally bumptious, she saw that as a trait he had to have to get on in the legal profession. He could also be loud and intimidating when he was crossed, but it had never once occurred to her that Tony would hurt her. Despite being indulged at every turn in his life, Tony had still been brought up in the God-fearing Italian way, and he continued to follow most of the rigid rules of life that came from a religious upbringing.

She was certain he was a good man at heart but his reaction to her inheritance had been out of all propor-tion, and she knew she could never marry someone who she could not confide in about Maggie one day.

She had just opened the door at the top of the stairs when Tony threw the sitting-room door wide open and flew at her like a madman.

'You're not going until this is resolved. I'm not letting you call it off. I'm not.'

He grabbed her by the wrist and tried to pull her back into the room, but she instinctively pulled away and to her horror she heard a crunch.

'You've broken my bloody arm,' she stated, more in shock than pain.

He let go as if he'd been stung, but as she put her foot on the stair he caught her around the waist in a bear hug and tried to swing her round. The pain was excruciating but still she fought. Her instincts told her to get out of there as quickly as she could. As he loosened his grip she fell forward, landing on her chest on the upright at the top of the banister; he tried to pull her back into the sitting room, but as they fought she lunged away back onto the landing, determined to get out whatever the pain.

'Stop it, Ruby. I'm telling you, stop. I just want to talk. You're not going, you're not—'

'Well, I don't want to talk to you. I want to get out of here and away from you. You're a maniac,' she screamed in his face.

Next thing she knew, his hands were grabbing at her neck, pulling her towards him, and he was trying to kiss her.

'I love you, Ruby, don't do this to me, I love you . . .'

Stumbling backwards, she lost her footing and as she started to fall back over the stairs, so Tony let go of her.

Barely conscious at the bottom of the steep stairs, she heard footsteps running down. As she cowered she sensed

Tony stepping over her and running out of the door. Instead of checking to see if she was OK he'd bolted.

It took all her willpower to get to the front door, which Tony had left open in his panic to flee; she crawled out onto the pavement. Everything ached but she knew she had to stay conscious.

'Help,' she shouted as loud as she could. 'Someone help me . . .'

'What's happened to you, dear?'

Ruby looked up and through the mist of semi-consciousness saw an elderly woman standing over her, looking bewildered.

'I need an ambulance,' she said before she passed out from a mixture of pain and relief.

When Ruby came round the second time she was out of post-operative care and in a hospital bed on a general ward with only a hazy memory of how she got there.

A passing nurse stopped and smiled. 'You look better already, would you like a cup of tea? The trolley will be here in a minute.'

'What happened to me? I can't really remember.'

'You had an accident, took a fall down the stairs. The doctors will be doing rounds later this morning and they'll explain to you.'

'I'm in such pain. My chest hurts so much.'

'I'll ask the doctor to prescribe something for the pain but I'm here to have a look at your dressings.'

The nurse pulled the covers back and examined her closely. When she touched Ruby's ribs she yelped in pain.

'I'm sorry but I do have to check everything is as it should be. You'll feel better once you've had a wash and you're wearing your own nightdress.'

'Does anyone know I'm here?' Ruby whispered, unable to raise her voice for the pain.

'Your fiancé was here last night while you were in theatre. He came as soon as he heard about your accident.'

'I don't have a fiancé any more.'

'Maybe the doctor got it wrong. Is there anyone you'd like us to inform?'

'Yes, my business partner, Gracie McCabe. She lives at the same address as me. Do you want the telephone number?'

'Yes, please.' The nurse pulled a piece of paper out of her uniform pocket and wrote the number down. 'I'll go and ring her now. You're going to need some essentials brought in. I think you'll be staying in for a while with those injuries.'

'Thank you.' Through hazy eyes Ruby watched the nurse as she walked away. In her crisp blue uniform with starched collar and cuffs, a white belt and a pert white hat pinned to her hair, she was the epitome of how Ruby had once dreamed of being herself.

Before going back to Walthamstow; before Johnnie; before Maggie.

Later in the day Babs Wheaton turned up at the hospital,

along with Gracie. George wasn't with them but once again he had been able to use his influence as a doctor to make sure they were able to see Ruby outside of normal hours. He had also got her moved to a small side-room where she was the only patient and had some privacy.

Gracie had phoned the Wheatons as soon as she'd heard, and they'd met in the foyer of the hospital and gone to the ward together.

Babs was calm and collected on the outside, but Gracie could see she was distraught.

'Do you know what happened?' Babs asked.

'Only what I told you on the phone. The hospital rang me to say Ruby had had an accident and an operation. I wondered why she didn't come home last night but thought she might have stayed at Tony's parents' place and forgotten to tell me.'

'Is he here?'

'I hope not, the creep. I can't help but think he's behind this. I was only telling Rube yesterday what I thought of him. Dark and dangerous.'

Babs Wheaton's head spun round. 'Is that what you think of him?'

'Can't stand the bloke, but Ruby says she's going to marry him. She's mad.'

'I see.'

They walked quickly along the corridor to the stairs that would take them up to the first floor.

'It's in here,' Gracie said.

They turned into the ward and were pointed in the direction of Ruby's room.

'Sweet Jesus, Ruby, you look like you've been bare-knuckle fighting,' Gracie said by way of a hello. 'What happened?'

'I fell down the stairs at the Alfredo flat.' Ruby looked at Gracie, willing her not to ask too many questions. She felt much more alert and she could remember what had happened.

'Where was Tony?'

'He left. I called off the engagement.'

Gracie crossed her arms and said nothing. She'd understood immediately what Ruby was trying to tell her.

'Did Yardley drive you down here?' Ruby asked, as if it was just a casual conversation question.

'No, I drove myself. I didn't want Yardley to bring me. Actually, I want to ask you about him – but another time . . . when you're better. Oh, Ruby, I couldn't believe it when Gracie telephoned me. We were so scared.'

'There's something I have to tell you,' Ruby said cautiously. 'It's about Yardley . . .'

'Not now, love. You need to sleep and I need to go and have a talk to the doctor. I'll be back in a minute.'

'But it's important. You have to know . . .'

But Babs was already out of the door.

Ruby closed her eyes until Babs had moved away from the bed, then she forced them open again.

'Johnnie is coming tomorrow and I can't contact him.'

359

'Ah! Oh, well, I'll deal with him when he gets there. Tell me about this accident. It was Tony, wasn't it? He pushed you down the stairs, didn't he? I'll kill him. I will . . .'

Unable to face the inevitable questions, Ruby closed her eyes and feigned sleep. Her concern was more with Yardley than with Tony at that moment, but then the pain relief took over and in a few moments she was snoring quietly.

TWENTY-NINE

Derek Yardley was pacing around his tiny flat like a captive wildcat as he tried to figure out what was happening. Everything was strangely different . . . George Wheaton was ensconced in a busy surgery and Babs Wheaton had taken the car to go somewhere on her own. Although she sometime drove George if they were going out socially she rarely went out in the car on her own. Yardley hated it when she took his precious car away at the best of times, but this time he was petrified that she'd gone off to talk to Ruby Blakeley. He was so worried he'd been physically sick several times during the day. As he paced so his headache started again.

He took the bucket down to rinse at the outside tap at the back of the garage and then, trying to look casual, he walked round to the front to see if there was any sign of her coming back. Swinging the bucket he stood by the hedge waiting and wondering if this particular day was going to be the one when the Wheatons threw him out.

As he stood there, moving from foot to foot, Mrs Alderton, a teacher from the village school, came into view. She was walking along holding little Maggie Wheaton by the hand.

Word travelled fast in a village and everyone except Derek Yardley had soon heard the news about Ruby Blakeley being in an accident. Mrs Alderton had phoned to offer to look after Maggie until Babs Wheaton returned but as George wasn't doing any house calls because he had no car, he was free to look after Maggie himself. All the teacher needed to do was drop her off.

'Hello, Yardley,' the elderly teacher said as she walked up the path with Maggie.

'Mrs Alderton,' he nodded in acknowledgment.

'I've brought Maggie home. Is Dr Wheaton around?'

'He's busy,' Yardley answered in his usual taciturn way.

'Right, well I've got to rush back so here she is. Delivered as promised. If you'll just take her to the doctor . . . The woman laughed and looked down at Maggie. 'Mr Yardley will take you to your father and I'll see you tomorrow.'

As she walked off Yardley stood there feeling ambushed. The last thing he needed was to have to take the child in to the doctor. He needed to be there on the drive, waiting for Mrs Wheaton to get back.

As he cussed to himself so the little girl looked up at him and smiled. He looked down at Maggie Wheatley and stared. As she continued smiling, waiting for him to reciprocate, so he continued staring.

Derek Yardley had never been bright, but because he had spent so much time alone, he had a brilliant memory and well-honed instincts. He'd had to be alert and cunning when he lived in the woods in order to survive, and although he no longer needed those skills in quite the same way, they had remained. He didn't need paper and pen to remember things, to work them out. His brain could do all that all by itself.

Ping, it went. And he knew.

He'd never really looked at the child before. He'd ignored her because he resented her very being – she was just a little girl who was there – but as she looked up at him his brain collated all the information and got a result. A good result, in chronological order.

He knew.

Ruby had gone back to London, aged fifteen, and then revisited the Wheatons a few months later with a man in tow. Johnnie Riordan. Yardley remembered it well. He'd felt the electricity between them and had been angry that she was responding to that man but had rejected him.

He'd been even more angry when Johnnie had tried to tap him for information about the Wheatons. Then three months later Ruby had turned up and stayed for a couple of weeks, tucked away of sight of everyone. But he'd known she was there. He'd always made a point of knowing everything.

Then the Wheatons had given him an extra day off and whisked Ruby away, with Babs driving.

Six months later the Wheatons went off in the car again, Babs driving again, and came back with a baby they were adopting.

Johnnie Riordan came sniffing around for information . . .

Ruby Blakeley threatened him with his life if he looked at Maggie.

Well, of course she did. Maggie was the illegitimate offspring of Ruby Blakeley and Johnnie Riordan. Just one look and any fool could see that!

He looked at Maggie again and saw both parents in her face.

'Uncle George is busy at the moment but I'm going out on my bicycle. Would you like a ride on the handlebars? Down the lane and back?'

'Oh, yes,' the little girl grinned up at him.

'George? Are you there, George?'

'I'm in the garden,' he shouted.

Babs went through and kissed him on the top of the head.

'How's Ruby?'

'Not very well at all at the moment, but she'll be OK. She took a nasty tumble and has some bad injuries. I think that Tony pushed her but she won't say. I'll have to leave it to Gracie to get to the root of it all. Ruby's more likely to tell her than us.' Babs looked around. 'Where's Maggie?'

'Still at Mrs Alderton's. She hasn't brought her back yet.'

'That's strange. I'd better ring her.'

After she'd spoken to the teacher Babs ran back through to George.

'Mrs Alderton said she brought Maggie back nearly two hours ago and left her with Yardley. He told her you were busy. He said he'd take her to you.'

They looked at each other, both immediately aware of the possible implications.

'Maybe he's around somewhere. I'll go and call. He wouldn't do anything to our Maggie. He wouldn't. We've done everything for him,' Babs said, trying to convince herself.

'You look all around and if he's not nearby then I'll go in and call the police. Two hours is far too long,' George replied.

Babs Wheaton's voice got louder and louder as she called Maggie and checked everywhere possible. There was just no sign of her or of Derek Yardley.

'Mrs Wheaton . . .'

Babs turned to see Mrs Alderton standing on the path in tears. 'I don't understand it. I left her with Derek Yardley. Two of the village children were playing out and they said they saw Derek Yardley on his bike with Maggie on the handlebars. He was heading out of Melton that way.' She pointed in the direction. 'They said Maggie waved at them.'

'George!' Babs screamed. 'George. She's with Yardley.

Tell the police he went through the village with her on his bicycle.'

Suddenly all hell broke loose in the village, with residents coming out of their shops and houses as word spread that Derek Yardley had abducted little Maggie Wheaton, the doctor's daughter. Search parties were organised and the evening dusk was lit up with the glow of flickering torches.

'What do we tell Ruby?' Babs asked. 'We have to tell her. Supposing something bad happens? She'll never forgive us.'

'Ring Gracie. She's the only person who knows about Maggie.'

'George, I feel so sick. What if he does something to her? She's only five years old. She trusts him. I knew something was wrong about him, but I didn't do anything.'

Yardley skidded his bike to a halt at the side of the road and jumped off. Then he lifted Maggie off and stood her on the ground.

'Do you want to see my den, Maggie? It's a secret. No one else knows it's here. We have to follow the marks high up on the trees. I put them there a long time ago so I could always find my way there and back again.'

He pushed his bike by the handlebars as far into the wood as it would go, then tucked it under some heavy foliage; he made sure it was well camouflaged, then took the little girl by the hand.

'Why have you got a den?'

'So that I have somewhere to be all alone. I like to be alone.'

'I want to see Mummy. She'll be home by now.'

'It's just a little bit further, come on,' Yardley sighed, and tugged at her hand, pulling her along roughly.

'I'm scared. It's too dark in here. I want to go home.' The child started to cry quietly.

'Oh, stop whining, will you? You're just like your mother.' He felt the child freeze. When she looked up at him, again he saw Ruby and Johnnie in her face.

He had the ultimate revenge in mind.

No one would ever find her in the woods, and the bitch Ruby would spend the rest of her life regretting the way she'd treated Derek Yardley. She had turned him down and then had sex with Johnnie Riordan. She'd ruined his life with the Wheatons.

It would serve her right.

'Come on, don't you dare try and run off without me because you'll get lost in the woods and then you'll die.'

As the child wailed, so he snatched her up under his arm and carried her to his secret hideaway.

'Ruby, I've got something to tell you.' Gracie had rushed back to the hospital the moment she'd put the phone down.

'Did Johnnie ring about coming down? Did you tell him where I was?'

'No, it's nothing like that. Ruby, I'm sorry but Babs

telephoned me a little while ago. It looks as if Yardley might have abducted Maggie. They're both missing.'

It took a few moments for the words to impact on her still-befuddled brain. She tried to sit up but couldn't.

'Abducted?'

'He took her off on his bike a few hours ago and hasn't come back. Babs said he'd been acting strangely. She's beside herself. Everyone is—'

'Oh God, this is all my fault,' was all Ruby said before she started coughing and bringing up blood.

Then she was rushed off to intensive care.

By the time they reached the den Maggie had calmed down a bit and even looked a bit interested.

Yardley pulled the tarpaulin from his bed of leaves.

'Look, this is where I lie when I have really bad headaches. I cover myself in these blankets to keep warm. I'll make a fire in a minute, but first come and sit with me.'

'No. I want to go home to Mummy and Daddy. Please?'

'No. Not yet. We've got to stay here tonight now. There's wild animals out there who'll eat us up. It's much too dangerous to try and get back.'

Maggie wailed in fear.

'Shut up . . . just shut up. I don't want to listen to that whining any more.'

He took hold of her, forced her to lie down and covered her with the dirty smelly blankets.

Again he looked at her face. She wasn't making a sound but tears were spilling over from her eyes, she was shivering with cold and he could see she was terrified. She turned onto her side and tucked herself into the foetal position with the eiderdown up round her neck.

'Don't move from there. I'm just getting some wood for a fire,' he ordered her. He went around the back of his den and pulled some ready-cut small logs round to the flattened area outside and piled them up. He reached into his knapsack and pulled out a box of matches but as he struck a match he saw Maggie Wheaton's face in the glow. Her eyes were wide open as she stared at him in terror.

Her expression shocked him and the fog started to clear from his head. Suddenly he realised exactly what he'd done. Because he was angry he'd taken a small child and scared the wits out of her.

He stared at her but this time instead of seeing Ruby and Johnnie he saw George and Babs Wheaton: the people who had been so good and kind to him; the people who had rescued him and given him a life away from the den. They were the ones he was hurting and he couldn't do it to them.

He jumped up and went back outside. Leaning against a tree, he breathed deeply, trying to get some air into the bottom of his sickly lungs as he'd been taught. It helped clear his head a little and lessened the pain of his excruciating headache.

Marie Maxwell

At the same time a second plan started to form. It would be too easy to let Ruby off scot-free, and if he was going to be homeless and jobless he would need money, and he wanted it from Ruby Blakeley. The one who started the whole thing. The one who had caused his house of cards to topple.

'Come on then, little Maggie. This was just a game. Let's go back. But you did like my den, didn't you?'

'Yes,' she sniffed hopefully.

'Good. You mustn't tell anyone about it, though. Now, we'll go and get my bike and take you home but I have to go to the phone box. We have another game to play first. It's called How Loud Can You Scream?'

'What about the wild animals? Won't they get us?'

'No. I've got special powers, but I'll carry you, just to be sure.'

Derek Yardley carried the little girl to where he had left his bike. He placed her on the handlebars and then went a longer way out of the dense woods so Maggie would lose her bearings. He didn't want anyone ever finding his secret place.

After propping his bike up against a tree he put the girl down, took her hand and cautiously crossed the road to the layby that was at the entrance to a quiet lane, where there was a line of tied cottages and a phone box.

'I want you to sit on the grass right there and don't move until I call you. And then I want you to scream really loudly down the phone to your mummy.'

He smiled at the irony and fumbled in his pocket for his diary where he had written all the details he had for Ruby.

He dialled the number for the Thamesview Hotel.

'I want to speak to Ruby Blakeley,' he said, confident in his plan. But Ruby wasn't there. He didn't know what to do next. He needed money to get away.

As he flicked through his diary, trying to decide what to do, he saw Maggie stand up and wander towards the road.

He flung the phone-box door open. 'Maggie, come back, come back here!' he shouted as loud as he could, but instead of stopping she ran. Straight into the path of a car.

Yardley didn't know what to do. He started to go towards where the child lay in the road, but when the driver got out he panicked and ran back over the road, jumped on his bike, took one last look over his shoulder and then rode like the wind back into the woods and back to his den.

When he got there he laid down on the lumpy mattress, pulled the cover over himself and savoured the excruciating pain of his headache.

It was his punishment.

Babs and George Wheaton were waiting down by the gate at nearly midnight when the police car pulled up outside.

'Your daughter is safe but she's got a few cuts and

bruises so she needs a check-up at the hospital tomorrow. She was hit by a car, but luckily it was someone on the lookout for her so it was going very slowly. She needs some other checks as well, but as you're a doctor . . . ?' The policeman conveyed exactly what he meant with those few words.

There was a queue of well-wishers outside the surgery who, after fearing the worst, were all waiting to see the little girl brought safely back home.

As the car door opened, so Babs, trying to pretend she wasn't crying, snatched her up and hugged her as tightly as she could. She had never felt such fear in her life.

'Mummy', Maggie cried, 'Yardley was all horrid and not nice. We went to his den in the woods but I didn't want to sleep there in the dark. It was smelly and dirty but the nice lady washed my face and wrapped me in her blanket.'

'Let's go inside into the warm and then you can tell us all about your adventure,' George said with a smile.

Once indoors, the two police officers explained as much as they knew: that one of the tenants at the cottages had helped the driver tend to Maggie and then taken her indoors to his wife before using the phone box to call the police. No one had seen Derek Yardley.

'Did he hurt you? Yardley, I mean – did Yardley hurt you?' Babs asked nervously.

'No, he carried me so the wild animals couldn't hurt me.'

'And where's Yardley now?' George asked, looking at

the policeman standing in the doorway. 'Why didn't he bring you all the way home?'

'After the car knocked me down he went away really fast on his bike.' The little girl turned the corners of her mouth down. 'He's horrid, I don't want him to live here any more.'

'He won't, darling, I promise. It's all right now.'

'Can I see Scruffy?'

George and Babs exchanged looks over her head. Neither of them needed to say a word.

THIRTY

Ruby was upstairs in the flat recovering from her life-threatening haemorrhage and trying to understand everything that had happened during the previous weeks. Her brain was still a bit befuddled from all the medication, but she kept thinking about it over and over and torturing herself with blame. It had been so dramatic she still palpitated thinking not only about what happened, but also what could have happened. And if the unthinkable had happened to Maggie, it would have been her fault. Now she was going to have to live with that.

By the time she had recovered consciousness after her collapse Gracie was at her bedside waiting to tell her that Maggie had been found and she was alive and well. The child was scared and clingy, but miraculously nothing irreparable had happened to her. Yardley hadn't hurt her physically, although he had badly frightened her.

When she heard what had happened to Maggie, Ruby had intended to tell George and Babs about what Yardley had done to her, and she had been about to do just that when she had collapsed, but even if she had told them at that moment it would have been too late to save Maggie. Now it was her dark secret and she was going to have to keep it; after failing to speak out at the right time she could never disclose it now.

Despite an intensive search the police hadn't found any trace of Yardley, or his den in the woods; everyone feared the worst for the mentally fragile man.

'Hey, Ruby, you've got a visitor,' Gracie shouted up the stairs, interrupting her dark thoughts. 'Shall I send him up?'

'Depends who it is?' Ruby said as loudly as she could, knowing full well it was Johnnie Riordan. She was expecting him and she had invited him.

The bunch of flowers came in the door first.

'Hello there, Red. How are you feeling? The shiners are impressive; do any boxer proud!'

'Bit by bit I'm improving,' she smiled. 'I can laugh now without thinking my chest is going to burst open. The ribs are so painful and the arm's going to be in plaster for a while, but I'm OK really.'

Ruby was ensconced in Aunt Leonora's old chair with her feet up, and her plastered arm was propped up on a cushion, but she'd drawn the line at the blanket Gracie had offered her. They was no denying that she was pale and poorly, and the bruises were still evident, but she'd put on some lipstick, patted some powder around her black eyes and let Gracie brush and shape her hair.

'So, I got your cryptic letter via our Betty and I even managed to figure out what you meant. I could have been a code-breaker in the war.'

'Did Betty know it was from me? I hoped typing the envelope would stop her from wondering about it.'

'Well, it did and it didn't. It never occurred to her it was personal so she decided I was in trouble and gave me gyp for it!' He laughed and looked at her. 'I'm not in trouble, am I?'

Ruby looked at him and felt the familiar lump in her throat. A part of her wanted him out of her life for ever, but another part wanted to be with him for ever.

'No trouble . . . well, not that I know of, anyway,' Ruby replied lightly. 'I just had no other way to contact you and I thought we still had unfinished business. Imagining I was going to kick the bucket made me think about my life and all the things I should have organised, and in a way that included you!'

Johnnie went over and sat on the arm of the sofa opposite Ruby.

'Imagining you were going to kick the bucket made me think as well. I really thought that was it for you, and when I turned up here, happy as Larry, to see you and Gracie told me what had happened I felt quite sick and I couldn't even go to visit you.' He looked at her intently.

'What did happen? Gracie seemed to think your fiancé was somehow involved.'

'Let's leave it that I tripped. It's not important now and Gracie shouldn't be gossiping.'

'She wasn't gossiping, she was upset, but yes, let's leave that for the minute. Unfinished business, you say? Does that mean there's going to be a finish for me? Is that what this is all about?'

'I suppose it is. There has to be, with things as they are,' she said sadly. 'A wife and children means there's no going back.'

'Hang on, let's not forget a fiancé . . .'

'He's not a fiancé any more. That's finished. Look . . .' she held her hand up and wiggled her fingers. 'No ring. The beautiful diamonds had to go!'

Johnnie walked over to the balcony and stepped outside.

'Bit nippy out here without a pullover!' He wrapped his arms around himself and hunched his shoulders as he looked from side to side at the vista of the Thames Estuary. 'It's so beautiful from up here. I can understand why you like working and living in this gaff. That view is fantastic. But how come you got the penthouse?'

'Because this is my hotel. I own it.' As he turned round Ruby stared him straight in the eye. It was a definite challenge so she could judge his reaction.

'Blimey,' Johnnie said after a few seconds' thought. 'And there was me thinking I was the entrepreneur of Elsmere!'

'Not quite an entrepreneur – I inherited it – but I've worked here since I left Walthamstow so I know it inside out, and now I own it. Isn't that odd? I must have done a good job for Leonora to leave it to me, mustn't I?'

'Not odd at all. There always was something special about you! How did it all happen?'

Ruby told him the story. It both amused and saddened her that they were so comfortable with each other. She knew she could tell him anything.

Anything but the secret about Maggie. His daughter. Not because she didn't want to but because she'd promised the Wheatons.

'Tell me about your life, your marriage and what happened to Ray and Bobbie that day.'

He looked at her and raised his eyebrows. 'Tall order, that . . .'

'I know,' she smiled sadly, 'but we might never see each other again after today so take a seat and let's dig all the skeletons out, eh?'

Johnnie walked over to the sofa and sat down.

'I've already told you about Sadie and my marriage . . .'

'Ray and Bobbie?'

'Yes, that was me. Well, not me – someone else did it – but I arranged for them to take a bit of a beating. But I gave them a pay rise when I became the boss!'

'They were badly hurt, really badly, especially Ray. It wasn't so much what happened, but your part in it.'

'That wasn't what I wanted. I used the wrong bloke. I

thought I knew best, but even Bill Morgan warned me against him. They were stealing my business. Now I wouldn't be so angry, but back then . . .'

Ruby thought for a moment and then smiled. 'And there was I thinking you'd done it for me. Ray and Bobbie warned me about you but I took no notice, so we're quits.'

'That is not fair. They weren't right. I never did anything to hurt you. I loved you, and you ran off and never came back – well, not until it was too late. I would never hurt you.'

Ruby stared at him and was surprised to see him turn red and look away.

'I shouldn't have said that.'

'Yes, you should. There were reasons I went. I know I should have told you, but . . .' She looked at him sadly. 'Oh, Johnnie, how could we both have been so daft?'

'I don't know, Red, but more to the point, what are we going to do about it?'

'Nothing. We can't.'

There was a subtle knock on the door and then a pause before Gracie opened it and looked around cautiously.

'Safe to come in? I've come bearing gifts from the kitchen: sandwiches and cake. I've even carried up a pot of tea. Don't say I never give you anything.'

'How's it going downstairs?'

'We're not talking about the hotel. You're sick and resting, and I'm dealing with it.'

Johnnie stood up and took the tray.

'Thank you kindly, sir,' she said as she bobbed in a curtsy.

Johnnie laughed. 'You two are as mad as each other. How did you meet?'

The glance that passed between Gracie and Ruby told nothing and everything, and after just a moment's pause Johnnie smiled. 'Forget I asked. That was nosy.'

'Well. Love you and leave you,' Gracie laughed nervously. 'Madame can ring the bell if Madame wants anything further.' She curtsied again and scuttled away demurely.

'Yes, both of you are mad. But where were we . . . ?' he asked.

'How trustworthy would you say you are, Johnnie Riordan?' Ruby asked, suddenly serious. 'I mean if I told you something really big would you blab or could you keep quiet?'

'I could keep quiet without a doubt. I may be a bit of a fly-boy, as our Betty says, but I'm loyal. You know I am. Why? What have you done? I'm worried now . . .'

'I need you to swear this will be our secret, that you won't betray me whatever happens, not ever.'

'You're scaring me now, but unless you're going to confess to being a secret mass murderer then I promise. Hand on heart.'

'Do you remember when I borrowed the train fare from you?'

'And you never came back or paid it back, naughty

girl. Yes, of course I remember,' he smiled. 'I did try and find you.'

'I didn't go off to see about nursing. I went to Melton, to the Wheatons. I was pregnant. With your baby.'

Johnnie looked at her, his expression hard to read, and she waited for this news to sink in.

'What happened to it?' he asked eventually.

'I came to live here, with George's sister, Leonora, and hid away until the baby was born. A girl. She was adopted. I was going to go back to Melton but I met Gracie and decided on a new start so I stayed here.'

Johnnie leaned forward, put his elbows on his knees and looked at her. Again she tried to read his expression but couldn't.

'You were so ambitious,' she continued, 'so sure of what you wanted, and that didn't include a shotgun wedding to a sixteen-year-old. I did what I thought was best at the time,' she smiled.

'Do you know anything about the baby?'

'Everything. She was adopted by George and Babs. Maggie is five years old and their daughter. I'm her godmother. No one knows apart from Gracie.'

'Does your fiancé know?'

'No, he doesn't, and I told you, he's not my fiancé any more.' She watched his face carefully, desperately hoping she hadn't made the wrong decision.

'Why are you telling me now?' he asked slowly.

'Because I saw your boys on the beach and I realised

they're related to Maggie and that you had a right to know. But you mustn't do anything or tell anyone.'

'I promised, didn't I? Am I allowed to see her?' Johnnie asked.

'I have to think about that. She mustn't know – not until she's older – but she's having the best life. George and Babs adore her; she is their daughter, not mine, not yours. The adoption was done properly and they never pressured me. They did it for me and Maggie. To save her being adopted by strangers and going out of our lives for ever. See over there on the sideboard, the photo frame that's laid down? That's Maggie. I turned it over so you wouldn't see it and maybe realise.'

He stood up and reached out for the frame. Turning it over he stared at the photo for what seemed an age without saying anything.

'Please don't hate me,' she said eventually.

'How could I hate you? You did what you had to do and it was probably right at the time. I wasn't ready for anything like that. I suppose you knew me better than I knew myself back then. But now . . .' He stared into her eyes. 'I wish we could turn back the clock in one way, but then I love my boys so I can't regret them.'

Ruby smiled. 'I know that. So the skeletons are out and it's time for you to go. I don't mind if you want to telephone sometimes and see how Maggie is doing, but apart from that, Johnnie Riordan, I think we missed the boat several years ago.'

They talked for a while longer until the moment came and Johnnie Riordan said goodbye to Ruby with a kiss on the top of her head and a quick wave. She said nothing as she bit her lip and breathed deeply, desperate not to cry.

As Johnnie drove away he looked up, hoping to see Ruby on the balcony or even at the window, but she wasn't there.

He was supposed to be out and about checking on Bill Morgan's various investments but he simply couldn't face it. He couldn't face anything to do with Bill Morgan at that moment.

So much had happened and his head was in turmoil as he tried to understand it all as he drove back down the arterial road to Wanstead. He knew he needed to lie down and clear his head – he needed time to think – so he decided to go home instead and tell Sadie he had a headache. He hoped that would persuade her to leave him alone and let him rest.

He let himself in the house. 'Sadie? Sadie? Where are you?'

He thought he heard a noise upstairs and guessed Sadie was up there with the children; he went into their bedroom and they were both asleep, but there was no sign of Sadie. He ran downstairs and checked everywhere before realising that Sadie had gone out and left the children alone.

He looked out in the back garden and then went out

the front to check the road, but there was no sign of her anywhere.

'Hello Johnnie,' his neighbour said as he saw him looking around. 'What's up mate?'

'I'm looking for Sadie. The kids are in bed but I can't find her.'

The man looked down at the ground. 'I didn't know she left the kids on their own. That's not on. You'll find her at number forty-eight. She'll be in there with the Greek bloke. Sorry . . .'

'What do you mean?'

'She's always in there, but I didn't know she left the kids in the house.'

Johnnie focused for a few seconds. 'Do me a favour, just stand by my front door and listen for the boys. I won't be long.'

He marched over the road and banged on the door of number forty-eight. When there was no answer he simply kicked the door in and ran straight up the stairs. He was confronted by a man wearing just a vest and socks. Without pause he grabbed him in a stranglehold round the neck.

'Where's Sadie? Quick, or you're going headfirst down those stairs.'

'In there . . .'

But then Sadie appeared on the landing, her hair in a mess and her blouse buttoned up wrong. Johnnie could see she'd tried to get dressed quickly.

'Do you know what you've done?' he shouted at her, his anger bubbling away.

'Exactly the same as what you've been doing,' Sadie smiled. 'But it's all right for you, out all day whoring, but not me.'

Johnnie looked at her and his temper evaporated down into cold fury. 'Oh, for Christ's sake, I don't care who you fuck, but I do care that you've left the boys on their own while you do it. Anything could happen to them, you stupid, stupid bitch. The whole house could have burned down with them in it.'

As Sadie stood on the landing looking bewildered, so the man, whose name Johnnie didn't even know, backed up against the wall.

'I'm sorry, mate. She just comes over here . . . what's a man to do when it's on a plate?'

Johnnie pulled his arm back and punched the man clean on the jaw.

'Wait for me, Johnnie,' Sadie said meekly in her silly girly voice that grated on him at the best of times.

'I'm taking the boys to Betty. You can do whatever you like to earn enough to pay the rent on your own.'

'Johnnie, Johnnie, I didn't mean it, Johnnie. Don't leave me. You were doing it as well. *Johnnie . . .*'

'I was not doing it, Sadie. I've never been unfaithful to you. Never.'

As he crossed the road he could still hear her shouting, 'I'm gonna tell Bill. You can't do this to me . . .'

THIRTY-ONE

'So you're not into adultery, then?' Gracie laughed, trying to cheer Ruby up. 'He's a bit of all right though your bloke.'

'He's not my bloke, so give over. I'm all alone and single again, and tomorrow I'm going to get a Pekingese. That's all I need in my life. I've got the hotel, I've got the genteel lady guests, what more do I need?'

'Johnnie Riordan!' Gracie did a little dance in front of her friend.

It was a few days after Johnnie's visit, and Ruby was still feeling fragile from both the emotion of their conversation and the aching of her slowly healing injuries. She had managed to get down the stairs and was sitting in the kitchen, out of sight and away from guests' questions.

'Just out of interest, have you seen Tony at all? I'm really worried about him being so close by, especially once I start going out.'

'Mamma and Papà Alfredo told Henry he'd gone to

386

live in London. They were also talking about his new girlfriend . . . Don't know what's true and what isn't. They idolise him and will cover up for him whatever. They're firmly stuck with the idea that you fell down their stairs drunk. That's why Tony called the engagement off.'

'That's what parents do, though, isn't it? Unconditional love. But if he's gone to London . . .'

'How unconditional is unconditional?' Gracie asked.

'Blimey, missus, that's a bit deep . . .'

'I'm learning, I'm learning. Oh, it's the phone. I'll get it.' She went out into the lobby and then put her head back around the door. 'Ruby, it's Johnnie. He says it's urgent.'

'I don't want to speak to him.'

'He says it's really urgent.'

'No. I can't speak to him, I can't. Tell him another time. If it's urgent he can tell you.'

She could hear Gracie talking to him but she couldn't hear the words. Then Gracie came back into the room.

'I don't want to hear it, Gracie.'

'Oh, you do, you really do.'

'I don't. I have to shut him off.'

Gracie smiled. 'When he left here the other day he went home and found the babies on their own and his missus over the road having it away with a neighbour, a Greek waiter from Soho . . . though I don't know why he told me that.'

'*Nooo*, I don't believe you, Gracie McCabe. You're lying to me.'

'Cross my heart and hope to die. He said he can't see you for a while because he's got the boys with him at his sister's and he doesn't want Sadie finding out anything and dragging you into it. Now there's a fine kettle of fish for you.'

Ruby leaned forward. She felt sick and faint. In a few moments everything had changed.

'He wants you to phone him on this number.' Gracie handed her a piece of paper. 'Shall I cancel the Pekingese?'

Ruby smiled. 'We'll see. At the moment I really need a brandy.'

That evening, after she'd spoken to Johnnie, Ruby sat out on the balcony thinking about everything that had happened and wondering how it might all pan out in the future. In a few short weeks her life had roller-coastered up and down so much she was scared to think about anything positively for fear of it all whooshing back down again.

Johnnie Riordan. Could it happen? She didn't know . . . His life was so tied up with Sadie and Bill Morgan. Despite what Sadie had done, the threat from Morgan was there. If he divorced Sadie then he lost everything: his home, his job, his car; but he would keep his boys, which was the most important thing to him.

But would he go that far? She wasn't sure. Only time

would tell. But the thought that maybe she and Johnnie Riordan, the love of her life, could be together one day was enough for the moment.

She picked up the binoculars and looked out across the water. It was damp and misty, but she could knew Leonora was out there somewhere, keeping an eye on her hotel and her protégée.

She was so far away she jumped when Gracie came up behind her.

'Babs rang. They've found Derek Yardley's body. He hanged himself with his belt in the place he'd called his den, so Maggie was right about that. Really spooky place, a proper hut in the woods, which was only found by chance by a farmer shooting rabbits and following his dog into the undergrowth. The police never found him.'

Ruby put her fingers in her ears. 'I don't want to hear about it, not now. I can't think about him because I feel sorry for him and I don't want to, he took Maggie.'

'That he did, but he brought her back and he didn't do anything bad to her. That's the main thing. There's good and bad in all of this, that's for sure.'

'I suppose you're right . . . Do you think we could both take a day off?' Ruby suddenly asked Gracie. 'Just one day. I really want to go and see my mother but I can't drive with my arm like this. I was thinking, it'll soon be a new year . . . a new year, a new start. I want to get everything cleared in my head and start afresh.'

'Sounds good to me.'

Gracie and Ruby stood together looking over the balcony.

'Are you watching, Lady Leonora?' Gracie shouted. 'We love you!'

EPILOGUE

Johnnie Riordan turned the car into the drive and pulled up in front of the garage.

'I'm dreading this, you know.'

'Well, don't. Just think of it as an extended family get-together. It happens all the time – aunts and uncles, nephews and nieces. Maggie is just like that.'

'It doesn't feel right.'

'I know, but you have to pretend it is. You'll get used to it. I have.'

'I know.' Although the engine was turned off his hands were still gripping the steering wheel.

Ruby smiled reassuringly. 'How's Betty coping with two babies in the house?'

'She's grumbling but she's loving it. It's a bit cramped, though, with me as well. Poor Betty . . .'

'So Bill hasn't put a hit out on you then?'

'No. Just sacked me, took the car, chucked me out of

the house and threatened to break my legs if I ever showed my face in Wanstead again, that's all.'

'But *she* was in the wrong . . .'

'Does it matter? Nope. Bill Morgan always had a soft spot for her so he was automatically going to believe her. She's even working in the Black Dog again!' Johnnie shook his head and grinned. 'Life, eh? So, shall we go in? I'm scared, if I'm honest.'

'It'll be OK. I'm her sister Ruby, and you're my friend Johnnie.'

'Sounds like a storybook.'

'It is a bit like a fairytale, and all's well that ends well. Right, here we go. Come and meet Maggie.'

'I can't believe we have a daughter.'

'You must never ever say that out loud.'

'What about us?'

'You know about us. We were meant to be.'

They both stopped when they heard voices.

'Mummy, it's Ruby!'

Ruby looked at Johnnie's face as his daughter ran towards them.

'One day,' she said to him quietly, 'one day she'll know. Hello, Maggie. Say hello to my friend Johnnie.'

An Interview with Marie Maxwell

What items couldn't you live without?
My iPad (I'm in love with it!); tinted moisturiser and waterproof mascara; cordless hot-brush (even though it's old fashioned technology); beautiful thick-papered notebooks; coloured gel pens; central heating and my gorgeous cashmere wrist warmers for when I'm typing! Oh and books, stacks of books. And a cat. Must have a cat.

Which authors inspire you?
Jilly Cooper, Harold Robbins, Jackie Collins, Barbara Taylor Bradford. All brilliant story-tellers of the blockbuster variety, and the one and only Agatha Christie who was never lost for a plot!

Do you spend a lot of time researching your novels?
With Ruby I had to do far more research than I ever had before. I was out of my comfort zone in a different era so I had to keep checking. Thank Heaven for Google and all the people who put information up on the internet. It was time-consuming but very interesting and sometimes I was so absorbed I fell way behind with the book itself!

What is a typical working day like for you?
I like to start work early and then have a siesta in the afternoon before carrying on into the evening. If I'm up against the clock (as I often am) then I'll get up at 3 or 4 am and start but I can't work into the night anymore, my brain shuts at 10pm.

If I'm 'Home Alone' then I usually work in the conservatory which is an office at one end. I also have a fully-equipped shed-office halfway down the garden which is a real bolt-hole away from everything. I love my shed!

Have you ever had writer's block? If so, how did you cope with it?
I do sometimes sit and stare at the screen and wonder if I'll ever be able to string a sentence together again so that's when I go and make a cup of coffee and read a magazine. Other times I'll just move ahead

of the story and start a whole new section before going back to where I was. Or I go shopping for handbags . . .

Do your characters ever surprise you?
Oh yes! They often take on a life of their own when the story gets going. Sometimes minor characters will push the main ones aside and put themselves centre stage, nice characters suddenly turn mean and occasionally just have to be banished or killed and new ones appear from nowhere. A writer's brain can work in very strange ways sometimes, especially in the middle of the night. I often wake up and think AHA, and a new plotline evolves.

Which give people, living or dead, would you invite to a dinner party?
BILL CLINTON he's such a charmer.
BEAR GRYLLS he could teach me how to make a meal from a shrub.
KEITH RICHARDS because he must have some rock'n'roll secrets
    to tell.
VIRGINIA MCKENNA I so admire her work with Born Free. Fab
    Lady.
CHERIE BLAIR I think she gets a rough deal from the media, I'd
    like to hear her side.

What's the strangest job you've ever had?
When I lived in Lagos, Nigeria, I worked for a short while as a receptionist for the father of a friend, a Lebanese importer and exporter of fabrics and clothing. Only he wasn't. The business was a front and he was a smooth con-man who fled the country one night with his family and a small fortune of other people's money. I never had a clue and I never got paid.

And what can you tell us about your next novel?
It's the story of GRACIE, a young woman who features in RUBY as her friend. Gracie's a lively young woman, full of personality and ambition whose life is full of both good and bad twists and turns. I really like her and I hope the readers will too.